PENGUIN BOOKS
IN THE NAME OF GOD

Ravi Subramanian, an alumnus of IIM Bangalore, has spent two decades working his way up the ladder of power in the amazingly exciting and adrenaline-pumping world of global banks in India. Four of Ravi's eight bestselling titles have been award winners. In 2008, his debut novel, *If God Was a Banker*, won the Golden Quill Readers' Choice Award. He won the Economist Crossword Book Award in 2012 for *The Incredible Banker*, the Crossword Book Award in 2013 for *The Bankster* and more recently in 2014 for his thriller *Bankerupt*.

He lives in Mumbai with his wife, Dharini, and daughter, Anusha. To know more about Ravi, visit www.ravisubramanian.in or email him at info@ravisubramanian.in. To connect with him, log on to Facebook at www.facebook.com/authorravisubramanian or tweet to @subramanianravi.

BY THE SAME AUTHOR

FICTION

If God Was a Banker
Devil in Pinstripes
The Incredible Banker
The Bankster
Bankerupt
God Is a Gamer
The Bestseller She Wrote

NON-FICTION

I Bought the Monk's Ferrari

RAVI SUBRAMANIAN

IN THE NAME OF GOD

PENGUIN BOOKS

An imprint of Penguin Random House

PENGUIN BOOKS

USA | Canada | UK | Ireland | Australia
New Zealand | India | South Africa | China

Penguin Books is part of the Penguin Random House group of companies
whose addresses can be found at global.penguinrandomhouse.com

Published by Penguin Random House India Pvt. Ltd
7th Floor, Infinity Tower C, DLF Cyber City,
Gurgaon 122 002, Haryana, India

First published in Penguin Books by Penguin Random House India 2017

Copyright © Ravi Subramanian 2017

All rights reserved

10 9 8 7 6 5 4 3 2

This is a work of fiction. Names, characters, places and incidents are
either the product of the author's imagination or are used fictitiously and
any resemblance to any actual person, living or dead, events or locales
is entirely coincidental.

ISBN 9780143425731

Typeset in Minion Pro by Manipal Digital Systems, Manipal
Printed at Replika Press Pvt. Ltd, India

This book is sold subject to the condition that it shall not, by way of trade
or otherwise, be lent, resold, hired out, or otherwise circulated without the
publisher's prior consent in any form of binding or cover other than that in
which it is published and without a similar condition including this condition
being imposed on the subsequent purchaser.

www.penguin.co.in

To you, the reader,
for reading it and making it worthwhile for me to have written this

and

to my daughter, Anusha,
for this is the first book of mine that she has ever read.

Author's Note

The book refers to real places and real titles of people who operate in these places and in the government and law-enforcement agencies. These have been used to lend an air of authenticity to the story, just as in a fictional story about the Pope or the prime minister of the nation or the President of the United States of America. The characters who occupy these positions in the book do not, and are not meant to, resemble the real-life incumbents in any manner. This story is entirely fictional and is not intended to be a depiction of the life of individuals who, in real life, occupy the exalted positions that their titles suggest. If, despite my best efforts, some similarities have crept in, I apologize. If you have this book in your hand, I recommend that you read it to enjoy what could be, rather than as a depiction of what is.

Part 1

Part 1

1

THIRUVANANTHAPURAM

He didn't notice the body immediately.

Not even when he dipped the holy vessel into the Padma Teertha Kulam, the divine pond, to fill it up for the Devaprasnam. It was only as he was lifting the vessel, filled to the brim with water, that the right hand of the floating body scraped against it and he saw it break through the surface of the weed-infested tank. His voice deserted him; he stood stupefied. The vessel dropped from his hand and sank to the bottom of the pond with a gurgling noise.

'Padmanabha! Padmanabha! Padmanabha!' he chanted loudly as he ran up the steps to the pond and sprinted towards the temple gates. Whether he was upset at having touched a dead body early in the morning or it was the shock of having found said body floating in the temple pond, or both, was difficult to say.

2

DUBAI
A few months ago

It was a deafening sound. The kind that is heard when metal crashes into glass, bringing the whole thing down. The ground shook. It almost felt like an earthquake.

Visitors at Wafi Mall, the largest and possibly most exquisitely designed luxury mall in the area, stood astounded. No one could fathom what was going on.

Gate 1 of the mall was to the right of the central courtyard and a few minutes away from the main parking lot. The ground floor, accessible from Gate 1, was home to a variety of luxury gold and jewellery and accessory brands—Chopard, Cartier, Damas, Rolex, Omega, Breitling and a few local biggies were within shouting distance from the gate.

Moments later another piece of glass came crashing down amid the perceptible sound of cars rumbling close by.

At precisely 12.48 p.m.—no one knew the significance of the time, if there was one—two Audi A6s, one black and one white, had driven up to Gate 1. It was not uncommon for cars to drive up to the mall entrance. It was some distance from the main parking and the mall clientele, the rich and famous of Dubai, were not used to walking with their shopping bags. Ordinarily, the cars stopped on the carriageway built for them, waited for a couple of minutes, picked up their masters and drove out. But at 12.48 that day, the two Audis did not stop at the main gate. However, that was only half as strange as the manner in which they drove up to the gate: The black Audi was furiously approaching in reverse, followed closely by the white one, their bonnets almost kissing each other.

By the time the lone security guard at the gate could react, the black Audi had already crashed through the glass-and-metal door with a deafening noise. It drove further into the mall, right up to the main lobby on the ground floor, and screeched to a halt, the white car following suit. It almost seemed as if the black Audi was the pilot car, clearing the way for the second car. But why was it being driven in reverse? No one knew. No one cared. All that anyone in the mall was worried about was saving his or her own life. What ensued was mass panic as scared shoppers started running helter-skelter.

Amidst the confusion, four masked men, all dressed in black, got out of the cars, while the drivers stayed back, keeping the engines running. Armed with Kalashnikovs, they fired indiscriminately in the air, sending the already panic-stricken crowd into a state of hysteria. Everyone assumed it was a terrorist attack. At the time, that's what it seemed like. Nervously vigilant, the four men strode towards the aisle to the right of the entrance. It was narrow, short and housed only three shops: Cartier, D'Damas and Ajmal Jewellers. At any given point in time, the cumulative stock in all the three stores put together was worth over a hundred million dollars.

The leader of the group stopped in front of Ajmal Jewellers and gestured to the other three to take up their positions. It took just one bullet to neutralize the shop attendant who was furiously rolling down the safety grille. The men entered the store. Once they were in, they were cut off from the rest of the mall. All anyone could hear was the sound of shattering glass and indiscriminate gunfire.

In three minutes the men came out of the store and ran back to the two Audis. Each of them had a bag in one hand—

clearly booty from Ajmal Jewellers. But as they were rushing, the last of the four tripped and fell. The bag slipped out of his hands and rolled ahead. The contents of the bag—jewellery and gemstones—spilled out on to the marble floor.

'Damn!' the leader swore. 'Quick! Three more minutes and the cops will be here. We need to go!' The fall had delayed them by forty-five seconds. They had to leave, else they would be sitting ducks for the Dubai Police. He continued towards the Audi even as his fallen team member recovered, and tried to gather the loot on the floor and put it back into the bag. He quickly got into the second Audi though he had not managed to collect everything that had fallen out of the bag.

Immediately the engines roared to life. The cars vroomed and this time, the white Audi reversed out of the shattered mall entrance followed closely by the black one. In no time, they had disappeared from sight.

The moment the cars left the mall, people rushed towards the jewellery showroom, a few stopping on the way to pick up the pieces of jewellery and curios that had fallen out of the robber's bag.

Ajmal Jewellers was in a shambles. Glass from broken windows and display units was strewn all over. There was blood everywhere. Seven people had been shot—six store staff and a sole shopper.

All of them were dead.

3

THIRUVANANTHAPURAM
1900 onwards

There is a history to why Kerala is called God's Own Country.

In the 1750s Travancore was ruled by Maharaja Anizham Thirunal Marthanda Varma. A pious and god-fearing king, Anizham gave up his entire kingdom to Lord Anantha Padmanabha in a ceremony called Thripadidaanam, thereby making God the owner of the kingdom of Travancore. Thus Travancore came to be known as God's Own Country, a legacy that Kerala has inherited.

After the Thripadidaanam ceremony, the prefix Padmanabhadasa—Dasa or Slave of Lord Padmanabha—was added to the king's name. Whenever a male child was born into the royal family of Travancore, he was laid on the ottakal mandapam, the single granite stone slab abutting the sanctum sanctorum, in front of Lord Anantha Padmanabha in the Anantha Padmanabha Swamy Temple in Thiruvananthapuram and holy water from the Padma Teertha Kulam, the temple pond, was sprinkled on him. Thereafter the child, possibly the future king, would be proclaimed as Sri Padmanabhadasa. Every king ruled Travancore and cared for its people and property on behalf of Lord Padmanabha.

Things changed around the time India attained independence in 1947. At that time, nearly a third of the subcontinent comprised princely states. Prior to Independence, the states were given an option to either accede to India or Pakistan or even stay independent. Since most of them were dependent on the government, they chose to accede to India. By 1949, all these kingdoms had merged with the nation and new states were created, as a result of which the kings lost all ruling rights. In return, the government announced a Privy Purse—an assured sum of money to be paid annually to the erstwhile king. The amount was determined by the economic importance of the state, the stature of the ruler, the relationship he enjoyed with the government and the longevity of the kingdom. The Privy Purse was abolished by the Indira Gandhi-led Congress government in 1971 in what came to be known as the 26th Amendment to the Constitution of India. Though the move was severely contested by the rulers, they couldn't do much once the amendment was passed by both the houses of Parliament.

The south Indian kingdoms of Travancore and Cochin merged to become the new state of Thiru–Kochi. Chithira Thirunal Balarama Varma, the last ruling king of Travancore, who signed the instruments of accession to India, died in 1991. It was after his death that his younger brother Aswathi Thirunal Dharmaraja Varma took over as the titular king of Travancore. And by virtue of that he became the trustee managing the affairs of the Lord Anantha Padmanabha Swamy Temple. He was referred to as Padmanabhadasa, and at times even as Thampuran, 'the lord', or Thirumanassu, a Malayalam word for His Highness. Kowdiar Palace, a 150-room architectural marvel, built by his predecessor Chithira Thirunal, became the seat of the titular king.

4

THIRUVANANTHAPURAM
A few years ago

Rajan's mornings were normally peaceful. According to him, it was the best time of the day. Time to introspect. Time to plan. He loved the solitude that morning offered. On a typical day, an old hand-wound Favre Leuba alarm clock with a greenish dial and radium-coated hands would wake him up at half past four. The erstwhile king of Travancore had gifted the alarm clock to his father, a trustee of the Anantha Padmanabha Swamy Temple, in the mid-fifties. Rajan's father had passed it on to him when he joined the Indian Civil Revenue, saying, 'A successful man always starts his day well before the world gets up.'

Rajan had recently retired and moved back to his ancestral home in Thiruvananthapuram in the narrow lane to the east of the Anantha Padmanabha Swamy Temple. He didn't have a family. He had never married. 'Never felt the need to,' he would say when asked. He now lived with his cousin who worked in a local school in the neighbourhood.

However, that day, uncharacteristically, Rajan was in an agitated frame of mind. His face red with anger, he was pacing up and down the poomukham, the portico of the house, impatiently. In his hand was a copy of the day's edition of *Kerala Kaumudi*, the local Malayalam newspaper. A large wooden reclining chair with long rails on either side stood in the northeast corner of the portico. He sat down on the chair, put his leg up on the rails and held the newspaper aloft. He didn't even have to turn the page. It was on the front page. The lead story. He read it once. Then a second time. Finally, he dumped the paper by the side of the chair and closed his eyes. His forehead showed signs of stress—or was it anger? He stayed like that for a long time till his cousin, Kamu, walked up to him and tapped his shoulder.

'What happened?' she asked.

'Nothing.' He shook his head. 'Nothing. Nothing,' he whispered, as he got up from the chair. He picked up his angavastram, the cloth that adorns the top half of the body of south Indian men, flipped it on his shoulder and walked out of the house. He didn't even bother to wear his slippers. He wasn't going too far. The temple was just a few hundred metres away.

'Did you see this?' Rajan demanded, tossing the paper on the table. There was anger in his voice, and fierce resolve in his eyes.

Gopi set his pen on the table, shut the register he had been writing in and looked up. He had a round face, and a bald head that was kept shining by regular application of coconut oil. A hairline moustache neatly divided his face in two, making him look stern even when he was not. He got up from his chair and walked around the table towards Rajan. 'Kaapi?' he asked calmly.

'What?' Rajan's eyes narrowed. 'Kaapi?' he repeated incredulously. 'Here my blood is boiling and all you are worried about is kaapi?'

The look of contentment on Gopi's face did not waver. 'Look, Rajan,' he said calmly, 'if it is not in your control, why lose sleep over it?'

'What do you mean?' Rajan stared at Gopi, his eyes red with anger. 'Are you saying that I must keep quiet and let this go?'

Gopi smiled. 'You know me better than that, Rajan,' he said with a shake of his head. Putting his arm around the other man's shoulders, he continued, 'If something is not directly in your control, try to influence it . . . try to change it. But don't let the consequences get to you. Anger invariably leads to mistakes. I suggest that you think calmly. Rather,' he took a deep breath, 'rather, think when you are calm.'

Rajan shrugged off Gopi's arm and began pacing. 'How could the Thampuran give such an interview? He is only the *titular* king. Just because the temple is under his control does not mean that he can do whatever he pleases!'

'He is within his rights to. Who are you to dictate what he should and what he shouldn't do?'

'He owes it to the people, to the temple, to the employees of the temple who have served him with so much devotion,' Rajan replied agitatedly. 'Everything is not *his*! He can't stake a claim to it. Everything belongs to the lord. And the lord is not for him alone. Padmanabha Swamy belongs to the people.'

'Is he staking a claim to it? I don't think the report says that.'

'Well, read it. Again. But this time, read between the lines,' Rajan instructed.

Gopi looked at the newspaper again. On the front page was an interview with Aswathi Thirunal Dharmaraja Varma, the king of Travancore. Accompanying the interview were two pictures—one of the king, standing firm and erect even in his old age, and the other of mounds of gold, diamonds, other precious stones and ornaments. Wealth which was allegedly locked up in the vaults of the Anantha Padmanabha Swamy Temple.

Gopi skipped the introduction and went straight to the Q&A.

You are one of the fittest kings in India. Even if one were to compare you to the other royal families in north India, you would be the fittest at 85. What is your secret?

It is all due to the will of God. I will remain alive and fit till the day Padmanabha Swamy wills it. The day he feels that my work on earth is over, I will be gone. And no one will even miss me.

You also live a life of frugality?

I am a man of limited needs. With Padmanabha's blessings, we have everything we want. The people of Travancore have given us so much respect, love and affection. What more can I want?

If one were to believe what insiders say, the temple is one of the richest in this part of the country. You are the custodian of this wealth. Aren't you ever tempted? Haven't your children demanded that you up your lifestyle? For that matter, do you even know how much wealth is there, locked up in the vaults?'

The wealth that the temple has is a result of the riches that have been passed down through the ages. In the seventeenth century our ancestors built the temple vaults to protect that wealth from the plunderers from the north. Our entire wealth belongs to Padmanabha. And we have faith in Him—when the time is right, He will give us what we need.

What is the value of the wealth in the temple vaults? There has been a lot of speculation.

It's difficult to say. Almost impossible. No one has ever inventoried those vaults. I have personally never visited them. You are welcome to inspect them and make a rough approximation for yourself.

Right in the middle of the interview was the image of the gold and jewellery allegedly in the vault. Gopi saw it and looked up, meeting Rajan's eyes.

'Who all are authorized to open the temple vaults?' Rajan asked in a low voice.

'There are six vaults,' Gopi answered, ignoring Rajan's question. 'Of these, four contain items of critical importance to the temple—utensils, puja paraphernalia, antiques and a few curios and statuettes.'

'Yes. And only three people are authorized to open these vaults. Right?' Rajan persisted

'Periya Nambi and Theekedathu Nambi, the priests of the temple, are the custodians of the four vaults. They keep opening them on a day-to-day basis. The other two vaults haven't been opened in the past eighty years. Vault A was last opened in 1931 and Vault B has apparently never been opened after it was sealed. God only knows when it was sealed!' Gopi ended with a shrug.

'And the keys to those two vaults?' Rajan prompted.

'Why are you asking me?' Gopi snapped. 'As if you don't know. Two of three—Theekedathu Nambi, Periya Nambi and I—need to be present to open the vault, along with the king.'

'So, if they wanted, the two of them could have independently opened the two vaults that contain unimaginable wealth, without your knowledge.'

'Correct. But it is not easy to open a vault without other people knowing. Specifically these vaults.'

'Then where did the paper get this image from. These pictures from?' Rajan argued, pointing to the second image on the page, which showed a pile of haphazardly dumped jewellery.

'This could just be a stock photo.' Gopi said. 'Is this what is making you angry?'

'I am not angry.'

'Then?'

'I am worried.'

'Worried about what?'

'Thampuran has never spoken about the temple's wealth openly. He has always skirted the issue. Until now. Not only is he being candid about the riches, he is also saying that the wealth was thanks to his ancestors. He is even inviting the journalist to photograph it.'

'So?'

'It indicates a changing climate, Gopi. The Privy Purse payable to these people . . . the royalty,' Rajan said with disdain, 'was stopped long ago. The temples, all of which were being run by private trusts, have come under state control. Temple-owned land has been taken away in the name of urban development, to make way for roads and infrastructure. All except the Anantha Padmanabha Swamy Temple. This one still remains in the control of the king. Do you think it's possible that Dharmaraja Varma might be tempted to siphon the entire wealth of the temple before the state decides to take control—whether voluntarily or by the courts' decree is another issue. Even if he doesn't give in to temptation, the next generation might force his hand.'

'I still don't understand why you are so upset about the interview!'

'Anything which deviates from routine worries me. If an old man does something which is out of character, it is a red flag. There is something fishy about this interview. When I saw this, I called the journalist who did the piece. He told me that the interview was done at the behest of Dharmaraja Varma. Why would someone who is camera-shy and hasn't spoken much to the media in fifteen years, despite his towering stature, suddenly ask to be interviewed? And . . .'

'And what?' Gopi asked with mounting impatience.

'The photographs were supplied by the Thampuran's media manager. I am not even arguing if these are stock photos or not. The assumption is that they are not.' He paused to catch his breath, then continued, 'Where did this photo come from if all the vaults are locked?'

This time Gopi did not dismiss him summarily. He thought for a while. 'If the idea is to siphon off this wealth, then why draw attention to it?'

'You don't understand. There is enough noise these days about wealth being hoarded by temples, churches and other religious institutions. At some point in time, if not today then a few years down the line, the vaults will be opened. No one knows what is inside them. Nothing is documented.'

Gopi listened intently. He knew Rajan well enough and didn't interrupt.

'Thus far, everyone has relied on the integrity of the kings. But times have changed. This could well be an attempt to tell the world that *this* is all there is in the vault, while the truth could be very different. The actual riches in the vault could be ten times more.'

'And you think the rest will be siphoned off?'

Rajan nodded. 'If it has not been already. Dharmaraja Varma's son has just returned from Stanford. The timing of this article somehow worries me.'

Gopi didn't need any explanation for what Rajan was referring to. The king was growing old. Since Kerala was a matrilineal society, his sister's son would become king upon his death, not his own son. It was natural to expect the king to worry about the future of his children and their inheritance.

'What do you want to do?' he asked.

'There's only one thing we can do. We must accelerate the process of the control of the temple passing into the hands of the state. Out of the king of Travancore's hands and into those of the Government of Kerala.'

'And how do you propose to do that?'

'By filing a writ in the court against the Thampuran and the temple. I'm going to ask that the entire wealth of the temple be catalogued in full and that the Thampuran be relieved of his temple duties and authority in the interim.' Rajan was clear in his intentions. He did not want the temple wealth to be used to fill personal coffers.

'You love playing with fire, don't you?' Gopi chuckled. 'Not many will support you. I hope you have considered that.'

'Gopi,' Rajan looked him in the eye, steely resolve in his own, 'never be scared of doing what your conscience tells you to do. If you think what you are doing is right, do it even if the whole world is against you. When you're doing what is right, nothing can harm you. Lord Padmanabha will be with you.' He walked up to Gopi, put a hand on his shoulder and smiled. 'I don't care about others. Are *you* with me?'

Gopi shrugged off his arm and walked towards the steel cupboard. 'Of course. What's there to doubt in that?' He opened the cupboard and dumped some papers on top of an existing pile. 'And this is not because I agree with you about the newspaper interview or because I have always stood by you. But because I believe that the state must take over the temple and manage its day-to-day affairs. The vast wealth that our temple is said to possess cannot be looked after by a private family. There is always the possibility of it falling in wrong hands. In the right hands, this wealth can do a lot for the people of this state.'

'Whatever you plan to do, do it soon,' Gopi said, sitting at his desk and opening the register he had been writing in. He was the treasurer of the temple. The chief trustee was his superior.

Rajan smiled and left. Once outside, he sat on a ledge on the temple premises for a couple of minutes. It was widely believed that whenever one visited a temple, one ought to sit down in the presence of the lord or at least inside the temple complex for a few minutes. If one didn't do that, the punya that one earned from paying obeisance to the lord passed to the first house right outside the temple door.

The mandatory two minutes over, Rajan got up and left the temple. The sun was shining overhead, heating up the tar roads—walking barefoot on them was out of the question. He started walking on the mud track by the side of the road. He had barely gone a few feet when an autorickshaw pulled up.

'Cheta! Get in. I will drop you.'

'Ah Kannan!' Rajan exclaimed. Kannan was the only one around who called him Cheta, Malayalam for elder brother. He was a trusted autorickshaw driver whose mother had worked in Rajan's house for many years. He also doubled up as a personal errand boy for Rajan.

Even though the house was only a short distance away, Rajan was happy that he didn't have to walk. In any case he could sense he had a long and lonely journey ahead.

5

Aditya was in seat 23A on the Amsterdam–Mumbai Jet Airways flight. He was ecstatic. And why not? He had just finished in the top three in an international jewellery design competition, organized by Piece de Resistance in Amsterdam.

The airhostess walked up to their row and started explaining the emergency exit procedures. Aditya watched her for a few minutes and then turned to look out of the window. As he thought of everything that had happened the previous evening, and the way events had unfolded over the past few days, his sharp eyes sighted two people talking across the barbed wire fence at the far end of the airport. One of them, a guy, was inside the fence, while the other, a girl, was on the outside. They continued speaking for a few minutes—the barbed wire between them. Then suddenly the girl threw something up in the air towards the guy. The airhostess had finished giving her instructions by now and disappeared to her post. Aditya tracked the package in the air and subconsciously curled his fingers into a fist and banged it against his leg as the package failed to make it across the fence, settling on top of it instead. The girl had given it the elevation but the package couldn't travel the distance. The guy walked close to the fence and pulled the packet towards him using a stick. Once the packet dropped to the ground, he tore it open, took out a jacket and wore it. It certainly was cold in Amsterdam. He blew

18

a kiss at the girl, turned and walked back towards the airport terminal.

Aditya smiled. The couple reminded him of his girlfriend back in India. For a minute the thought of lapses in airport perimeter security crossed his mind, but the romantic appeal was so strong that he didn't let it spoil the moment. He closed his eyes and leaned back in his seat. As he thought about his girlfriend back home, the events of the previous days kept barging in on his reflections. He ignored them as he pushed back the seat and stretched his legs.

Divya would be at the airport, waiting for him to land.

6

Nirav Choksi, a name the who's who of Mumbai had on their speed dial, designed and manufactured customized jewellery for the rich and famous all over the world. He was often referred to as the Indian Joel Arthur Rosenthal, one of the world's most exclusive jewellers whose high-flying clientele included Elizabeth Taylor, Elle Macpherson, Kim Kardashian, Michelle Obama and even the Princess of Jordan. Nirav Choksi's client list boasted the marquee names on the social circuit—politicians, wealthy Indian businessmen, film stars. Choksi wielded a fair bit of clout on the jewellery trade in the country. A man with both contacts and influence, he was an extremely sought-after guy in the political circuit for skills which went beyond jewellery design.

Like Rosenthal, he too made fifty to sixty pieces of jewellery a year. Connoisseurs recognized an NC piece the moment they saw it. From traditional to contemporary, he designed them all, never repeating a design. A man with a huge ego, Nirav crafted his own designs and would get very upset if a client tried to dictate to him. He was once overheard saying that he preferred international clients to Indians, not because they paid more, but because in India every woman thought she was the best designer in the world. There were times when he had refused to sell a piece of jewellery because he felt the ornament would not look good on the client—such was his pride in his craft. Every stone is a canvas and every item of jewellery is a piece of art, he would say. Advertisements and self-promotion were not Nirav's style. According to him, 'word of mouth' was what helped him get and retain clients. Even his office in Zaveri Bazaar was a thousand-square-foot pigeonhole in the basement of Pancharathna Complex.

Zaveri Bazaar was the nerve centre of the jewellery trade not only in Mumbai, but the whole of India. Roughly sixty per cent of India's gold trade passed through the narrow overcrowded lanes of the bazaar. The shabby buildings lining the sides of the main road held crores of rupees worth of gold, diamonds and jewellery, all stored in lockers built into the walls of the small stores, said to be strong enough to withstand any kind of robbery attempt, earthquake or bomb blast. The Government of India's attempts to move the diamond and jewellery trade to a snazzy new building in Bandra Kurla Complex, an upmarket suburb in Mumbai, had been met with resistance. Many jewellers, led by Nirav Choksi, were Zaveri Bazaar loyalists and unwilling to move to the government-sponsored yet privately owned BKC Diamond Bourse.

Nirav had one more office in the neighbourhood. Apart from the basement office in Pancharathna Complex, he also had a small workshop a few buildings away where his trusted and most skilled workers crafted the pieces that he so painstakingly designed.

That day, he had just stepped into his basement office when his phone rang.

'Hi beta!'

'Dad, where are you?'

'Just reached the office.'

'So late? You left over an hour ago.'

Zaveri Bazaar was a fifteen-minute drive from Nirav's house, after which he would get down from his car and walk for another ten minutes to reach his office. In all, twenty-five minutes from door to door.

'Traffic was terrible.'

'Why do you even go there, Dad? It is an apology for an office.'

Nirav smiled. He was the third generation in the business to operate out of that office. His grandfather had begun a small bullion trading business in that same thousand-square-foot office. Nirav's emotional bond with it ran deep. Becoming a famous, immensely successful designer was not reason enough for him to shift out. The space he needed was for him to sit alone, think and sketch. His office was more than sufficient for that. For the few clients who insisted on meeting in his office, he had had a small comfortable lounge built.

'Dad, why don't we shift to the diamond bourse in BKC? We can get a large, spacious office there worthy of your stature.' Nirav's daughter hated coming to Zaveri Bazaar. The crowds drove her mad, and the area was too downmarket for her.

'People come to us because of our designs. When they go to parties and social events wearing the jewellery we've made, other people admire the pieces. They appreciate our designs. Not our office. That's the way it is supposed to be.'

'There you go!' came the exasperated response.

'We built our business here. This building helped us realize our self-worth, beta. We will stay here. Besides, none of the others are moving. The bourse at BKC is barely occupied. It is a bhoot bangla.'

'The other jewellers are not moving because you are not. The day you decide to leave, they will follow.'

'Can we discuss this at home?' Nirav cut the conversation short. 'I need to work on a design.'

'Okay okay!' she hurriedly replied. 'I completely forgot what I had called for. I am going to the airport to pick up Aditya. He is coming back from Amsterdam today.'

'Fine. Call me once you return.'

Nirav had not met Aditya yet. It had been a bit difficult for him to accept him. Until Aditya, Nirav had been the only man in Divya's life. Nirav's wife—Divya's mother—had died of cervical cancer eight years ago. After her death, Nirav had almost given up everything. But his love for Divya brought him back from the brink and made him rebuild his business. Today, he had money, fame and respect, but the only things that truly mattered to him were Divya and his jewellery designs, in that order. Everything else, according to him, was incidental.

7

The telephone on the shining laminated table of the commander-in-chief of Dubai Police, Mohammed Jilani, rang three times before it was picked up.

'Assalam waleikum.'

'Waleikum assalam,' the chief replied.

'The Audis have been traced. Found abandoned about sixty miles outside of Dubai . . . On the route to . . .' the caller informed him, excitement in his voice.

'It has taken us two days.' The chief was not impressed.

Silence.

'And what else do we know now?'

'Forensic teams are on the scene, sir, but it's unlikely that we will find any clues. The cars were completely burnt, destroying every bit of evidence that we could have relied on. No fingerprints. No DNA.'

Jilani asked a few more questions and hung up. He was a worried man. The media had been closely following the story from the time the two Audis had crashed through the gates of Wafi Mall. The CCTV camera footage of the first Audi crashing into the gate in reverse, immediately followed by the second Audi, was playing on a loop on all the local TV channels. An angry Jilani stared at the TV, wondering who could it be. The police had sought out all their informers, checked out all the leads they had and investigated potential suspects. In vain. Now, the two cars had finally been traced. But they weren't expected to yield any fresh clues.

A knock on the door interrupted his thoughts. He looked up. There were three officers standing at the door. He waved them in.

'What do we have now, Iqbal?' he began without even waiting for them to be seated. Iqbal was the officer in charge of the investigation into the Wafi Mall heist.

'Nothing,' Iqbal replied matter-of-factly. He knew he was the best that the Dubai Police had. If he could not get to the bottom of the robbery, no one else could. 'No trace of the perpetrators. No records. They seem to be a team of first-timers.'

'For first-timers they were pretty good,' Jilani commented. 'Almost like professionals.'

'Yes, sir. They had done their homework. They knew what they were doing. Ordinarily, a novice driving into the mall to conduct a robbery would have armoured the front of the car and driven straight in. Had they done that, they would have run the risk of the airbags getting deployed. In Audis . . . in most cars for that matter, air bags deploy in case of a frontal collision, but not when the car is driven in reverse. These guys were smart. They drove in the first car in reverse. The rear of the car collided with the gate and brought it down, clearing the way for the car that was following. Unless they were professionals, they wouldn't have planned the heist in such detail.'

'Seems like you have become a fan, Iqbal,' Jilani commented. He didn't want to hear paeans of praise for the rogues who had blurred his impeccable record.

'Not a fan, janaab. But they executed such a clean job, one cannot help but admire.'

'In my thirty-two years with the Dubai Police, I have yet to come across a perfect crime. There is always something. There has to be a clue somewhere. Don't let your admiration for those crooks cloud your judgement, officer.'

Iqbal smiled. 'It is always good to admire competition, sir. Helps you stay ahead of them.' He extended his left hand towards the officer next to him, who promptly handed him the packet he was carrying. Iqbal carefully laid the packet on the table, and pulled out a transparent pouch with some markings on it.

'We recovered this from the robbery site.'

Jilani slowly picked up the pouch and looked at it.

'When they were running back to the Audis, one of the robbers stumbled and fell. Even though he recovered quickly and managed to gather a significant portion of the loot, he couldn't pick up everything that had fallen out.'

Jilani had not taken his eyes off the pouch.

'This is one of the things he failed to gather.'

The silence in the room was deafening. Finally, Jilani raised his eyebrows and looked at Iqbal.

'Damn! How old is this?'

8

A few weeks later

Rajan had been up since 4 a.m. Sleep had deserted him of late and he was feeling too restless to try falling asleep again. It was probably the excitement of the day ahead, coursing through his body like adrenaline. He tiptoed to the kitchen, and set about making himself some coffee. He had barely kept the container of milk on the stove when Kamu walked in.

'You could have woken me up.'

'Didn't want to. You were sleeping soundly. Snoring, in fact.'

'What's happened to you? You seem to have forgotten how to sleep.' Kamu walked up to him and put her arm around his shoulders. 'Is it the court case?' she asked.

Rajan smiled and hugged her back. 'You know,' he said, 'today is the day when the courts will be tested. They will have to make a choice.' He walked up to the stove and checked on the milk; it was simmering. 'Religion or monarchy. History or propriety. They will have to take sides. For years Dharmaraja Varma and his predecessors have run this temple like their private fiefdom,' he said, shutting off the gas. The milk had come to a boil. 'The court will pronounce its verdict on the case Gopi and I filed against the royal family and their mismanagement of the temple and misuse of the wealth in the temple vaults,' he finished, pouring out his coffee.

After his morning dose of filter coffee, he took a bath and stepped out of his house. It was 5.15 a.m. He could see the temple gopuram in the distance. On his way he crossed the Padma Teertha Kulam, the holy pond. He stopped, pushed open a small gate and went down a few steps to the water's edge. Dipping his hands in the water, he brought up a palmful and sprinkled a few drops on his head. With the same wet hands, he touched his eyes as a mark of respect.

As he got out of the enclosure, he saw a group of people walking hurriedly towards the temple. They were probably getting late for the morning abhishekam, the holy ritual of bathing the deity.

Upon entering the temple, Rajan walked straight into the sanctum sanctorum. He bowed his head before the huge monolith of Padmanabha Swamy reclining on the five-hooded serpent Anantha, also known as Adi Sesha. He said a silent prayer and went to the temple office. Gopi had not come in yet; it was too early for any office bearer to report for work. Rajan stepped out into the corridor—called sannidhi—that ran all round the sanctorum, providing a covered area for devotees to sit and sing verses in praise of the lord. On the northeastern side of the temple, the sannidhi branched out into a small passage to the left. Rajan walked down the passage to an open area. He was the only one there. To his right was a small flight of stairs that went down one level. He climbed down the twenty-four steps. As he reached the bottom he could see it: a large door on his right. He stood for a long time looking at it.

Behind those doors lay the secret of the treasures of the Anantha Padmanabha Swamy Temple. There were six vaults named A to F for bookkeeping purposes. Vaults C to F had been opened multiple times and the temple utilities and gold and jewellery found inside were used for the running of the temple. Vaults A and B had not been opened in the recent past. Legend had it that Vaults A and B contained riches beyond belief, unseen and unheard of in any temple in the world. Riches that had not been claimed by anyone—except the family of the king. Strangely enough, despite having these unimaginable riches, the security cover provided to the temple was surprisingly lax. Probably because people believed that no one would attempt a robbery at a temple guarded by Padmanabha Swamy himself.

As he stood there, wondering what lay in the two unopened vaults, his phone rang. It was Gopi. Rajan glanced at his watch. It was already 7.30 a.m. He had to be at the high court by 9 a.m.

It was judgement day.

9

The high court was teeming with people. A posse of journalists waited patiently in one corner. It was a landmark case and everyone was eagerly awaiting the verdict.

When the judge walked in, everyone stood up as a mark of respect. The judge took his seat and began cautiously. The first one and a half pages that he read out were nothing dramatic. That was just the preamble.

Finally, he came to the verdict.

'Based on the arguments presented by both sides, it has been decided by the court that the administrative control of the temple will pass from the current office bearers to those appointed by the state. The Government of Kerala will take over the day-to-day running and management of the Anantha Padmanabha Swamy Temple. The state will also set up a committee to evaluate the need to open the vaults in the temple and submit their recommendations to the court within forty-five days. Dharmaraja Varma, on account of his position and stature, will continue to be the chief trustee of the temple.'

Rajan and Gopi were thrilled. The former had tears in his eyes. It was a great victory for them. They had protected the riches of Padmanabha. They had performed a service for the lord, which everyone would be proud of. Or so he thought.

Outside, a huge crowd was assembled, shouting slogans in favour of the king. It was an emotional issue and the king's public relations machinery had worked overtime to influence public sentiment and drive people into a frenzy. The moment the court delivered the verdict, the restless crowd became violent. Despite the presence of a large contingent of the police, people started pelting stones, breaking barricades and damaging the cars parked in the compound.

Policemen took up positions outside the main door of the courtroom. The petitioners were not allowed to leave, for fear of their safety. Gopi and Rajan walked up to the window and looked outside in disbelief. A riot had broken out. This was a public sentiment that they had failed to read. A power they had failed to assess. Rajan couldn't understand what the brouhaha was all about. Hadn't they saved crores worth of public wealth from being usurped by the king? Why then this backlash?

Rajan turned towards the assistant commissioner of police who was in charge.

'Is there another route from where we can exit?' he asked the ACP. After all, they could not be holed up in the small room for the entire day.

'There is one, on the eastern side. Seldom used but—'

'Aaaaah!'

The sudden moan from behind Rajan interrupted the ACP mid-sentence. When they turned to see what the matter was, they realized Gopi was on the floor. He was clutching the right side of his face with one hand, and vigorously rubbing his chest with the other. He seemed to be in severe pain. Rajan rushed to his side.

'Gopi! What happened?' he asked, a worried look on his face.

Such was his agony that Gopi could barely speak; he kept groaning. Rajan went down on his knees and tried to raise Gopi's head into his lap. The moment he touched Gopi's face, he screamed and pulled his hand away. He shook his hand a few times as if to get rid of whatever was on it. It felt like it was on fire. Grinding his teeth against the burning sensation, he wiped his palm on his shirt. To his horror, the shirt fabric started crumbling instantly. Shocked, Rajan looked at Gopi helplessly. That's when he noticed the broken vial on the floor near Gopi's feet. The carpet around it seemed like it had burnt away. Suddenly everything became clear. Someone had hurled a vial of acid into the courtroom through the open window and it had struck Gopi. Had he not stepped away to talk to the ACP, it could have hit Rajan.

Gopi was in terrible pain. His shirt had dissolved in the acid, exposing rapidly blistering skin, but it was his face that had borne the brunt of the attack. The acid had eaten through skin and flesh. The strong pungent smell of acid and burning flesh filled the courtroom.

The policemen were busy on the walkie-talkie, presumably calling for an ambulance.

Five minutes passed. There was still no sign of the ambulance. Rajan was getting paranoid. The crowd was swelling by the minute.

'The ambulance is stuck at the court gates,' a constable announced. 'Unable to get in.'

Rajan put his arms around Gopi, hauled him up and stumbled towards the entrance, determined to take him to the hospital himself.

One of the policemen barred the way. 'You need to wait. It is not safe to go outside.'

'I can't leave him to die!' Rajan yelled at him and staggered out with Gopi. The moment they emerged, a few protesters noticed them and started running in their direction, shouting slogans against the court verdict.

Rajan turned and hurried towards the eastern gate of the court, the one the ACP had mentioned. Though it was further away, he had no choice; the front gate was blocked. Gopi was in excruciating pain and couldn't walk as fast. Rajan had to literally drag him. A few police constables too stepped out and walked alongside them. The distance between the protesters and them was decreasing steadily. Rajan kept glancing back to see how much of a lead they had. Even at that moment, he feared more for Gopi's life that his. If he could not take Gopi to the hospital nearby he was almost certain his friend would die. A friend who had stood by him as he fought the biggest case of his life. He couldn't let that happen. 'Please, Padmanabha,' he implored silently, 'he was standing by my side—for you. Help me save him.'

A few in the crowd started pelting stones at them. The policemen took up positions behind them. When the crowd didn't stop, they fired in the air, but the crowd remained undeterred. In another forty-five seconds they would be overrun by the mob.

'Cheta! Rajan Cheta!'

Rajan heard someone call his name over all the noise. It was Kannan! He had managed to enter through the rear gate and was almost next to them.

'Get in,' Kannan implored. 'Quickly! Quickly! Before those guys reach us,' he said, revving the autorickshaw engine.

In no time at all, the three of them were roaring towards the hospital. By the time the doctors took him inside, Gopi had passed out from the pain.

Three days later, Gopi died.

'Had he been brought in ten minutes earlier we might have been able to save him,' the doctors told Rajan. 'But what can we do if Lord Padmanabha wills it.'

10

They were the only two people in the northeastern corner of the coffee shop at the Four Seasons hotel in Worli. Divya was wearing fitted blue jeans and a maroon top. Aditya was in formals. He had come straight from college where the placement session was on. He didn't look too pleased.

'I don't want to join just any company. I *won* the world design competition. I beat the best in the world! I would rather start my own jewellery design business than work for someone else. Besides, as someone once said, "No one gets rich saving on their salary."'

'And you want to be rich.'

'Rich and famous,' Aditya corrected. 'Who doesn't? I want to be the best jewellery designer in the world. The most exclusive diamantaire for the rich and famous.'

'Join my father then,' Divya suggested, squeezing Aditya's hand in a reassuring manner. 'He will be only too happy to have you. He sees me as a disappointment. God's cruel joke on him. Nirav Choksi's daughter . . . not interested in jewellery—it's all a bit unpalatable for him, to say the least.' She smiled.

'He hasn't even met me. What makes you think he will be happy to have me join him?'

'Come on. You know him, don't you?'

'Whatever I know about him has come from you and business magazines.'

Divya rolled her eyes at that. 'I keep talking about you to him. He wants to meet you only after you have told your parents about us.'

Now it was Aditya's turn to make a face. 'This is the one thing I just don't get. What does him meeting me have to do with my parents?'

'Simple. He thinks that once he has met you, keeping our relationship a secret from your parents will be tantamount to treachery. He is like that. You can't argue with him; no one can. At some point in time, sooner rather than later, you're going to have to talk to your parents.'

'You know the story, Divya. Why do you want me to repeat it?' Aditya snapped, frustrated.

'I know but . . .' She stopped. Divya knew that he had been away from home for years. Any discussion about his parents would irritate him. 'Anyway, forget all that,' she said brightly. 'Should I talk to my dad about you joining him?'

'No. Not right now.'

'Why?'

'After winning an international competition, you want me to work in Zaveri Bazaar? The slum of the diamond industry?' Aditya smiled. He knew how much Divya loathed the bazaar.

'In that case, you'll never be able to work with him. I have tried talking to him multiple times about moving out of Zaveri Bazaar, but he is wedded to that place.'

'Wedded?' Aditya said with a glint in his eyes. 'Generous choice of words, sweetheart. He is a don there.'

'Of course not! Everyone loves him.'

'Love and fear often bring out the same reaction—compliance,' he said and laughed. 'Okay! Okay!' Aditya protested as Divya punched his arm. 'I was just kidding! Maybe if I join him, I'll convince him, maybe arm-twist him into moving.'

'Arm-twist?' Divya grinned. 'I didn't know you had this violent streak in you.'

Aditya quickly changed track. 'Let him enjoy his life in that dungeon while we celebrate our togetherness.' He raised his cup of coffee. Divya responded with a smile and raised her own cup.

Later that evening, as he was walking Divya to her car, Aditya asked, 'If, God forbid, he refuses to let you be with me, what will you do?'

Divya rolled her eyes and looked at him. 'Are you asking whose side I will take if it comes to that?'

'Hmm.' Aditya loved to put her on the spot.

'It's simple. My dad is the most important person in my life. I will never marry you without his blessings. I love you, Aditya, but not enough to go against his will.'

11

Gopi's body lay in the thatched veranda of his house. To anyone standing next to his body, the gopuram of the Anantha Padmanabha Swamy Temple was clearly visible. A crowd of friends and relatives had gathered for his last rites. The heart-wrenching cries of the womenfolk that rang through the house would have melted even the strongest of hearts.

Rajan stood by the door, a few feet from the body. His eyes burned with rage. Why had Gopi become the victim of the acid attack? What was his fault? It could have been anybody standing inside the courtroom. Even Rajan himself. That last was a particularly disconcerting thought.

Gopi was one of Rajan's closest friends. They had first met in school over fifty years ago, and been together ever since. Rajan greeted everyone who walked in and accepted their condolences on behalf of Gopi's family. A sudden chatter disturbed the silence in the veranda. Out of the corner of his eye Rajan saw a puff of dust on the right, where the street in front of Gopi's house joined the main city road. Four white Benz cars could be seen in the distance.

Rajan stepped out of the house and waited on the street. He knew who it was.

A few minutes later the cars stopped in front of Gopi's house. Just as suddenly as it had begun, the chatter died down, and a hush descended on the gathering. Everyone got up and stood with folded hands, heads bowed in respect. Everyone except Rajan. He calmly stood his ground and stared at the cars. The rear door of the second car opened and an old man stepped out. He was wearing a dhoti, a white shirt that extended a few inches below his waist, and black Quovadis sandals. He shuffled up to Rajan, put a hand on his shoulder, shook his head and said, 'It is sad that he went this way. He was a good man.' Rajan didn't respond. Before the king could say anything further, the sound of two more doors being shut was heard and his wife and daughter stepped out of the car. They started to approach the house, but the look in Rajan's eyes stopped them.

Meanwhile, word of the visitors' arrival had spread through the house, and close relatives of Gopi who were inside with his wife came out.

'Thampuran,' they said and bowed before him.

Thampuran's wife walked ahead and hugged the woman of the house. His daughter stayed next to him, a grim expression on her face.

'You should not have come here,' Rajan said softly, glaring at the two of them.

The king's daughter looked at her father, who obviously didn't like what he was being told. Nor did he like Rajan. After all, wasn't he the one who had precipitated the court case?

'Well!' began the king. Judging by the way he began, he had obviously come prepared. 'This is all a result of going against the will of the lord. When Lord Padmanabha is angry, his rage knows no bounds. Had you not invited the ire of the lord this would not have happened.' He then turned towards the crowd that had gathered there and said, 'Had this man here not angered the lord, Gopi would be alive today. Everything that has occurred is the will of Padmanabha. No one can escape his fury. The temple and its riches have remained untouched for centuries. If someone tries to defile the temple, natural justice will prevail. This man here misled Gopi, and poor Gopi paid the price. He was a good man. May his soul rest in peace.'

Often, in matters of death, rationality takes a beating. The moment the king uttered these words, Gopi's relatives turned on Rajan.

'This is how you repaid Gopi for supporting you!' one of them said, an angry look on his face.

'Had you not dragged him into your battle with the king, he would be alive right now,' another added.

'If you had an axe to grind against Thampuran, why drag innocent Gopi into it?'

Accusations flew thick and fast, and in no time the crowd became aggressive. Someone even pushed Rajan. By the time the king left, the scene had almost turned violent.

Rajan had no choice but to leave. He returned home, ferried from Gopi's house by Kannan. The only regret Rajan had about the day was not that the king had won round one but that he could not bid farewell to his friend on his last journey.

Three days later, the legal counsel of Dharmaraja Varma filed an appeal in the Supreme Court, challenging the verdict of the high court.

12

Mohammed Jilani walked into the head office of the Central Bureau of Investigation in Delhi at 10 a.m. sharp. A meeting had been set up for him through the ministry of external affairs with the director of the CBI, C.S. Inamdar.

'Hey! Good morning!' Inamdar got up from his chair the moment Jilani pushed open the door to his cabin. He had met the Dubai chief of police earlier at an Interpol conference. The men shook hands and then took seats on either side of Inamdar's desk. A curious Inamdar waited while Jilani opened his briefcase and pulled out a file.

'Have you heard of the Wafi Mall heist?' Jilani asked as he handed over the file to Inamdar.

'Who hasn't!' Inamdar confirmed. 'It made headlines even in India.' He opened the file and looked at the first page, squinting just enough to get a clearer view. 'But what does the heist have to do with this?'

'This was found at the site of the heist. While making their getaway, one of the robbers stumbled and fell. This fell from his bag,' Jilani said. 'Probably.'

Inamdar scrutinized the picture from every angle. Finally, he set the file down and leaned back in his seat, his eyes trained on the ceiling. 'What else do you know about this?'

'Nothing,' Jilani admitted. 'This fell from his bag. Whether it is the robbers', or the jewellery store's or belongs

40

to the customer who died in the heist . . . we don't know.' He handed over a photograph of the customer who was shot to Inamdar.

'Well, you will have to give me a little bit more than that to go on,' Inamdar said as he came forward and rested his hands on the desk.

'That's all we have,' Jilani reiterated. 'We believe that if we can get to the bottom of this, we will know who the perpetrators were. At least we will have a good chance.'

'How old is this?'

'Six hundred years.'

Inamdar looked at Jilani in shock. '*Six hundred years?*'

Jilani nodded.

'Taking a figurine outside the country, especially one that is six hundred years old, is a criminal offence.'

'Will you be able to figure out where this came from?' Jilani asked. 'Maybe the origins will tell us something about what actually happened.'

Inamdar continued to stare at the printout. After about a minute he tapped the bell in front of him. Almost immediately a peon walked in, followed by his secretary.

'Get me Dr Bose, director general of National Museums.' The secretary nodded and turned back. 'Now!' barked Inamdar.

Within a minute, the phone on his table rang. His secretary was on the line. 'Dr Bose for you, sir,' she said and hung up.

'Yes, Director Inamdar. How can I help you?'

'Chief Mohammed Jilani of Dubai Police is with me. He needs some help.'

'Sure. Tell me.'

'I am sending you an image. There's no time for a formal request. I just need to know any details that you might be able to pull out. This is extremely urgent!' he said and hung up. Next, he took a picture of the image on his phone and messaged it to Dr Bose.

Dr Bose called back soon after.

'I'm putting you on speaker, so that Chief Jilani can also hear what you are saying.'

'Well, Chief Jilani,' Bose began, 'the statuette in the image you just sent is a very ancient piece. From the looks of it, it is from the Chola period. About six hundred years ago.'

'Great, so it is from India.'

'Yes, looks like it.'

'If it is from here, it must have been stolen. Any records of such a theft?'

'It's hard to say. The Chola dynasty spanned all of Tamil Nadu and parts of the other south Indian states as well. The statuette must be from one of the temples down there, most likely in Tamil Nadu, though it'll be difficult for me to pinpoint a particular one. There are hundreds of them,' he said apologetically. 'Let me see. If I find a match, I will let you know.'

'Thank you, Dr Bose,' Jilani said, a tad disheartened, even as Inamdar pressed the button to cut the call.

Half an hour later, Dr Bose called Inamdar again. 'What I suspected is sadly true. There is no official cataloguing of temple idols in Tamil Nadu. So it will be impossible to determine which temple this idol was stolen from. The only way to do this is to go from temple to temple and figure out which idol is missing. But even that is a fairly far-fetched plan for if we don't have any record of what was there in the temple to begin with, how will we know what is missing? We will have to rely on local knowledge.'

This call was even more disappointing than the first, especially for Jilani. It told him in no uncertain terms that it would be almost impossible to figure out the origins of the statuette. He had been counting on it to decipher the secret of the Wafi heist.

Inamdar walked a desolate Jilani to his car. 'I will depute a senior officer to help you with this. He will get in touch with you soon.'

'Thank you.' Jilani shook Inamdar's hand and got into his car.

On the way to his hotel, Jilani saw a large contingent of media personnel and OB vans blocking the road. A large board to his left announced that the building was that of the Supreme Court of India.

'These media people. They are a law unto themselves. Do whatever they want,' the car driver complained. 'They always descend in hordes and block traffic in this area whenever an important case comes up for hearing.'

Jilani glanced at the paper lying on the seat by his side. The headline on the front page was: Lord Padmanabha Swamy Wealth Case in Supreme Court Today.

13

The lawyer representing King Dharmaraja Varma made a fervent plea in the Supreme Court, protesting the high court verdict which transferred the charge of the temple and its wealth to the state. Strangely, the Kerala government too joined the petition, filing a statement in the court stating that they were comfortable with the way the Anantha Padmanabha Swamy Temple was being managed and that they did not see any need for the temple to be taken over by the state.

The court adjourned the case for a few weeks.

14

At 6 p.m., Nirav locked everything up and was about to leave the store when he saw a young man walk in. He seemed to be in his late twenties. Smartly dressed, in jeans and a semi-formal shirt, he looked like he belonged to an affluent family.

The security guard at the gate stopped him. That was the default option for him. Nirav Choksi did not entertain walk-ins.

'I'm not a customer,' the young man was explaining to the guard when Nirav walked up to him.

'What brings you here, young man?'

'I came here to meet you.'

Nirav nodded. 'Go ahead. I am listening.' His support staff was still hanging around to ensure the guy didn't cause any trouble.

'Aditya,' he said, extending his right hand.

'Right! Aditya. Nice to mee—' Nirav said absently. Then suddenly: 'Oh! Aditya! It's wonderful to see you. Divya didn't tell me you'd be coming.' He shook hands with him warmly. 'Come on in!'

'She doesn't know. I haven't told her.' Aditya looked at the other people standing around.

Nirav understood his discomfort and gestured to his staff to leave 'Come, come.' The two of them walked up to Nirav's office and sat down on the sofa.

'What will you have?' Nirav asked, wondering what the was protocol when meeting one's daughter's boyfriend for the first time!

'Nothing, sir. I just came to meet you because I wanted to talk to you alone. Divya mentioned that you didn't want to meet me unless I had spoken to my family and told them about Divya and my relationship.'

'Aaah, yes,' Nirav said. 'I did say that. I wanted to make sure that you were serious about the relationship. For Divya, my endorsement is critical. And I did not want to endorse someone who had an exit option. When you are serious about a relationship, you willingly give up all exit options. You commit wholeheartedly. That's what I'm looking for in you, or for that matter anyone who wants to be a part of her life. Informing one's parents, to me, is just one way of demonstrating that commitment. That aside, I trust Divya's judgment completely.'

'Is there any other way?'

'What do you mean?' Nirav was intrigued. And then as he understood what Aditya wanted, he clarified. 'You mean to say that you don't want to tell your parents about your relationship?'

'Not don't. Can't,' Aditya spoke. Seeing Nirav's confusion he elaborated, 'My father left us—my mother and me—when I was six years old.'

Nirav nodded. 'Yes. Divya did tell me about this.'

'My mother raised me alone, as a single parent. But I never missed having a father. She has always made sure that I have everything I need. Thankfully I got a scholarship to fund my jewellery design course. I left home about eight years ago and came to Mumbai. I stayed with an aunt for a few years.' He paused for a moment, then continued. 'If you insist, I will tell my mother now but if I have a choice, I would rather speak to her when I am independent and have become successful enough to take care of all her needs for the rest of her life. She has her expectations and I don't want to disappoint her.'

Nirav looked at Aditya thoughtfully. It was as if he was judging him. Reading his character through his face. Eventually Aditya squirmed under Nirav's scrutiny and moved a bit.

'You know Aditya, Divya is my only daughter. I have to make sure that she makes the right decisions in life.'

'Of course, sir.'

'I have to be certain that she's not fallen for someone inappropriate, Sometimes when boys know that the girl's father is rich . . . well, you know what all they do. I just wanted to make sure that you are not one of them. The fact that you did not take money from your mother for this jewellery design course is praiseworthy, as is the fact that you have no idea what I do or how big my business is.'

Aditya smiled. 'Except that you operate out of this pigeon hole, even though you can afford a much bigger office in any of the diamond bourses around the globe.'

Nirav laughed. He liked Aditya. 'You're right! I could have moved. Bourses around the globe, I am not too sure. But certainly to the BKC Diamond Bourse. But you know what Aditya, the people who launched that bourse could not take much of Zaveri Bazaar with them. If they wanted us to move they should have kept our interests in mind too. Which they didn't. There are a lot of small-time traders, who won't be able to afford a space in the BKC Diamond Bourse. Too much money for something which is not significantly better than what they have here in Zaveri Bazar. That's why none of us have moved there. And in any case this is a comfortable and lucky office for me. Three generations of my family have operated out of this office. It's a legacy I have inherited and don't want to give up. And for generations our family has protected the small traders here. We will continue to do that.'

'I am sorry,' Aditya apologized. He realized that he had touched a raw nerve. 'I didn't mean to be rude.'

'It's all right. Divya keeps nagging me about this as well. In any case, what were we talking about?' He looked upwards, at the ceiling. 'Aah yes. I have convinced myself that you are the right choice for Divya.'

Aditya just smiled. 'Then why insist on the parents bit?'

A cornered Nirav just shrugged his shoulders. 'Maybe . . . I was testing your resolve, your commitment to your own goals.'

'To your daughter you mean,' Aditya said.

Nirav laughed again. That's when Aditya understood. Nirav had made his choice. He had given his blessings to the relationship. He had just been waiting to see if he would fight for Divya. Today's visit had sealed it for him.

By the end of that conversation, Nirav was so confortable with Aditya that he offered him an apprenticeship with him, an offer that Aditya politely turned down.

He had other aspirations.

15

Bhaskar Iyer, commissioner of police, Chennai, was in his office when K.S. Murgavel, the head of the CBI for the southern region, walked in, accompanied by a stranger. Though it was not uncommon for the CBI and the local police to be at loggerheads, Murgavel enjoyed a cordial relationship with the police commissioner

'When I got a call this morning saying that you wanted to meet, I was a bit concerned,' the commissioner admitted as he shook Murgavel's hand. He looked inquiringly at the clean-shaven man who had accompanied Murgavel.

Murgavel didn't need much prodding. 'Meet Kabir Khan, additional director, CBI.'

Iyer was surprised—and a little miffed. According to protocol if an additional director with the CBI was to come calling, the commissioner had to be informed in advance. However, he tamped down his anger, albeit momentarily, and held out his right hand.

'Hello!' The visitor shook his hand and smiled. 'Kabir Khan, additional director, heritage and environment crimes.'

Often we like or dislike people not for who they are, but for the circumstances under which we first meet them. The breach of protocol had not only angered Iyer but also given him an instant dislike for Kabir Khan. 'And what brings the CBI to my doorstep?' he asked curtly.

'We need your help.'

His tone dripping with sarcasm, Iyer asked, 'Help? Since when does the CBI need the assistance of the local police?'

'Well,' Kabir Khan replied, ignoring the sarcasm, 'Director Inamdar has been approached by the commander-in-chief of Dubai Police. They have recovered a small idol of Ganesha, six inches tall, at the Wafi Mall heist. They believe the idol is a clue to the identity of whoever was behind the heist. When we checked, we found that it was a bronze idol, most likely from the Chola era. Hence we wanted your assistance in figuring out which temple it belongs to.' And he placed the image on the table. 'This is the idol.'

'Aah. Mr Khan, you must know—' the commissioner started and then abruptly stopped. 'How will you know? You don't worship idols, do you?'

Kabir Khan was infuriated. He had had no hand in his appointment as the head of heritage and environment crimes. He knew it was a transit posting. He had been the head of cyber crime earlier, a role in which he had served effectively for two and a half years until he was transferred out of the unit for taking on a powerful politician and getting on the wrong side of him. At the time, this was the only unit which was available. He had accepted the posting under the explicit understanding that he would be reassigned at the first available opportunity.

'And what is it that you think I am *not* likely to know, Commissioner?' he asked, refusing to let the slight pass unanswered.

'Idols like these are found all over the temples in south India. How can we tell which temple this one belongs to?'

'You can't. Had there existed a detailed catalogue of all the idols in all the temples in Tamil Nadu, you could have told me what I want to know. Rather, I would have figured it out myself.' Kabir leaned forward, his hands on the table between them. 'Sadly, there isn't any such catalogue in existence.'

Not one to be intimidated, the commissioner stood his
ground and said, 'Even if there was one, you would still have
a problem, Mr Khan. Similar idols can be found in multiple
temples.'

'And it's very easy to steal them, isn't it? These ancient
treasures . . . ' Kabir persisted.

Murgavel was a silent spectator to the entire discussion. He
did not know how to react. Embarrassed and a tad confused, he
kept quiet.

'Mr Khan, there are *thirty-three thousand* temples in Tamil
Nadu alone. How is the government supposed to protect all of
them? We don't have the manpower to provide security to even
one-tenth of that number. It is left to the local village councils
to manage them. I understand there are issues here, but we have
bigger problems to deal with. Your missing idol does not fit into
our priority list.'

'I am sure.' Kabir stood up to leave. 'Thank you for your time.'

16

When Kabir Khan walked into the lobby of the Taj Coromandel in Nungambakkam, Ashokan was already waiting for him. As soon as he saw Kabir, Ashokan sprang up from the sofa and hurried towards him.

The men shook hands warmly. It was evident that they knew each other well.

'So, what do you have?' Kabir asked him when they had settled into an isolated corner. He didn't have time for polite conversation. 'Were you able to figure out where the statuette is from?'

'No, not yet, sir.' Ashokan was always nervous in Khan's presence, and the latter's brusque manner only made it worse.

'Then why are you wasting my time?' Kabir snapped.

'Not sure how much it is worth, but . . . ' He fidgeted with his phone for a bit and then showed a picture to Kabir.

The expression on Kabir's face changed as he looked at it. 'Where is this?'

'I can take you there. But this is an old picture.'

'How old?'

'A few months for sure. One of my contacts sent this to me.' Ashokan let out the breath that he had been holding. He was happy that Khan saw value in what he had shown. For informers like him, their place in the system was linked to the value of the information they brought to the table. And Kabir Khan's sudden interest suggested that the information was significant. 'When do you want to go?'

Kabir looked at his watch. He had a flight back to Delhi later that night. But what Ashokan had shown him had piqued his interest. Delhi could wait. 'How about now?' he said.

'Now?'

'Is there a problem?'

'Not at all. Let's go.'

17

Their destination was 26 kilometres outside Chennai, on the road to Sriperumbudur. As a result of heavy traffic, it took Kabir Khan and Ashokan over an hour and a half to get there. About a kilometre ahead of Sriperumbudur, Ashokan took a left turn on to a muddy track. In the growing darkness, they continued on that track for another 1.5 kilometres, occasionally passing clusters of huts on the way. The land was quite barren and dry. Two dusty Ambassadors went by in the opposite direction. Ambassadors were very common in rural Tamil Nadu, and by the looks of it, Kabir and Ashokan were almost in rural Tamil Nadu.

For a minute, Kabir wondered if he had done the right thing in trusting Ashokan and coming with him without his regular entourage. But then the information he had brought was too exciting not to follow up on. Kabir pulled out the image Ashokan had shown him at the hotel and looked at it. He swiped his way to the image of the statuette that Mohammed Jilani had sent Inamdar. He swiped back and forth a few times.

The images were very similar.

'How much further?' he asked, looking up from his phone.

'Almost there.'

Five minutes later, they stopped outside a makeshift gate made of planks of wood that had been nailed together. A huge compound wall enclosed what looked like a workshop. There was no sign of human civilization for acres and acres. Inside, it was pitch dark. Kabir patted his holster to confirm the presence of his service revolver. He wondered if he should send his coordinates to his team, to call for backup, but dropped the idea; it was too late now.

Ashokan cut the ignition, stepped out of the car and walked through the gate. Kabir followed him in the eerie silence, walking stealthily, trying to crouch in the shadows.

'It is okay. You don't need to do that.' Ashokan smiled, not bothering to keep his voice down, much to Kabir's despair. Something was not right. Kabir's intuition was usually bang on target. But Ashokan was not bothered.

'Annaiya!' he called out. Loud and clear.

No response.

'Annaiya! Annaiya!' he called again as he walked into the workshop. While the outside light was on, there was no light inside. He walked to his left and switched on the lights. He had been here before. He knew the lay of the land.

'Annaiya!'

Still no response.

'Must be drunk,' Ashokan remarked, looking at Kabir. 'These guys spend all their money on arrack. Make money during the day and blow it all up in the evening. Had this guy been in America, he would have earned millions.'

'Nobody earns millions making plaster of Paris impressions,' Kabir retorted.

'Ah, but this guy is very good.'

'That's fine, but all he does is make moulds and then cast copies of statues to be sold in some third-rate curio store.'

'Maybe. But even that requires talent.'

'Talent!'

'Of course!' Ashokan insisted, walking into the room next to the main hall. 'If he didn't have the talent, he wouldn't have got the contract for making so many impressions of the Ganesha statuette. Didn't you see how close to the original the replicas look? Simply perfect!'

Kabir looked at his phone, at the image that Ashokan had sent him—over one hundred plaster of Paris imitations of the statue that resembled the statuette found after the Wafi Mall heist were lined up as if waiting to be packed and dispatched. It was not the number of statuettes that bothered Kabir; it was their similarity to the original. There was a possibility that these were dummies produced for sale in the normal course of business—they would know once they interrogated Annaiya, the owner of the manufacturing unit where all these had been produced.

Kabir opened the rear door and walked into the deserted backyard. A few coconut trees. A tin-roof shed. It seemed as if at one point in time a few cows might have been tied there. A large tank. He had seen those before. In the days when open bathrooms were popular, such tanks were used to store water. But this guy, Annaiya, was using them for a different purpose. The white marks on the sides of the three-foot-tall tank, which shone in the moonlight, told Kabir that Annaiya was using it to mix industrial quantities of plaster of Paris prior to pouring it in moulds. A primitive way of manufacturing plaster of Paris artefacts, but effective nevertheless.

As he turned to go inside his foot brushed against something. He stopped and looked down. It was a slipper. A Bata rubber slipper. He bent down and picked it up. It looked new. He flipped it over and saw that the price tag was intact. He stared at the slipper for a moment, then—

'Ashokan! Come here. Now!'

Kabir rushed to the tank, Ashokan in close pursuit. There was something on the side wall of the tank that had caught his eye. He picked it up. It was the other slipper.

Apprehensively, he looked down into the water tank. It was all white. Plaster of Paris. As he had suspected, Annaiya was using the tank for mixing the plaster of Paris. However, what caught his attention was the smooth round bulge in the otherwise flat surface of the plaster of Paris in the tank. Kabir swore angrily.

Ashokan followed Kabir's gaze and immediately realized what he was looking at. 'Annaiya!' he gasped. 'How could this have happened?'

Kabir Khan didn't answer. He just pulled out his phone and dialled a number. 'There has been a murder.'

Annaiya was lying in the plaster of Paris, his curved paunch the only part of his body visible above the plaster. Whether he was killed and then thrown into the tank or whether he was drowned in the tank, Kabir Khan couldn't say.

'The plaster is wet,' Ashokan said.

'This can only mean that he was killed a short while ago.'

'We need to leave.'

'You go,' Kabir whispered. 'I will wait for the police to arrive.'

18

Dharmaraja Varma arrived at the temple at 7.20 a.m. that day, as he had been doing ever since he was crowned king of Travancore. As per the rules of the temple, the king was duty-bound to visit the lord every morning and brief him on the happenings in the kingdom. Now, even at the age of ninety-one, the king still followed the ritual. He would go to the temple and spend about ten minutes in the sanctum sanctorum, locked in with the deity, before continuing with his day.

That day when the king ascended the ottakal mandapam, the elevated and enclosed platform in the centre of the temple from where one can get darshan of the deity, he ran into Rajan. In the normal course, the king's representatives would have cleared the temple of all unwanted elements, but knowing Rajan's litigious nature and thinking of the case pending hearing in the Supreme Court, they didn't force him to leave.

The king stood on the mandapam, facing the statue of a reclining Padmanabha. The statue was so large that it could not be viewed all at once. Three large viewing doors stood between the king and the statue of Padmanabha, the first offered a glimpse of the visage of the reclining lord; the second, Brahma seated on a lotus emanating from the lord's navel; and the third, the lord's feet.

Rajan was also in the mandapam, right in front of the middle door. The king looked at Rajan and smiled. A smile full of mockery.

'So you visit the same god you have stolen from all these years . . . eh?' Rajan asked unabashedly. Dharmaraja Varma might be the king, but for Rajan, he was an ordinary mortal. No different from him. Rajan was far from intimidated.

The king was taken aback. He looked around hurriedly to see if anyone had heard Rajan. His entourage never stayed on the mandapam with him. They escorted him to the mandapam and then left, returning only when summoned.

Displaying great self-control, possibly because he was in front of the lord, Dharmaraja Varma ignored Rajan's words, closed his eyes and said his morning prayers. He sat down on the mandapam and kept muttering something to himself. Possibly updating the lord on everything that was going on. After about ten minutes he got up. Rajan was still standing there, staring at the lord, as if in a trance. The king slowly bent down and touched his forehead to the ground, a gesture of subservience before the lord, his master. As he rose, he looked at Rajan and said, 'Do you have the courage to do this? If you want to take everything from the lord, have the courage to give him everything you have.'

As per folklore, prostrating oneself in front of Lord Anantha Padmanabha meant surrendering all of one's worldly belongings to the lord. By offering oneself to the lord, a person formally declared themselves his slave. Since the king had ritualistically offered everything to the lord, there was nothing left for him to offer and hence it was an acceptable practice for him to prostrate himself in front of the lord. But for everyone else, the belief had deteriorated to such an extent that if they were to accidentally drop something on the ground while standing on the mandapam, it was considered an irretrievable offering to the lord.

Rajan smiled again and said, 'I have nothing left to offer to the lord but myself. So I have nothing to fear.' He folded his hands as he dropped to his knees and kowtowed to the lord. 'All that I have is yours, Padmanabha,' he said, touching his forehead to the ground.

The king turned and started walking away from the mandapam. At the top of the steps he turned around. His calm demeanour gave way momentarily as he thundered, 'What you are doing is not right! It will only anger the gods. Beware, foolish man! You and only you will be responsible for the misfortune that will befall this province.' He stopped as abruptly as he had begun and walked down the few steps to where his entourage awaited him.

19

Kabir Khan was at the office of Union Transport and Logistics Pvt. Ltd when he received a call from Commissioner Iyer's office.

'The commissioner has requested your presence in his office at noon,' a voice at the other end curtly informed him.

'I will be there,' he said and disconnected the call. A frown appeared on his face. He was just about to get his hands on some information from the logistics company.

The previous night, once Ashokan had left and before the police arrived, Kabir had scanned the workshop thoroughly for any clues. The only item of relevance that he found was a receipt that showed that Annaiya had shipped some replicas from Chennai to Hong Kong through Union Transport and Logistics. That explained Kabir's presence at the company's office.

'Here it is.' The customer service executive handed over a piece of paper to Kabir.

'Was the consignment inspected before it was shipped out?' Kabir demanded, glaring at the young man.

The executive shook his head. 'Unlikely.' Seeing the expression on Kabir's face darken, he hastily added, 'The consignment had a "Not required to be checked" clearance from customs. Not only that, given that it was a handmade consignment, it even had a government-issued certificate that said "Modern Handcrafted Replicas". Hence it is quite unlikely that the consignment would have been checked at our end or even by the on-site customs team.'

'Hmm.' Kabir nodded. He walked up and down the room for a few seconds and then turned towards the executive. 'Were any other consignments shipped out by the same person?'

The executive stared into his computer for a few seconds and then looked up. 'No. This is the only one.'

'Never ever?'

'No. Not in the last five years. Not unless he used a different name.'

'And what about the receiver? Has he been sent any other shipments from here?'

A few minutes of silence followed. Then the executive looked up again, a curious mix of triumph and fear on his face. 'Yes,' he said. 'There is one consignment. Shipping out.'

'When?' Kabir barked.

The young man looked at his computer again, as if he was reconfirming, and whispered. 'Tonight. It leaves the port tonight.'

'What!'

'Yes. Tonight. The manifest says that it is garden furniture.'

'Damn!' Kabir exclaimed and looked at his watch. 'Damn!'

20

Kabir had been waiting in the conference room of the Chennai Police headquarters for nearly fifteen minutes when Commissioner Iyer walked in. He was not alone; there was someone with him.

'Mr Khan,' Iyer exclaimed as he shook Kabir's hand and nodded.

Kabir forced a smile in response.

The commissioner looked to his left at the apology of a snowman. He was short, fat, balding, and it looked like if he didn't run and get himself suspenders, he ran the risk of his trousers falling victim to gravity.

'Meet Mr Madhavan.'

His mind elsewhere, Kabir nodded and absently shook hands with the snowman. 'Hello, Mr Madhavan.' It sounded more like a question than a greeting.

'Mr Madhavan is the DIG of the idol wing of Tamil Nadu Police.'

'Aah!' Kabir tilted his head and raised his eyebrows. So that's why he had been summoned to the commissioner's office.

'Do you have any explanation for your actions yesterday, Mr Khan?' Madhavan asked.

If Kabir was still undecided on what stance to take, the question, or rather Madhavan's tone, made the decision for him. He took an instant dislike to Madhavan.

'Yes. Indeed,' he said. 'My informer had shown me a picture which suggested that someone was manufacturing replicas of the idol that had been found in Dubai. I went to the location to check out the lead.'

'Don't you think you should have taken Tamil Nadu Police into confidence?'

'Really?' Kabir scoffed. 'You expected me to keep you in the loop? For what?'

'Your actions have resulted in the death of a human being. Someone who could have been a valuable source of information.'

'Aaaah!' Kabir exclaimed. 'If you think my actions resulted in him being killed, I am sure you also know who killed him, Mr Madhavan. Why not just spill the beans and kill the surprise?'

Stunned by Khan's vitriol, Madhavan looked at the commissioner for guidance.

'And if he was such a valuable source of information for you,' Kabir continued, 'where was Tamil Nadu Police when he was being dumped in a tub of plaster of Paris? And,' he turned to Iyer, 'when I met you yesterday, you showed little inclination to be of assistance. Why then should I have kept you in the loop while following up on a task assigned to me by the director himself?' He paused before adding, 'Albeit unofficially.'

Madhavan fumbled. He didn't know what to say. 'There isn't even an FIR in the state. Why should we follow up on someone's whims and fancies?'

'Interpol is on it. The case came to us at the Centre through Dubai Police. Director Inamdar is personally interested in it. Isn't that enough?'

'We don't have any formal intimation on it. Nothing, apart from your discussion with the commissioner yesterday,' Madhavan argued.

'It's not like you would have done much had you had any information,' Kabir mocked. He was angry. Rather than helping him, Madhavan was throwing the rule book at him. 'And by the way, you have a case now. The murder of an idol replica manufacturer. And just to set the record straight, you are dealing with the murder of a smuggler here. Not a saint.'

'How can you be so sure, Mr Khan? Let's not get ahead of ourselves.'

'Well, he shipped two hundred idols to a Hong Kong-based company.'

'That doesn't make him a smuggler.'

'You're right, that doesn't. But what about the fact that he had clearance from customs and the department of handicrafts of the Central government? For a simple, uneducated man, which is what I gather he was, those clearances are nearly impossible to get.' Kabir was fuming. 'And just to let you know, the company he shipped the replicas to doesn't exist. I had my contact in Hong Kong check it out on my way here. It is a fake company.

'So here's how it is. Our dead friend in Chennai ships a consignment of idols to someone in Hong Kong, who in turn clears the consignment and has it reshipped to another country under a different name, rendering the chain untraceable. At the final destination—or even an interim one, who knows—the real antique is pulled out from among the replicas and sold in the black market for a huge price. No?' Kabir looked at Madhavan. 'What do you say, Mr Madhavan? Is this possible?'

'You are a great storyteller, Mr Khan. Where is the evidence?'

'Even an idiot will tell you that this was what happened. You don't need a really high IQ to figure it out.' He raised his voice enough to intimidate Madhavan. 'And if you want evidence, you will get it tonight. A consignment is sailing for Hong Kong tonight from Chennai port. Shipped by Union Transport. Intercept it. Prevent it from leaving the country. The manifest lists it as garden furniture. I can guarantee that it is something else. It is likely to be a consignment similar to what our dead man had sent.'

'If so,' Commissioner Iyer intervened—he had been watching Kabir and Madhavan squabble all this while—'shouldn't we let the consignment go, and track it at the destination?'

'Futile,' said Kabir confidently. 'The fact that Annaiya was murdered suggests that the smugglers know that the police is on their trail. It's unlikely that someone will receive the shipment in Hong Kong and get it cleared from the port. Your only chance is to intercept it here.'

'I think you are right,' Iyer declared. Kabir smiled. 'Madhavan, get the consignment checked, and if necessary confiscate it before the ship sails tonight. I'll sign the search orders.'

Madhavan just nodded.

'Before we disperse, any luck with the image I showed you yesterday?' Kabir asked Iyer. 'Were you able to figure out which temple the statuette was stolen from?'

The commissioner turned towards Madhavan inquiringly.

'There are thirty-three thousand temples in Tamil Nadu alone, Mr Khan. All under the jurisdiction of the HR&CE.' Noticing the puzzled look on Kabir's face, Madhavan clarified, 'The Hindu Religious and Charitable Endowments Board. We have sent them the image. The problem is that they don't have a database of temple sculptures. They have started the process of building one now. As in a couple of years ago. But covering all these temples will take time. However . . .' He paused.

'However . . .?' Kabir prompted.

'The French Institute of Pondicherry has chronicled most of the temples in Tamil Nadu, Karnataka and Kerala. They have a repository of over one lakh photographs of temple architecture, statues and idols.'

'That should help. Are these in digital form or as actual photographs?'

'These are all old photographs. Largely black-and-white. The project was carried out in the late sixties. As of now, that is the only authentic database of temples and their architecture in south India. The institute started the process of digitizing the old images in 2009, so that they could be shared and studied. We have sent them the image that you gave us to see if there is a match. But it will take time. If we are lucky, we will have an answer in a few weeks.'

'And if there isn't a match?'

'Well, we have better things to do than to go about personally checking thirty-three thousand temples,' Madhavan snapped. 'That too for a robbery involving the sheikhs.'

21

That night, led by DIG Madhavan, a police team raided the *MV Symphony*, a cargo vessel, carrying, among other things, a consignment for Fabulous Furnishings HK Plc. According to the ship's manifest, the small container was carrying garden furniture.

Later, Madhavan called Commissioner Iyer.

'Yes, Madhavan,' the commissioner's groggy voice came on the line. 'Tell me.'

'He was right, sir.'

'What?'

'Kabir Khan. He was right, sir. The consignment does not have furniture. It has largely useless household goods. Items of no commercial value.'

'Is that what you called to tell me at 1 a.m.?' Iyer snapped.

'No, sir.'

'Then?'

'The consignment also had two hundred and fifty Shiva statues. We checked each one of them—two hundred and forty-nine were replicas. Only one was a heavy piece. Looks like an original antique, like the ones found in the Varadaraja Perumal Temple near Suthamalli village.'

'Suthamalli?'

'Yes, sir.'

'How can you be so sure?'

'My family temple is in Suthamalli, sir. Until a few years ago, I used to visit that temple annually.'

Neither of them spoke for the next few seconds. The commissioner was lost in deep thought.

'Sir?' Madhavan finally spoke just to make sure the call hadn't got disconnected.

'Speak to the French Institute.' The commissioner was still on the line. 'Tell them that they need to prioritize finding a match for the image we sent them. Dispatch a team to the sender's address and see if we get something there. We need to stop this plunder of our heritage.'

'Already sent, sir. It is a residential address which has been lying locked for years. The sender used fake KYC documents.'

'What about the CCTV footage from the shipping company's offices and the container depot? Any clues from there?'

'I have asked for it. But I will be surprised if anything comes out of it. These guys are too smart.'

'Hmm. Call Kabir Khan. Ask him to come and see me tomorrow morning.'

'Done, sir.'

22

the courtroom was packed with journalists, social influencers, a few politicians and security personnel.

Rajan sat in a corner, alone. The events at the high court playing on his mind. He had lost his best friend to an acid attack after one such hearing.

'During the last hearing,' Chief Justice Raj Sharma began the proceedings, 'we had requested the Kerala government, through the chief secretary, to table their views on plaintiff S.S. Rajan vs. Dharmaraja Varma representing the Anantha Padmanabha Swamy Temple in Thiruvananthapuram.' He extracted a letter from an envelope lying on the table and read it. 'I wanted to know the views of the state government, which are detailed in this letter, before I give my verdict.'

There was pin-drop silence in the court. Rajan was waiting in anticipation.

'The state clearly says in this notice that it does not want to take over management of the temple or its wealth. It believes the temple is the abode of the lord and any wealth in it belongs to Him.'

Oblivious to the turmoil in Rajan's mind, the chief justice continued. 'I am not surprised at this stance of the state. The temple is one of the most popular temples in Kerala and any attempts to usurp control forcibly by ousting the king might be construed as unpopular and might result in the erosion of the vote bank. The stance the state has taken, that too in the election year, while not necessarily accepted, is understandable. But it is the logic they put forward that is incomprehensible.' And he paused. He took off his glasses and looked at the crowd in front of him.

'If the state is to be believed, any attempts to take control will anger the lord and will invite his wrath, thereby bringing misfortune to the people of Kerala. In today's day and age, this argument sounds very far-fetched and tantamount to taking the court for granted. However,' said the chief justice, 'I don't subscribe to this point of view.'

Rajan suddenly straightened up in his chair. What had just happened?

'Yes, I don't subscribe to this point of view,' the chief justice repeated.

A sudden chatter broke out in the courtroom. The chief justice banged his gavel, asking for the crowd to be silent. 'But we cannot ignore the wishes of the state completely. The fact that it has stated that it does not want to take charge must be taken into consideration. But the security and safety of the temple are paramount. The state says that the temple and its wealth can be taken care of by the existing administrators and the descendants of the king. Fine! But how many guards are stationed at the entrance of the temple today?' He paused for effect, looking all around the courtroom. 'Three constables! As of now, anyone can walk into the temple unhindered. As word of the wealth in the temple spreads, there could be attempts made to loot the temple, maybe even terror attacks. You are counting on the fear of the lord keeping out unsavoury elements! And not fear of the law! Which to my mind is being supremely foolish. Or seriously naive.'

He rummaged through the papers kept on the table before him and pulled out a sheet of paper.

Beep. A mobile phone in the courtroom beeped. The judge looked up angrily. Mobile phones were banned in the courtroom. *Beep.* Another cell phone. Everyone looked around to see whose phones these were. As more phones began to ring people realized the sounds were coming from the press corner. The guilty journalists hurriedly put their phones on silent.

One journalist, from NDTV, quickly checked the messages on his phone. There were two, both from his boss.

'How much longer? Get to Race Course NOW! PMO won't wait.'

And:

'Serial blasts in Mumbai.'

23

MUMBAI

The first blast rocked Zaveri Bazaar around lunchtime. Moments later, a second bomb exploded in a taxi near Chhatrapati Shivaji International Airport. The third explosion took place in a Mumbai local that was passing through Matunga Railway Station. Initial reports put the number of the deceased at six.

Divya and Aditya were at a mall in Central Mumbai when the bombs went off. Within a matter of minutes the entire mobile network of the city had collapsed. She tried reaching Nirav, but was unable to. Panicked, she dragged Aditya out of the mall. 'Come on, let's go!' she said. 'We need to check on Dad.' Fear was written all over her face.

By the time they got out of the mall and on to the main Tulsi Pipe Road towards South Mumbai, the roads were jammed. Police checkposts had been set up every 200 metres, and the roadblocks had thrown the entire traffic system out of gear. As their car inched forward, a near-hysterical Divya continued to try Nirav's number. Suddenly her phone rang.

'It's Dad!' she exclaimed. 'Daaad!' she yelled when Nirav's voice was heard on the car Bluetooth. 'We were so worried.'

'I have been trying to reach you for a while now, Divya. But I couldn't get through. I knew you would panic so I even SMS'd you a few times.'

'I didn't get any, Dad. But I am so relieved you are safe.' Divya had calmed down somewhat and her breathing had settled. 'Is everyone safe, Dad?' she asked.

'Akhil Uncle has been hit.'

'What?' Divya was shocked. Akhil Shah had occupied the office next door to Nirav's for over four decades, from the time they had first met. 'How bad is it?'

'He was right next to the scooter when the bomb went off. I was just a few feet behind him. I saw his body blow up . . .' Nirav's voice faltered. Divya could sense the anguish in his voice. It was as if he was about to break down.

'I'm so sorry, Dad,' Divya consoled him.

'Thank you, beta. I . . . I'll see you at home.'

As soon as the call disconnected, Aditya extended his left arm and hugged her. Divya just turned towards him, buried her face in his shirt and started sobbing. Wordlessly, Aditya tightened his grip and simply held her.

The car in front had moved a few inches. Immediately, the car behind them started honking. Biting back a retort, Aditya pressed on the accelerator and crawled forward.

By the end of the day, the blasts had claimed the lives of seven people and injured countless others. That night, as Divya lay in bed, she marvelled at the way Aditya had kept his composure in the near-panic situation. The events of the afternoon had brought her a lot closer to him. She wanted to spend her life in the arms of the man who had held her firmly, comforted her and allowed her to grieve, who had been there for her.

24

The chief justice looked up again, 'I am tempted to ask the court receiver to book everyone whose mobiles are not turned off for contempt of court.' There was a momentary bustle in the courtroom following the judge's announcement as everyone hurriedly turned off their phones.

'Based on the information presented before the court in the matter of S.S. Rajan vs. Dharmaraja Varma representing the Anantha Padmanabha Swamy Temple, the court hereby orders that adequate security cover be provided to the Anantha Padmanabha Swamy Temple to prevent any untoward incident. The CRPF must provide manpower and take charge of temple security. An area of five hundred metres around the temple will be out of bounds for vehicular traffic except for people living in that area, or for people with specific permissions. The preliminary exploration around the temple complex for finding subterranean structures will continue as is, but with additional security from the CRPF. The area over the temple will be a no fly zone. The state government will have to make sure that the temple, its legacy and its wealth are adequately protected.

'As for the temple vaults—the four vaults that are currently open will be sealed with immediate effect. A special audit of the temple and its properties shall be conducted as early as possible. The court hereby appoints Vikram Rai, former comptroller and auditor general of India, to head the audit. He will be at liberty to request the services or assistance of any other person or persons for the completion of this task. Starting eight weeks from now, and every fortnight thereafter, the committee will give a report to the court on the progress of the exercise and also the efficacy of the steps taken to protect the temple, its resources and its people.

'Furthermore, no property of the temple shall be transferred or disposed of in any manner whatsoever until the audit is complete.'

The moment he heard this, Rajan stood up and started clapping. He had finally got what he wanted. Mission accomplished.

25

CHENNAI

Kabir Khan walked into Commissioner Iyer's office—this time no one tried to stop him.

'You were right,' the commissioner said the moment he saw Kabir. The animosity was gone, replaced by a newfound respect and admiration for Kabir's ability to see things from a different perspective. 'Have a seat.'

Kabir raised his eyebrows. 'It would be nice if you would elaborate,' he said as he sat down, a touch irritated. He had wanted to be a part of the raid on the container the night before, but he had not been allowed to join the team.

'The consignment had a Shiva statue,' Iyer began. 'You know Lord Shiva, right?' The sarcasm was clearly a force of habit.

'Just so that you dump your sarcasm and don't do this a third time, let me tell you. My mother is a Hindu; father a practising Muslim,' he said. 'As for me? I am an atheist. I believe in the power of human beings and science. Not God, irrespective of the name you call him by or the manner in which you worship him. Now can we move on?'

An embarrassed Iyer hurriedly changed track. 'The Shiva statue is apparently from the Varadaraja Perumal Temple near Suthamalli, a village sixty kilometres south of Trichy. No one knows how it reached the container.'

'Are you sure it is from Suthamalli?' Kabir struggled to pronounce the name of the village.

'Madhavan is.'

'And how is he so sure?'

'It is his family temple. He used to visit that temple often until a few years ago.'

'Are we going to Suthamalli?' Kabir asked. He seemed restless, itching to do something, anything. 'Am I going to Suthamalli with someone?'

'Yes.' Iyer nodded. 'We better.' He pointed to a few papers on his table. 'Madhavan will be coming shortly. I want you to go with him. Let's figure out what happened in Suthamalli.'

'And . . .' Kabir paused and looked at him. 'And whether there are more Suthamallis out there . . .'

'I know. However, I do not want to create panic. We don't want to make a song and dance about it. Keep the investigation under wraps until we have something concrete.'

Kabir nodded and got up from his chair. Just then the front door opened and Madhavan walked in.

'Let's go,' he said.

26

'When was the last time you saw the statue in the temple?' Kabir Khan asked Madhavan as they got into the car. Suthamalli was over 300 kilometres away and the drive would take them a while.

'A few years ago. Five, maybe,' Madhavan responded.

'And you haven't been there ever since?'

'Looks like you don't know the background.' Madhavan looked out of the window for a moment, then turned back to Kabir. 'The temple is over eight hundred years old, dedicated to Shiva, the Destroyer. The villagers look after the temple these days. About ten years ago, the local priest packed his bags and left for Chennai. In pursuit of a more glamorous lifestyle. Once he left, the daily prayers became intermittent. Eventually they stopped.'

'Just because the local priest left?'

'No,' Madhavan said. 'The prayers became intermittent, as I said. But his leaving was not why they stopped.'

'Then?'

'The villagers had a tradition of bringing an idol of Goddess Kali to the temple once every three years to celebrate the harvest. The last time I visited the temple with my family was for this ceremony.'

'That was five years ago?'

Madhavan nodded. 'Maybe six.'

'Okay.'

'At that time I noticed a few things. The temple was not being maintained. Probably because there was no one to oversee. There were cobwebs in the corners. Exposed beams, textured by time, were cracking. The air was very musty, unhygienic even. The ceiling was sagging. It was almost as if the temple would collapse if not repaired immediately. Thankfully the event passed off without any untoward incidents.'

Kabir was listening intently. He had always thought that temples were overflowing with wealth. Yet Madhavan was telling him about a temple which had not been maintained and was on the verge of collapsing.

Madhavan continued: 'I came back to Chennai and lodged a request with the HR&CE asking them to do something about the condition of the temple.' There was anger in his eyes. 'But they didn't do anything.' He paused. 'And then came the killer bees.'

'Killer bees!'

'Three months after the harvest celebration, the entire village came under attack from giant hornets. Some claimed they were poisonous, others disagreed. Whatever the case may be, over one hundred people in the village fell ill, forcing the government to take notice. As an indirect consequence the condition of the Shiva temple came into the public domain. The government was forced to act. They shifted all the idols to the Varadaraja Perumal Temple in the neighbouring village. The idols have since been locked away behind iron gates and are cared for by the local village staff. The idol we recovered from the container in Chennai is one of the idols that was brought from Suthamalli. In fact it is the principal one.'

'How did it make its way to the container?'

'Who knows!' a concerned Madhavan replied. 'But the main question is,' he sighed deeply, 'is it the only one?'

They reached the Ariyalur HR&CE, under whose jurisdiction both the temples were, by mid-afternoon.

'Impossible!' The man in charge of the Ariyalur subdivision vehemently denied that the idol could have been stolen from the temple. 'We visit the temple once a week to check. The idols are all locked away. From the time they were shifted to the Varadaraja Perumal Temple, they haven't been brought out even once.'

Kabir Khan didn't show an iota of emotion on his face. 'Can we check the storage facility?'

'There's no storage facility. It is just a room in the temple which has been locked.'

'And who has the key?'

The officer pointed to himself. He walked to a glass key cupboard and took out a bunch. 'Let's go,' he said. 'You can see for yourself.'

The Varadaraja Perumal Temple was some distance from the admin office. A broken path wound round the village, past old mud-walled huts and randomly wandering cattle, to a quiet structure which in its glory days would have been the heart of the village. Weeds had overrun the pathway that led from the main road to the temple. The lack of funds had severely affected the temple's upkeep and only certain portions of the building were regularly maintained. The main door of the temple stood open, a stone warrior standing guard on either side. The gopuram rose majestically for over fifty feet. It desperately needed a coat of paint though. To the left of the temple door stood a statue of Ganesha. An old statue which looked almost green in colour, thanks to the moss that had gathered on it. It was the rainy season and no one had cleaned the temple thoroughly in ages.

'Can we go in?' Kabir asked. He was beginning to lose his patience.

'You!' scoffed the officer before turning to Madhavan. 'He can come in?'

'Why? Is there an issue?' Madhavan asked.

'He is not a Hindu!' exclaimed the in-charge. 'Non-Hindus are not allowed.'

'Who will know?' asked Kabir

'God will!' was the indignant answer.

'That is,' Kabir ridiculed, 'if he is still inside.'

'He is only here to help. I don't think the lord will find that objectionable,' Madhavan declared. 'Let's go.'

The HR&CE officer reluctantly led Madhavan and Kabir through several dismal corridors to a room in the rear of the temple where the Suthamalli statues were stored.

'See? It is locked,' he said triumphantly, pointing to the lock on the door.

'Open it.'

When the officer hesitated, Madhavan stepped forward and took the keys from him. The moment he touched the lock, it sprang open. Someone had opened it, and then just put it back in a locked position. Horrified, he looked at Kabir.

'What the hell!' Kabir exclaimed. Both of them looked at the HR&CE officer. 'Didn't you say the door was locked?'

'It was locked. I'm sure it was,' he mumbled.

'God knows how long it has been like this!' Madhavan said.

The officer entered the room, and froze. He turned back and looked at Kabir and Madhavan.

'Gone?' Kabir Khan asked nonchalantly. 'I knew it. Didn't I say, Madhavan, that god might take offence *if* he is inside? But obviously he isn't.'

Madhavan turned to the officer. 'When did you last see the statues?' he demanded angrily.

'This room hasn't been opened since the time the statues were brought in.'

'And that was over five years ago.'

'Yes.'

'So the statue could have been stolen any time in the last five years.'

The HR&CE officer looked lost. He had no idea what was going on. His team had visited the temple week after week for the last many years. They had merely seen that the room was locked and gone back assuming the statues were safe.

'Do we know what all was there in the Suthamalli temple?' Kabir asked.

'I know,' Madhavan volunteered. 'Apart from the statue that we found in the shipment in Chennai, there was a large, five-foot-tall statue of Nataraja, called the Lord of the Cosmic Dance. It's centuries old and worth a fortune.'

'Stealing a five-foot statue would mean bringing a truck to shift it from here. It would have been very difficult to move without the help of the local authorities.' He looked at the officer. 'Would you have a picture?'

'Back in the office, for sure.'

'There is nothing left here. Let's go,' said Kabir.

The moment they stepped out of the temple, flashbulbs went off. The press had got wind of the story.

'Who the hell told these guys?' Kabir demanded furiously. In such situations, it always helped to conduct the investigation secretly. The involvement of the press invariably ruined matters. Kabir knew that it was only going to get worse from here.

The next morning, the story about the theft of antiques from the Varadaraja Perumal Temple in Suthamalli was front-page news in most of the dailies in south India. A few creative reporters had even managed to get old pictures of the statues from the villagers.

In Commissioner Iyer's office in Chennai, a furious Kabir flung the newspaper away and looked at the commissioner. 'Is there a way we can stop the media from covering this?'

'Not without an injunction from the court. And for that we have to prove that the media writing about this will hinder the investigation.' He walked up to Kabir and patted his shoulder. 'You know how difficult it will be to prove something like that in court.'

27

It was midday in Singapore when stories about the Suthamalli temple theft came out in the newspapers in India.

Monna Yates was updating her blog chariotsoffire.com when a beep signalled a new mail in her inbox. Monna was one of the most popular bloggers writing about antiques, sculptures and religious artefacts. Considered an expert in this space, she had a huge readership amongst people who cared for and had an interest in history and architecture.

The mail in the inbox was an innocuous Google alert. She had set an alert for news items related to artefacts and their sale, theft, smuggling or transfer of ownership, especially in the Asia-Pacific region.

The Hindu's story on the theft of artefacts from the Suthamalli temple had made it into her inbox. She read through the article with bated breath. At the bottom was a small image of the statues that were missing. Monna had been closely tracking a number of transactions that had taken place in the region over the last few years and suspected that they were all smuggled from south Indian or Sri Lankan temples. This was the first time when the actual source of the artefacts had been identified, though their destination was not known.

Monna decided to get to work. She had to find where the statues stolen from Suthamalli had gone.

28

Two hundred people had gathered at a prayer meeting in the Sofitel Hotel in Bandra. On the stage, smoke from the incense sticks curling in front of it, was the giant picture of a man who had died in one of the bomb blasts—the one in the taxi outside the airport.

The entire diamond and bullion fraternity had assembled to bid him farewell One by one the mourners spoke about him. Lauded his foresight. His business acumen. And above all his compassion for his colleagues. He loved his manager as much as he cared for his driver, they all said.

Finally Nirav went up to speak. 'This is a tremendous loss for the diamond trade. Gokul Shah Bhai was an extremely popular member of our community, and one of the most respected. Relationships, for him, were far more important than money. He loved everyone in the trade. In fact, the trade was his family. He lived for all of us. He was so passionate about the diamond business that he dedicated his life to it. He never married. I have lost two friends in these bomb blasts. Akhil Bhai, my neighbour of four decades, and Gokul Shah Bhai, whom I admired greatly. May god punish the perpetrators of this heinous act. Only then will the souls of those whom we have lost rest in peace.'

He passed the microphone back to the person who was managing the proceedings and stepped down from the stage. He had barely taken a few steps when Gokul Shah's brother, Jinesh Shah, confronted him.

'My brother would have died a happy man, had all of you moved to the Bandra Kurla Complex Diamond Bourse. As promoter and chairman of the bourse, he wanted to see the entire diamond community united and in one location. He wanted to make this one of the largest and most prestigious diamond trading bourses in the world. Had all of you moved here, his dream would have been realized. But you, like a jerk, refused to budge from Zaveri Bazaar. Not only did *you* not move, you did not let others shift either! Never before has this trade been so divided. And all because of one person. You! Nirav Choksi!'

Nirav was taken aback by this onslaught. He could feel the rage in Jinesh's eyes. Divya started to say something in response, but Nirav held her back. 'This is not the time to talk about this. We can discuss this later,' he said in a calm voice that belied his anxiety. Most of the people present at the venue were traders who had moved to the BKC bourse. Their loyalties clearly lay with the deceased and his family. And in situations like these passions tended to rise and logic took a beating.

Within moments, many of Gokul Shah's supporters had joined in.

'Zaveri Bazaar is unsafe—' claimed one.

'No security there. Crowded—' said another.

'Home to many unsavoury elements—'

'What are you waiting for? A bigger terrorist attack? More death—is that what you want?'

A few of the women sitting in one corner of the hall became nervous. They didn't want this to deteriorate into a street fight. One of them quietly walked up to Jinesh Shah and, unbeknownst to anyone, whispered something in his ear.

Nirav had consciously kept quiet all this while. He didn't want to get into an argument. The people who continued to work at Zaveri Bazaar had stayed back despite knowing that the BKC Diamond Bourse had better infrastructure, was safer and easier to operate from. Obviously, they had their own reasons for making the choice.

'Let us talk about this in a few days. Now I need to go,' he said and walked towards the main door with Divya. Suddenly in his peripheral vision he noticed something coming towards him. He stepped to the side instinctively and took the blow of the lathi on his shoulder. The knock upset his balance and he tumbled forward.

Divya turned and challenged Jinesh Shah, the aggressor. She had seen the lathi in the woman's hand a few moments before she handed it over to Jinesh.

'What is wrong with you?' she yelled. Her voice rang through the hall.

What was intended to be a peaceful prayer meeting was quickly deteriorating into a madhouse. The woman who had spoken to Jinesh Shah moments ago was now on the phone. Divya suspected that the woman was up to some mischief and tapped Nirav on the shoulder. 'You need to leave. Now!' she insisted, before turning back to the crowd.

'You are so taken in by the entire issue that it is clouding your judgement,' she said. 'You're all making it seem that the BKC bourse is tottering because some businesses stayed back in Zaveri Bazaar. Come on! Had all of them moved to the bourse, would Shah Bhai still be alive? Don't forget, the blast that killed Shah Bhai was outside the airport; *not* in Zaveri Bazaar. In what way is Zaveri Bazaar responsible for his death?' A note of hysteria had crept into her voice. 'Is this the time to discuss this?' she yelled.

Just then Aditya rushed into the hall. He had accompanied Nirav and Divya to the venue, but since he was not family, he had chosen to wait for them in one of the hotel's cafes. However, the raised voices and gathering crowd outside the hall had caught his attention. Seeing what had happened, he walked up to Jinesh Shah. 'You guys have gone crazy. It's almost as if you are using

Shah Bhai's death and the Zaveri Bazaar bomb blast to convince merchants to move to the BKC bourse. If that's what you want to do with Shah Bhai's death, it is unfortunate.' He turned away from them and took Divya's hand. 'Come, let's go.'

Divya and Aditya supported Nirav between them and together the three of them walked out of the prayer session. No one had the courage to challenge them again. Jinesh Shah turned and looked at the crowd. A sinister smile lit up his face. As if he was extremely proud of what he had done.

'Thanks, Divya. I wonder what stunts those guys would have tried had you not been there.' Nirav smiled at her once they were out of the hotel. 'They don't realize that no one will move from Zaveri Bazaar. We cannot alter our lives just because of the bomb blasts.' He looked at Aditya and said, 'Beta, you must stay out of these battles. You are just about to embark on your career. No point taking sides and getting branded even before you've begun.'

Aditya nodded mutely.

Divya spoke up. 'Aditya will be fine, Dad. It's you I'm worried about. You need to be careful. You could have died!'

'Those who are protected by God, don't die so soon, my sweetheart,' Nirav responded. Divya didn't understand the context and rolled her eyes.

'Well, see for yourself.' Nirav pulled out a folded sheet of paper from his pocket and gave it to her.

'Supreme Court!' Divya exclaimed.

Nirav looked at Divya and smiled. 'It came this morning. The media has not yet caught wind of this.'

'But you must have known earlier.' Divya smiled and turned her attention to the notification.

From the first few lines of the letter it was clear that this document was related to a case that had been filed in the Supreme Court. Hurriedly she skipped the next few lines and reached the core content of the letter.

The Supreme Court of India, on the advice of Vikram Rai, former Comptroller and Auditor General of India, has decided to appoint you to the committee that will be tasked with conducting a thorough audit of the Anantha Padmanabha Swamy Temple, Thiruvananthapuram, Kerala, and its properties. You will be a part of a seven-member team:

Mr Vikram Rai, Former Comptroller and Auditor General of India

Retd Chief Justice Kamal Nadkarni

Mr S.S. Rajan, the Complainant

Mr R. Dalawa, Chief Secretary, Government of Kerala

Mr Subhash Parikh

Mr Ranjit Dubey

Mr Nirav Choksi

Apart from the audit, this panel will also inspect the temple's vaults and be accountable for reviewing the security measures in place to protect the temple and its heritage.

A detailed scope of work is in the annexure.

'Where is the annexure?' asked Divya.

'I haven't received it yet.'

'What does it have to do with God protecting you and saving you from the bomb blast?'

'Well, God wants me to protect the temple. So he saved me from the bombs and Jinesh Bhai's cowardly attack,' Nirav said as he got into the driver's seat of the car the parking attendant had just brought up to them.

29

'So we finally get to work together.' Subhash Parikh clasped his hands in glee. He was meeting Nirav Choksi after a very long time. They had known each other for many years. They had grown up in the same neighbourhood, worked in similar professions, but never together. Nirav had stayed on in India to manage the family business and work at acquiring an exclusive client base while Subhash Parikh went overseas, to become a more global, mass player. Focusing more on antiques.

'Not the most pleasant of assignments, though,' Nirav countered.

'Does it really matter, Nirav?' Subhash argued. 'The way I look at it, it is just another job to be done. Mind you, it is not going to be easy, but let's see . . .'

'True,' Nirav said. Subhash's words reminded Nirav of an incident that had occurred years ago when they were teenagers. Subhash had attacked one of their acquaintances for making derogatory remarks about his family. Had it been a normal fight, it would have been fine. But the acquaintance nearly died. Subhash had been arrested and almost sent to a juvenile remand home. Nirav's father had intervened on Subhash's father's request. 'It's not going to be easy. Let's see,' he had said then, before he used all his clout with the police and politicians to get Subhash released and the records sealed. The Parikhs had moved to America after that, and eventually Subhash had set up his business in New York.

'When do we have to be there?' Parikh queried, and then answered the question himself. 'Next week, right?'

'Yes.' Nirav nodded.

Just then the door to the small lounge in Nirav's basement office opened and Aditya walked in. He looked at Nirav and smiled. 'Oops!' he exclaimed. 'I am sorry. I didn't mean to intrude.'

'That's okay. Come on in.' Nirav waved Aditya over to one of the chairs.

'I thought Divya was with you. I am supposed to pick her up from here.'

'She is about to reach. She got held up at home.' He turned towards Subhash. 'Meet Aditya, a good friend of Divya,' he said with a note of pride in his voice, and then went on to introduce Subhash as a long-standing acquaintance.

'How do you do, young man?' Subhash said as he shook hands with Aditya. 'What do you do?'

'I just finished a jewellery design course, sir,' Aditya replied diffidently. 'Figuring out the next course of action.'

'With Nirav here that bit should be easy. No?'

Aditya smiled. He didn't like the idea of using Nirav's status and connections when it came to his career. 'Or maybe just that much difficult,' he said. 'He is a towering personality. Intimidating too at times.'

'Hahaha. That is true. You used the right words. Towering! Intimidating! He knows you so well, Nirav.' Subhash smiled at his friend. 'But you missed out one word, my boy: Influential.'

'Rubbish!' Nirav laughed.

'He is one of the most influential jewellers I know. Be it wielding influence on his family, his clients, his business colleagues, this man can sway almost anyone.'

'Don't believe him, Aditya.' Nirav laughed.

Subhash shook his head. 'The day he decides to move from here, trust me, Aditya, the whole of Zaveri Bazaar will follow him.'

'I am sure.' Aditya just smiled. He didn't know what else to say. The direction the conversation was taking was making him uncomfortable.

'Yes, yes. Absolutely! The converse is also true. No one will leave Zaveri Bazaar until he does.' He laughed. 'And as far as your career is concerned, whatever you decide to do, I am sure you will be successful. Let me know if I can help in any way.'

'Sure, sir.'

'In case you need any space to start up on your own, don't hesitate to ask. I can offer you some free space in Mumbai. I have also just bought some land, about twenty-five acres, in Surat. So irrespective of the scale of your operations, I will be able to offer you something there too.'

'Thank you so much for the offer, sir. I'll definitely let you know,' Aditya said. At that precise moment his phone rang. 'Hey!' he said, taking the call. 'Yes, yes. I'm coming out. See you in ten minutes.' He got up. 'Divya is here. I need to run. She won't be able to park.' He shook hands with Nirav and Subhash and walked out of the office.

'Nice fellow,' Subhash remarked. 'It's difficult to find guys like these, these days.'

Nirav just smiled. The two of them gossiped for an hour more before Subhash finally stood up, pleading another appointment.

'I'll see you in Thiruvananthapuram,' he said as he left. 'In a fortnight?'

'Given government procedures, not before two months,' said Nirav as he waved him off.

30

The security around the Anantha Padmanabha Swamy Temple was airtight. The public had been barred from entering the temple for the first half of the day. Dharmaraja Varma had visited the temple early in the morning to update the lord, albeit notionally, on the key happenings in his kingdom. And today there was an important update that he had had to give.

There was a sudden bustle in the gathered crowd when four Ambassadors followed by three Kerala Police vans turned left from the arterial Mahatma Gandhi Road on to the Padmanabha Swamy Temple Road. The pilot car crossed the arch marking the intersection of the two roads and drove for another 150 metres. The crowd was getting restless; some of them even started shouting slogans.

The motorcade drove past the Ramachandran Street crossing. The Padma Teertha Kulam, the sacred pond of the temple, came into view on the right. The cavalcade slowed down and finally came to a stop outside the clock tower a short distance from the temple gates.

Vikram Rai stepped out of the pilot car and looked around him. His gaze rested for a moment on the weed-infested dirty green water of the Padma Teertha Kulam. T.P.R. Krishnan, the director general of police, Kerala, emerged from the other side of the car. Since this was a high-visibility operation, his team was involved right from the beginning.

'Methan Mani, the clock tower,' Krishnan volunteered when he noticed Vikram observing the building to their left. On top of the building was a huge clock.

Vikram nodded. The clock tower had a very peculiar look to it. 'What is that?' he asked, pointing towards something on top of the clock.

'It's a bearded man, with two rams on the side of his cheeks,' Krishnan explained. By then the others had also got out of their cars and gathered around. 'Whenever the clock strikes, the rams hit the cheeks of the man.' Krishnan smiled. 'It's operated through a highly complex pulley system that's been operational for years.'

'Interesting,' Vikram commented.

'And what is behind that?' Ranjit Dubey asked, looking at the huge building behind the clock tower. Ranjit suffered from chronic diabetes; his kidneys were in bad shape. The sight of water would trigger a tingling sensation in his body and make him want to rush to the bathroom. He had agreed to join the team because he needed the money that came with the job.

'That's the Swati Thirunal Palace.' Krishnan didn't volunteer any further information. He was the DGP, not a tourist guide.

Ahead of them was the imposing gopuram of the Anantha Padmanabha Swamy Temple. 'Shall we?' he asked and started walking towards the temple. He was one of those who did not subscribe to what the court-appointed auditors had come to do. Yet he was duty-bound to provide them protection.

Just as they were entering the temple they were stopped by a temple official, who was glowering at Ranjit Dubey.

Krishnan glanced at Ranjit. 'You need to tie it on top of your trousers,' he clarified, pointing at his veshti, 'and make sure it falls below your knees.'

All the team members had worn a veshti on top of their trousers. Temple rules prohibited anyone not wearing a veshti from entering the temple premises. Everyone had worn it properly, except for Ranjit who was not used to a dhoti and had worn it in a very peculiar manner.

As they approached the temple gates, Dharmaraja Varma walked out, leaning on his walking stick, to receive them along with the temple trustee. When he saw Rajan in their midst, the king was consumed by anger. However, he recovered quickly and by the time he reached them, he was smiling again. Pleasantries were exchanged, introductions made.

'I have requested the trustee to escort you through the temple,' Dharmaraja Varma said, smiling in a benevolent manner.

'That won't be necessary, Mr Varma,' Vikram Rai said, politely declining the offer. 'Mr Rajan will guide us through the temple. He knows everything about the temple and has been involved in its day-to-day affairs as well.'

Dharmaraja Varma was stumped by this refusal. And a little peeved at being addressed as 'Mr Varma' instead of Your Highness. He wanted to be in control of the flow of events and dissemination of information, but he was being kept out of it. More than anything else, he wanted to know what was going on.

'There is no harm in Thirumanassu being a part of the team,' Rajan said. 'He is also the chief trustee of the temple.'

Vikram nodded and followed the trustee into the temple. They walked through the sanctum sanctorum, and then up to the mandapam where they offered prayers to Lord Anantha Padmanabha Swamy. There was an atmosphere of serenity inside the temple. At every stage the team was impressed with what it saw. Though centuries old, everything was gorgeous.

'This is one of the one hundred and eight divya desams in India,' Rajan said.

'Divya desams?' Ranjit asked.

'The sacred Vishnu temples as referred to by the Tamil azhvars,' Rajan said. 'Tamil saints,' he added hurriedly when he saw the confused look on Ranjit's face.

He took them around the temple and finally led them down a flight of steps to a dimly lit corridor. They crossed a large door made of thick planks of wood.

'We are entering the vault area,' Rajan explained as they walked ahead.

To their right was a door made of solid wood. Criss-crossing across the length and breadth of the door were iron strips lending strength to it. In the middle of the door, shaped like the sun, was a keyhole. The door had not been polished in a long while and there were cobwebs along the top.

'This is the door to Vault F,' Rajan said as they walked past the door.

'Aren't we opening it?' Nirav stopped and asked.

'Not unless you want to,' Rajan replied. 'This vault has been opened and closed a number of times. I would be surprised if we found anything of substance inside it. In fact Vaults C to F have been opened and closed at will. That's what prompted this litigation. Now that we have sealed them all, we can come back to this one after the more important tasks have been completed.' Rajan looked at Nirav intently and waited for a response. Nothing was forthcoming. This was the first time Nirav was involved in this kind of activity.

'I think what he is saying makes sense.' Vikram Rai put an end to the discussion. Rajan looked at Dharmaraja Varma and smiled. The latter just turned away.

They walked ahead and crossed three more similar-looking doors. Finally Rajan stopped in front of the fifth door. He turned towards the others. 'This, gentlemen, is the first of the two vaults which we have been asked to open and see what's inside.'

'So this is Vault A?' Subhash asked curiously. He remembered the two vaults being mentioned as Vaults A and B in the Supreme Court judgement.

'Yes. That's right,' Dharmaraja Varma confirmed.

Ranjit slowly shook his legs and held them together tightly. He had been lagging behind for a bit, but then he hurried and caught up with the rest of them.

Unlike the other doors that they had seen so far, this one was a solid iron door and looked like it protected something precious.

'This one needs two keys to open it,' Rajan continued. 'Two of three people—the king of Travancore, the treasurer and the trustee of the temple—have to be present for the vault to be opened.'

'But it has not been opened in the recent past,' Dharmaraja Varma protested. 'At least not in my lifetime.'

'When was it last opened?' Vikram Rai asked. It was not an interrogation. Interrogating the king, or anyone else for that matter, was not in the purview of the task assigned to him by the Supreme Court. He was just curious.

'There is no record of this vault ever being opened,' the king responded. 'Ever. So if we open it—'

'When we open it,' Rajan corrected him. 'When. Not if.'

'Yes, yes, of course!' The king didn't want to engage in a discussion. 'When we open it, we might be the first in decades to do so.'

'Hmm.' A pensive Vikram Rai sighed. 'Can you have the keys brought in?' He looked at the king. 'Right now.' It did cross his mind that if the king was the administrator and the interested party too the chances of finding anything inside the vault were slim. But then, that was not for him to think about. He was there to do a job.

'Do you want to open it now?' Dharmaraja Varma panicked.

'Is there a problem?' Vikram asked. 'Isn't that what we are here for?'

'I would strongly recommend against opening it today.'

Vikram was beginning to get irritated. 'The reason being . . .?'

31

MUMBAI

The night before the team's arrival at the Anantha Padmanabha Swamy Temple, the chief minister of Maharashtra was in a troubled mood when the police commissioner of Mumbai met with him. The news was not good. They had not had any significant breakthroughs in the Mumbai blasts case, and as a result no arrests had been made.

'It's been close to two months, Commissioner. We look like idiots in front of the public! Easy meat for the opposition. What is going on?' the chief minister demanded.

'The modus operandi of the perpetrators is very different. We checked out the usual suspects as well, but every one of them has a solid alibi. What do we do?'

'Do you really care who did it?' the chief minister asked, suddenly calm.

The commissioner looked at him, but didn't say anything.

'Answers! We need answers. No one really cares if they are right or wrong, as long as we have them.'

The commissioner's lips curled into a sinister smile. 'I understand, sir.'

The chief minister nodded. 'The elections are in six months. Your next move is due in less than that,' he said and walked off to his next meeting.

The next morning, while Vikram Rai was going with his team to the Anantha Padmanabha Swamy Temple, the commissioner of police, Mumbai, released a statement to the media:

In a raid conducted late last night in Dongri, the key perpetrators of the Mumbai blasts were arrested from their hideout. In the brief exchange of fire, two of the militants were killed. The operation was masterminded by the Laskhar-e-Taiba in collusion with the ISI of Pakistan. The government has been apprised of the situation. Any further course of action will be in consultation with the Central government. A state of alert has been declared all over Maharashtra.

Within a few minutes, the chief minister tweeted a congratulatory message to Mumbai Police. 'Great job #mumbaipolice. Best in the country. An inspiration. Proud of the team.'

By evening, the tweet had been favourited 5831 times and retweeted 6749 times.

32

'As I just said, the vault has not been opened in decades,' the king began.

'So?' Vikram demanded. He hated being stalled. Whenever he had asked questions during his tenure as the CAG of India, it was what people around him seemed to do.

'The air inside the vault is bound to be stale. It could even be poisonous. After all, we don't know what's inside. Maybe we should open it only after adequate precautions have been taken.'

Vikram pondered over the king's words. 'You're right. We need to be armed with oxygen cylinders. Maybe have some fresh air pumped in so that the air inside is breathable.'

'And an ambulance,' Ranjit added. 'Just in case.'

'Let's move on then,' Vikram said, and they followed Rajan to Vault B.

'Do the keys to Vault A also open Vault B?' Subhash asked as they walked towards it.

'There are no keys to Vault B,' Dharmaraja Varma replied haughtily. 'I'm surprised you didn't do your research before coming to the temple.'

'What?' Subhash was surprised. So were the others.

'See for yourself,' the king said, pointing to the right.

As they turned to the right, their mouths fell open. In front of them was a towering door made of solid iron. It was roughly twelve feet by seven feet, much bigger than any other temple door that they had ever seen. On closer inspection, they realized that it was actually two doors that joined seamlessly in the middle. A snake was carved on each door, and together the pair of serpents appeared to be protecting the vault. There were scratches along the middle where the doors joined, but none too deep to suggest that the vault had ever been forced open.

'There are no nuts, bolts or latches on the door. The seal was affixed to the vault by a naga bandham, a snake spell, by siddhapurushas. It can only be opened when one chants the Garuda Mantra.'

'Let's do that then,' Subhash suggested.

Dharmaraja Varma glared at him, the way a teacher might glare at an errant student in class. 'The Garuda Mantra is no ordinary mantra! Only highly erudite sadhus who know how to extricate the naga bandham can chant it. If chanted correctly, the Garuda Mantra will drive away the serpents and clear the vault; the door will open automatically, without any human effort.'

'Okay . . . so what will it take to get those individuals here?'

'As of now there are no known siddhapurushas who can come and open the vault.'

'Then we have no option but to force the vault open,' Subhash argued. He had got stuck into the discussion and was trying to prove a point. There was a part of him that was annoyed with Dharmaraja Varma for talking down to him in front of the others.

'We can't do that,' insisted Varma, pleading almost. 'It is recommended that we do *not*. Legend says that if we force the door open without chanting the mantra, catastrophe will befall the temple, maybe even the city, the state or the country.' And then, as if to prove a point, he said, 'Try putting your ear to the door.'

Nirav walked up to the door and listened.

'Can you hear anything?' Dharmaraja Varma asked him.

'Yes,' answered Nirav. 'But I am not sure if it is the sound of sea waves or hissing snakes.'

'It is a bit of both. It is believed that if any person forces the door open, he will come face-to-face with a large snake guarding the vault.' He paused for a moment, then continued, 'Besides, it is almost impossible to open the door without the Garuda Mantra.'

'Rubbish!' Subhash scoffed. 'It is superstitions like these that keep people from asking questions. Fear is the key! Instil fear in the minds of the public so that no one questions you. And when that happens, it gives you the authority to do whatever you want.'

'Hold it!' Vikram Rai checked Subhash. 'We are not here to level allegations against anyone. The purpose of our visit today was to get to know the topography of the temple. We will come back once all arrangements are made.' He turned around and walked back towards the temple mandapam, the rest of the team following.

Outside, it was pouring. Caught unawares in an area which was exposed to the elements, they ran helter-skelter, clutching their veshtis lest they come undone.

Nirav was the first to run up to the mandapam, where his attention was immediately drawn to the imposing statue of Lord Padmanabha Swamy. Seeing him, the rest of the team followed. Vikram Rai was first, then came the others. Subhash was last. He was completely drenched. As he rushed on to the mandapam, his foot slipped. He managed to break his fall with his hands but his head still struck the floor. Nirav reached out and pulled him up. 'Careful. Careful,' he muttered as he helped Subhash back on his feet.

While they waited for the rain to subside, Vikram Rai looked at Dharmaraja Varma and said, 'We will come back tomorrow. The arrangements will have been made by then.'

Varma nodded.

'And we have to figure out a way to open Vault B. We can't wait for a siddhapurusha to turn up.'

As Vikram walked away, the king muttered: 'There is a way.'

Vikram Rai stopped and turned. 'What?' he asked. 'What did you say?'

'I said there is a way.'

'And that is?'

'Devaprasnam. Divine permission. We need to seek divine permission from the gods to open the vault. If we get the permission, then we will be allowed to do whatever we need to in order to open the vault door.'

Vikram Rai had heard about Devaprasnam. 'What if the outcome of the Devaprasnam is a no?'

'Then you would be advised not to try to open the vault,' Dharmaraja Varma said firmly. 'But just imagine, what if the outcome is a yes? Everything will go as per your will.' And he smiled. 'For the gods' will shall be proven to be no different from yours.'

Vikram turned on his heel and strode out of the temple, followed by his team. The king remained on the mandapam, a worried look on his face. He needed time to think.

33

Divya's and Aditya's lives were entering a critical phase. Aditya wanted to establish his career before they settled down together. All their discussions these days centred on what Aditya should do with his career. Join a leading firm as an apprentice? Start out on his own? Work with Nirav? His indecision was beginning to irk Divya.

They were having dinner at St Regis that night when Divya's phone rang.

'How are you, Aunty?' she said the moment she answered the phone. 'Hmm . . . mmhmm,' she said, listening intently. 'I know, Aunty. It is very tough. All of us miss him. I can only imagine how hard it must be for all of you. . . . Oh! . . . But why? You really want to do that, Aunty? . . . Hmm . . .'

Aditya waited patiently while Divya finished her conversation.

'Sure, I will check with Dad and get back to you.'

After disconnecting the call, she turned towards Aditya. 'Akhil Uncle's wife.'

'Akhil Uncle?' Aditya asked. 'Am I supposed to know him?'

'Akhil Uncle! The one who owned the neighbouring shop.'

'Oh yes, yes,' said Aditya. 'The one who died in the Mumbai blasts.'

'Hmm. Yes, him,' Divya confirmed. 'That was his wife.'

'What did she want?'

'They want to move back to Rajkot. She has family there. They want to sell and consolidate all their holdings. She wanted to speak to Dad. Apparently she's been trying to reach him, but can't get through. She wants to know if he is interested in buying that property. I told her I would check with Dad and let her know.'

'What do you think he'll say?'

'Oh, I'm sure he'll be keen. And knowing him, he will even pay a premium to Akhil Uncle's family. He is very close to them. He was the one who convinced Akhil Uncle, and a few of the other merchants, to stay back in Zaveri Bazaar when they were planning to shift to the BKC bourse.'

'Do you really want him to buy it?' Aditya asked her. 'If he buys it, he will never feel a space crunch. All he'll need to do is break down the wall connecting the two offices. The space will be more than enough for him. He will stay in bloody Zaveri Bazaar for the rest of his life!'

'I know! But that's his call. I can't make that choice for him.'

'Why don't you quietly turn down the offer? In any case, he's tied up with the temple issue for a few weeks. By the time he comes back, the property will have been sold.'

'Aditya!' Divya exclaimed, rolling her eyes. 'You know I can't do that.'

'One thing's certain, Divya,' Aditya said in a firm tone, 'I will never work with your dad if he doesn't move out of Zaveri Bazaar. That place stinks!'

Even though Divya agreed with almost everything Aditya had said, she didn't like the way he wanted her to manipulate her father. She too was not in favour of Nirav's continuing to work out of Zaveri Bazaar, but she had left the decision to him. He had built his business from nothing operating from that small dungeon of an office; rather, he had built his life from there. She couldn't trick him into giving it up. 'Well, that's your call. I will never lie on behalf of Dad or to him,' she responded curtly, and then sulked for what remained of the evening.

After a tense dinner, Aditya dropped her home. He parked his car on the road outside the building and walked her to the gate. An uncomfortable silence stretched between them. At the gate Divya gave him a quick hug and walked into the building without saying a word. Aditya waited outside until she got into the lift and then stomped back to his car, irritated by the way things had progressed that evening.

As he pulled out the keys from his pocket, a tap on his shoulder made him turn.

'We need to talk. Care for some coffee?'

'What the—'

Before he could complete his question, Aditya had fallen on the bonnet of his car. His mouth was sealed.

34

Kabir Khan was in an extremely volatile mood. He had been summoned back to Delhi for a discussion with Director Inamdar. Unfortunately, it had not gone well. Inamdar had just returned from a two-day trip to Dubai where he had met Mohammed Jilani. Obviously the Wafi Mall heist had been discussed. The repercussions of that conversation were felt in Inamdar's meeting with Kabir.

To make matters worse, he had not made any headway in the Tamil Nadu case. In fact they had hit a dead end in the Varadaraja Perumal Temple and in Suthamalli. Madhavan and he had visited the temple, and while their hypothesis was right, and they had indeed identified where the theft had taken place, they had not got any more leads. The villagers had no idea who was behind the robbery or when it might have occurred. The last that anyone had seen the sculptures in the temple was over four years ago. The Nataraja statue and the one found in Dubai could have been stolen any time in the intervening period.

He walked back to his personal bar and poured himself a refill: single malt, Laphroaig was his favourite. Glass in hand, he walked back to his desk, picked up his iPhone and scrolled through the numerous messages on WhatsApp. He stopped at the one Inamdar had sent him from Dubai.

'Our credibility has been seriously impacted. Wonder if I did the right thing by asking you to manage a case related to disappearance of TEMPLE sculptures. Back tomorrow morning. Please meet me.'

In his entire career this was the first time someone had reprimanded Kabir in this manner. And what did Inamdar mean by typing the word temple in capitals? Why was it that his religion always came in the way? Why did people always judge him? Inamdar was now seemingly accusing him of being a Muslim and hence not focusing on the temple sculpture case. He gulped down the large peg of whisky in one go. He was feeling a bit heavy. He had been drinking from the moment he got back from Inamdar's office. That made it four and a half hours of drinking. Drinking alone!

Kabir set down his glass and opened his email. There were sixteen unread messages. He looked at all of them. Most were pointless forwards; a few were spam, which he deleted before he tossed his phone on the sofa. Then he staggered to his bedroom, fell face down on the bed and passed out.

35

THIRUVANANTHAPURAM

The rains didn't abate the following day either. Word on the street, thanks to Dharmaraja Varma's PR machinery, was that this was the lord's way of expressing displeasure at what was going on in the temple.

For Vikram Rai and his team, it was a big day. The vaults were going to be opened. They couldn't afford to be distracted by such superstition. Meanwhile, spurred by the story about the lord's displeasure, a large crowd had gathered outside the temple, completely blocking access to it. The moment the cars carrying Vikram and the others turned into the street the crowd became violent, a few people even pelting stones at the pilot car. Thankfully, this time, the law enforcers were well prepared. In no time, they cleared the road and ensured that the team could reach the temple premises.

Everyone got out of their cars and hurried in, Subhash taking a little longer than the rest. He was limping—he had injured himself in the fall on the temple mandapam the day before.

Dharmaraja Varma was already there. He had not returned to his residence after his early morning routine.

The audit team, the temple office bearers and the king made their way to Vault A. Nirav brought up the rear with a limping Subhash, helping him down the steps into the vault area.

When they reached the vault, Vikram Rai took out the keys and handed them to the trustee. He inserted them in the slots and turned them clockwise. It took some time, but eventually the door opened with a clank. It was heavy and it took considerable effort to push it open.

Inside the vault it was pitch dark. A few technicians in moon suits with oxygen cylinders strapped to their backs went in to assess the quality of the air in the vault and set up lights. The audit team waited outside for about ten minutes before the technicians gave the all-clear. Vikram Rai closed his eyes for an instant and then raised his right foot and stepped into the vault. A silent prayer of thanks escaped his lips when nothing happened. One by one the entire team followed.

The vault was really just a large chamber, twenty feet by twenty-five feet, with no light save that coming from the LEDs brought in by the technicians. The chamber had nothing except for four walls and a roof. It was empty . . . Almost.

In the floor, to the rear of the chamber, was a small trapdoor, at best three feet by three feet. Vikram and Nirav walked to the trapdoor while the others stayed back near the entrance to the vault. Vikram went down on his knees and peered inside. Three of the technicians had gone down into the space below the trapdoor.

'This is unbelievable!' one of them yelled. 'You have to see this!'

There were roughly fifteen steps leading into the enclosure where the technician was standing with a light. Vikram carefully turned and manoeuvred himself through the trapdoor and climbed down the stepladder. As his eyes adjusted to the dim lights and saw what the technician was pointing at, his jaw dropped.

'What the hell!'

36

Kabir Khan was finding it difficult to open his eyes. It was as if something heavy was weighing down his eyelids and preventing them from opening. But the ring of the phone was persistent. He had ignored it once. Maybe twice. Perhaps even more times; he did not know.

With a sense of foreboding Kabir stumbled to the living room and looked around for his phone. The ringing had stopped, making it difficult for him to figure out where it was. He remembered checking his messages on it before tossing it somewhere in a drunken haze. But where? The ringing started up once again, painfully loud now that he was in the same room as the phone. He looked around and realized the sound was coming from the sofa. He pulled it out from under the cushions and answered it.

'Where are you, Mr Khan?' Madhavan asked testily. 'I have been trying to reach you since last night. I was about to call Delhi Police and lodge a missing person's report.'

'Sorry . . . sorry,' Kabir mumbled. 'Don't know what happened last night.' Flashes of his conversation with Inamdar came to him.

'I must have called your number at least thirty, forty times.'

'What the hell was so important?' Kabir rubbed his hand over his face wearily. 'Maniac!'

'Have you checked your mail?'

'For the last ten hours that I was sleeping? No!'

'Check your mail. Right now!'

'Wait,' Kabir said shortly. He put the call on speaker and tapped his way into his inbox. He quickly scanned the new messages, but didn't find anything which seemed significant. He was about to tell Madhavan to go to hell when he remembered that he had deleted quite a few mails the night before. Those would still be in the trash folder. He quickly checked. He had deleted four mails the night before. One of them was from Flipkart, one from Urban Ladder, one from some loan company. It was the fourth which didn't seem to belong there. It was from information@chennaipolice.com. The unfamiliar ID and his drunken stupor had made him think it was spam and delete it.

'Well?' Madhavan's voice floated over the speaker.

'Yes, yes, hang on!' Kabir opened the mail and quickly read through it. The iPhone almost slipped out of his hands. He read it again.

'Damn. This is awesome stuff.'

'So what do we do now?'

'We have to talk to them.' Kabir was wide awake now. 'Maybe even go there.' After a pause, he asked. 'Are you scared?'

Madhavan laughed.

'Okay, look,' Kabir suggested. 'I'll write to these guys. Let's see what they say.'

'Not in your jurisdiction,' Madhavan reminded him. 'The case is still with the state. I need to talk to the commissioner about it. And remember, she has written to me, not to you.'

'Okay. But whatever you have to do, do it today.'

'Right away.'

'I am taking the afternoon flight; I'll see you once I land.'

After he hung up, Kabir looked at his screen. The mail was still there. He read it again.

Dear Mr Madhavan,

Please allow me to introduce myself: I am Monna Yates, a blogger at chariotsoffire.com. I came across an article in one of your newspapers about the theft of a statue, identified as the Lord of Cosmic Dance from a temple in south India. We are a group of bloggers who trace, track and unite stolen artefacts from across the world with their rightful owners. You could go to our blog to learn more about our work.

The Lord of Cosmic Dance is a very intriguing statue. When I saw the image in the newspaper, I was quite agitated because I knew I had seen the statue somewhere but couldn't remember where. I mailed our group of volunteers across the globe the same day.

This morning, I got a response from one of our volunteers in Australia. The National Museum of Australia has recently acquired a statue for five million dollars. Our volunteer sent us a picture of the statue. I have attached the photo to this email. As you will notice, it bears an uncanny resemblance to the statue that was stolen.

Should you wish to pursue the matter, you can take it up with the National Museum of Australia.

With regards
Monna Yates

37

THIRUVANANTHAPURAM

Vikram Rai wore a dazzled look when Nirav joined him in the room below the vault.

'Look!' he said, the excitement in his eyes unmistakable.

Nirav was shocked when he looked around. Mounds of jewellery, diamonds and other precious stones, utensils made of gold, idols, weapons and gold bars covered every inch of the large room. Chains and necklaces more than twenty feet long, sacks upon sacks of gold coins, antique sculptures, pots overflowing with precious stones, jewellery and gold nuggets. Vikram Rai and Nirav had similar expressions of disbelief on their faces. They were now standing in the midst of treasure which could easily qualify as one of the richest finds in modern-day history. The thought itself was making Vikram Rai nervous. Just the treasure in front of them would be enough to make the temple one of the wealthiest in the world.

'Wow!' exclaimed Nirav, struggling to take his eyes off the floor. By that time a few of the others had also come down.

'How long will it take to catalogue all this?' Vikram asked Nirav. The room was almost four times as large as the one above it, maybe even bigger. And it was full of gold.

'Cataloguing will not take as long as valuing all this will,' Nirav said. He looked up and noticed Subhash peeping through the trapdoor. 'Hurry up and get well! You're missing out!' He laughed, then turned back to Vikram. 'Are we planning to establish the worth of these riches here itself? It is going to be a tough task.'

'What is the option?'

'First, we ought to transfer everything to a sterile environment. Working indefinitely in this dungeon will be impossible.'

'Security will be an issue,' countered Vikram.

'That can be dealt with,' Nirav responded.

'Even so, there will be enormous resistance to taking all this wealth out of the vault. People here are very emotional, particularly about anything that pertains to the temple. We can't take the chance of antagonizing them,' Vikram replied.

'Fair point,' Nirav conceded. 'But to do our job, we need a well-lit place. Equipment. Manpower. And, most importantly, *space* to work. Can you imagine what it would be like if we brought twenty jewellers in here? The whole place will be crowded. No matter how much security you have, you won't know if someone walks out with a pocket full of rubies.'

'Let's think about our options.'

Vikram Rai was not comfortable with the idea of transferring all that wealth outside the vault. He walked around the room, stopping every now and then to look at a piece of jewellery or examine a statue. He had never seen so much of wealth. It was mind-boggling.

'Okay. Here is what we're going to do,' he said after some time. 'We'll use the room upstairs. It will be easier to light up, and will be safe too. I know it is small, but it is empty. Seven to ten valuers can fit in there. And nothing will leave the vault.'

Nirav thought about it for a moment. 'It will be tight, yes, but it's possible.'

'If we get ten valuers working round the clock, how much time do you think we will take to complete the task on hand.'

'Judging by the looks of it . . . at least three months. And don't forget, this is Kerala! Getting people to work round the clock will be a challenge.'

'Even three months is a long time.'

'The number of pieces dictates the timeline. If there are one hundred coins in a bag, we can't assume that all of them are of the same value. We have to individually value thousands of pieces lying all over the place.'

'Hmm.' Vikram had a circumspect look on his face.

'What's on your mind?' Nirav asked him. 'Say it.'

'The public reaction to the opening of the vault has been pretty hostile. You saw the protests outside the temple. I am a bit worried about the safety of the team. Though security has been beefed up, I am concerned.'

Nirav just stood there listening to him. He had no idea what Vikram was hinting at.

'If the work on Vault A is going to take us three months, let's not rush to open Vault B. With so much negativity surrounding it, we might as well delay opening it. Three months is enough time for people to become obsessed with something else. Let public sentiment settle down. We can do the needful after that. Right now, even the media is following this story. Hopefully, they'll find something else to distract them soon.'

'But won't the court object?'

'The Supreme Court merely told us what we have to do. It didn't specify any timelines,' Vikram clarified. 'At best it has asked for a fortnightly report.'

Nirav was not convinced. 'But if we do so, we will be seen as spineless. We are being watched very closely.'

'There is a way out,' Vikram said triumphantly. 'In fact, Dharmaraja Varma recommended it . . . Something which will take the heat off us for some time, and will eventually allow us to do what we have to do, in peace.'

Nirav stared back at him blankly. He hadn't understood a word of what Vikram Rai had just said.

'What if we let them conduct the Devaprasnam?' Vikram clarified.

38

CHENNAI

Kabir Khan landed in Chennai late in the afternoon. Madhavan's car was waiting for him at the airport. He called Madhavan from the car to let him know he had arrived.

'Great! I'll brief you when you get here,' Madhavan said.

It took him forty-five minutes to reach the office.

'So what is the latest on the Nataraja statue?' Kabir demanded the moment he entered Madhavan's cabin. There were three other people in the room, but they excused themselves the moment he walked in.

'After looping in the commissioner, I wrote to the National Museum in Australia, asking for details of the statue that is in their possession.'

'Is it confirmed that it is ours?'

'Yes.'

'And how have we confirmed that?'

Madhavan rummaged through the pile of papers on his table and pulled out a printout. 'Here,' he said, handing it over to Kabir.

Kabir looked at the printout. It was a photo of the Nataraja statue that had gone missing from the Varadaraja Perumal Temple. He looked at Madhavan, wondering why he was showing him the same image.

'This is the image of the statue that I pulled out from their site. It is the same.'

'It could be a similar one,' Kabir argued.

'Yes, it could,' agreed Madhavan. 'But not all Nataraja statues have "Suthamalli" engraved on their base. Look closely at this image, you'll see what I mean. That in more ways than one confirms that this is indeed the statue that was right here in Tamil Nadu.'

Kabir peered at the photograph and, sure enough, he saw 'Suthamalli' engraved along the base of the statue. 'Let's demand that they give it back!' he said excitedly.

'We did.'

'And?'

'And? And nothing,' Madhavan answered matter-of-factly. 'They have come back. They're denying that it is a stolen statue. They paid five million dollars to buy it and even have the provenance.'

'Provenance?'

'That's what happens when they ask people who have no knowledge of antiques to investigate such crimes,' Madhavan said ruefully.

'Oh shut up!'

Madhavan grinned. 'Provenance is the record of ownership of a work of art or an antique. It is often used to authenticate the genuineness and quality of such pieces.'

'That's fine. The guy who sold it to them could have faked it.'

'If you are the National Museum of Australia, being taken for a ride and paying five million dollars on the basis of fake provenance is shameful, isn't it?'

Kabir began to see what Madhavan was getting at. He nodded mutely.

'Then what makes you think they will accept that their provenance was fake?' Madhavan asked.

Kabir had no answer. 'Do we know who sold it to them?'

'They refused to share details with us,' Madhavan said, a touch of irritation creeping into his voice. 'They say that we do not have any jurisdiction over the statue and that we do not have the authority to ask them any questions.'

'Really?' Kabir was surprised.

'Verbatim.' Madhavan handed Kabir a printout of the museum's reply.

As Kabir read through the reply from the National Museum of Australia a look of anger came on his face. 'Bastards!'

'Their refusal pissed me off too. But they don't know us. We need to go to them through proper diplomatic channels.'

'Who has the time for all that?'

'Well, there's no other choice,' Madhavan reminded Kabir.

Kabir didn't respond. He was furiously pacing up and down the room, wondering what to do. There had to be a way to force the National Museum of Australia to take them seriously and respond. He racked his brain. Suddenly, a mischievous look came on his face and he pulled out his iPhone from his pocket.

'What are you doing?' Madhavan asked him, warily.

Kabir didn't respond. He was furiously typing away. Once he was done, he turned towards Madhavan. 'Here, see,' he said, giving him his phone

On the screen was a tweet.

Indian Nataraja statue, stolen from temple in Tamil Nadu (Suthamalli) found in National Museum Australia @pmoindia please help bring it back.

'Are you crazy?' Madhavan yelled. He turned and walked behind his desk. 'I don't know you! No way! Which idiot tweets to the PMO with a complaint while in government service?' Madhavan was both shocked and surprised. He was not sure if Kabir had done the right thing.

'A Muslim complaining about the theft of a Hindu idol, requesting the PMO to help bring it back, is surely going to be a story that everyone will talk about. And a story that everyone is talking about will force the Indian government to act.'

'And when the Indian government acts, it will force Australia's hand and get them to respond!' Madhavan smiled. 'Damn! You really are a mad genius.'

'But a genius nevertheless!'

Around the same time at a press conference in New Delhi, the finance minister made a significant announcement.

'Last week, we received names of 750 Indian who hold bank accounts with the Geneva branch of HSBC. The details of the monies that have passed through the Swiss accounts of these individuals have also been received and passed on to the respective departments for investigation. We are validating the data. Notices have been sent out to a few of those named. You will see some traction on this soon.'

39

Work in the vault had been on for three days now. Sixteen local government-empanelled jewellers had been called in to work with the audit team to assess the value of the jewels and catalogue the same. Life had taken a hectic turn for Vikram Rai and his team.

That day, as any other, lunch for the audit team had been laid out in the room adjoining the king's chamber. Dharmaraja Varma had a lavish, artistically anointed chamber near the entrance of the temple. Next to it was a small room, which was always locked, and adjoining that was the lunchroom.

'What do you all think of the Devaprasnam?' Vikram Rai asked everyone as they settled down for lunch.

Rajan looked up from his plate. Kannan had brought food for him from his house. 'Devaprasnam? Why would that thought even cross your mind?'

'First tell me what do you think of it.'

'It is a bad idea,' Rajan said, looking at the other members of the team. 'But why do you ask?'

Vikram explained: 'The public has not taken kindly to this court-ordered audit. Protests have intensified, our families are being threatened—'

'So?' Rajan cut him off. 'Are you scared? If you are scared, why don't you ask the court to appoint someone else in your place and recuse yourself.'

Vikram Rai ignored the jibe. 'It is not fear,' he said. 'I have dealt with problems far more severe than this. Have you seen the number of people on the road every morning, protesting the opening of the vaults?'

'They are all Varma's men. He has mobilized them to drum up support for himself.'

'They are someone's family,' Vikram argued. 'A family that loves them, prays for their safety. Yesterday there was lathi charge outside the Secretariat. Six people were hurt. If we don't do anything about it, these protests will only intensify. In any case, valuing everything in Vault A will take about three months. Two, if we do it fast. Which means that for the next two months we will not be able to open Vault B. So why not let them do the Devaprasnam? It will satisfy the temple authorities *and* the public. If the Devaprasnam rejects the idea of opening the second vault, we will have two months to figure out our next course of action. If it confirms the lord's will in opening the second vault, the protesters will have no choice but to back down.'

'It will not be the latter. For sure. Ever,' Rajan argued. 'Dharmaraja Varma will manipulate the process to suit his objective.'

'Fine. If that happens, we will agree to abide by the result of the Devaprasnam and not open the vault. Then we will report the findings to the Supreme Court. The court is bound to find all this unacceptable. It is quite possible that another team will be charged with the task of opening Vault B. I'm just buying some peace. Some time.'

'I think it is a brilliant idea. We can go about doing what is expected of us, peacefully. And the public will also remain calm and mind its own business,' Nirav added. Now that he had had some time to think about Vikram's idea, it did seem logical to him.

Rajan thought about it for a while. 'The temple has been specifically banned from organizing any special events during the period that the audit team is here. So even if they want to, they can't.'

'That's why we are discussing it,' Vikram said, looking around the table at the other members of the team. 'If all of us agree, then we can give them permission to conduct the Devaprasnam. To find out the lord's will.' There was a touch of ridicule in his voice, which Rajan didn't like. 'But it has to be passed unanimously,' he said as he walked back into the vault. Rajan was not listening. He was looking out for Kannan, who was nowhere to be seen. Grudgingly, Rajan followed Vikram into the vault. Five minutes later, he came out of the vault and finding Kannan, who had come back by then, handed over his lunch bag to him to take back home.

That evening, when the work for the day came to a close, the entire team walked out of the lower level of the temple, the vault area, to the ground level where Dharmaraja Varma was waiting for them. It was a daily routine. He waited till they finished the day's work, saw them off and then went home. There was not a single day when he left them alone in the temple.

'I need to talk to you,' Vikram Rai told the king when he greeted them. The latter was accompanied by two of his coterie. 'Alone.'

'I discussed it with the team,' Vikram said when they were some distance away from the rest. 'We don't have any objection to the Devaprasnam.'

'Wonderful.' The king seemed elated. 'I will announce it tomorrow and find an auspicious date.'

'But we will not be a party to it. We will not give it the recognition that you might want us to.'

'What do you mean?' The king was perplexed.

'You go ahead with the Devaprasnam, on your own. We won't object or create a scene about it. If it gives you and your people satisfaction, we won't get in the way,' he said as he walked back towards the group.

The next morning, the king called a press conference at his mansion and announced that the Devaprasnam, the three-day ceremony invoking the gods to seek their permission, would begin in four days.

40

The tweet worked. The PMO intervened.

As a result, the National Museum of Australia found itself in the unenviable position of being asked by their government to issue a press release clarifying their position.

There has been a lot of speculation in the Indian media about the statue of Nataraja, known as the Lord of Cosmic Dance, that was installed in the National Museum of Australia eighteen months ago. The administrators of the NMA would like to confirm that all acquisitions go through a rigorous process of due diligence and only after we are satisfied that these are genuine and legally obtained pieces, does the NMA engage in discussions for acquiring the artefacts.

In the case of the Lord of Cosmic Dance, the acquisition was made through an art dealer in Singapore— CreARTor. We have been dealing with Shreyasi Sinha, the proprietor of the art agency, for fifteen years and have had no complaints thus far.

Even the provenance for the said artefact has been verified at our end and found to be genuine.

We believe it is a wonderful work of art acquired through genuine channels. However, if it is found to be

otherwise, we would be happy to engage with the concerned
authorities to arrive at an acceptable resolution.

'There we go!' whooped Madhavan when he read the press
release online.

'It doesn't say anything,' Kabir grumbled. 'No acceptance of
the fact that it is a stolen artefact. The only thing is that we now
know that they acquired it from CreARTor in Singapore.'

'Which means CreARTor is the guy we are looking for.'
Madhavan was thrilled at finally getting a lead to follow up on.

'Or maybe, CreARTor was just a front. It could even mean
that they are also one of those who were conned by our artefact
thief.'

'How do we find out?'

'Shreyasi Sinha,' declared Kabir. 'She holds the key.'

'Let's get some help from Singapore Police.'

'Hmm.' Kabir nodded. He pulled out his phone and called a
number. 'Hi. Can I speak to Arnab Basu?'

Arnab was a very popular secretary in the ministry of
external affairs. All state requests for assistance had to be routed
through his office.

'I am aware of the chaos you created, Kabir,' Arnab said
when Kabir tried to give him the background. After hearing
Kabir out, he added, 'I will speak to my counterpart there and
apprise them of this request. I'll try and get you an informal
acceptance by tomorrow.'

'Thank you, Arnab.'

Kabir was delighted with Arnab's proactive approach
and thanked him profusely before hanging up. Madhavan got
into the act and forwarded all the relevant papers to Arnab.
This was a breach of protocol as the request should have been
routed through the commissioner's office. However, on Kabir's
insistence, they just spoke to the commissioner once before
sending the documents to Arnab Basu.

41

Later that night Arnab Basu called Kabir Khan.

'I have good news and bad news,' he said. 'Singapore has responded positively to your request. They are willing to help. I have sent them the details. I have also spoken with Director Inamdar. Madhavan and you can travel to Singapore as early as tomorrow.'

'Thank you, Arnab! You've been a great help. We'll leave tomorrow itself.'

'And now for the bad news. Shreyasi Sinha has gone into hiding. She is not at the address that the Singapore government has. Her office and home are both locked. Sinha has not been seen by anyone for the last four days. She seems to have packed her bags and left on the day the controversy broke.'

'Damn!'

'It's not as bad as you think.'

'She was our only hope, Arnab! How can you say it is not bad?' an irritated Kabir snapped at Basu.

'Because she is in India. I had the immigration records checked out for the last three days. A passenger by the name of Shreyasi Sinha, same passport number, has entered India. She arrived on a Singapore–Thiruvananthapuram flight.'

'Thiruvananthapuram? Why . . .?' Kabir wondered out loud.

'Your guess is as good as mine,' said Basu.

'Hmm.' Khan didn't know what to say. He was considering his options when Basu added, 'In fact, if I were you, I would not pack my bags for Singapore. I would head to Thiruvananthapuram instead.'

Kabir and Madhavan landed in Thiruvananthapuram on a warm Sunday afternoon and drove straight to Hotel Lotus Pond. To their surprise the lobby was bustling with media personnel carrying microphones and cameras in their hands. When Kabir asked the receptionist, she told him that this had become a daily occurrence ever since the court-ordered audit team had checked into the hotel.

Kabir turned to Madhavan. 'Do you think this could have something to do with our case?'

Madhavan merely shrugged in response and collected his room key from the receptionist. 'I will freshen up and come down to the lobby.'

Kabir nodded. 'Yeah. Me too.'

They were to meet the local police in connection with the whereabouts of Shreyasi Sinha.

42

Even with sixteen jewellers assisting them, it was taking the audit team far longer to evaluate the contents of Vault A than they had imagined. The valuation process itself was extremely cumbersome. The jewellers would inspect every item in the vault, affix a value to it, wrap it in diamond paper, place it in a pouch and tag it appropriately.

Subhash was the first to protest. 'At this pace, it will take over a year to value all of this! What happens to our businesses? I need to be back in Mumbai and then Gujarat for a day and then New York. If I don't go my business will suffer.'

'But this has to be done, too,' Nirav reasoned.

'Is there a way we can hand this over to someone else and exit this project? Or maybe get a bigger team to manage this?'

Nirav nodded. 'There's no harm in asking. Let's chat with Vikram at dinner. This is not the right place to bring this up.'

The jewellers had moved to a heap of coins lying at the far end of the large attic. The coins would be easy to value. They just had to establish that they were made of gold and then weigh them. There were no precious stones to value in that mound.

Shortly after noon, the team came out of the vault for lunch. As usual, Kannan was waiting for them in the temple precinct. He saw Rajan and handed over his lunch. Rajan was very particular about eating lunch prepared at home. He had health issues and at his age he didn't want outside food to complicate things for him. As it was the stress of the audit was getting to him.

'It's been a while and yet it looks like we have achieved nothing,' Vikram Rai commented once they had settled.

'Oh, you will feel the same a few weeks down the line,' said Ranjit Dubey.

Vikram smiled and looked at the others. 'The wealth is staggering. Isn't it?'

Subhash immediately stopped poking around on his plate and looked up. 'Oh yes. Must be worth over fifteen billion dollars, well over one lakh crore rupees. Maybe even significantly more than that.'

'And we haven't even finished work on one vault,' Vikram added.

'Precisely.'

'Just imagine what the government could do with such wealth . . . the possibilities are endless.' Nirav joined the conversation. 'Kerala will soon become the most progressive state in the country.'

Ranjit nodded. 'This is a huge sum of money for the people of Kerala. It could take care of almost all the development and infrastructure needs of the state for a decade.'

'This is a huge sum of money even for the country. It exceeds the education outlay in this year's budget. In fact, it is larger than the budget for most states in the nation,' R. Dalawa, the chief secretary of the state of Kerala who was also on the audit team, said.

'This money is not the government's to take and spend!' Rajan burst out. 'Why should any government stake claim to this money? It belongs to the temple. It is the lord's wealth. Neither the Kerala government nor the Central government should take it. Irrespective of how much it is.'

'But you didn't file this case to see the money rot here, did you?' Ranjit Dubey questioned, surreptitiously rubbing his thighs together. The urge to pass urine was back. He had gone to the toilet on the vault level right before they had sat down to eat. It was too soon for him to have that urge in the normal course. He took a deep breath and turned his attention to Rajan.

'You don't understand,' Rajan insisted. 'I never wanted the wealth to be taken out of the temple. What I wanted was a clear, documented record of how much wealth is in the temple. That's it.' He looked around. No one spoke. They were clearly not in agreement. 'This wealth is the temple's. No one can touch it. Neither the king. Nor the government.'

An uncomfortable silence descended on the room. Everyone focused on finishing their food before they had to return to the vault. Vikram Rai excused himself as he had some calls to make. As always, Rajan handed over his lunch bag to Kannan and continued towards the vault.

'Is this guy your man Friday?' Nirav asked Rajan as Kannan left.

'He has been with us for a really long time. His mother worked for my family for years. After his father died, my family took him in and looked after him. Now he helps us with small errands. He's a very dependable soul.'

Nirav smiled. 'You don't get people like these, these days.'

'Absolutely. He will even give his life for us should the need arise. He is that kind of person.'

'Touch wood,' said Nirav as he stepped inside the vault.

43

Kabir and Madhavan returned to the hotel after a long day's work. At their insistence, Kerala Police had checked every single hotel in the city for Shreyasi Sinha, but was unable to trace her. While it was unlikely that the staff would remember everyone who had walked into their hotel, the investigators were not taking chances. They showed her photograph around but nobody could recognize her. Next, they scanned all the ID proofs the hotels had collected while checking in guests, to no avail. In the end they left photographs at every hotel reception with instructions to call the police control room the moment they saw the woman in the picture.

'What makes you think she is still in Thiruvananthapuram?' Madhavan asked as they walked into the coffee shop at the Lotus Pond.

'We need to start somewhere. This is where she landed and airlines' manifests show that she has not yet flown out of the city.'

'She could have left by train or by road!' Madhavan responded, stunned by Kabir's apparent naivety.

Kabir let out a puff of air. 'That's a possibility,' he agreed irritably. 'If you have a better plan, we will go with that.'

Sensing his mood, Madhavan quietly walked ahead and pressed the button to summon the lift. He was hungry and wanted some food but was scared to even mention it to Kabir. A quiet meal in his room would be better than dinner in the hotel restaurant with an ill-tempered Kabir Khan.

The lift arrived with a *bing* sound and as soon as the doors opened a young couple stepped out. They looked around suspiciously and walked towards the coffee shop. Kabir turned. There was something fishy about them. He wanted to stop them. His hands even went to the picture in his shirt pocket to confirm if the girl was not Shreyasi. She couldn't have been; Shreyasi was far older, in her early forties. The couple looked like they were in their twenties.

'Don't be paranoid!' Madhavan scolded as the lift doors closed behind them

'There was something odd about their behaviour. As if they didn't want to be seen.'

'Maybe they are lovers having a tryst in this hotel.'

'If that were the case, they wouldn't have come out together. They would make sure they were not seen with each other. It is something else,' Kabir said thoughtfully.

'Let's not get distracted, Kabir,' Madhavan reminded him. Kabir nodded reluctantly.

Back in his room, Kabir Khan spent some time reflecting on the case. What had begun as an isolated case of robbery at the Wafi Mall in Dubai had now blown up into a full-fledged investigation into an international case of stolen antiques. Temple loot, smuggling, frauds . . . this had become a lot bigger than anything he had imagined. His tweet to the prime minister and the Australian government's subsequent response had caught the attention of the national media. Kabir needed a bigger team. He couldn't just rely on Tamil Nadu Police for assistance. After weeks of investigation they had only one clue, one link in the entire racket. Shreyasi Sinha. Who seemed to have disappeared. How deep was her involvement? Only time would tell.

Kabir switched on the TV. He hated being in a silent room. From the room service menu he ordered some dal and veg fried rice—the safest north Indian meal in a Kerala hotel. Then he dialled Madhavan's number and apologized for his paranoia. 'If you are not in the mood to eat alone, you can join me for dinner,' he suggested.

As he hung up the phone, the headline on the local edition of the *Times of India* lying on the centre table caught his eye.

'God's will vs. Court Order: 48 hours to Devaprasnam' it said.

44

Thud! Thud! Thud!

Nirav woke up with a start. He switched on the bedside lamp and looked at his phone. It was midnight, merely fifteen minutes since he had gone to sleep. Someone was at the door.

Thud! Thud! Thud! The banging persisted.

'Who is it?'

There was no reply. The banging continued. How could the hotel allow such unruly people to simply walk up to people's rooms! Especially on a floor with additional security.

'Who is it?' he asked again as he shuffled towards the door, the hotel slippers slowing him down. He peered through the peephole, but couldn't see anything. There was something, possibly a hand, covering it. He panicked.

'Who is it?' he repeated. A little softly this time.

No response.

Slowly, after making sure that the safety chain was in place, he turned the latch and pulled the door open.

The temple was bustling with people even at midnight. The temple thantri and several other temple officials were making arrangements for the Devaprasnam that would begin in a little over thirty-six hours.

Through the complex astrological procedure of the Devaprasnam, the temple priests would determine the will of the reigning deity. The thantris of the temple would draw up two astrological charts, referred to as the Rasi Chakra. Each of its twelve cells denoted a particular planetary position which depended on the time and date of the construction of the temple and the installation of the deities as well as certain key happenings in the course of the temple's existence. The puja would begin with the lighting of two lamps and prayers invoking the blessings of Dakshina Murthy, the god of astrology. A gold coin, called puthu panam, would be kept in the centre of the Rasi Chakra. Once the puja ended, the puthu panam would be given to a child less than seven years old and therefore uncorrupted by worldly desires. The child would then be asked to place the coin on one of the cells of the Rasi Chakra. Using the Vedic analysis of this and various divine signs—nimithams—the priests would arrive at their interpretation of the will of the deity.

The entire process would take three days. This was the first time that a Devaprasnam was being held in the Anantha Padmanabha Swamy Temple. Public interest was at its peak. Hectic preparations were on to ensure that nothing went wrong with the prestigious event.

Vikram Rai and his team had neither sanctioned the event nor denied permission.

Nirav couldn't believe what he was seeing.

'H . . . how did you get here?' he stammered, as he unhooked the safety chain and pulled the door open.

'Happy birthday, Dad!' Divya shouted gleefully and hugged Nirav. 'Tell me,' she said, 'how many of your birthdays have I missed till date?' And then without even waiting for him to answer, she volunteered, 'None! Then how could I have missed this one?'

Aditya had been observing the reunion of father and daughter with a quiet smile. Now he stepped forward and wished Nirav.

'Come in! Come in!' Nirav said ushering them inside. He quickly dismissed the security guard who had accompanied Aditya and Divya with a nod and a muttered 'thank you'.

'When did you arrive?' Nirav asked as soon as he shut the door.

'This morning,' said Divya. 'You were at the temple when I came.'

'I'm so glad you came! Such a wonderful surprise.' Nirav was grinning from ear to ear.

'How could I have not come, Dad? I thought you'd come back in the afternoon, but the manager told me that your team usually returns late at night. That's when I coaxed Aditya into coming.' She smiled at Aditya. 'He landed in the evening.'

'She wouldn't have missed your special day for anything, sir.'

Nirav's smile widened, and he pulled Divya into a hug. Suddenly, he turned to Aditya and, with narrowed eyes, demanded, 'Where are you staying?'

'Daaad! Come on!' Divya exclaimed in mock anger before Aditya could respond. 'In the same hotel,' she said with a touch of defiance, her hands on her hips, head tilted to the right. After a pause she added, 'In another room.'

'That's fine then.' Nirav smiled and went back to hugging his daughter.

'Do you realize that in the recent past, this is the longest that I have gone without seeing you? Particularly since Mom . . .' Divya had tears in her eyes.

Bored with the waterworks and family drama, Aditya excused himself with a nod and returned to his room after a while.

That night Nirav slept well. He was happy to have met his daughter after so long. Divya stayed with him for some time and then went back to her room. She had initially planned to sleep in Nirav's room, but the AC in his room was too cold for her comfort. The thermostat had blown and was not responding to their attempts at adjusting the temperature. Nirav was not too bothered. Divya called him 'thick-skinned' and left.

45

Back in her room, Divya picked up her phone to send Aditya a message. She opened her WhatsApp and saw that he was online. She wondered why he was still awake at that hour—it was almost 3 a.m. She went to her contacts and tapped on his name. Just as the phone was dialling his number, the screen blacked out and the phone turned off. It had run out of battery. Mumbling a curse, Divya connected it to the charger.

Rather than wait for the phone to charge, she picked up the hotel telephone and called Aditya's room. The phone rang a few times, but there was no answer. 'He's probably turned off the ringer,' she said to herself. She was about to give up and go to sleep when she remembered that she had one of the key cards for Aditya's room. She pulled it out from her bag and hurried to room 704. She inserted the key card in the slot and the door opened with a click. She walked in.

There was no one in the room.

A shocked and worried Divya walked up to the hotel phone kept on the side table, next to the bed. She picked it up and was about to dial Aditya's number when on a whim, she pressed another button. She looked at the screen of the phone, thought for a while, put down the receiver and walked out of the room.

Her eyes were red with unshed tears. She went back to her room, grabbed her phone and waited for the lift. When it stopped on her floor, she got in and pressed the button to go up to a higher floor.

46

Day of Devaprasnam

When the audit team arrived at the Anantha Padmanabha Swamy Temple at 6 a.m., the place was buzzing with activity. The king, who normally greeted them every day, was in his room.

It was a large, lavishly appointed room—thirty feet in length and about the same in width. There was a separate lounge area where a massive ancient swing made of teak wood hung from the rafters. In front of it, in a semicircle, stood four ornate chairs, which were clearly a few centuries old. Beyond the swing was a wall made of rough grey blocks of stone.

'You are early today?' the king said as Vikram Rai and the team entered, and smiled.

'So are you, Thirumanassu,' Rajan replied, rather curtly.

'Of course. It's a great day for all of us. I came in because of the Ashtamangala Devaprasnam. Just to make sure that everything goes fine.'

'And is it?' Vikram asked. 'Going fine, I mean.'

Dharmaraja Varma nodded. 'All arrangements have been made. We are now waiting for the Daivajnas to arrive.'

'Daivajnas?'

'Vedic jyotishis. Astrologers,' Rajan clarified. 'They are the ones who will perform the Devaprasnam over the next three days and find out the Devahitam—the divine will of Lord Anantha Padmanabha Swamy.'

Ranjit Dubey twitched in his seat. His discomfort was mounting. He wouldn't be able to hold on for long.

Vikram nodded and looked at the others.

'Expecting a crowd?' Nirav asked Rajan.

'No,' the king spoke up. 'It is not a very public event. There will be a few people, but not many outsiders. The chief minister and a few important people may drop by tomorrow.'

Suddenly a young boy, not more than sixteen years old, darted in. He stopped for a second, looked at the people in the room, and then at the king and said, 'Brahmashree is here.'

'I will be right there,' replied the king and got up from his chair. 'Excuse me, gentlemen. I will be back soon.'

The moment the king left the room, Vikram turned to Rajan. 'Explain!'

'Brahmashree Narayana Bhatt. He is the head of the Daivajnas. The one who controls the Devaprasnam.'

Ranjit Dubey squirmed again. It was time to go.

Outside, there was a fair bit of activity going on. A group of people was fussing over a child.

'So this is the child through whom the lord will give his verdict?' Nirav asked Rajan as they headed for the vault.

The latter didn't like the tone of Nirav's question. 'Look,' he said. 'Faith is something which is inherent. I cannot teach you to believe. You either do or you don't. You may not believe in the rituals that are being performed here. That is your choice. But don't ridicule them.'

'Oh no!' Nirav was suddenly on the defensive. 'I was just curious.'

Rajan didn't labour the point. 'Yes, based on the timing of the puja and the activities which the child does, the astrologers arrive at a conclusion. They claim this is science, not superstition.'

'What do you think?'

'Well, it is part science for sure. Part experience. I don't know what you would call it. The proponents of this are specially trained and experienced astrologers.' And he began explaining the concept of the Devaprasnam. Nirav stopped short of rolling his eyes; he was hearing it for the seventh time.

Ranjit Dubey was desperate now. It had been two hours since he last went to the bathroom and his bladder was about to burst. No one in the team was really bothered about it. There was no sympathy for him. How he hated his stint here! But there was no choice. He hurriedly turned back in search of a bathroom.

Brahmashree Narayana Bhatt walked up to the site which had been chosen for the Devaprasnam, to the right of the mandapam, just above Vault B. He sat down on the ground, and started giving instructions to get things moving. The Devaprasnam was supposed to begin at 8.28 a.m. There was no way they could miss that deadline.

He set up the agni kund in front of him, muttering some shlokas all the while. He dipped his hand into his bag and pulled out some of the things he needed for the puja and arranged them on the floor next to him. Someone brought him a cup of coffee, which he happily accepted.

Coffee done, he looked around. Something was missing.

'Kindi evite!' he yelled at no one in particular. Kindi—the snake-shaped vessel, containing water—was not to be seen. He needed that. 'Kindi!' he called again.

Narayana Bhatt's anger was legendary, and just a stern look was enough to send people scurrying. Within moments someone noticed that the kindi was in a bag along with the other puja samagri. It was immediately brought out and handed over to him.

'What is this?' he thundered. 'Where is the water? What were you people doing all night that you couldn't even get this basic thing right.'

'I will fetch the water,' said one of the volunteers. He picked up the kindi and ran out of the temple, towards the Padma Teertha Kulam. The water had to come from the holy tank.

'Apashakunam! Apashakunam!' Narayana Bhatt muttered under his breath as he went about his work. Lines of worry appeared on his forehead. He had been doing this long enough to know that these were merely a sign of things to come.

Ranjit Dubey looked around anxiously. Any longer and he would soil his pants. The only toilet that he was aware of was on the lower level and slightly far. There had to be one close by. He rushed back to the king's room and walked in. He was alone there. He looked around. Beyond the wooden swing, there was a small door. That had to be a bathroom. There was a small sign above of it that said 'Private'.

He opened the door and walked in.

Jayaraj Panicker cursed himself as he ran towards the Padma Teertha Kulam. It was his responsibility to keep the samagri needed for the Devaprasnam ready. How had he not noticed that the filled-up kindi was missing? Narayana Bhatt had just had coffee and there wasn't any holy water that he could use to cleanse his hand before touching anything else.

He leapt over the small iron gate that secured the tank compound and hurried down the steps to the edge of the water. He dipped the kindi into the water. As he was lifting the vessel, filled to the brim with water, something scraped against it. He looked up to see what it was. His voice deserted him; he stood shocked. The kindi dropped from his hand and sank to the bottom of the pond with a gurgling noise.

'Padmanabha! Padmanabha! Padmanabha!' he chanted loudly as he ran up the steps to the pond and sprinted towards the temple gates. Whether he was upset at having touched a dead body early in the morning or if it was the shock of having found a body floating in the temple pond was difficult to say.

Half an hour later the bloated body was fished out of the holy tank.

Part 2

47

Ranjit Dubey was sweating when he emerged from the room. What he had seen was shocking, completely unexpected. But perhaps that had also been the will of Lord Padmanabha. As he walked towards the vault to join the rest of his team, he saw people rushing out of the temple. He panicked. Suspecting a terrorist attack, he joined the horde heading for the temple exit.

Outside, a crowd had gathered next to the Padma Teertha Kulam. Ranjit looked around and finally spotted Vikram Rai standing near the iron gate with Nirav Choksi. Not far away from them was Subhash. Kamal Nadkarni and R. Dalawa were talking to a few men in uniform. Armed commandos of the CRPF who were responsible for temple security had surrounded the place. A few of the temple staff were huddled up to the left, talking in hushed voices. Panting heavily, he walked over to where Vikram Rai and Nirav were standing. That's when he saw it.

Lying on the step closest to the water was a lifeless body. It seemed as if it had just been fished out of water. Rajan stood next to it, a grim expression on his face. Ranjit watched as he knelt beside the body and covered the face with a white sheet.

'Oh my god!' he exclaimed as he reached Vikram's side. 'Isn't that . . .? Isn't it . . .?' Words failed him.

Vikram Rai put a hand on his shoulder. 'Yes. That's Kannan.'

Kannan's body was put in an ambulance and taken to the Thiruvananthapuram Medical College Hospital for an autopsy. At Vikram Rai's insistence, Ranjit Dubey and Subhash accompanied the body, while Rajan went to the young man's house to inform his wife and bring her to the hospital. However, by the time he reached, someone had already broken the news to her. She was in an inconsolable state. Rajan waited till she calmed down a bit and then escorted her to the hospital in an autorickshaw. Kannan's relatives and other villagers followed.

At the hospital, the situation threatened to get out of hand. A few relatives started raising slogans against the administration and even the king. Two teams of Kerala Police had to be deployed to control the situation.

Kabir Khan was in the police headquarters when he heard of the events at the temple. His meeting with DGP Krishnan was cut short because the latter had just received news of the body in the temple pond and had to rush there to take stock.

'Come with me,' the DGP had said. 'We can chat on the way.'

In the car, despite his best efforts, Kabir found it extremely difficult to get Krishnan to focus on the issue topmost on Kabir's mind—the disappearance of Shreyasi Sinha.

'I appreciate your predicament, Mr Khan, but at the same time, you need to understand that the state police are overwhelmed by this sudden world interest in the Padmanabha Swamy Temple and its issues. If the discovery of the enormous wealth in its vaults had merely disturbed the peace of the temple and its neighbouring areas, today that peace has been blown to smithereens. A dead body! That too in the Padma Teertha Kulam. It defies all logic.' He paused and took a deep breath. 'Anyone in Kerala Police who promises to help with your case is not doing his duty. Not a single constable will have time to spare. More so now.'

'Are you saying that you will not be able to help the CBI in this investigation at all?'

'Well, is the CBI investigating this formally?' Krishnan asked.

Kabir nodded. 'The case of the stolen Lord of the Cosmic Dance statue found in Australia is being investigated by the CBI, and this is part of that investigation. We get to Shreyasi Sinha, we get to the perpetrators of the crime. And we will be able to bring the stolen statue back to India.'

'I must say, Mr Khan, your obsession with this Ms Sinha seems to have clouded your judgement. So much so that you are not following the progress in your own case.'

'Care to explain that allegation?' a furious Kabir asked.

'Maybe your office hasn't updated you. As of this morning, the Government of Australia has agreed to return the statue. As far as I am concerned,' he said with a smile that made Kabir's blood boil, 'case closed.'

The constant squabbling between the central agency and the local police had created a problem in investigating any matter that fell under the agencies' joint jurisdiction.

Kabir Khan's phone rang. 'Yes, sir?' he said into the phone.

'You've been told about the Dancing Nataraja statue?' Director Inamdar asked.

'Yes, sir. Just now.'

'Great. Good work on that. Now for the reason I called.' Inamdar was a man of few words. To the point. 'The PMO called. They are following the Anantha Padmanabha Swamy Temple issue closely. They've asked the CBI to investigate a murder on the temple premises. The Centre does not trust the local government to conduct a fair investigation. It is heavily biased in favour of the local king—at least such is the perception. I want you to take the lead on this investigation, at least till we can put another team together.'

'Another team?'

'Oh come on, Khan! As if you don't know. How will you investigate a case inside a temple? Only Hindus are allowed inside. Muslims are not.'

'That has to change sometime, sir. We don't live in the Stone Age, do we?'

'We were better off then. The Stone Age didn't have these barriers; the Modern Age does. This is not the time to force change. The government will make the announcement on the CBI taking over the case later in the day. Till then, keep a low profile. Besides, your position as head of heritage and environment crimes is only a short-term assignment, until we can find another assignment worthy of your talents.'

'Sure. Thank you, sir.' Kabir hung up. Muslims not being allowed inside temples was still bothering him, but it was a larger social issue which he could not do anything about immediately. He let that pass.

'I take it you're heading the investigation for the CBI?'

'You knew?' Kabir was stunned.

'No, I didn't. But I'd have to be a fool not to expect it. I am going to retire in less than two months. I am seen as a Dharmaraja loyalist. The temple issue is in the Supreme Court now. The community is disturbed. And now there's been a murder. Of course the CBI will be asked to step in. It will hurt me to hand over this case to the CBI or any other agency. If you are with me, you will have all the details. I won't need to debrief the CBI team.'

Kabir Khan smiled. For the second time in the past few weeks he had experienced the complexities in the relationship between the state police and the CBI, particularly in states not ruled by the government at the Centre.

'Besides, once the CBI takes over, the state police will be free to hunt for your girlfriend.'

'Girlfriend?'

'Ms Sinha.' The two of them laughed heartily.

They had arrived at the hospital.

48

'You're kidding!' Subhash looked at Ranjit Dubey, eyes wide with disbelief.

'I'm telling you it was there! Right there as I walked in. I thought it was the way to a toilet. It was actually a small passage. The washroom was at the other end. And then I saw it. Right there. Behind the door—'

'Have you told Vikram?' Subhash interrupted worriedly.

'No. Not yet. When I came out of the room, there was complete chaos. And then Kannan's death . . . I couldn't tell him at the time.'

'I think we should tell Vikram as soon as possible.' He looked at his watch. It was approaching noon.

They stopped talking when they heard footsteps coming from the other end of the corridor. Two men, one of them in uniform, walked towards them.

'Mr Dubey, Mr Parikh.' The DGP nodded in acknowledgement and shook hands with both of them. 'This is Mr Kabir Khan. CBI.'

Ranjit felt the tingle again. Whenever he was stressed, it became difficult for him to control his bladder. But he couldn't leave until the conversation ended.

Subhash glanced at Kabir curiously. 'CBI? Is the CBI investi—'

'I'm sorry, I can't say anything about the investigation right now,' the DGP interrupted. He gestured to Khan, and the two of them walked to the morgue. Kannan's wife and a few other relatives were huddled around Rajan outside the room. She looked as if she would collapse any moment.

When Rajan saw the DGP, he broke away from the crowd and strode towards them purposefully. The coroner too came out at the same time.

'Preliminary cause of death?' the DGP asked.

'Death due to drowning—'

Rajan interrupted instantly. 'He was a good swimmer. It couldn't have been that!'

The coroner ignored him. 'Murder,' he added wearily.

The DGP didn't show any emotion. 'It usually is.'

'We have found alcohol in his system. Extremely high levels. There was even unabsorbed alcohol in his stoma—'

'How is that possible?' a shocked Rajan asked. 'Kannan never drank!'

Irritated, Khan hit out, 'It means your precious Kannan drank more than he should have, stumbled up to the tank and fell in! His state of intoxication prevented him from using his Olympic-level swimming skills to save himself.' He glared at Rajan. 'Now that we've solved that, will you let him finish what he is saying? Without interrupting?'

Rajan was shaking his head violently, albeit silently.

Taking advantage of Rajan's unexpected silence, the coroner continued, 'There are traces of carbon in his right nostril as if someone thrust a tube into his nose and forced him to inhale the exhaust fumes of a running vehicle. The abrasions on his wrist and neck suggest that he was forcibly held down. It is likely that carbon monoxide would have knocked him out. And to make it appear like he was drunk, alcohol was forced down his throat. And then he would have been pushed over the tank wall and left to die.'

'But why would anyone want to kill him?' Rajan seemed visibly shaken by the findings of the autopsy.

'Maybe for this?' The DGP extended his mobile phone towards Rajan. 'This was found in his auto. It's been sent to Forensics.'

'How did Kannan get it?'

'That's something we will try and figure out once the forensic examination is over.' When the DGP said this, Rajan just nodded. 'And this is not in the public domain yet.'

'Of course.' Rajan said hastily.

On his way out, Kabir Khan asked the DGP, 'You did not tell him the entire story?'

The DGP smiled. 'He will have figured it out if he is in on it.'

Kannan's cremation that evening was a volatile affair. The police were on high alert. Anything could go wrong. Religion was an emotional subject and they did not want to take chances.

The results of the post-mortem were not made public. Nor was the recovery of a gold bar from the victim's autorickshaw. The announcement of the CBI taking over the case had not been made either. Ranjit Dubey didn't mention anything to Vikram Rai or the others. A terrified Subhash even talked him out of sharing the details with anyone else. They were scared. Scared that there might be consequences.

The Devaprasnam continued on schedule. Narayana Bhatt had insisted on it. The audit of the temple's riches continued as well. Only Rajan was not involved that day as he was tied up with Kannan's cremation.

Kabir Khan was in the police headquarters that evening, fiddling with the paperweight on the table, when he got a call.

'Saar wants to see you.' It was the DGP's assistant.

'I'll be right there!'

When he walked into the DGP's office, there was another person present. The DGP introduced him as K. Menon, the head of forensics.

'Menon says that the gold dates back four hundred years. Possibly more.'

Kabir turned towards Menon. 'So it is from the temple vaults?'

'Most likely,' confirmed Menon. 'But it is not the entire piece,' he added.

'How can you say that?' Kabir asked him

Menon pulled out a few images from the file that he was carrying and spread them out on the table. They were close-ups of the gold bar. As Kabir and the DGP peered at them, he explained, 'If you observe carefully, while the sides of the gold bar are dull, this face is glittering like new. It is clear that a larger gold bar has been cut into two, or maybe more, pieces. While this is clear from a visual inspection, our forensic examination confirms the same. The side which is shinier contains particles and fragments of the iron blade that was used to cut this. The clean edge suggests that the blade used is new. Old blades will not cut as smoothly as this one has.'

'So.' The DGP looked at Kabir. 'What should our approach be, Mr CBI?'

'We should bring him in.'

'Do we have enough evidence against him?'

'What we have is enough to question him. Isn't it?' Kabir Khan asked.

The DGP merely shrugged.

49

Ranjit Dubey was uncharacteristically quiet at dinner that night. Subhash, Dalawa and he were eating in the hotel restaurant together. Vikram Rai had stepped out to meet a friend, and the others had retired to their rooms.

Kabir Khan walked into the restaurant. Seeing the three of them, he strolled up to their table and pulled out a chair.

'How have you been, gentlemen?' He had met them all at the hospital.

'As good as can be under the circumstances,' Subhash answered.

'I can understand.'

'Who could have killed him?' Subhash asked.

'We're not sure yet. But we hope to make some progress tonight. We have rounded up some suspects. Let's see.'

'Why would someone kill him?'

'Well, Mr Dubey.' Khan sighed. 'Someone once said that there are six reasons why a person commits a crime: love, faith, greed, boredom, fear or revenge. In this case, the motive seems to have been greed. But nothing can be ruled out.'

'Very true.' Subhash nodded sagely.

'Anyway, you guys have a good time. I have to run. Your friend must be waiting.' He was gone before the three men at the table could ask him what he meant by that last remark.

Shortly afterwards, Dalawa got up and went to his room. As soon as he left, Ranjit turned to Subhash and asked in a whisper: 'What have we got ourselves into?'

Subhash burst out laughing. 'Don't be such a pussy, Ranjit! Life is full of excitement. Embrace it! Trust me, it will be fun.'

'Someone was *murdered* this morning.' The fear was evident in Ranjit's voice. 'And we know that something is not quite right here.'

'Where money is involved, there will be intimidation. There will be fear.'

'I don't want to die.' Ranjit squeezed his thighs together. He was scared. The TV in the restaurant was plying images of Kannan's murder. 'Especially at this man's hands,' he added, pointing to the TV. Subhash turned. Dharmaraja Varma was on the news, giving a statement.

'Increase the volume, please,' Subhash called out to the attendant.

'—was someone who was very popular with the crowd in and around the temple. His death is very unfortunate. First it was Gopi, and now Kannan. Isn't it clear? It is the will of the lord. Anyone who goes against Him, must be ready to face the punishment. How, when and where He will punish you cannot be predicted. But if you incur His wrath, you will pay for it in this life itself.' Dharmaraja Varma spoke softly, but firmly to Asianet Television Channel.

'What if I recuse myself from the exercise?' Ranjit asked.

'Are you crazy? What reason will you give? An autorickshaw driver's death? No one even knows the reason for his dea—'

His phone rang. He glanced at the screen, then got up and walked away from the table to take the call. Ranjit waited for some time for him to return. Suddenly he felt the tingling sensation again. He stood up hastily and went to the washroom, muttering curses. It had become a serious irritant for him. He had to run to the toilet twice before he could finish even one drink.

Subhash was already sitting when Ranjit returned from the washroom. He was looking a bit worried. Ranjit noticed the change immediately. 'Is everything okay?' he asked.

'Yes, yes.' Subhash faked a smile. 'I got a bit worked up, that's all. This idiot says that we will suffer if we go against the lord's will. And for all practical purposes, that's what we are doing.'

Ranjit nodded in understanding. 'Let's take it one day at a time,' he suggested. 'And forget about what I told you this morning. I don't want to talk about it. It is too risky. Let's just value whatever wealth is kept inside the vaults and get out of here. Nothing more than what is expected from us.'

While Kabir was waiting in the porch for his car, he saw a young couple walk into the hotel. It was the same couple he had seen exiting the lift the other day. The girl had a big frown on her face and was on her phone. He caught a few words from her conversation: '. . . down, Dad. We'll wait in the coffee shop . . .'

Twenty minutes later, Kabir was running up the steps of the Thiruvananthapuram police headquarters. He took the elevator to the fourth floor and walked to the conference room. He pushed open the door and entered.

'Good evening, Mr Rajan. How are we doing today?' he asked with a smile.

50

'Why am I here?' Rajan demanded angrily.

'Hold on! Hold on! What's the hurry, Mr Rajan?' the DGP said, walking into the room seconds after Kabir. 'We will come to that.'

'How long did you know Kannan?'

'From the time he was a child. Maybe six years old. After his father died, my family brought him up.'

'That's how you know he was a good swimmer and a teetotaller?'

'Yes. He was completely against drinking. His father died of liver cirrhosis. But that doesn't answer my question. Why am I here?' He looked nervous. 'Do you think I killed Kannan?' he asked, quiver in his voice, swagger gone.

The DGP ignored his question. 'So what all did Kannan do for you?'

'Household chores. Run errands. Drive us around etc. etc.'

'Did he ever help you hoard?'

'Hoard? Hoard what?'

'Jewellery,' Kabir said matter-of-factly. 'Gold perhaps?' His tone bordered on ridicule.

'What? Are you crazy?'

'Not yet,' Kabir said flippantly, and followed it up with a question. 'He brought you lunch every day?'

'Yes, he did.'

'He would walk up to the vault entrance and hand it over to you. And collect it from you afterwards?'

'Yes. That's correct.'

'Yesterday, after lunch, did he collect the lunch bag from you?'

'Yes, he did. He waited there till we finished lunch. And then he took the bag home.'

'Did he take the bag home yesterday?'

'I cannot say. I will have to check.'

'Don't you check if everything you've pilfered has made its way back to you?'

'WHAT! What rubbish!'

'Calm down, Mr Rajan. What if I told you that the gold bar, the one in the photograph I showed you in the hospital, was found in your lunch bag, in Kannan's autorickshaw.'

Rajan's eyes widened and a shocked expression appeared on his face. 'I don't know anything about that. Only Kannan can tell you how you it got there. And he is dead.'

'And you killed him,' the DGP stated grimly.

'Are you out of your mind? Why would I do that? We all loved Kannan!'

'Oh yes. We know that. Don't we? A brotherly love . . . eh!'

Rajan looked at Krishnan in surprise.

'Many years ago, when Kannan's father was on his deathbed in the hospital, and you and your father were outside the general ward, ASI T.P. Ramakrishnan was sent to investigate the case. He was shunted out in no time for getting too nosey,' Krishnan explained.

Rajan slowly moved his eyes from the DGP's face to his uniform. The badge. And that's when it hit him. DGP T.P.R. Krishnan *was* ASI T.P. Ramakrishnan! He had never realized it because he had forgotten the name of the ASI who had come to visit Kannan's father that day. He was very young at the time.

'So, Mr Rajan,' the DGP continued sternly, 'we do know how much you loved Kannan and why. So stop playing games and tell us what exactly happened.'

'Yes, Kannan was my stepbrother,' Rajan admitted, head hung low, ashamed. 'No one knew that.'

'Except me,' DGP Krishnan reconfirmed. 'I knew it the day I saw Kannan's father in the hospital. The purple mark around his wrist confirmed my suspicion that something was wrong. But I was asked to back down because of your family's proximity to the king. Your father was the trustee of the temple.'

Rajan nodded. 'Kannan was my younger brother. The age difference between us was significant. His mother was my father's mistress. When all this was happening we were too young to comprehend what was going on. I learnt about this much later, when my mother confided in us.'

'And did Kannan know that?'

'No. This was kept from him.'

'How sure are you?'

'His mother passed away a couple of years after his father. Kannan was too young to know anything at that stage. No one in my family knew about it except for my parents. So it is unlikely that anyone told him about it.'

'Okay. Let's move on.' Kabir stepped into the conversation. This family saga was all very well, but he wanted to focus on the case. 'Tell us what went wrong between the two of you.'

'Nothing went wrong between us. And for the record'—he raised his volume just a little bit—'I did NOT KILL Kannan.' He seemed flustered. 'And why am I being interrogated in this fashion? You cannot intimidate an honourable citizen in this manner. Has Dharmaraja Varma put you up to this?' He sighed deeply. 'I need to speak to my lawyer.'

Kabir Khan merely laughed.

The door opened and the AGP, Thiruvananthapuram Range, walked in. DGP Krishnan glanced at him dismissively, not bothering to conceal his irritation. The AGP handed over a sheet of paper to Kabir, whispered something in his ear and left. Kabir scanned the sheet quickly and then turned to Rajan.

'So . . .' he said

'So?' Rajan responded.

'It was all about money?'

'What nonsense!'

Kabir offered DGP Krishnan the sheet the AGP had given him. It was a list with 750 names; the 439th name, highlighted with a yellow marker, was that of Kannan Ramalingam.

Kabir slammed his hand hard on the table. His eyes glittering with rage, he glared at Rajan. 'How much?' he bellowed. 'How much did Kannan siphon out for you?'

DGP Krishnan set the sheet on the table. Rajan's eyes widened and almost popped out of his head as he read what was written on the sheet of paper in front of him. It was a note issued by the ministry of finance to the Central Board of Direct Taxes, CBI, Enforcement Directorate and the Economic Offences Wing, giving them the details they had received from the whistle-blower in the HSBC Swiss account scandal.

As he scanned the list, he stopped at number 439: Kannan Ramalingam, and next to it was the figure $4,563,826.

'Where did Kannan get all this money from?'

'We thought you might want to tell us that . . .' Kabir said as he picked up a bottle of water from the table and glugged it down. 'Start.'

Rajan held his head in his hands and whispered. 'I didn't kill him. Why don't you believe me? It was not me.'

When Kabir and DGP Krishnan finally emerged from the room, they were exhausted. They had interrogated Rajan for over two hours, but he had stuck to his story: he had not killed Kannan.

'What do you think?' Krishnan asked Kabir Khan.

'Honestly? I don't know.'

'We can't hold him for much longer. If we keep him overnight, we will get into trouble. There will be allegations of us using the murder investigation to stall the temple audit.'

'As of now, we have nothing against him. Absolutely nothing.' Kabir swore angrily. He paced up and down the corridor for a few minutes, trying to calm himself. 'What's the hospital story?' he asked the DGP suddenly. 'The one where you were ingloriously shunted out of the investigation into Rajan and his father?'

'The focus of our investigation was Rajan's father. Not him. He was a child himself. We suspected that Rajan's father had killed Kannan's father because he was involved with the latter's wife. When Kannan's father found out about the affair and threatened to tell the king, he was eliminated. Rajan's family was very reputed, and his father was a trustee of the temple . . . they couldn't afford to take the hit from this disclosure. They would've lost everything. A story was put out that he had died of liver cirrhosis. Given that Kannan's father was a drunkard, everyone bought the story.'

Kabir and the DGP fell silent for some time, each lost in his thoughts.

At last, Kabir spoke. 'But the point is, is he telling the truth?'

'He obviously knows more than he is letting on, but the only reason he gets the benefit of the doubt is that his relationship with Kannan was perfectly normal. Possibly you may not know, but Kannan put his life on the line to save Rajan and take Gopi to the hospital the day the mob attacked the high court. Besides, you yourself said we have nothing on him.'

Kabir Khan nodded. 'You're right. Cut him loose.'

51

The next afternoon came the news that Dharmaraja Varma's counsel had filed a special leave petition in the Supreme Court asking for a stay on the opening of Vault B of the Anantha Padmanabha Swamy Temple, citing the results of the Devaprasnam as the reason. Brahmashree Narayana Bhatt had categorically stated that the last vault should not be opened and the currently open vaults should be immediately sealed. Not doing so would be flouting the lord's will and would attract serious consequences, such as the one faced by Kannan and Gopi. They hadn't waited for the three-day Devaprasnam to get over. In fact the Devaprasnam had been declared a failure on account of the discovery of the body in the holy pond on the morning of the ritual. 'It was the lord's way of indicating that trouble is round the corner,' Brahmashree had said in his statement.

Vikram Rai was thrilled with the recent developments. He was confident that the petition against the opening of Vault B would be looked at by the Supreme Court in a positive manner. After all, nudging Dharmaraja Varma towards the Devaprasnam had been his idea. The same evening, at dinner, Vikram Rai spoke to Nirav Choksi. 'Didn't I say it was a good idea to let the Devaprasnam go through and use that as a reason to delay the opening of Vault B? Now we don't look like people who are scared of doing a job. The public will also get a compromise: they'll have saved Vault B.'

'For the time being.'

'Yes. Still it is a win–win for everybody.'

'I always knew you were a genius,' Nirav commented dryly.

'Who is a genius?' Subhash asked, joining the two men.

'At the end of this entire exercise, the world will value all of us as geniuses,' Vikram boasted. 'Convincing people to do what they think we don't want them to do is also an act of genius, isn't it?' he asked with a smile on his face.

Subhash laughed. 'Sure. Anyway, I am off to sleep. I have an early morning flight tomorrow. Goodnight!'

'Where to?' Nirav asked, but Subhash had walked away by then.

'Mumbai. He is going to Mumbai,' Vikram responded. 'He told me this afternoon that he has some urgent work to attend to. He'll be back by the weekend. Now that there is a possibility that the Supreme Court will accede to Dharmaraja Varma's request on Vault B, I felt it would be fine.'

'Oh? Okay . . . ' Nirav wondered why Subhash hadn't told him that he was going to Mumbai.

'You didn't know?' Vikram asked as if reading Nirav's mind. 'I thought he would have told you. After all he is closest to you in the group.'

'I'm sure he had his reasons,' Nirav responded and then excused himself when he saw Aditya and Divya walk in.

'How was your trip?' he asked them. They were returning from a day trip to Kanyakumari, a three-hour drive from Thiruvananthapuram.

'It was awesome, Dad. The Vivekananda Rock Memorial is so inspiring! And that statue of Thiruvalluvar . . .' she said enthusiastically, but her expression belied the excitement in her voice. 'Why are you wrapped up like this?' She pointed to the jacket and muffler that Nirav was wearing.

'The AC. It finally got too cold.'

'Dad! It's been so long! I told you that day itself. There is nothing wrong in saying that the AC is too cold. What is wrong with you men?' She glanced at Aditya then went back to scolding Nirav. 'You were going to ask for a change of room. What happened?'

'Calm down! Calm down!' Nirav implored. 'They changed it today. Gave me the next room.' He coughed. 'Tell me more about your trip. What took you so long?'

'The sunset at Kanyakumari is simply amazing. Divya wanted to wait to catch a glimpse of the sun going down.' Aditya smiled. The look on Divya's face said otherwise, but she didn't contradict him.

'How long are you folks here?' Vikram Rai asked them as he rose to go back to his room.

'I have a few interviews lined up so we're leaving tomorrow morning,' Aditya responded, putting his arm around Divya's shoulders.

'Oh! Quite a short trip.'

Divya squirmed out of Aditya's embrace and said, 'Well, I wanted to be with my dad for his birthday. I am glad I came.' She smiled and turned to leave. 'I have lots of packing to do. Please excuse me. Are you coming up, Dad?'

'Yes. In some time. Don't go to sleep.'

Divya nodded. 'Goodnight Mr Rai. Good luck with the rest of the audit,' she said as she stepped into the lift.

When she got out on the fourth floor, she gave Aditya a quick hug and said, 'I will call you once I am done packing.'

Aditya's room was on the seventh floor.

52

The mood of the team was low the next day. Rajan had stayed home; he was still recovering from the ignominy of having been interrogated as a suspect. He had not told anyone about the incident, lest people began believing the lies the police was spinning. Subhash was away. Nirav was a bit edgy and irritable, probably because of his cold.

Lunch was also a bit low key. Everyone was sitting quietly and eating the food which had been brought from the hotel. The workers and jewellers had gone for lunch as well, leaving Vault A sealed for the duration of the break. The TV in the lunchroom was on. The Supreme Court verdict had just come in.

'A special bench of the Supreme Court today announced a stay on its own order thereby stalling the opening of Vault B of the Anantha Padmanabha Swamy Temple until further notice,' the news anchor reported. 'This was in response to a plea filed by Dharmaraja Varma, the king of Travancore. While dismissing the arguments, which the court called regressive, the court took note of the lack of objection from the state and issued a temporary stay order. The court has directed the amicus curiae to submit a report once the evaluation of the contents of Vault A is completed. In other news—'

'Finally.' Vikram sighed, pressing the mute button on the remote. 'Some peace will return.'

Nirav smiled. He knew where Vikram was coming from.

'I'm not sure if this is the best thing that could have happened.'

Everyone turned towards the speaker. It was Ranjit Dubey. He had just come back from the restroom.

He pulled out his chair and sat down. 'Stopping the entire exercise just because we were worried about public retaliation was wrong. We should have asked for more people to finish this faster. There is something very fishy going on here.'

'Conjecture, Ranjit,' Vikram said. 'We have not come across any serious irregularities.'

'What if I say I have?'

There was stunned silence in the room.

'What do you mean?' Nirav asked in a hushed tone.

'I have been thinking of this ever since. My conscience has been pricking me . . . I have not been able to sleep, and this has made my condition worse. I would rather get this off my chest. The morning of the Devaprasnam, when we were all waiting in Dharmaraja Varma's room, after all of you left I went back looking for a restroom. I went through a door hoping to find the toilet, but ended up in a corridor. When I continued down the passage I found something unexpected.'

'And what was that?'

'A gold-plating machine.'

'A what?' Vikram Rai burst out.

'You heard me. A gold-plating machine.'

'What use could a temple possibly have for a gold-plating machine?' Nirav asked.

'I even took a few pictures.' He brought up the photos on his smartphone and passed it around so that everyone could see.

There was a shocked look on Vikram's face. 'Why didn't you tell us earlier?'

'Well, that was the day Kannan died. I was terrified. I didn't want to spill the beans and become the next body to be fished out of the pond. I mentioned it to Subhash and he too advised me to stay quiet. I did. But today when I saw all of you happy at the court verdict, I couldn't help but think that if we put this off for long, the plunderers will not leave anything of worth in the vaults.'

'*Subhash* asked you to keep quiet?' Nirav looked at him, wondering what his friend was up to.

'We should ask for an explanation. The discovery of a gold-plating machine on the temple premises changes everything. Something is definitely going on!' Vikram was furious.

'It is not in your jurisdiction to look at anything beyond the vaults,' Nirav reminded him. 'Isn't that what you said to me, Mr Rai?'

'Yes, I did, but there is something called legal jurisdiction, and something called moral jurisdiction. The rights the latter gives you cannot be defined by any court. Only your conscience can—'

'Let's not go down that path, Mr Rai,' Nirav argued. 'Where was your conscience when you wholeheartedly supported the Devaprasnam?'

'It was not for us to support or oppose,' Vikram replied heatedly.

'That may have been the case, but you cannot deny that you orchestrated it!'

Vikram ignored him and picked up his phone to make a call.

'Whom are you calling?' Nirav asked him. 'The police?'

'No,' he said. 'I'm trying to call Subhash. I want to ask him why he stopped Ranjit from telling us about it.'

'Wha—'

'Quiet! It's ringing.'

After about ten rings, the call was automatically disconnected.

'I think we should call the police and inform them,' Vikram Rai suggested.

Nirav was opposed to the idea. 'Do you really want to do that?' he asked, a concerned look on his face. And then he added, 'This is getting messier. I thought Kannan's death was a mishap. But now I'm beginning to think it was foul play.'

Vikram nodded in agreement. 'I know I was the one who wanted to restrict ourselves to Vault A, but now I think we need to hurry the entire operation. Any delay could prove costly. Perhaps even fatal.' Lost in thought he walked out of the lunchroom and headed for the vault; the others followed. As he entered the vault he turned and said, 'Let's wait till Subhash comes back.'

'Good idea,' said Nirav as he followed Vikram into the vault. The others too walked in behind them, slowly.

Even though all of them got busy with the jewellers and valuers inside the vault, something was bothering Vikram. Questions kept clamouring in his mind: Why hadn't Ranjit told them about the machine? Why had Subhash asked him to keep quiet? Was it only fear? Or was there something more? Was Subh— Oh god! How had he not realized it sooner!

Vikram picked up his phone and dialled a number. A few feet away, the phone in Nirav's pocket rang.

'Why are you calling me?' perplexed, Nirav asked Vikram. 'Pressed a wrong button?'

'Don't cut the call!' Vikram warned as he dialled Nirav's number again.

This time Nirav let it ring until the call got disconnected on its own.

Vikram looked up at him. 'Something is not right here.'

The others had gathered around them by now.

'What happened?' Ranjit asked. Nirav shook his head and looked at Vikram.

'Why did Subhash lie to all of us?'

'What!' Nirav was shocked.

'He never went to Mumbai. He is here, in Thiruvananthapuram,' Vikram explained.

'How do you know that?'

'Just now, when I called him, the subscriber-busy message played in Malayalam. Had he been in Mumbai, the message would've been in Hindi or Marathi. Apart from English, of course.'

'It can't be! He booked his tickets in front of me. He even spoke to someone to book a cab for him. I was with him when he did all this,' Ranjit Dubey countered.

'Check for yourself,' Vikram said. 'In any case, let him come back. We will ask him then.'

As he walked back to the temporary working space erected for the team just outside the vault, his mind was elsewhere. Something was wrong. 'Why don't you check with your daughter if he was on the flight with them? They were on the same flight, right?'

'The kids didn't go. I guess they were so tired after the Kanyakumari trip yesterday that they overslept,' Nirav informed Vikram.

Kabir Khan was getting ready for bed when he got a call from Delhi.

'Hello?'

'Interpol is putting out a red corner notice on your Shreyasi Sinha,' Arnab Basu began without preamble. 'They wanted to inform us in advance because she is an Indian citizen.'

'How does that matter now? She is in India. And from the looks of it, it's unlikely that she's left the country. We have notified the airports,' Khan said.

'After the hue and cry over the Nataraja statue, the Singapore government began an investigation and discovered that there are no import records for the statue. Sinha should have declared it as a part of her filings, but she didn't. That gave Singapore Police reason to investigate her. And since she disappeared soon after, they have grounds to declare her an offender and file a case.'

'Aah. Now that she's being sought by Interpol as well, it might make our job a little easier.'

'On paper at least,' Arnab said and disconnected the call.

53

'I felt the jewellers were taking longer than usual today,' Ranjit Dubey remarked as he exited the lift with Vikram Rai. They were returning to their rooms after dinner.

'A distracted lot,' Vikram said dismissively. 'Kannan's murder has them worried and scared.'

Ranjit shook his head. 'Now it will take longer to complete the task. My condition may prevent me from seeing this through till the end.' He quickened his pace just a tad; it was time to get to a toilet.

'Don't worry about it.' Vikram tried to sound very concerned. 'We can ask for a replacement for the team. If you are unwell, you are unwell.' He actually felt bad for Ranjit. 'You should have just told us in the beginning that you have a problem. We would have asked someone else.'

'The fear of incurring god's wrath is getting to me. I haven't been getting proper sleep, and it's making the condition go from bad to worse.'

'Hmm,' said Vikram as he crossed Subhash's room. Nirav's room was a few doors down the corridor on the opposite side. 'I'll file an interim report intimating the Supreme Court about a change in team. Give me some time, I'll fix it. Okay?' Oddly, there was no response. He turned around and saw Ranjit standing outside Subhash's room.

'Ranjit! What happened? I thought you were in a hurry to go to your room!'

'Isn't Subhash supposed to be in Mumbai?' Ranjit asked him. He had started sweating from the effort it was taking to control his bladder.

'Yes. That's what he said.' He patted Ranjit's back. 'Though I do think he lied to us. Still, he'd have to be really thick-headed to have stayed back in the same hotel, in the same room.'

'Then why is the do-not-disturb light in his room green?' Ranjit pointed to the lights by the side of the door.

Vikram looked at the panel. 'Relax, Ranjit,' Vikram said. 'You're overthinking this. Maybe he turned it on at some point and forgot to switch it off before leaving.'

'You are not getting it.' Ranjit was visibly shaking now. 'The light will remain on as long as there is power in the room. The moment the power is cut the light will go off.'

'So?'

'Subhash would have taken the room key with him. And the moment he pulled the key card out of the slot, the power to the room would have been cut. The very fact that this light is on indicates that there is someone inside the room.'

'Or that he left in a hurry and didn't take the key card out of the slot.'

'Whatever!' Ranjit was flustered. 'I think we should check the room.'

Not wanting to get into trouble, Vikram stepped up and pressed the doorbell. It didn't ring. He was about to press it again when he realized it wasn't ringing because of the do-not-disturb setting. He walked up to the house phone in the hallway and called the reception. Within a couple of minutes a steward and the duty manager arrived. The steward swiped his card on the key console and the door unlatched with a click.

The duty manager pushed open the door and stepped inside. Vikram and Ranjit were about to follow when he shouted, 'Call the doctor! Right now!'

54

Subhash was lying on the bed. Sprawled on his back. Eyes open. Motionless. A towel lay in a heap on the carpet next to the bed.

Vikram walked up to him and touched his wrist. It was cold. He turned and looked at the others. His eyes said everything they needed to know.

'The doctor's on his way. Five minutes,' the duty manager announced, putting away his phone.

'He can take his time.' Vikram stepped away from the bed and walked towards the window. The curtains were not drawn. He stared out into the night, the fronds of the coconut trees in the distance swaying under the moonlit sky. 'How did this happen?' he muttered under his breath, running his fingers through his hair. This was not the way he had expected things to go.

The police arrived shortly after and took charge of the situation.

55

DGP Krishnan called Kabir to tell him what had happened.

'I'll be right there!' Kabir hurriedly changed out of his nightclothes and rushed out of his room. On the way to the lift, he messaged Madhavan asking him to come to the fourth floor, 'ASAP'. He didn't give any details. He didn't have any.

He made his way through a posse of constables and a few other onlookers and entered Subhash's room. There were several people inside—two police photographers, a bunch of forensics specialists, a crime scene investigator and the remaining members of the audit team.

Vikram Rai looked up as he entered. 'Mr Khan.' He smiled. Kabir wondered how he could smile in the presence of a corpse.

'Who is the doctor?' Kabir asked. The doctor came forward. 'Initial assessment?'

'It's difficult to say. There're no visible injuries, no marks on the body, no signs of a struggle. The bed is undisturbed. Everything points to a heart attack. But I'd like to reserve my comments till after the autopsy.'

Kabir nodded and turned to the others in the room. 'Who here saw him last?'

'We were in the coffee shop last night when we saw him. That was the last time,' Nirav responded. He had come a few moments ago, along with the rest of the audit team. They seemed more anxious than sad. Fear seemed to have set in, 'He had to catch an early flight to Mumbai this morning,' Nirav added, looking at Ranjit for confirmation.

Ranjit's face too was white with fear. 'Is it the curse of the lord? Or is it something else,' he whispered, unable to keep his voice from shaking.

Kabir Khan questioned them for some time on various things that happened that day, taking notes all the while. Finally, he took Vikram Rai aside. 'Mr Rai, was Mr Parikh's life at risk? Was he under threat from anyone? Would you know?'

Vikram Rai just shook his head.

'Could someone in your team have an interest in eliminating Mr Parikh?'

Vikram Rai was horrified. 'Tell me that was not a serious question, Mr Khan!' he burst out.

Kabir placed a hand on Vikram's shoulder and tried to placate him. 'I am not trying to insinuate anything. I just wanted to be sure. Part of my job, you see.' He patted Vikram's shoulder.

Vikram shrugged off Khan's hand and stepped back. 'I don't think anyone here had any interest in killing Mr Parikh, that is assuming he was murdered.'

'Oh, in most of these cases, that's the way it is,' Kabir said nonchalantly. 'Thanks a lot. I might call you in case we need more information. I hope that's okay.'

'Of course.'

And then, as if he had just remembered, he asked, 'By the way, do you know why he was going to Mumbai?'

'No. He said he had some business dealings to finish,' Vikram responded.

'Any idea where he was planning on staying in Mumbai? Family? Friends? Hotel?'

'Sorry, I won't be able to help you. But yes, Ranjit Dubey might know. He was with Subhash when he was making his travel arrangements.'

'Wonderful. Where is Mr Dubey?' Kabir asked. 'I can't see him.'

Vikram Rai looked around. He couldn't see Ranjit Dubey either. He peeked into the corridor, but Ranjit was not there.

Just then they heard the sound of the toilet being flushed. Seconds later the bathroom door opened and Ranjit Dubey walked out, wearing a look of relief.

'Are you out of your bloody mind?' Kabir yelled in disbelief. 'Everybody OUT!'

DGP Krishnan was talking to the general manager of the hotel outside the room. Upon hearing the commotion he walked in to see what the matter was.

'No more corrupting my crime scene. Get the hell out of here. ALL OF YOU!' Kabir was furious.

'He has a problem,' Vikram Rai tried to explain. 'Unstable bladder. It is a long-standing problem.'

Ranjit was terrified. 'I . . . I'm sorry, I couldn't control . . .' he stammered as he exited the room.

Kabir just threw up his hands in frustration and waited until everyone had left.

'What do you think?' Krishnan asked him when they were alone.

'Murder? This seems to be one of those cases where the motive is far more important than the murder itself.' He turned and looked at Krishnan. 'What's your take?'

'Were I not in possession of a vital piece of information that you don't have I would've said it's a freak case. Maybe even a heart attack. But . . .'

'But?'

'The CCTV camera on this floor has not been working since last night. The service engineers haven't come by yet. I don't believe in coincidences, Khan,' Krishnan finished thoughtfully.

Kabir was shocked.

'Interesting, isn't it, Khan? There is a lot more going on here than we realize.' He scanned the room as he spoke, his eyes flipping past something shiny in a corner. It took him a moment to realize that he had missed something. He walked to the corner and looked behind the floor lamp. Hidden there were three strips of Alprax. Three *empty* strips of Alprax.

'Ah! Whoever killed him wanted it to look like a suicide,' he said, showing Kabir the strips of Alprax, an anti-anxiety, sleep-inducing drug—an overdose of which could be potentially fatal. 'I am sure you will find traces of Alprax in his bloodstream as well.'

56

'Mr Dubey!' Kabir called out. A nervous Ranjit stepped away from the rest of his team and walked with Khan to the lift lobby and sat down on a sofa.

'Any idea where Mr Parikh was headed?' Kabir asked once they had settled down on the sofa.

'Not sure,' he said. 'I just heard him speak to someone about his trip. He said he would do the needful when he got there. He did rent a car for two days.'

'Does he have an office in Mumbai?

'I remember him saying once that whenever he was in Mumbai, he operated out of a hotel. He has a skeletal operation in Gujarat. The main operations are based out of New York City.'

'Understood. Would you know who he was talking to?'

'No, sorry!'

'Okay. If you do remember something else, do call me.' Kabir got up, feeling more frustrated than enlightened after that conversation.

'Certainly,' said Ranjit. 'But—'

Kabir Khan turned around immediately. So there was indeed something else.

'Yes?'

'I am very worried for my life.'

'Oh?' Kabir had expected some sort of revelation that was pertinent to the case, not the imaginings of a scared man. 'Don't. We are all here to take care of you and the team.'

'Forgive me if I don't put much trust in your security measures. First Kannan. Now Subhash. God only knows what's in store for all of us. I have half a mind to quit this assignment. Why would I knowingly put my life in danger?'

'I couldn't agree with you more.' Dharmaraja Varma had arrived on the scene.

'Thirumanassu?' DGP Krishnan walked up to him. 'I was about to call and brief you.'

'Yes, well, that's thoughtful of you, but Mr Rai already called and informed me,' he said dismissively. Turning to face Ranjit Dubey, he said, 'Mr Dubey, you are a mere human. Everything is in the hands of the mighty Anantha Padmanabha Swamy. Whatever he wills, will happen. That day, when Mr Parikh slipped on the mandapam, I knew it was only a matter of time before the lord claimed him. You see, Mr Dubey, in our part of the world, we believe that anything which is dropped on the mandapam belongs to the Almighty. As I said, it was only a matter of time. And when the team continued to insult and challenge the lord by defiling the temple vaults, He was bound to get angry. Anything is possible when the lord is upset. Cyclones, winds, floods, earthquakes are all a consequence of the lord's anger. Once Padmanabha Swamy made up his mind, Subhash Parikh never stood a chance.'

'We'll be the judge of that, Mr Varma, if you don't mind,' Kabir retorted. The king's lecture was beginning to infuriate him.

'Well, Mr Khan, your religion, possibly your religious leanings, will not allow you to understand what goes on in ours—'

'Then I am reasonably safe,' Kabir interrupted. 'Your lord's jurisdiction does not extend to my religion. So regardless of what I do, He won't be able to get back at me,' he said with a smirk and walked away, leaving a red-faced Dharmaraja Varma to glare impotently at him.

'Look for his phone,' Kabir instructed the forensic team combing the room for clues. When DGP Krishnan entered, after having spent several minutes pacifying Dharmaraja Varma, Kabir simply rolled his eyes. 'Jerk!'

'It is all right. He is a strong believer in the lord. At his level and position, one doesn't have a choice. Even if you don't want to, you will have to believe.'

Khan ignored the explanation. 'Parikh's phone holds the key. I need to find out who his contact in Mumbai was. Once we get to that person, we might be able to unearth some more information about what our guy was up to.'

'There is an easier way to find out whom he was meeting in Mumbai,' Krishnan said mysteriously. 'Let me make a few calls.'

57

The investigation into the non-working of the CCTV cameras and the absence of housekeeping staff on the floor occupied by the audit team led to a dead end. The police could not pin the responsibility on any individual. Background checks were done on all hotel personnel, but they were all found to be clean.

'All of them are sympathizers,' Kabir complained.

'Sympathizers?' Madhavan asked.

'In this state, not many support the vaults being opened. There is a huge difference between what is right and what is *considered* right. Opening the vaults is the right thing to do. But does the public at large think so? Maybe not.'

'Hmm.'

'That's why no one has come forward with any information.'

Kabir's phone rang just then. It was Krishnan. He was waiting in the hotel lobby.

Within the next two minutes, Khan was with him.

'I think we have some info on the person who Subhash Parikh was to meet in Mumbai,' Krishnan told him as he led him to a quiet corner of the lobby. Beyond the glass facade Kabir could see a throng of media personnel waiting to get a sound byte from the people in the know. Confusion reigned supreme.

'Oh wonderful. That was fast.'

Krishnan rifled through his files and pulled out a photograph. 'Here is your guy.'

Kabir looked intently at the balding, middle-aged man dressed in a grey safari suit in the photo. 'Who is he?'

'This is the man who came to the airport to receive Subhash Parikh. CCTV footage at the arrival gate shows him holding the placard with Parikh's name on it.'

'Impressive!' Kabir Khan complimented.

Krishnan acknowledged the compliment with a grin. 'I told you I had to make a few phone calls. Mumbai Police has been informed. Everyone is looking for him. We even got his vehicle number from the parking lot.'

'Do we have a fix on where all Subhash Parikh went the night he died?'

'Yes. The mobile phone company was able to give us his location pings. Contrary to his normal routine, he didn't move around much that evening. You see, he was quite the explorer. Every evening he would go out and come back late. But, on the evening in question, he stayed in the hotel only.'

He handed over the papers to Kabir. As the DGP had mentioned, the document which traced Parikh's whereabouts on the night he died didn't show much movement. However, he seemed to have done a fair bit of travelling the night before that. One of the places he had visited was just six kilometres away. Apparently he had spent a few hours there and returned to the hotel. Why would he do that, Kabir wondered.

'Any idea where this place is?' he asked Krishnan.

'It is some place closer to the sea. Near Kovalam.'

'Why would Subhash go there at night?'

Krishnan shrugged. 'A team has been dispatched to investigate. We will know in a while . . . ' He realized he was talking to himself. Kabir had disappeared. 'Where has he gone?' he asked Madhavan, who was equally perplexed.

Within five minutes, Kabir was back in the lobby, clutching a folder.

'Sorry!' he said, pulling out a sheet from the folder and placing it on the table, next to Subhash Parikh's mobile phone tracking record. 'See?' He looked at both men and pointed to the two sheets. 'He followed him. Everywhere!'

'Who followed whom everywhere?' Krishnan was confused.

Kabir let out a little huff of breath. How could they not see it, he wondered with a touch of exasperation. 'This one, the one on the right is Subhash Parikh's mobile tracking map. The one on the left is identical, except for the time stamps. They are just about twenty seconds apart, give or take a few. It's as if Subhash Parikh was trailing the person on the left all evening.'

'Whose is the data on the second sheet?'

'Kannan's,' Kabir answered. 'The moment I saw the tracking data for Subhash, I knew I had seen it earlier.'

The DGP looked at both tracking maps for a few seconds and then spoke. 'What is even stranger is the fact that both the trails mirror each other towards the latter part of the evening and then at one point, one of the trails disappears.'

'The Padma Teertha Kulam,' Madhavan whispered. 'That's where Kannan died. Subhash was there when Kannan was killed.'

'Yes,' Kabir said grimly. 'Maybe that's why he was killed.'

58

Most of the local jewellers whose help had been solicited in valuing the contents of the vault stopped coming to work, fearing for their lives. Dharmaraja Varma's reiterations that these deaths were the result of the curse of the Anantha Padmanabha Swamy Temple weren't helping matters.

That morning, DGP Krishnan, Kabir Khan, Madhavan and a team of officers descended on the premises of the Anantha Padmanabha Swamy Temple. They wanted to scout around for some clues in the Subhash Parikh murder case.

Kabir stayed back and explored the area around the Padma Teertha Kulam while Krishnan, Madhavan and the others went in. For once he didn't make a fuss when Krishnan asked him to stay put; he knew that it was because of his religion.

Dharmaraja Varma was waiting at the temple gates; he was the only one who had been intimated of the police's arrival.

'It is unfortunate that you have had to come under such circumstances,' Dharmaraja Varma said, his words measured, his voice cold and his face expressionless.

By that time, they had been joined by Vikram Rai and Nirav.

'Who could have killed Subhash Parikh?' Krishnan asked Vikram the moment they were ahead of the pack, as they took the customary round of the temple. 'I know we have asked you this before, but now that you have had a chance to introspect . . .?'

'He was quite popular. Everyone liked him. I have no idea why anyone would kill him.'

'Any fights? Any conflicts? Any arguments you are aware of?'

'None whatsoever. Although—' Vikram hesitated.

'Please! Any information, however inconsequential, might give us our next lead,' Krishnan begged.

'I . . . He knew about something strange happening in the temple. One of our team members, Mr Dubey, saw something inside the temple and mentioned it to Subhash. I don't know how relevant it was, but Ranjit thinks that it might have had something to do with his death. He is worried that he is next in line.'

'What was it? What did Mr Dubey see?'

'A gold-plating machine. In the king's chamber. But when they went looking for it again, it was not there.'

'What?' Krishnan was surprised. 'A gold-plating machine. Why does the temple have one? And why didn't you tell us earlier?'

'And what would you have done?' Vikram Rai was sarcastic. 'Precisely,' he said when Krishnan remained silent. 'Nothing! You would have done nothing. These guys enjoy political patronage. You can't touch them, can you?'

Krishnan's silence spoke volumes. The two of them kept walking, each preoccupied with his own thoughts. On the way they crossed the temple elephant. It had been freshly decorated; a promotional banner of India Cements Limited hung right behind it.

'I was present when N. Srinivasan came in person and donated this to the temple. It's been a little over a year now,' Krishnan remarked. He wanted to keep the conversation going.

'That's the problem, Mr Krishnan. This temple enjoys immense political patronage. The who's who of India's polity and business is a devotee. Anything that changes the status quo will face huge resistance.'

'You are telling me? All of us know what goes on here, but can do nothing. The state government is in the king's pocket. They need the votes, so they turn a blind eye to whatever he does. Why else would they give a declaration in court saying they are very happy with the temple remaining under the control of the king?'

Vikram Rai stopped abruptly and walked back to the elephant. The banner behind the elephant was new, he noticed with interest. 'Are you saying that this elephant was donated by N. Srinivasan of India Cements?'

'Yes. Why?' the DGP asked him. 'In fact, Mr Srinivasan is expected here today. This will be his first public appearance after the match-fixing scandal broke out. We have been asked to beef up security for him.'

'That explains the new banner! The Kerala division of India Cements must have come in to make sure it was put up properly,' Vikram commented

'Sycophants!' Krishnan declared.

As they approached the king's chamber, they crossed a room on their left that was locked. It was the only locked room on that level of the temple.

'What is in that room?' Madhavan asked out of curiosity.

'Just some old temple stuff,' one of the king's representatives answered.

'Why is the room locked? Anything which is out of the ordinary is cause for suspicion.'

'I'm not sure, but I'll check,' was the response.

'Can we see what is inside?' Krishnan asked in an almost apologetic tone.

'Let me see where the keys are.'

Madhavan and Krishnan waited for about five minutes and then walked to the king's chamber, deciding to sit there till the keys came.

They met with all the jewellers and valuers, who had been specifically called in, one by one. The interrogation process lasted over a couple of hours. Krishnan had offered to have Kabir Khan dropped back, but Kabir declined politely. He wanted to be around and in the thick of things.

59

Kabir walked around the Padma Teertha Kulam, his thoughts in a jumble. He wondered what could have caused the deaths of Kannan and Subhash Parikh. Both in different parts of the city, both by different means—one violent, the other peaceful. Yet, instinct told him that the two murders were related. He turned around and looked at the temple. From here, he could see the gopuram. Were the killings related to the happenings in the temple? But then, he thought, religion was made to protect. In every religion, *people* killed in the name of god. Just that they had got used to blaming him for everything.

After walking around a bit, he called Madhavan, who was in the king's chamber with Krishnan.

'Did you ask to see what's inside those rooms?'

'Not in my jurisdiction. I did tell the DGP,' Madhavan responded.

'And?'

'At first they tried to stall us, then the DGP asked Dharmaraja Varma. That's when we were told that the keys are not available; the person who has them hasn't come in.'

'Break open the locks, man!' Kabir thundered. 'I am sure there is something there which the king wants to hide.'

'As I said, not under my jurisdiction. This is Krishnan's call. I am just an observer.' He handed over the phone to Krishnan.

'Is there a problem?' Dharmaraja Varma sensed something was amiss. No one responded.

'Yes, Kabir.' Krishnan walked away from the king's table as he spoke. He did not want the latter to overhear him.

Kabir didn't have to convince Krishnan to break open the lock. 'You will need court permission, sir. But not the amicus curiae.' He had read the terms of reference of the job that was entrusted to the amicus curiae. 'The court-appointed team can check any room they want to. They have unhindered access to every corner of the temple complex. If Vikram Rai asks for it, no one can refuse. It is well within his powers. Powers that have been granted by the Supreme Court.'

The moment he hung up, the DGP walked up to Vikram Rai and tapped him on the shoulder. 'Mr Rai, may I have a word?'

Vikram was only too happy to sign the orders to break open the padlock. 'I don't have a problem. You are the person who should be worried about the effect of this on public perception. Not me. I will sign the request to open the door under police bandobast.'

'Thank you. I will get the letter ready.'

60

Divya and Aditya were still in Thiruvananthapuram. Divya was worried about Nirav and had insisted on staying back till the situation resolved itself. Aditya concurred, not that he had a choice. Over the last couple of days a certain chill had crept into their relationship. Divya was no longer as friendly as she used to be. She had become snappy and would take off on him at the smallest pretext.

Divya was in her room when she got a call.

'Hello, Aunty.'

'I spoke to you earlier too, sweetheart. Were you able to talk to your father about this property?'

'Oh no! I completely forgot about it, Aunty. Too many things are happening here. You must have read about them in the papers.' She paused for breath. 'But don't worry. I will speak to him. Tonight. For sure.'

'Okay, my love. Just let me know. After Ankit went overseas, your uncle was managing all this. Now that he is not with us any longer, I only have you to turn to.'

'Don't worry, Aunty. I will speak to Dad.' She hung up.

'What happened?' Aditya inquired.

'Nothing important.' Divya didn't elaborate.

'Fine!' Aditya shrugged in frustration and stormed off.

She was feeling the heat of the past few days and her behaviour was possibly the result of that, he consoled himself.

61

Vikram walked up to the door, one last time, to check the lock. It was a new Godrej seven-lever padlock. 'We shall break the lock. And if need be, the door too.'

'Is that really necessary?' Dharmaraja Varma tried arguing. 'If you'd wait for just one day, we'll get you the keys!'

Vikram Rai was in a confrontational mood. 'Either give us the keys *now*, or we will break down the door.' He glared at the king.

Varma stared back resolutely.

'So be it,' Vikram said and in no time, the padlock was hammered into submission by two of Krishnan's men.

Vikram pushed open the door and entered the dark room. He ran his fingers along the wall lightly, trying to locate the light switches. The moment he turned the lights on, there was an audible gasp from the men behind him. Vikram was shocked by what he saw. In the centre of the room was a gold-plating machine. On closer inspection he noticed that it was a West Houghten and Blake model. The year on the manufacturers stamp read 2014.

Ranjit hurried up to Vikram and nudged him. 'This is the one I saw in the corridor near the bathroom.'

Vikram looked at Dharmaraja Varma. The king looked utterly composed.

'Why does a temple need a gold-plating machine?' Rajan asked.

Dharmaraja Varma ignored the question. He refused to be drawn into a conversation with Rajan of all people.

'Well?' Vikram asked irritably. 'The man asked you a question.'

'Oh. It is used all the time. This is one of the largest temples in south India. We have so many smaller temples inside and festivities are held all through the year.'

'So?' Vikram was getting impatient.

'So during these festivals the deities have to be decked up with jewellery.' Dharmaraja Varma spoke slowly, as if explaining the intricacies of temple procedure to a child. 'And because the jewellery tends to get roughed up a lot, the pieces often suffer damage. The gold-plating machine is to make sure that the damaged pieces can be repaired on the temple premises itself.'

'How come I have never seen this?' asked Rajan, only to be ignored by the king once again.

'Is that why these pieces are here?' Nirav pointed at a miniature statue of Goddess Lakshmi lying in one corner of the room. 'It doesn't seem to be bro—' He stopped abruptly, walked over to the statue and moved it to the side. Partially concealed behind the statue was a pot studded with precious stones and full of glittering gold coins. Coins which appeared to be centuries old. DGP Krishnan was shocked when he saw the pot.

Nirav carefully picked up the pot and brought it to Vikram and Rajan. Together they peered at the marking on the pot.

'1648,' Rajan said, reading the numbers inscribed on the neck of the pot.

Both Vikram and Nirav looked at each other.

'Which means there were at least 1648 pots.'

62

Vikram Rai looked at Dharmaraja Varma in shock. 'Wasn't this in Vault A?'

Varma looked as unaffected as ever. 'Vault A?' He chuckled. 'You must be joking!' Suddenly his expression changed. His face became red and mouth quivered with rage. 'Are you insinuating . . . ?'

'I am not insinuating anything, Thirumanassu. I am just asking you a question. The answer to which all of us can see.'

'This pot has been outside ever since I can remember!' Varma blustered. 'I don't know what makes you think that this belongs to Vault A. I have no idea.'

'For starters, it is numbered 1648,' Nirav began. 'There are a few hundred of these gold pots and large urns numbered in this manner inside Vault A. Not only numbered in this manner, but the look and feel is exactly the same. If I remember correctly, the largest number I have seen on those pots is 869. If this is pot 1648, there should have been at least 1647, if not more, pots inside the vault. Where are the rest?' Nirav demanded aggressively.

'Watch your tone!' Dharmaraja Varma thundered. 'And lower your voice. No one speaks to *me* in this fashion.'

'Bullsh—' Nirav burst out, but Vikram squeezed his shoulder in warning.

'Gold, statues and figurines which should be in the vaults are here in this room. A gold-plating machine of industrial scale is on the premises. What are we to make of it, Thirumanassu?' DGP Krishnan asked forcefully, yet respectfully.

The king was outraged. 'How dare you!' he thundered. 'The gold-plating machine was imported from Switzerland through proper channels. You can see the papers. We have the required import permits. No one questioned us then, so what gives you the right to question us now? As far as the rest of the antiques and jewellery that you are seeing here, they have been outside the vault for generations. They are in this room for repairs,' Dharmaraja Varma snapped, not bothering to conceal his anger. 'And now if you're done with your insinuations and your accusations, gentlemen, I need to leave. The chief trustee of the temple will accompany you.' And he stalked off.

The moment he left, Nirav turned to Vikram Rai. 'Why the hell didn't you pin him down? This was our best chance to nail him.'

'Calm down, Nirav.'

But Vikram's reassurances only irked Nirav further. '*Calm down?* We had him. The cops were here. The evidence of pilferage was here—'

'We are not sure it is pilferage. We *think* it is.' Rajan spoke for the first time.

'Isn't it obvious? Pot 1648 is here. We have only 869 pots in the vault. Which means that roughly *seven hundred* pots are missing! Each pot containing almost one kilo of gold. Seven hundred kilograms of gold that was probably melted in this contraption standing in front of you.' And he pointed to the gold-plating machine. 'At today's price, the gold alone will be worth over two hundred crore. And you say that you *think* it is pilferage. I tell you this fraud should be in jail for what remains of his godforsaken life! No bail, no parole.' Nirav moved his hands in the air, gesticulating wildly. 'And you!' He pounced on Vikram. 'You sounded like you didn't want to tread on his toes! As if you *wanted* to let him go. Without any explanation!'

'Nirav! Stop and think for a moment,' Vikram retorted. 'Our brief is only to report any suspicious activity and irregularities. Not take action on them. Our job is to tell the court what we saw. What we've seen in the past thirty minutes will certainly make its way into our report. Over two hundred crore rupees worth of gold seems to have been systematically pilfered, as you have said. And there is no way that can be condoned. But we're not the ones sitting in judgement here. Our job is to simply let the courts know, and let these gentlemen do theirs,' he said pointing to Krishnan and Madhavan.

He looked at Rajan and requested, 'Could you arrange to have the evidence in the room photographed and recorded, and take charge of the gold-plating machine?'

Rajan just nodded. 'I will also get the lock replaced.'

'Thanks!' said Vikram as he walked out with Nirav.

63

Back at the hotel Kabir waited in his room for Madhavan and Krishnan to return. Plagued incessantly by a variety of thoughts, he finally decided to go out. As he exited the hotel a few security guards saw him and hurriedly came up to him. Wanting to be left alone, he shooed them away. In his hand was a sheet of paper—a map that tracked Subhash Parikh's movements the night before he was murdered. He got into the car given to him by Kerala Police and told the driver where to go.

The trail began near their hotel where Padmanabha Swamy Temple Road intersected with MG Road. From there it went past the Kovalam Bypass Road and on to the highway. Subhash could not have covered this distance on foot. He must have taken a cab. Kabir made a mental note to ask the reception for the cab details.

The highway curved towards the sea. Thiruvananthapuram, by virtue of being on the western coast of India, had a long coastline. While parts of it were rocky, the bulk of it was sandy and made for a picturesque shoreline. Kabir drove for about 14 kilometres. At which point the trail turned right, towards the beach where a number of five-star hotels were located. Vivanta by Taj – Green Cove, Kovalam, was to the right and a few kilometres ahead was the Leela Hotel.

Kabir got out of the car and looked around. To his right was the main gate of the Taj. To his left, according to a sign, was a small passage that led to the private beach of the Taj Hotel. A strange configuration for a hotel, he thought. A public road separating the residences from the private beach—he hadn't seen that in many hotels.

He ignored the thought and let his eyes wander. Going by the tracking data, Subhash had waited somewhere close by for about five to seven minutes that night. As he looked about he noticed two security cameras atop the main gate of the Taj. He stared at them for a few seconds before he got into the car, and asked the driver to enter the hotel.

The car dropped him outside the hotel lobby and drove away to the parking. Kabir walked up to the desk, showed his badge and asked to see the head of security.

'Can I get you the manager?' the receptionist asked.

'Anyone who can guide me through the property,' he said. The head of security would have been ideal but in his absence Kabir was willing to settle for someone else.

Within minutes, a sari-clad young lady, who looked to be in her early thirties, walked up to him.

'Excuse me?' she said, handing him her card. 'I'm Pallavi, the assistant general manager.'

Kabir, who had been expecting to see a middle-aged man dressed in a suit, was pleasantly surprised. The look on his face was a dead giveaway. 'You must have been a star performer, Pallavi!' he couldn't resist saying.

Pallavi laughed. 'It's nice to see that people think that way. But that's not true. This is one of the smaller hotels in the group and finding people to work here is always a bit of an issue. If someone puts their hand up, they are picked almost immediately. I am not a star, just an ordinary girl who put her hand up.' She smiled again. Her smile was gorgeous. 'Now tell me, how can I help you, sir?'

'I'd like to see the security footage from the main gate for Saturday night.'

'And what makes you think I would oblige?' Although she was still smiling, ice had crept into her voice.

How can someone be so pretty, yet so rude, Kabir wondered. 'Oh, I am sorry,' he said. 'I should have introduced myself.' He brought out his ID and offered it to her. 'Kabir Khan. CBI.'

Pallavi's demeanour changed instantly. 'Of course! If you could give me some background, it will help me get things done. I will, however, need to check with the group head of security.'

'On Saturday, an individual went past your hotel gates at 9.36 p.m. and then again at 10.23 p.m. I want to see if he was with someone.'

'Our feed is held in our server in Mumbai. I will have to requisition the footage.'

'How long do you think it will take?'

'I'm not sure. But they will need some more details. They won't release the feed on the basis of an oral instruction. Yet I will ask.'

'Perhaps you can tell whoever it is that this is an ongoing murder investigation?' Kabir said coolly, ignoring Pallavi's gasp. 'The man whose footage I am looking for was found dead on Monday. He was a member of the Padmanabha Swamy Temple audit team. His death raises many questions, some of which point to the highest seat in the monarchy and possibly even in the government. We must get to the bottom of this. Quickly. Any delay will make it easier for the killer to escape.'

'I will do my best to expedite the request, Mr Khan.'

Before he left Kabir gave her his card and said that he would be expecting a call from her. 'We are staying at the Lotus Pond.'

Pallavi smiled ruefully. 'I know. We tried our best to host the audit team. We were even willing to give out the rooms for free! This is a better hotel, certainly a better-managed one. Yet everyone chose to stay there.' She shook her head. 'We figured that the Lotus Pond management probably used their connections to help them swing the deal. It's unfortunate, losing a deal like this. But, we move on in life, don't we?'

Khan didn't know what to say. He just smiled and walked out of the hotel to his car.

At the main gate he turned right on to the public road. About a kilometre ahead was the Shiva Parvathy Temple in Kuzhivilakom. The road passed through some areas where construction activity seemed to be going on. Kabir stopped the car and looked around. A portion of the land on the right was cordoned off and huge pits had been dug up. He couldn't exactly figure out what was going on inside. He ignored that and walked; the Shiva Parvathy Temple was just about one hundred steps ahead.

At the temple gate Kabir consulted the map in his hand. Subhash had come here on Saturday night and spent over twenty minutes before turning back towards Thiruvananthapuram. Kabir looked around, puzzled. Something didn't seem right. An enormous padlock hung on the gate along with a board that said the temple was closed for renovation. The date on the notification was from two years ago.

What was Subhash Parikh doing here that night?

64

Later that evening Kabir got a call from Pallavi. She came straight to the point. 'Mr Khan, unfortunately the CCTV cameras at the gates were not working that night. They were repaired on Sunday morn—'

'Is this a joke?' Kabir snapped. 'Is the entire state involved in this cover-up? Whenever we need any footage, CCTV cameras across the state seem to malfunction. How convenient! How can you not have camera feed for the gate at that time?'

'Mr Khan,' Pallavi responded calmly, refusing to take the bait. 'I told you that the gate cameras were malfunctioning that night. I did not say that we don't have any camera footage for that time.' There was tremendous poise in her voice. Kabir realized why she had become the assistant general manager of the hotel at such a young age.

'I'm sorry?' he said.

'I said, that I told you that the cameras were malfunctioning. I never said that the feed was not available.'

'Isn't that the same thing?'

'Almost, but not quite,' she said.

Kabir resisted the urge to ask her what she meant. Her mind games were irritating him, but he was also beginning to enjoy them.

'On Saturday night there was a wedding in the hotel. The wedding procession was at the gate around the same time that you wanted the feed for.'

'Hmm' was all Kabir Khan could say.

'I asked for the wedding videographer's recording. Fortunately, it covers the gate and the area that you want. If I recollect correctly, you want the footage from 9.20 to 9.38 p.m.? Right?'

'Excellent!' Kabir said admiringly. 'Can you send it to me?'

'On its way, *sir*!' He could hear the smile in her voice. 'But please do not drag the hotel or its employees into this.'

'I shall do my best,' Kabir promised.

'The courier left with the CD some ten minutes ago. He should be reaching your hotel soon.'

Sure enough, the CD was in Kabir's hands fifteen minutes later. Madhavan had joined him in his room by then as well. Without wasting a minute, Kabir opened his laptop and played the CD. It was a Punjabi wedding. The baraat was dancing in a crazed manner around the groom as he approached on horseback while the band belted out a hip-hop tune.

At 9.36 p.m. in the video clock, wearing a cream shirt and jeans, Subhash Parikh came into view. He was carrying an iPhone in his right hand and was walking by the side of the road, trying to avoid the baraat. He was alone. The audit team had been advised not to venture out alone, but there he was, all by himself.

Subhash walked past the baraat and stopped right in front of the hotel. He looked around—perhaps to make sure he had not been followed or maybe to look for someone. He stood there, fiddling with his phone. As Kabir watched the video he made a mental note to ask for a higher resolution image of the screen of the phone, just to try and see if he could make out what was on it.

After a couple of minutes Subhash suddenly brought the phone to his ear. The fact that he didn't speak immediately suggested he was the one making the call. A few moments passed and then he could be seen shouting into the phone, possibly trying to be heard over the noise being made by the band. He was still gesticulating furiously and speaking agitatedly when the camera started to pan across. In a few seconds Subhash would no longer be in the frame. The call over, he could be seen putting the phone in his pocket.

Kabir watched intently. The video had just five seconds remaining. Two seconds before the end he hurriedly tapped the spacebar and paused the video. He peered at the screen for a moment, then turned and looked at Madhavan.

'Did you see what I just saw?'

Madhavan nodded.

'How could this happen?' Kabir looked shocked.

65

DGP Krishnan was in office early that day. Kabir Khan had called him at 5 a.m. and asked to meet him as soon as possible. It was 6.45 a.m. by the time they met. Kabir inserted a pen drive into the DGP's computer and brought up the video on the screen.

'Whose wedding is it?' Krishnan asked.

'Does it matter?'

'Not really, no . . .' Krishnan said as he went back to watching the video. 'Can't we just watch the relevant portions?' he complained as an office boy brought in some fresh filter coffee, and poured it out for him.

'No,' Kabir said shortly.

'The video's about to end, Khan,' Krishnan said, reaching for his filter coffee. 'What's so important about watching Parikh yell on the pho—' He stopped speaking abruptly, the tumbler of coffee halfway to his mouth, his eyes focused on the screen. Turning towards Kabir, he muttered, 'What does *she* have to do with Subhash Parikh?'

'My guess is as good as yours.'

'What do we do now?' he asked Kabir.

Madhavan had been silent all this while. Now he said, 'This proves that this woman is in Thiruvananthapuram. But where is she now? Where has she been hiding? We have activated all our information channels—every single bit of information we could get, we have got.'

'We have her number. We can track her down,' Kabir declared.

'We have?' Madhavan asked.

'Can't you see? Subhash must be calling her. The moment he disconnects the call, she appears. I can only imagine he was calling her to locate her. And when he saw her, he hung up.'

'I don't think it was Shreyasi that he called.' Madhavan was firm. He replayed the last few seconds of the video again. 'It's true, the moment he disconnects, Shreyasi does appear. But she doesn't have a phone in her hand.'

'How long does it take to slip it inside the bag?' Kabir countered.

'Not long, but where is her bag?' Madhavan paused the video at the point when she entered the frame. Kabir looked carefully. Madhavan was right. She didn't have a bag in her hand. And she was wearing a sari.

'It could have been a normal call to someone else,' Madhavan reasoned.

'But to whom?' Krishnan was lost in thought. This someone could be the key to the entire case.

DGP Krishnan picked up his intercom and pressed a button. 'I need you to run a check on Subhash Parikh's mobile number. On Saturday, a day before he died, I want to know who all he called between 9.30 p.m. and 9.45 p.m., and if he received any calls during that time. You have ten minutes.'

'This is an interesting connection,' Kabir remarked thoughtfully. 'There is something extremely fishy about this.'

'Knowing Parikh could be a coincidence. They are in similar trades.' Krishnan played the devil's advocate.

'Hmm . . . It's possible. Possible but not probable. We won't know unless we get to the bottom of this. And until we do that, all possibilities have to be considered.'

The intercom rang.

'Yes?' Krishnan barked. 'That was quick. Tell me.'

The DGP's face transformed as he heard the answer. One didn't need to be a genius to figure out that everything was not right.

'Are you sure?' Krishnan asked and waited for the answer before he hung up. He grabbed a glass of water kept on the table and gulped down half its contents.

'Parikh neither made nor received any calls that night.'

'Or maybe he did,' Kabir reasoned. 'Just that he made them from a different phone. A second phone.'

66

Concerned at the turn of events the chief minister of Kerala called for a meeting of the top officials of the state police that day. Krishnan asked Kabir to accompany him to the meeting. Vikram Rai was also summoned.

As expected Dharmaraja Varma and the chief minister walked into the room together.

'So, Mr Krishnan,' the chief minister began, 'this is proving to be a lot more complicated than what it had seemed when it all began.'

'If the loss of two lives is "complicated", then yes, sir.'

'Human life is precious, Krishnan. Two people have died. The press is baying for my blood. If we can't protect people in and around the temple, whom can we protect? If we cannot safeguard the lives of guests in high-security areas, then that raises questions about the effectiveness of our police force.'

'Respectfully, sir,' Kabir Khan said, 'if more than two hundred crore worth of gold can be pilfered from under our noses, where is the guarantee that we can protect anybody?'

'Don't speak out of turn, officer,' the chief minister chided Kabir and turned to Krishnan, ignoring what Kabir had said. 'What are we doing to give people the confidence that things are under control?'

'Another investigation?' Vikram Rai butted in with a straight face and a hint of derision in his tone. 'An open, honest and *thorough* investigation for a change . . .' He looked pointedly at Dharmaraja Varma.

'What do you mean, Mr Rai?'

'Well, sir, with due respect, you call for this meeting and then walk into it arm in arm with Dharmaraja Varma . . . It doesn't instil confidence in the idea of a fair investigation, does it?' Kabir responded even though the chief minister had directed the question at Vikram. He was furious that the chief minister was taking them to task when he should have been asking them the facts of the case and taking an update. He was reasonably certain that the king had given him his own version of events and the chief minister had believed it to be gospel.

'Do you know what I think, Mr Khan?' The chief minister spoke with barely concealed rancour. 'Within the four walls of the room, I think a Muslim investigating a murder . . . *two* murders . . . that involve a temple is possibly the most blasphemous thing I have ever heard.' He looked around the table for support. Only Dharmaraja Varma was nodding. 'So, I am going to recommend to the CBI that you be taken off the investigating team and someone who understands Hindu culture and its practices take the lead.'

Kabir stood up. 'In that case, sir, I shall be forced to make sure that everyone knows about the gold-plating machine in the temple and the two hundred crore worth of gold that is missing. Mind you, this is only *one* instance. The more time the audit team spends in the temple, the more discrepancies we shall find. Although, to cast aspersions even a small act of indiscretion is enough. Who needs two hundred crore when twenty-one lakh will do? And by the way, lest we forget, we have documentary evidence. The temple paid from its bank account a sum of twenty-one lakh to allegedly acquire an elephant when the animal was actually *donated* by N. Srinivasan of India Cements! Your own records show it. Would you like me to produce the paperwork?'

Sitting beside Kabir, Vikram Rai smirked. After all, it was he who had told Kabir about the elephant and given him the evidence to support that claim.

Trust is really a delicate thing. It doesn't always require a twenty tonne hammer to break it. Sometimes, even a small pat of indiscretion is enough to shatter it to bits. And once destroyed, recovering it is almost impossible. Dharmaraja Varma realized that, as did the chief minister.

'And, sir,' Kabir continued, 'the CBI does not look at caste, creed or religion. That's for politicians like yourself. There may be some black sheep in the force, but they are also everywhere. In every organization, every religion. Please don't taint everyone with the same brush, sir. If there are any other questions, I am happy to answer, else please excuse me.'

When no reply was forthcoming, Kabir turned away and walked out of the meeting, leaving both the chief minister and Dharmaraja Varma red-faced.

The chief minister got up from his chair and gestured to DGP Krishnan to join him in the adjacent room.

'Look, Krishnan,' he said as soon as the DGP shut the door. 'The king is an old man. A foot and three quarters in the grave. How much longer will he live? But as long as he does, he is critical to us. People look at him as a protector of the temple, their faith. If we touch him, it won't be without political ramifications. We need to make sure that he is protected. Else our vote base will gravitate towards the opposition. Dharmaraja Varma is our insurance—insurance that we will win the next elections, which, as you know, are not too far away. Once we win the next term, we will act on him. Till then keep Kabir Khan on a very short leash.'

Krishnan just smiled and nodded.

The meeting was over.

On his way out, Krishnan requested Vikram Rai to join him in the car since they were both headed to the temple.

'What kind of man was Subhash Parikh? Do you think he could have been involved in a racket of any kind?'

'What kind of a racket?'

'Something illegal.'

'Not that I know of. Why?'

'He was seen with a woman who we believe was involved in the smuggling of the Nataraja statue from Suthamalli which was eventually recovered from the National Museum in Australia.'

Vikram Rai seemed concerned with this allegation. 'No, no! He has a highly reputed antiques showroom in New York.'

'Do you have his telephone number?'

'Of course. Why?'

'Can you share it with me?'

Vikram Rai browsed through his contacts and gave Krishnan Subhash's number. It was the same number the police had.

'Did he have an alternate number?'

'If he did, he didn't share it with us.'

'Did you ever see him use another phone?'

Vikram shook his head. 'He used to carry an iPhone. I don't recall seeing him use another phone.'

'Well, the other phone could have been an iPhone as well!'

'Everyone has a secret these days.' Vikram gave a hollow laugh.

Krishnan smiled grimly. 'I wonder what yours is.'

Vikram was taken aback. 'What!'

67

CHENNAI

C.G. Sumangali, the head of the Tamil Nadu HR&CE board, was attending a concert by renowned vocalist T.M. Krishna when her phone rang. It was an unfamiliar number so she quickly cancelled the call before the people around her could object to the buzzing and put the phone on silent. She refused to be disturbed during a concert. Moments later there was a second call from the same number. Then a third. And a fourth. She determinedly ignored them all.

The fifth call was from the culture minister of Tamil Nadu. She hurriedly got up from her chair and exited the auditorium.

'Where are you, madam?' the minister bellowed the moment he heard her voice.

'Good evening, sir,' Sumangali stammered into the phone. 'I have come to listen to T.M. Krishna, sir.'

'Madurai Police has been trying to reach you!'

'Oh, I . . . I didn't know it was Madurai Police. I will call them back, sir.'

'Immediately! And update me after you have spoken to them.'

'Yes, sir,' Sumangali said. As she waited for the minister to disconnect the phone, she wondered why, if he already knew what had happened, he wanted an update from her.

She called the number from where she had got the missed calls. After talking to them, she called the minister back.

'Who is in charge of this in Tamil Nadu Police?' he asked her.

'Mr Madhavan,' Sumangali said. 'He is the DIG of the Idol wing of Tamil Nadu Police.'

'Call him. Tell him to get to work.' The minister hung up.

Sumangali's next call was to Madhavan who was in the DGP's office in Thiruvananthapuram.

Subhash's post-mortem report was expected the next morning. Kannan's murder investigation had taken a back seat. A Subhash Parikh, with his contacts, influence and wealth, was a bigger case than a 'nobody' autorickshaw driver. As the media shifted its focus to the Subhash Parikh investigation, Kannan was forgotten, much to Rajan's frustration. He tried chasing the police and Krishnan to hasten the investigation, but was forced to maintain a low profile, for fear that the secrets he and his family had kept for so long would come tumbling out. The only factor that kept the cops interested in Kannan's murder was the theory that, on some level, his and Subhash Parikh's deaths were related.

Mumbai Police had been unable to trace the person who had been waiting at the airport with the placard bearing Subhash's name.

'How can that be?' Madhavan was bewildered. 'They have the vehicle number. They have his photo. They just need to land up at the address in the RC book of the vehicle.'

'They did that,' Kabir said. 'But it turned out that the address is fake. There is a peculiar problem in Mumbai. If someone buys a car from a dealer and registers it at an address within Mumbai city, the car costs about two to three per cent more on account of octroi being levied when it is brought inside Mumbai. So, a lot of people give a fake address and register the car outside

Mumbai. This particular vehicle is registered in Thane. For now they have put out an alert for this car number. All toll plazas and entry points into the city have been intimated. Hopefully, we'll hear something soon.' He paused for a second and added, 'Ask them to put his photograph out on TV channels. Particularly the Marathi and Tamil channels.'

'Tamil?'

'Yes, many drivers in Mumbai are Tamilians. They stay in Dharavi and work in Bandra and other affluent neighbourhoods. It's worth a try,' Kabir Khan said.

'I will let them know,' Krishnan agreed.

'If we can find out whom Subhash was going to meet in Mumbai, it might help us figure out the motive behind his murder.' Madhavan's phone rang just then. 'Sollu,' he answered. It was his subordinate in Chennai. 'Hmm . . . Okay.'

The sombre look on Madhavan's face suggested that something was wrong.

'What happened?' Kabir asked.

'Madurai Police has intercepted a group involved in smuggling artefacts.'

68

THIRUVANANTHAPURAM

Krishnan's secretary walked in with a copy of a fax that had just come in.

'Subhash Parikh's post-mortem report,' he said, offering the document to Krishnan.

Before the DGP could take the report, Kabir swooped in and plucked it out of the secretary's hands. He perused the report very carefully, and then handed it over to Krishnan, who had been observing the change in his expression as he read it.

'Nothing dramatic in this,' Kabir Khan volunteered.

Krishnan read through the report. 'The toxicology results are inconclusive. They say that his death could have been because of the Alprax, which might have compounded his sugar problem. There are needle punctures on his thighs which could be because of insulin jabs. But there is nothing to explain the divots on his back, just above his buttocks. That's what prompted the toxicology test,' Krishnan replied.

'Whoever killed him is smart. They know that most toxins don't normally show up in regular tests, unless specifically tested for. And to test for a particular toxin, one needs to know which one it is. Very smart work,' Kabir responded.

'This just means, Khan, that all our hypotheses have an equal chance of being correct. We can't drop a single hypothesis as improbable.'

69

The deaths of Kannan and Subhash, particularly of the latter, refocused the media's attention on the temple. The story that at one point in time seemed to be settling down and losing traction, was back on the front page of every major newspaper; each one peddling a unique conspiracy theory. News channels went ballistic, discussing Anantha Padmanabha's wealth and how it should be handled. 'Don't mix religion and commerce!' a popular news anchor shouted during a prime-time debate.

At lunch that day, Vikram asked Nirav, 'What scares you more: god's fury or human anxiety?'

'A bit of both,' Nirav replied.

Work in the temple had almost come to a standstill. Only a quarter of the people initially hired to work in the vaults remained; the rest had left. Vikram was worried about the stance the Supreme Court would take if things came to a head and they were unable to complete the work entrusted to them.

Kabir Khan was in the Thiruvananthapuram police headquarters when his phone rang.

'Hi Madhavan, how have you been?' he said, answering the call.

'Good.'

'You ditched us right in the middle of an important assignment!' Kabir chuckled. 'You better be busy with something worthwhile.'

'You'll be surprised when you hear what I am doing right now.'

'Really?'

'You know we Indians are probably the most hypocritical race in the world.'

Kabir was surprised at this tangent in the conversation, but he detected frustration in Madhavan's tone and so he didn't interrupt. He knew that when someone was frustrated, the best thing to do was to let them speak their mind. Interrupting their flow of thought would only result in incoherence. Left to themselves, they would eventually come to the point.

'On the face of it,' Madhavan was complaining, 'we are so god-fearing. Yet we do not let slip a single opportunity to strip our gods of all the dignity and plunder their temples. That's our culture. We are possibly the most corrupt race in the world.'

Kabir remained silent.

'Hello?'

'I'm here, waiting for you to finish.'

'The truck that was seized in Madurai was a sand truck. It was being taken to a construction site in Rajapalayam. When it was inspected the police found small statues buried deep in the sand. They were en route to the port of Tuticorin.'

'And what was the intent?'

'Kabir!' Madhavan said, clearly exasperated with Kabir's question. 'Obviously they weren't for a temple there. They were meant to be smuggled out of the country and sold in the international market.'

'So another Shreyasi Sinha at play here,' Kabir remarked.

'Or maybe our own Shreyasi Sinha.'

'Any idea whom the truck belongs to?'

'I don't want to say anything yet. Give me a day.'

70

'I need to bring in Dharmaraja Varma.'

When Kabir Khan said this, the tumbler of hot filter coffee nearly slipped out of Krishnan's hands.

'Are you out of your mind!'

'Why? Is there a ban on questioning him?'

'Oh come on!' Krishnan exclaimed. 'Don't you know what you are asking is impossible. He is one of the most powerful men in Kerala. He is the gatekeeper to god, the controller of Hindu votes. He is the man whom every politician in the state bows to. He may be living the life of a recluse in a very middle-class mansion—'

'That itself is an oxymoron. "Middle-class mansion" indeed!' Kabir rolled his eyes.

'Whatever. You will not get permission to bring him in. Period. I don't want to fade into oblivion, Khan, especially at the fag end of my career.'

'Can we meet him at least?'

'Not at this point in time. Not till we have some evidence which shows his involvement. The state will not give you permission,' he repeated.

A phone started ringing in the background. Krishnan walked across the room and took out a phone from his bag and spoke into it. He was back at his desk after a couple of minutes. 'Sorry. Wife. Can't not take her calls.'

Kabir smiled. 'You have a separate phone for her.'

Krishnan nodded. 'Only for Sundari. Sometimes, when I am in meetings, I leave my other phone behind. But this phone is always with me. Ever since our younger daughter went to Columbia to pursue her engineering, Sundari has become very lonely. Depressed. I try to do what I can, but I am also worried. I don't want to be in a situation when she cannot reach me. She doesn't talk to anyone else these days, doesn't even answer other calls; she's muted all her contacts. Only if I call from this number will she respond, for she knows it is me.' Kabir saw his eyes become moist. 'Parents find it very difficult to reconcile to life after their children leave the nest, Khan. It is not easy,' he said, wiping a tear. 'You are lucky, Khan. You don't have kids.'

Kabir smiled. Krishnan was a different police officer. He was a very simple, down-to-earth, family-oriented man. Kabir had seen him in action. While at work, he was aggressive, calculative, a quick thinker and a go-getter. But with family, his softer side came out.

They got back to discussing the arrest of Dharmaraja Varma, but Krishnan put his foot down. Kabir could have gone against the DGP, but he dropped his idea of interrogating Dharmaraja Varma.

Instead, he got up. 'I am heading back to the hotel.'

'Call me in case you need anything.'

On the way out, Kabir kept playing his earlier conversation with Madhavan in his head. There was something in that conversation which Kabir Khan didn't quite feel comfortable about. But what it was, he couldn't say.

The reason he had wanted to interrogate Dharmaraja Varma was the discovery of a numbered pot among the gold and silver ornaments found in the sand-laden truck. There were a few other articles which were from temples in Tamil Nadu, which a few experts from the HR&CE had identified, but it was the pot that was bothering Kabir. Krishnan had mentioned that numbered pots had been found inside the vault that had been opened in the Anantha Padmanabha Swamy Temple. Were these pots also from the same vault? The truck which had been seized belonged to a TPS Cargo Ltd. Unfortunately, the company was fake as was the truck's registration number. And the truck driver had escaped. Assuming for a moment that the pot was indeed from the vault of the Anantha Padmanabha Swamy Temple, it begged the question: how had it made its way into a sand-laden truck in Madurai en route to the international market? It pointed towards the involvement of someone on the inside.

As did the misappropriation of the twenty-one lakh rupees in the name of the elephant that Vikram had pointed out. While twenty-one lakh in itself was a small amount, it indicated a rot within the system. It was always the small frauds that lay the pathway for a larger malaise. If one paid attention to the small frauds in the system it became very easy to unearth the decay within. For him, it was difficult to ignore the elephant payout as a small one-time fraud committed by someone from within.

Back in his hotel room Kabir kept going over everything that he had learnt so far. Which was nothing, really. They had not got any leads from Subhash's hotel room, except for the Alprax; it had been wiped clear of any forensic traces. The murderers had probably been professionals. But then in such cases, where the scene of crime is a public place like a hotel from where all traces of murder had disappeared, there is always the possibility that someone on the inside is involved. The mysterious death of Sunanda Pushkar, the wife of a senior Congress party functionary, at a hotel in Delhi started playing out in his mind. Similar premise. He made a mental note to speak to the investigating officer in that case. However, in this case, what did insider mean. Family? Subhash was a bachelor with no living family members. A friend then? Someone from the audit team? But why would they want him dead? Their association largely began and ended at the temple. Could it be the person he was talking to over the phone outside the Taj the night before he was killed? But there too they had no way of knowing the number Subhash was using. Had they got that number, it might have given them some new leads. Until this morning he had thought it strange that no one in the audit team knew that Subhash had carried two phones, but then despite having spent so much time with him over the past few days, he had found out only recently that DGP Krishnan had a second phone.

As he stood at the window looking out into the distance, he couldn't help but wonder at what all people were willing to do in the name of God.

71

The next morning as Vikram Rai was entering the temple complex, he saw a crowd beside the southeastern end of the outer boundary wall of the temple. Over fifty people were huddled over something; a few of them were leaning against the outer wall of the Padma Teertha Kulam. That was the area where some workers working for a private security company were digging trenches to instal electro-hydraulic bollards and other security equipment as mandated by the Supreme Court. The installation was to be on the road leading to the northern entrance to the temple.

Vikram and his security entourage walked up to the epicentre of the commotion and summoned the security in-charge who was keeping the crowd at bay.

'The workers have stumbled upon something which looks like steps leading down,' the executive engineer replied when he was asked the reason for the commotion. 'The workers from the security company were digging a trench when they hit red bricks and large blocks of laterite just below the tarred surface of the road. They look like the remains of some old building; it might be an underground chamber or even steps leading to one. We stopped the digging. The Archaeological Survey of India has taken over.'

'ASI?'

'Yes. They monitor all the digging activity around all heritage buildings and buildings of historical significance. Since this is right next to the temple complex they had come in the beginning. Over a week ago.'

'When will we know what it is?' Vikram asked. There were signs of worry on his face. He was also a bit upset that they had not noticed the ASI intervention on site, and the same had not been discussed or mentioned to him. But that was the way the various departments worked. Very limited coordination between them.

'We have written to the government asking for permission to excavate. We can begin only after our request is approved.'

'All right. Be careful. Keep the crowds away. Keep the area secure. And make sure temple property is not damaged.'

'Yes, sir, we have been very careful. The entire process is supervised day and night. Even when people are not working this area is monitored to prevent anyone from playing a prank.'

'Thank you,' said Vikram, walking back into the temple.

When he reached the vault, a pensive-looking Nirav and the retired chief secretary were overseeing the work. Soon after, Rajan and Ranjit arrived.

'Do you think the structure they found this morning are steps? If they are, where do you think they lead to?' Vikram asked Rajan the moment he saw him. 'Could they lead to some corner of these vaults? An escape route maybe?'

'Do you remember the hissing noise you heard when you put your ear to Vault B?'

'Yes. Although it was unclear whether it was the hissing of snakes or the swishing of waves,' Vikram recollected. 'But why?'

'Underneath the town of Thiruvananthapuram lies a complex maze of drains. No one knows the extent of these drains. A few of these are believed to extend below the temple too. Whether this network can be accessed from within the temple, nobody knows. According to legend, there *is* an underground tunnel that connects Vault B to the sea.'

'Are you saying that these steps that have been discovered could lead to that?'

'Maybe.' Rajan shrugged.

'If there is an access . . .' Vikram trailed off as if he was contemplating something. 'If there is an access, and the access is inside Vault B, it would pose an enormous risk to everything that is inside the vault.'

'Why do you think I have been shouting myself hoarse about opening Vault B? I was completely opposed to having the Devaprasnam. Allowing them to organize the Devaprasnam was asking for trouble! But you took that call anyway.' He began to walk away, then stopped and said, 'I wouldn't be surprised if the granite steps discovered last night are in fact an ancient access to the underground tunnel, or maybe to the drain. Whichever it is, it spells doom.'

72

It was Nirav Choksi's turn to be summoned for questioning that afternoon. The police were not calling it an interrogation. Yet.

'So Subhash Parikh was a close friend?' Kabir Khan asked him as they sipped green tea in Krishnan's office.

'Not a very close friend. But a friend nevertheless. I had known him for over forty years. He too lived in South Mumbai, in the same neighbourhood. He moved overseas, I stayed back. Still, we ended up in similar businesses. He built a large set-up in Antwerp and the US. Antwerp for his diamond trade, and the US for his antiques business. We stayed in touch over the years. It's hard to cut off someone who has been a part of your growing-up years. There's a lot of history. My father had saved him from being sent to a juvenile remand home years ago. That sense of gratitude was still intact.'

'Any business dealings between—'

'Us?' Nirav finished Kabir's question. 'None.' He glanced at Krishnan. 'As I said, though both of us belonged to the jewellery trade, our constructs were very different, so there were no business dealings between the two of us. And because I deal with exclusive clients, there were no common clients on the jewellery side.'

'In the last two weeks that you have been here, did Mr Parikh seem stressed, worried, or anxious about something? Did you notice anything that you thought was abnormal?'

'No, nothing! In fact he was an extremely jovial, happy-go-lucky kind of a person. It is sad that something like this happened to him.' The rapid blinking of his eyes indicated to Khan that he was fighting back his tears.

'Do you know if he had any enemies?'

'No, he never mentioned anything or anyone that might have been bothering him. And why would someone track him all the way here and kill him?' Nirav nervously wiped the sweat on his forehead with his hand.

'Why are you sweating, Mr Choksi?' Khan asked him, casually offering him a napkin to wipe his forehead.

He swallowed anxiously. 'Could I be next in line?'

'I wouldn't worry about that, Mr Choksi. We have increased security in and around your hotel, and along your route. And needless to say, the temple is now a fortress.'

'Oh, that's a relief!'

They spoke for some more time, Nirav answering all their questions confidently and without any hesitation.

'Last two questions,' Kabir said, rising from his chair and walking round the table to the other side. He opened a folder kept on the table and handed a photograph to Nirav. 'Do you know her?'

Nirav looked at the woman in the photograph. He shook his head. 'No.'

'You've never met her?' Krishnan asked. 'Ever?'

'You heard me. Never,' Nirav replied testily.

'As expected,' Kabir muttered. He slid a chit pad across the table to Nirav. 'Can you give us Subhash Parikh's number?'

Nirav looked at him, slightly amused by the question. 'You don't have his number?' Realizing the futility of his comment, he pulled out his phone and copied down a number on the pad.

Kabir Khan looked at it and asked him, 'Is there another number?'

'Not that I know of.'

'Thank you, Mr Choksi,' Krishnan said at a glance from Kabir. 'I'll walk you out.'

When Nirav left, a motorcade of three cars followed him all the way back to the hotel. Krishnan had been serious when he said that they had increased the security cover provided to the entire team.

'What do you think?' Khan asked him the moment he returned to the room.

'Think? As in?'

'Do you think he is lying?'

'Not sure.'

'We'll know soon,' said Kabir.

He sat down at the table and opened an app on his laptop. In no time they were watching the video recording of the conversation with Nirav, recorded with the help of a camera affixed on the ceiling, right above Nirav's head. Kabir quickly fast forwarded the recording to the point where Nirav had turned on his phone to copy Subhash's number. At the point where Nirav set the phone on the table while he wrote the number, Kabir paused the video and zoomed in until the only thing visible on the screen was Nirav's mobile phone and Subhash's contact card.

There were two numbers on the screen.

73

Slumped in the back seat of the Toyota Innova that was taking him back to the hotel, Kabir was lost in thought. He had a call scheduled with Director Inamdar in half an hour. His phone rang. It was Krishnan. Wondering what could have necessitated the call, considering he had been with Krishnan till about twenty-five minutes ago, he took the call.

'False alarm,' said Krishnan the moment he heard Kabir's voice.

'Huh?'

'The second number on Nirav Choksi's phone is an old number, which Subhash had till about four years ago, when he switched service providers. It hasn't been operational since.'

The car stopped outside the Lotus Pond. Kabir got out of the car and entered the hotel.

'So Nirav was telling the truth. He genuinely doesn't know about Subhash's second number.'

'Looks like it. We can talk about this when you come back in the evening for Ranjit's interview. He's coming at 5 p.m. You need to be back here by then.'

'Absolutely! Let me just get rid of some clerical stuff,' Kabir said and hung up. The call with the director would begin in twenty minutes.

He had barely stepped into his room when his phone rang again.

'What?' he barked into it, irritated with the consecutive calls.

'Well, hello to you too.' It was Madhavan.

'Oh sorry,' Kabir apologized. 'I was preoccupied.'

'That's okay. I do it all the time, so I can understand.' Madhavan empathized with Khan. 'Okay, now for the reason I called. I have something interesting for you. The sand-laden truck that was seized in Madurai? The one with the fake registration? We did some digging and we've found that a truck with the same chassis number is actually registered in Kerala, Thiruvananthapuram to be precise. Not Tamil Nadu. TPS Transport, under whose permit the truck was plying, is denying any connection with the truck and all the stuff found inside the truck, hidden in the sand. In fact they're claiming that the truck does not belong to them.'

'Okay?' It was more of a question.

'Records show that this truck crossed the Kerala border near Nagercoil, two days ago.'

'Go on . . .'

'Right before it crossed the border, it had a Kerala number plate. Once it entered Tamil Nadu, the number plate was replaced with a local Tamil Nadu number plate, probably stolen from a truck belonging to TPS Transport.'

'Send me the details. I will talk to Krishnan.'

'I am coming back there. Tonight. A request has already gone out to Kerala Police.'

Within five minutes of Madhavan hanging up, Kabir's phone beeped. Madhavan had sent the details. The moment he saw the name of the transport company, APS Transport Pvt. Ltd, he had a niggling feeling that he had seen it somewhere. Where . . .?

The phone rang again. It was Inamdar's office. The conference call was about to begin.

The meeting with Ranjit that evening went along the same lines as the others. As expected, nothing significant came of it. Ranjit told them again about his discovery of the gold-plating machine in the king's chamber and his subsequent discussions with Subhash Parikh. He too had never seen Shreyasi before. Nor did he know anything about Parikh's second number. The meeting took a little over an hour, including the two toilet breaks that Ranjit took.

Madhavan returned that night along with a few officers of the Idol wing of Tamil Nadu Police.

74

The police jeep, in which Madhavan and his fellow officers from Kerala Police were travelling, screeched to a halt in front of an unimpressive-looking building on the busy street in Attingal, the truck transport hub in Kerala. All transport companies and truck owners had offices in this area. Radhakrishnan Nair was in his office, quietly reading a copy of the local Malayalam daily, when there was a knock on the door. Dumping the newspaper on the table, he hitched up his lungi and walked to the door. The moment he opened it, the business end of a rifle was shoved in his face.

'Radhakrishnan Nair?' Madhavan asked calmly.

A confused Nair nodded warily. He was promptly bundled into the police jeep and carted away to the police headquarters, where Kabir and Krishnan were waiting for him.

'APS Transport,' Krishnan began.

Nair sat on the floor next to the sofa in the DGP's cabin, his eyes red with rage. He had never been treated with such insolence, certainly not by the police. He had not been offered any explanation whatsoever, and that made him even more furious. 'What about it?' he demanded, scratching his armpit.

'Your company?'

'Yes. It is my company. What about it?' he asked through gritted teeth.

'How long have you been doing all this?'

'Doing what? Will someone tell me what the hell is going on?' Nair yelled, giving vent to his frustration.

'How long have you been smuggling gold and priceless antiques in trucks filled with sand?'

Radhakrishnan Nair shot up from his place on the floor, his eyes almost popping out. '*What?* Smuggling? Are you out of your mind!!!' he shouted. 'I have lived all my life with dignity. And now, at this age, you are accusing me of smuggling. ARE YOU SERIO—'

Whack!

Radhakrishnan Nair lost his balance and fell to the floor, cradling his right cheek in his palm.

Kabir shook his hand a couple of time to ease the stinging. 'This was for screaming in the office of the DGP of Kerala Police, and that too in the presence of the additional director of the CBI.' He looked at Madhavan sheepishly—he had forgotten to mention him. Madhavan grinned.

'Now pay attention,' Kabir continued. 'Answer whatever is asked of you. Politely. One more outburst like that one and you'll end up in some obscure prison somewhere. No one will even know where you are. Understood?'

Dumbstruck, Nair simply stared back at him. He could still feel the imprint of Khan's fingers on his cheek.

'Excellent!' Kabir said, and gestured to the DGP to carry on.

'So,' Krishnan repeated, 'how long have you been smuggling gold and jewellery and artefacts, in sand-filled trucks.'

'I . . . I don't know what you are talking about. I'm not involved in any smuggling or illegal activity.'

'Don't lie to us,' Madhavan warned. 'Who are your partners in this?'

'Partners? In what? Smuggling? But I am not involved in smuggling! I'm not lying!' he said in shrill voice.

'Do you operate from Attingal or do you have a den somewhere else?'

By this time the initially belligerent Radhakrishnan Nair was in tears. 'How do I convince you—I know nothing about what you are saying.'

'Maybe this will remind you,' Madhavan said, thrusting a few pictures at him. Pictures of a truck filled with sand and the loot in front of the truck.'

'This is not even APS Transport,' Nair protested. 'The name of the truck company is different! How can it be mine?'

Madhavan leaned forward and slammed his palm on the table. 'TPS! Even an idiot can make out that the name painted on the truck is fake. The chassis number of this truck matches a truck that was bought by APS Transport. Your company.' He looked into Nair's eyes.

Something about the man's expression bothered him. While there was fear in his eyes, it looked more like fear born out of public humiliation, rather than remorse.

Nair shook his head. 'There has been a mistake.'

'There has been no mistake, Mr Nair. None at all. It's just that you have been cornered at last. So out with the truth. How long have you been doing this? And who are your partners?'

'Partners? Padmanabha! What has come upon you? This truck is not mine!' Nair repeated. 'Ask anyone in the Attingal market. Everyone there knows me. I have been working in the same apology of an office for the last twenty-two years.'

'Maybe that's why you thought you would get away with it. Tell me,' Kabir barked, 'how many trucks do you have in this trade?'

'None!' Nair begged. 'Believe me! I got out of the transport business eight years ago! When my father died.'

'What?' Kabir Khan retorted in disbelief, wondering why Nair had not mentioned that at the first instance. But then everything happened so fast that he would not have had a chance. 'What do you mean?'

'It was a business my father started. Over twenty years ago. He was extremely successful. When I took over, I didn't want to continue it. But the business was so close to my father's heart that had I closed it down then, it would surely have killed him. I reluctantly ran the business for a time. The year he died, I shut it down. Even his masters, who had funded the business for him initially, didn't have any objection to it. Because they also knew that I was running it only for my father. Tell me, if I shut down the business over eight years ago, how can I be running trucks and a cross-border smuggling operation?'

'You said partner?' Kabir walked up to him.

'Masters. I said masters, not partners. They could never be partners. They helped him set up the transport business in return for the loyalty demonstrated by our family. And to show our gratitude, we insisted that they take a small stake in the company. Which they hesitatingly did.'

'Who is *they*?' asked Krishnan. 'And how much stake do they own?'

'When the company was operational they owned five per cent of the company. It was more for optical purposes.'

'Didn't you hear me, Nair?' Krishnan thundered. 'WHO IS THEY?'

'Thirumanassu.'

75

The discovery of granite steps leading into the ground just outside the temple complex had created a stir in the neighbourhood. Speculation was rife that the staircase was one of the access points to the temple vaults. It also gave rise to innumerable stories about the possibility of the city's drainage system being linked to this access point. The civic authorities were a worried lot. There were two drainage pipes, three feet by three feet, which ran parallel to the boundary of the temple. Big enough for an adult to get through. Possibly these drainpipes shared a common wall with the vault. No one could say with certainty. Strangely for a well-developed city like Thiruvananthapuram, no blueprints of the underground drainage system were available, except for a few archaic papers kept in the nearby Swati Thirunal Museum. It was estimated that only thirty per cent of the drainpipes that criss-crossed the city were in use at any point in time. Until the recent public debate and media attention on the treasure in the temple, no one was even remotely interested in the drainage system or its history. Now almost everyone wanted a look at the papers. The government had quickly stepped in and banned access to them, stating that they contained sensitive information which might put the temple at risk.

Standing next to the granite steps, Vikram Rai was speculating about their similarity to the steps inside the vault area of the temple when his phone rang. It was DGP Krishnan.

'I need to speak with you, in person,' Krishnan said. 'Can you come over to the HQ?'

'Now?' Vikram asked him. 'Is it okay if I come after we've shut shop here? Say around 6.30 p.m.?'

'Sure,' Krishnan agreed. He hung up the phone and turned to Kabir. 'He'll come at 6.30 p.m.'

'We have spoken to everyone except him and Thirumanassu. How long will you avoid interrogating the king? He is probably the one person who knows everything that is going on.'

Krishnan waved his hand dismissively and walked away. 'Let it go. Interrogating the king in this environment will be next to impossible. We'll need state sanction for that. Something we will never get.'

The meeting with Vikram Rai that evening was cordial.

'Damp squib!' Kabir said when he left. 'Bloody waste of time.'

Madhavan, who had stayed away from the meeting, walked into the room. He looked at Krishnan and said, 'I want to take Radhakrishnan Nair to Chennai, for further interrogation. I need a transit remand. I hope I have your permission.'

Krishnan glared at him. 'Absolutely not!' he spat and strode away, leaving an irritated Madhavan with Kabir.

76

While Vikram was meeting Krishnan and Kabir in the police headquarters, Divya was sitting with Nirav in his hotel room. She had decided to stay in Thiruvananthapuram after Subhash Parikh's body was discovered.

'Aunty called again,' she complained. 'Why doesn't she call you?' She had become very irritable of late and it showed in the tone of her conversations. Nirav put it down to the stress of the circumstances and tried to be considerate towards her. He walked up to her and put his arm around her shoulder.

'About the property?' he asked, dropping a kiss on her forehead.

Divya smiled. It wasn't something she did a lot these days. 'Yes. It's harassment! I don't understand why she wants to sell the property only to you. This time I told her to go ahead and sell it to anyone she wants to if she doesn't hear from you.'

'She is alone, beta.' Nirav tried to calm her down. 'We have a responsibility towards her.'

'Yesterday she became hysterical. I don't know what the problem was.'

'Poor thing. She must be missing Akhil Bhai and Ankit.'

'Why does she want to sell it to you and not to anyone else?'

'It is a long story, Divya. There was a time when Akhil Bhai wanted to sell the property and move to the BKC Diamond

Bourse. At that time, he was getting a good price for the Zaveri Bazaar property. But I convinced him against doing that. And then property prices crashed. His wife blamed me for it. She holds me responsible for convincing Akhil Bhai to stay back in Zaveri Bazaar.'

'So?'

'I guess she is worried about her future now. I had told them at the time that if he stayed in the Bazaar instead of shifting to the bourse, I would make sure he didn't lose money on the sale of his property no matter when he sold. I even told them that I would buy it, that too at pre-2011 prices. Now that the widow is trying to get a grip on her life and consolidate her finances, I suppose she wants her pound of flesh.'

'Why would you commit to something like this?'

'Because he stayed back on my word! I didn't want him to go, he had been my neighbour for over four decades in that congested office. I could have bought it then, but I didn't want to expand at the time. Nor did I want anyone else to come in. Having someone there whom you can trust is additional security. We have crores of diamonds lying there. Besides, had he gone, a number of other merchants would have left with him. The unity of Zaveri Bazaar was at stake. I couldn't have let him go.' He walked to the table, picked up a bottle of water and took a long swallow. He was thirsty. 'In any case you know the details. Don't you? You saw how it blew up when we went to the prayer meeting for Gopal Shah. You were the one who came to my rescue that day. Didn't you?'

'Things would have been very different had Ankit been there.'

'True.'

'So what will you do about the property?'

'If she asks you again, tell her that I will buy it. At whatever rate she thinks is reasonable. I don't have a choice. I made a promise.'

'Okay, Dad.' She got up to leave. At the door she looked around and said, 'This room is bigger than the earlier one. No? They should have given you this room in the beginning itself. It is quite comfortable. And your cold too seems to be under control.'

77

'Nair seems to be a part of a larger network which smuggles artefacts. He is lying.' Madhavan was not happy that his request to take Nair to Chennai had been scuttled by Krishnan. 'That guy Krishnan, is he working for the police department or the king?'

'Well . . .' Kabir hedged. He understood Madhavan's frustration. 'You don't need his nod to arrest Nair. Just get a court order. He will be forced to cooperate with you.'

The two of them were waiting outside Krishnan's cabin. Krishnan had just got another call from his wife, Sundari, and was speaking to her. In the short time that Kabir had worked alongside Krishnan, he had seen the stress on the home front increase several fold. The investigation into the two murders had been keeping him away from home. His wife's depression had intensified as a result. Husband and wife had been speaking for over thirty minutes, and Krishnan was still at it. Kabir and Madhavan were on their second cup of coffee.

'Why does he have a separate phone for his wife?'

'So that she can reach him at all times. There are times when he might switch off his office cell phone, especially when he is in meetings, but his personal phone is always on. That number's only for his family.'

'I am sure he is having an affair.' Madhavan chuckled.

'At this age. He is almost sixty?'

'So what?' Madhavan asked. 'Film stars marry at sixty all the time. Why can't police officers have affairs? All of us are smart and fit.' He patted his 42-inch potbelly affectionately.

'Shut up, Madhavan!' Kabir chided. 'Not everyone who has a second phone is like Subhash Parikh, leading two lives.'

Madhavan laughed.

'Who is leading two lives here?'

The question startled Kabir and Madhavan. Krishnan stood in the doorway.

'He says you are leading a dual life.' Kabir pointed at Madhavan, earning a glare from him.

'*Me?*' Krishnan's face was a mix of anger and embarrassment.

Kabir burst out laughing. 'The life of a devoted husband and a tough policeman. It's tough to balance, isn't it?'

Krishnan smiled at Kabir's comment. 'I'm sorry to have kept you guys waiting for so long. Come, let's go.'

'I just spoke to Commissioner Iyer in Chennai.'

'I am quaking in my boots already.' Krishnan smirked.

'He says that if Kerala Police doesn't cooperate, we will file in the court for custody.'

Krishnan didn't respond. He sat down with a sigh.

'Look here, Inspector.'

'DIG,' Madhavan corrected.

'Yes, yes, that too . . . This is one problem I can do without. If we arrest him now word will spread. A few fingers will be pointed at Dharmaraja Varma. His followers, whose numbers are significant, might feel compelled to protest, and not necessarily peacefully. A potential law and order situation is the last thing I need.'

'So what do we do? He is a suspect in a case Tamil Nadu Police is investigating. A suspected criminal wanted for smuggling treasure which belongs to the nation.'

'Okay, here is what we will do. Give it a week. Maybe two. Let this case cool down a bit. And then we will do what it takes to hand him over to you guys.'

'I think that is fair,' Kabir said before Madhavan could refuse.

Madhavan just nodded. 'I will speak with the commissioner.'

'Thank you,' Krishnan said as he stood up. 'I have a meeting with the chief minister. I'll come back and talk to you.'

78

Kabir used the time Krishnan was away to visit Kannan's wife. It was the first time someone from the team investigating the murders was meeting her. She had been in the hospital under observation for several days. Kannan's death had sent her in a downward spiral of grief and depression which had affected her health severely. She had returned from the hospital for home care only recently.

Kabir was not allowed into the house. Although he was told that the family was in mourning and hence he couldn't come inside, he knew the real reason was different. It was the house of a chaste Hindu. Allowing a Muslim male inside the house was not acceptable. While Kannan's wife seemed to be a fairly forward-looking woman, it was the other members of the joint family she lived in who got their way.

'Do you suspect anyone?' Kabir asked her after the initial round of introductions was done and condolences had been offered and accepted.

'No.'

'Did your husband have any enemies? Any feuds within the family?'

'No.'

'Could there be any reason why someone would want him out of the way? Any business dealings gone sour? Any loans not repaid?'

'No.'

Kabir was a bit taken aback at her cold responses. He had expected her to be eager to share everything she knew with the police, but she seemed reluctant to give anything other than monosyllabic responses.

'We are here to help you.' Kabir tried to convince her.

'I don't think she believes you,' someone said from behind him.

Kabir turned towards the door and saw Rajan standing there, hand on the door frame, folded dhoti landing just above his knees. It was clear he had been listening to their conversation.

'We are not here to talk to you, Mr Rajan,' Kabir snapped. 'Please leave us alone.'

'Well, she refuses to talk to you unless her lawyer is present,' Rajan said categorically.

Furious, Kabir got up and stalked over to him. When he was within sniffing distance, he whispered, firmly, 'I'm sure you would not want her to know about your relationship with Kannan.'

'Be my guest, tell her.' Rajan smiled. 'Do you think I don't know you guys? I couldn't leave that Achilles heel unattended, could I?' He walked up to Kannan's wife and stood next to her. 'She knows who Kannan was.'

Kabir didn't like what he heard. 'Don't you want your brother's murderers to be brought to book?'

'I do. But how can I trust you?'

Kabir looked around the room. 'I don't see anyone else here,' he taunted.

'I don't need to trust anybody,' Rajan said vehemently. 'She made that mistake once.' He pointed to Kannan's wife.

'What do you mean?'

'The day you guys called me to the police headquarters, your guys landed here.'

'Our guys?' Kabir was surprised.

'Yes, your guys.'

'But no one from our team has been to talk to Kannan's wife. We were waiting for her to be in a position to talk.'

'See. Obviously you are not in the loop. If no one told you about it, then how can you trust them? And if *you* can't, how can you expect us to?'

Kabir was taken aback. So someone was playing games. Was it Krishnan? If Kannan's wife had already been interrogated, why had he been kept in the dark? Kabir was upset—more angry than upset. The behaviour of Kerala Police had caused him extreme embarrassment. It was unlikely that the police would have questioned her without Krishnan's sanction. And if Krishnan hadn't told him about it, it was clearly with the intent to hide it. Why would he want to hide anything unless he wanted to protect someone?

Kabir mellowed down after Rajan talked tough with him. In this case, particularly because it was so much in the limelight, it was important that he tread carefully. 'Can we just speak to her for a few minutes? If she could just tell us what she said during the earlier meeting, that will be fine.'

'Spare her the harassment. I'll tell you what you need to know. All she told them was that Kannan had no enemies. He was a very friendly guy. Everyone who knew him, everyone in town loved him. He never cared about money. If he did, he wouldn't be happy being an autorickshaw driver. That's why the gold you recovered from his autorickshaw, in my lunch bag, doesn't make sense. If he knew that I was stealing gold, especially from the temple, he would have personally delivered me to the police. The day he died . . . Well, the day he was killed he had called his wife and told her that he had seen something which was damning. When she asked what it was he said he was going to see Dharmaraja Varma and would tell her about it when he came home.'

'Dharmaraja Varma?' So that's why Krishnan had not told him about the questioning.

'Yes, Dharmaraja Varma. That was the last time she heard from him. The next morning, his body was found.'

'When he didn't come back home that night, didn't she find it suspicious?'

'No. It is very normal for autorickshaw drivers to ply the whole night and return in the morning.'

'Did he tell his wife what it was that he had seen? What he found necessary to share with Dharmaraja Varma.'

'The other men spent a lot of time questioning and cross-questioning her. But no. He had told her that he would come home and share it with her. All he told her was that it was shocking.'

'Anything else?'

'No.'

'Thank you, Mr Rajan.' Kabir got up, bid goodbye to Rajan and to Kannan's wife who had been a silent witness to their conversation, offered her condolences again and left.

He had to confront Krishnan.

79

DGP Krishnan had not yet returned from his meeting with the chief minister when Kabir reached the police headquarters. While he waited in Krishnan's office, he went over the sequence of events in his mind. His first meeting with Krishnan, the latter being too friendly with him, happily handing over the case to the CBI, involving him from the initial investigations, his resistance to the king being questioned, hiding behind law and order issues. All of these had seemed reasonable at the time. But now, when he looked back on them in light of his meeting with Kannan's wife, it all appeared to be a carefully thought-out, well-executed plan. That the case would be passed on to the CBI was a known thing. By cooperating fully, Krishnan made sure that he remained involved in the investigation. Was he the mole in the system? Could he trust Krishnan? How much should he share with him? Thus far they had worked as a team. What now?

The door opened and Krishnan walked in. 'You wanted to bring in Dharmaraja Varma, right?'

Kabir nodded, unsure of where the DGP was going with this.

'I mentioned it to the chief minister.'

Kabir didn't respond.

'He hesitated, but eventually agreed to it. His only condition was that we do not summon him here, or question him in the temple.'

Kabir was stumped by this sudden change in stance. He didn't know how to react. 'Then?' was all he could say.

'He thinks we should do it in Thirumanassu's palace, away from the public eye. We can't be seen to be questioning a man of god. And we'll have to leave when Dharmaraja Varma tells us to.'

'Is this an interrogation or a media interview?' Khan rolled his eyes.

'Think of it however you want. This is the best you're going to get!' Krishnan ended the discussion.

'Let's do it.'

Something was better than nothing. He would at least get a chance to evaluate Dharmaraja Varma's body language, if not anything else. Criminals, not the hardened ones, often gave it all away in their body language. It was often not about what they said, but *how* they said it.

'Great. I will set it up. Let me call Thirumanassu. It has to be just the two of us. I did it only for your peace of mind. I am convinced that you are on the wrong track. But unless you get it out of your head that Dharmaraja Varma has some role to play in the murders, you won't be able to focus on the true perpetrator.'

'Well, since you know so much already, maybe you can share it with me.' Kabir fired his first salvo. The probable interrogation of the king had confused matters. If Kannan's wife's interrogation was a negative for Krishnan, getting permission from the chief minister to question the king almost nullified it.

'What?' Krishnan raised his eyebrows.

Kabir rose from the sofa. 'Why didn't you tell me that you sent a team to investigate Kannan's murder and interrogate his wife?'

Krishnan looked at Kabir, shocked. 'What!' he said, his voice barely a whisper.

'I went there today. Met his wife. The day we met Rajan here, a Kerala Police team met the wife and interrogated her.'

DGP Krishnan finally found his voice. 'I don't know what you're talking about! Till you told me a few moments ago, I didn't even know that she had come back from the hospital. I did not authorize anyone to speak to the wife.' He paused to catch his breath. 'And my team would not do anything like this without my authorization. Which can only mean that Rajan and the wife are lying.'

'Or . . .' Kabir frowned. 'Someone went there in the guise of Kerala Police to find out how much she knows. Someone is worried about what Kannan discovered. And as we suspected, the clue to both the murders lies on the route that Kannan took that night.'

'Damn,' was all Krishnan could say.

80

The meeting with the king was set up for the same night. Krishnan had called up Dharmaraja Varma directly. The king had been expecting the call; he had been briefed by the chief minister's office.

At 12.30 that night, Krishnan and Kabir arrived at Dharmaraja Varma's palace in an unmarked car. They did not want to raise any eyebrows. The king received them at the main door. He was extremely courteous.

'Welcome! Welcome!' he greeted them warmly—after all, they were his guests—and led them to the living room. Though large in size, the room was not lavishly appointed. An eight-seater sofa, an old carpet, and a few other accessories were all that were in the room. Dharmaraja Varma lived a frugal life.

Krishnan touched Varma's feet, probably to ensure the king knew whose side he was on. Kabir settled on the sofa and looked around the room, waiting for the niceties to end. As far as he was concerned, they were here to interrogate a murder suspect. Kannan had gone to see him before he was killed. The king had too much at stake and would have wanted to end the audit of the vaults at any cost.

'So, Mr Khan,' Dharmaraja Varma began the conversation. 'The chief minister tells me you want to ask me something.' He laughed. 'I wonder why they should be so worried about anyone talking to me.'

Kabir completely ignored everything the king said. 'What do you have to say about the murders of Kannan Ramalingam and Mr Subhash Parikh?'

'About the murders?' The king thought for a moment and then said, 'Unfortunate. What else can I say? Anyone dies, it hurts. Every man is the lord's creation.' He glanced at Krishnan and looked back at Kabir. 'In our religion, at least, that's the way it is. What do you say, Krishnan?'

The latter smiled and nodded. Kabir kept his cool. He realized that Krishnan would never be able to act against the king if such a need were to arise.

'It's the same in every religion, Mr Varma,' Kabir retorted, promising himself that he wouldn't get angry. 'I know you had a fundamental disagreement with the team taking stock of the vaults, but did you have any arguments with them over the past few days.'

'None. I always maintain a cordial relationship with everyone.' Dharmaraja Varma smiled. 'Maybe because of who I am, no one enters into arguments with me. Occasionally, non-believers like you come along.'

'Non-believers.'

'Yes. People who don't have faith in the Hindu religion?'

'What does not having faith in the Hindu religion have to do with these killings?'

'If you had faith, you wouldn't ask me these questions. Both these deaths, three, if we include poor Gopi, happened because of the will of Padmanabha. He is unhappy with what is happening. Didn't the Devaprasnam prove this?'

'Rubbish,' Kabir burst out.

'Careful, young man!' the king reprimanded. 'Be conscious of where you are right now.'

'Forget where I am,' Kabir continued. 'Where were you on the nights when Kannan and Subhash were killed?'

'Is it so easy to become a CBI officer these days?' Dharmaraja Varma looked at Krishnan and asked. Gradually shifting his glance towards Khan he added, 'Can just anyone become a CBI officer?'

'Excuse me?' Kabir was taken aback.

'You asked me a stupid question. You think if I wanted to kill someone at this age, I would go myself, chase them and slit their throats? If I wanted to kill the two of them, there are enough means at my disposal to do so without moving from my seat. If it were me, I would make sure I stayed at home, and had a rock-solid alibi. In this country money can buy anything. Even human life.' Dharmaraja Varma smirked.

'Mere moments ago you said that in your religion, every life is considered god's creation. So you mean to say that you have the power to buy out god's own creation. Well done, sir. I didn't realize how powerful you are.' Kabir gave the king a thumbs-up. 'However, I'll let that pass.' And he smiled. An arrogant smile. 'Would you know of anyone who would want to kill Kannan?'

'I hardly knew Kannan, Officer. It is not the job of royalty to keep track of commoners. There are hundreds and thousands of autorickshaw drivers in Thiruvananthapuram. Should I know all of them?'

'What about Subhash Parikh?'

'I knew him for a week.'

'And Mr Nair? Mr Radhakrishnan Nair?'

'What about him?'

'Do you know him?'

'Yes, I do. His father was a loyal subject of my predecessor.'

'Then you are aware that you made an investment in Mr Nair's transport company many years ago.'

'Did I?' He thought about it for a minute, then said, 'Yes. Yes, I recall. He had borrowed money from me and in return he insisted that I take a stake in the company. We keep doing such charity. Helping those in need.'

'How many such companies have you invested in like this, sir?'

'I can't say. Everything I have is the lord's. And whatever the lord gives me is used to take care of his people.'

'Umm . . . the stake?' Kabir reminded him.

'I really don't remember.'

'We checked your tax returns for the last few years. This is the only investment that shows up.'

'How dare you?' the king roared, red-faced. 'How dare you check my documents without a proper order? This is ridiculous! I am going to take it up with the CBI director and the state.'

'I'm sure you'd want this discussion to remain private, sir.' Kabir smiled.

The king was seething, but he calmed down in the face of Kabir's veiled threat. 'I don't recollect any other investments. Even this one I remember because Nair's father was close to the previous king.'

'You must have heard about a truck belonging to APS Transport being seized in Madurai from which some artefacts were recovered. It seems the truck was taking them to the port in Tuticorin from where they would be smuggled out of the country. An offence punishable with up to ten years in jail.'

'Are you teaching me the law, son?'

'Apologies, sir.' Kabir quickly tried to calm him down. He wanted to finish this interrogation before he got thrown out. 'In the truck there were expensive ancient artefacts. Some of them could be from your vaults.'

Dharmaraja Varma was reaching the limits of his patience. He wanted the interview to end. 'Look, Officer. The truck you are referring to does not belong to Nair. Nair's wife called me after your third-degree treatment of him. His business shut down years ago. So the trucks are not his.'

'The signature on the RTO papers are his.'

'Maybe.'

'Validated by a handwriting expert.'

'That may be. But the items you found in the truck could be from anywhere. Not necessarily from the Anantha Padmanabha Swamy Temple's vaults. Pots like those were very common in the olden days. And the jewellery styles were the same across temples and kingdoms. I am sure there has been a mistake.'

'We will look into that, sir. We will be matching the jewellery in your vaults with the jewellery that was recovered to confirm if the source is the same.'

'Of course,' the king responded nonchalantly.

'Anything else you would like to tell us, Mr Varma? Any questions?' Kabir asked him, abruptly cutting the conversation.

'You're the ones who requested this interview. Left to myself, I would not have said anything.'

'Thank you, Mr Varma.' Kabir Khan rose and walked out of the room. Krishnan stopped to touch the king's feet and then turned to leave.

'Manage him. He is trying to get ahead of himself.'

Kabir was already in the car when Krishnan came out.

'Don't you think you were a bit too arrogant with him?' he asked, starting the engine.

'He put me off initially by talking about my religion. Where does religion come in here? We are talking about two people who have been killed. We don't know who killed them. We have come here to ask him a few questions and that guy throws attitude. Touch me if you can! What do you expect me to do?'

'He is the king. The whole of Kerala looks up to him.'

'And that gives him the right to do what he wants?'

Krishnan shook his head in exasperation. 'Anyway, are you happy now? Satisfied that he is not involved?'

'He is.'

'Sorry?'

'I said he is involved.'

'And what in today's conversation makes you say that.'

'No one except you, me and Madhavan knows exactly what was found in the sand truck; the press release only says artefacts.' He looked at Krishnan, eyebrows raised.

A confused Krishnan asked him, 'What?'

'Unless you told him.'

81

Krishnan looked at him indignantly. 'No, I didn't.'

Kabir was so taken in by the mature way in which Krishnan had handled the accusation that he felt sorry for what he had done. But he had to get to the bottom of this.

'Then how did he know about the numbered golden pots that were found in the truck? Either he saw the news and independently found out what was seized—our system is so porous that somebody or other could have squealed to him—or he is involved in the actual crime in some way. But how deep his involvement runs? I don't know.' He turned and looked at Krishnan who was staring at the road ahead. 'Yet!'

Krishnan didn't utter a word the rest of the drive back to the Lotus Pond. After dropping Kabir at the hotel, he drove back home.

As Kabir walked into the hotel lobby, his mobile phone beeped. He looked at it. A smile lit up his face. He hurriedly dialled a number.

'Hey, sorry for calling so late. I just saw your message.' As the conversation went on, Kabir's smile widened. 'No, no. I was awake. Just came back from an interrogation. This is the best news I've got in weeks! How did it happen? . . . Wonderful. Have you started the interrogation yet? . . . Okay, good. Hold on. I will be there tomorrow morning. We can do it together. Bye!'

Kabir disconnected the call and immediately dialled Krishnan's number. He had just reached home, and was parking his car. 'I need to go to Mumbai tomorrow morning.'

'Is everything okay?' Krishnan asked. He was still feeling uncomfortable about the discussion with Dharmaraja Varma, more so about Kabir's conversation with him in the car.

'The driver is in custody.'

'Which driver?'

'The one who was waiting at Mumbai airport to receive Subhash Parikh. They caught him at a checkpoint. He didn't know that Mumbai Police was on the lookout for him, and drove straight into a trap. From the look of things, he is a regular taxi driver who occasionally works on contract with Travel House. When they have more customers than cars, they outsource work to empanelled drivers like him. I am glad that they were able to nab him. I had lost hope when we couldn't get his number from Subhash's phone.'

'Hmm. Okay. Do you want to take someone with you?'

'No. I'll let you know.'

The next day Kabir Khan was on the 6 a.m. flight to Mumbai. He had a feeling that it was going to be a defining day for him and the investigation.

82

'Let's go!' said an excited Kabir Khan the moment he walked into the Marine Lines office of Mumbai Police.

ACP Patil looked up from his desk and smiled. 'Hello, Khan,' he said. 'You are looking fit as ever.'

The two of them had worked together several years ago when terrorists had attacked the Taj Mahal Hotel in Mumbai. Patil was now ACP in the crime branch of Mumbai Police.

Kabir gave Patil a quick hug. 'Yeah, yeah. Come on! Let's go!' he hurried the ACP. There was a spring in his step.

'Hold on, man. What's the rush? You just walked in.'

'We can't afford to lose time, Patil! There is a lot happening. Every second, those fuckers are getting ahead of us.'

An attendant brought in a glass of water, which Kabir gulped down. He was thirsty, but more than that he was anxious. Patil asked the attendant for some tea, and then led Kabir to a sofa in one corner of the room. 'Sit. Just for five minutes,' he said over Kabir's protests.

'You have not changed a bit,' Patil said some time later and glanced at Kabir's midriff, 'except for a few inches down there.' He smiled.

'It is stress, I guess. Once I am done with this case, I will be back to normal,' Kabir said defensively.

'That's okay. Even now you are likely to put all of us to shame,' he said, and the two of them laughed.

'So what's keeping you awake in Mumbai these days?'

'Mumbai is hell, my friend. You are lucky that you are not here. Crime syndicates, mafia, drugs, murders, violence, political apathy, terrorism, they're all here, making sure I don't get a moment's peace.' He pointed to a document lying on the table. 'I didn't sleep a wink last night.'

Kabir reached out and picked up the document. It was the charge sheet in the Mumbai blasts case. Next to the table was a large carton full of thousands of sheets of paper, which he assumed were the supporting documents. He casually flipped through the charge sheet and dropped it back on the table. Tea had been brought in. He asked after Patil's wife and children, his hurry forgotten momentarily. The conversation was more therapeutic than any he had had in the last few weeks.

'Ready to leave?' It was Patil's turn to hustle now. Kabir set down his cup and followed Patil. At the door, Kabir abruptly turned back. There was something in the charge sheet that was niggling at him.

'Khan?' Patil asked from the door.

'Just one second.' Kabir walked back to the table, picked up the charge sheet and flipped through it again. Three men had been arrested in the case. He looked at their pictures. That's when it struck him.

'Patil,' he called out over his shoulder.

'Yeah?'

'Are you sure this guy was involved in the blasts?'

'That's what the charge sheet says. Why?'

'Wasn't this guy an informer? The guy who worked with us when we were struggling with identifying the insiders in the Taj Mahal Hotel terrorist attack case, remember?'

Patil walked up to him and took the charge sheet from him. He looked at the picture carefully. 'Can't recollect.'

'I am positive. Do check on this. He can't be a terrorist. He helped us that time. People don't change allegiances so easily.'

'Well, informers always lead a dual life. They play the system from both sides. They normally become informers to settle personal scores. That's how it works, Khan. You know that as well as I do,' ACP Patil said. 'Shall we leave?'

Khan smiled. 'Yes, we don't have much time, do we?'

The two of them exited the building and set off in Patil's jeep. Throughout the drive the thought of his informer being involved in the Mumbai blasts bothered Kabir. It even took the sheen off the fact that he was meeting the man who had come to receive Subhash at the airport. Their first proper lead in weeks.

Twenty minutes later, they drove into Arthur Road Jail and parked in front of the admin blocks. Nobody had stopped them at the gate, nor did anyone check them as they walked into the building. Mobile phones were not allowed in Arthur Raid Jail, not even for jailors, but no one asked them to surrender theirs at the front desk. The chief warden met them and led them through a maze of passages to a solitary confinement cell. He inserted a key into the door of the cell and pushed it open. Slouched in one corner was the old man Kabir had seen in the picture that Krishnan had pulled out from the CCTV feed from the airport. Lakshmi Narain Sharma was in his seventies. He hardly looked like a criminal. The moment Kabir and Patil entered, Sharma stood up and slid along the wall, moving to the far corner.

'I haven't done anything,' Sharma said. 'Nothing. Absolutely nothing. I don't know what is happening.'

'We'll be the judge of that,' Patil thundered. His demeanour had changed the moment he entered the cell.

Kabir could see the fear in the old man's eyes. There was a large scar on his forehead. Most likely from a blow inflicted by a sharp weapon, Kabir concluded.

'You are the owner of a white Innova, number 4008?' Kabir started the conversation. He was not one to waste time.

'Yes, sir.'

'You were at the airport a few days ago to receive a man by the name Subhash Parikh?'

The driver nodded. 'It was like any other pickup, sir. Travel House had contracted someone else. When he couldn't go, they asked me.'

'Who asked you to go? And where were you supposed to take Subhash Parikh?'

'I got a call asking me to go to the airport to pick him up. As I said, the driver who was contracted by Travel House for the trip had fallen sick. I don't know where he was going. No details were given.'

'So you are saying that if anyone calls and tells you to go to somewhere to pick someone up, you will go? Even if you don't know who called you.'

'No, no, sir. I know the person who called. What I was not told was where the client wanted to go. Normally, we take them wherever they tell us.'

'Who called you?'

'We call him Dallu Driver. Dallu as in "Dalal". He is a go-between. He gets us assignments.'

'Can you call him now? And ask him to meet you?'

'Now?'

'Here.' Patil handed over his cell phone to Sharma. 'Call him and ask him to meet you outside the Parsi Dairy in Marine Lines. Give him whatever reason you want . . . maybe say you want to discuss a business opportunity.'

Sharma took the phone from him and dialled a number. 'Switched off,' he said a few seconds later looking at Patil and Khan.

'Okay,' said Khan, bringing the discussion back on track. 'When did you get the call?'

Maybe 6 or 6.30 p.m. I was at the temple at the time.'

'When did you realize Subhash was not coming? Did you get a call telling you that you could leave?'

'No, sir. I waited for over two hours after his flight had landed. Sometimes clients miss their flight and take the next one. But in this case the next flight was in the evening. When he didn't come out of the airport, I thought he might have stopped to eat something inside or had got stuck at the luggage bay. When he didn't show up even after two hours, I left.'

'Did you have another pickup?'

'No, sir. I was booked for two days. I was told that I had to stay with him and drop him back at the airport whenever he wanted. So I did not accept any other assignments.'

'Did Mr Parikh ever call you? Which number did he call you from?'

'His regular number.'

'Can you check your phone and tell us the number?'

'It is an old phone, sir, doesn't save so many numbers. But Travel House will have it.'

'Okay. Why did he call you?'

'He called me a couple of times. Once, the night before he was to come to Mumbai, just to confirm the timings, and then around midnight.'

'Midnight?' Kabir was curious.

Sharma nodded. 'Yes.'

'What for?'

'I think the second call was a mistake. He didn't say anything. I could overhear some conversation at the other end, but couldn't make head or tail of it. After staying on the line for a few seconds I disconnected.'

'Could you tell how many people were there in the conversation you overheard?'

'Three maybe?'

'Will you be able to recognize their voices if you heard them again?'

He shook his head. 'I barely heard them for thirty seconds. They were speaking so fast that I could not understand anything.'

'Do you remember what you heard? Any words? Phrases? What were they talking about?'

Lakshmi Narain Sharma thought about it for a while, his brow furrowed in concentration, and then nodded slowly.

83

Back in the ACP's office in Marine Lines, Kabir asked Patil: 'That scar the guy had, running across his forehead and down one side of his face? Makes him look rather ghastly, doesn't it?'

'That's the result of an injury he sustained during the Mumbai blasts. He was driving the taxi that blew up near the airport. Even then he was stepping in to cover up for absenteeism in taxi companies. He survived but his passenger died. In fact, he came back to work only a couple of weeks ago.'

'Lucky him. But, poor fellow, he was scarred for life.'

'Are you headed back tonight?'

'Yeah!' said Khan. 'Please get me that data I asked for. It will really help,' said Kabir in a worried tone. Patil nodded.

84

'One thing is certain, then,' Krishnan said after Kabir briefed him upon his return from Mumbai. 'Subhash was alive till midnight. Whatever happened, happened after that. This could also mean that the men the driver heard on the call were the ones who killed Subhash.'

'It's possible. The post-mortem puts the time of death between 2.30 and 3.30 a.m.,' Kabir said. 'We'll hopefully know whom Subhash was meeting in Mumbai in a day or two. I've asked for the phone records of Dallu Driver. He's the one who fixed up the taxi driver for Subhash's visit. Mumbai Police is also on the lookout for him.'

'We are running out of time,' Krishnan lamented. 'We know nothing.'

'It's like a pack of dominoes, sir. The moment one piece falls, the fortress will collapse. We just have to find the right piece to topple.'

'I hope you are right. I don't want an embarrassment just before my retirement.'

Before Kabir could reply, Krishnan's phone started ringing.

'Yes, Sundari,' he said, taking the call with an apologetic smile. He spoke to her for a few minutes and ended the call with, 'I will send the car. Go to the doctor. I will let him know you're coming . . . No! The doctor won't come. You will have to go, Sundari. You can't stay at home forever. Go out. Meet people.

That's the only way you will start getting back into your normal frame of mind.' He hung up.

'Sorry about that,' Krishnan said to Kabir. 'That was Sundari. Same old problem. Depression. She hasn't stepped out of the house even once in the last ten days.'

'I am sure she will get better.'

Krishnan gave a small smile. 'I hope so. By the way, Dharmaraja Varma complained about you to the chief minister. I got a call yesterday.'

'What did he complain about? That I called a crook a crook?'

'No. He was upset at the *manner* in which you asked the questions, not the questions per se.'

'That's quite generous.'

'He is not a bad human being. He is quite reasonable. Expecting a certain respect because he is royalty is not wrong. After all he is the king.'

'Not in my eyes,' Kabir said dismissively. 'That Nair fellow and Dharmaraja Varma have some connection which we haven't figured out yet. If we take Nair into custody and thrash him, I bet he will sing like a canary.'

'He is already inside.'

'Are you suggesting something?'

'He is seventy years old. If you thrash him he is likely to die.' Krishnan didn't want anything controversial to mar his tenure as police chief.

He excused himself for a moment and called the psychiatrist to tell him that his wife would be coming for a session. The psychiatrist must have reassured him because Krishnan smiled in response and hung up. He then called his driver and told him to go home and take madam to the doctor.

'So, where were we?' he said, turning back to Kabir once again.

'You could have told your secretary to do this . . .' Kabir was curious to know why Krishnan hadn't taken the easy way out.

'If I ask my secretary to do this, it will become gossip. I don't want that.' There was a hint of a pain in his eyes. 'Give me just one more minute. I'll tell her to be ready.' He walked to his table, and looked around. 'Where did I keep my phone?' he said, searching for the phone he used to communicate with Sundari.

'Call from the landline,' Khan suggested.

'Won't help. She doesn't answer any calls, unless they're from this number.' He finally pulled out his regular phone and dialled the second number. Seconds later, his pocket began ringing, and he sheepishly pulled out his other phone from it. Kabir smiled; he had seen him do this a few times in the past too.

While Krishnan spoke to his wife, Kabir stood to the side, trying to block out the conversation between husband and wife. He tried to divert his mind and started thinking of Subhash. The night Subhash died. Who were the men in Subhash's room? What was the number of Subhash's second phone? Whom had he called that night outside the Taj. Everything seemed so simple but was proving to be so complex.

'I'll call you once you are done with the doctor,' Krishnan was telling his wife, one phone clutched in one hand and the other one pressed to his ear. 'Bye.'

'Sorry,' he said to Kabir. 'I am done now.'

Kabir didn't respond. He was looking at the DGP as if in a trance. He pointed at the phone. 'That's your second phone.'

'Yes,' a confused Krishnan responded.

'What you just did . . . Subhash must have too.'

'Which is?'

'Dialled the second number from the first to find out where the phone was.'

'Right!'

'If we look at his phone records, specifically at calls he made that didn't get connected, we might be able to find his second phone number. In fact, once we have the list, we can pare it down to those numbers which were in the vicinity of his primary number at the time the call was made—that should definitely help us determine his second number. We can confirm it by checking the location of that number at the time Subhash was outside Taj Kovalam. If all of these match, we'll have the number we want.'

'Brilliant!' exclaimed Krishnan. 'This might just be the breakthrough we need.' He walked out of his room, and called his assistant. 'Call the mobile intercept and telecom surveillance team to my room right now.'

When he walked back into the room, Kabir just raised his eyebrows and said, 'Dominoes. We need only one to topple.'

85

'I need to take up a job,' Aditya said to Divya that afternoon. 'Dior has offered me the position of an intern in Paris. 'Do you think I should take it?'

Divya was taken aback when Aditya said this. 'You never even told me that you applied.'

'I didn't.'

'Then?'

'They sent me this offer.' He showed her the mail from Dior.

Divya looked at it and forced a smile. In the mail, the person from Dior had mentioned his win at the competition in Amsterdam, said how impressed they were with his work and made him an offer. Below it was a mail from Aditya, declining their offer. When she looked up, she had tears in her eyes.

'You think I'd leave you and go, you idiot!' Aditya said, hugging her tightly. 'I'll figure something out in Mumbai.'

Divya returned his embrace, but the warmth in her hug was missing.

'How would I know?' A tear squeezed itself out of Divya's eyes.

'What if I don't go? What if I stay here and end up becoming a bigger designer than your dad and then he has ego issues with me?' he asked, trying to lighten the mood.

'We will deal with it.'

'That's why I keep telling you to marry me soon, so that he can hand the business over to me and retire peacefully.'

'It will be his call if and when it happens,' Divya said curtly, pulling away from him.

Aditya didn't try to stop her. 'Is everything okay, Divya?' he asked.

'Yes, of course,' she responded flippantly. 'Let it be, Aditya. No man can be like my father.'

She had noticed that the printout that Aditya had shown her didn't have a 'sent time stamp' on the mail. She decided to ignore that for the time being.

A harried Aditya got up and walked out of the room.

86

The analysis of Subhash's phone records was taking longer than expected. A data storage and retrieval upgrade at Vodafone had rendered the phone records partially inaccessible, frustrating Krishnan and Kabir.

Madhavan arrived later that morning after a brief trip to Chennai. Upon his return from Mumbai, Kabir had asked him to join the investigation formally. He had spoken to both DGP Krishnan and Commissioner Iyer in Chennai.

'Your logic in locating Parikh's second number was brilliant. Let's hope it gives you the desired result,' Madhavan said the moment he came in.

'We will know only tomorrow.' And he explained the reason for the delay.

'Great. So what do we do today?' Madhavan asked. 'Kerala ayurvedic massage?' he recommended, gleefully rubbing his hands together.

Kabir glared at him. 'Maybe you could check out the Kuzhivilakom temple for me.'

Madhavan just looked at him with raised eyebrows. He didn't understand what was being said.

'About one kilometre from Taj Kovalam is a temple. It is right opposite a construction site. On the board outside the temple is an image of Lord Ganesha. It resembles the small figurine that we have – the one found in the Wafi Mall heist. I'm not sure if it is the same one. Could you do a cursory check?'

'You could have checked it yourself. You have an image of the statue.'

'With a name like Kabir Khan, it is almost impossible to enter a temple, let alone entering *and* investigating. And I was so drawn into these murders that it completely slipped my mind.'

'I thought I was the one who was growing old,' Krishnan said, and the three of them started laughing. 'I will ask my assistant to organize a car for you,' he volunteered.

'Thank you, sir!' Madhavan bowed to the two of them and smiled.

'And a last piece of advice,' Krishnan offered. 'Go in plain clothes. People in Kerala get really defensive if they see a policeman asking questions. And the only reason why we are asking you to go is that sending someone from the local police force is a guaranteed way of attracting media attention.'

'Thank you. It is the same in Tamil Nadu too. I will change and go.'

After Madhavan left the two of them started discussing the temple. 'No one there is what they seem,' said Krishnan.

Kabir readily agreed. 'I really do not know whom to trust and whom not to.'

'How about no one!'

'We don't have any other option,' Khan lamented. But soon, realizing that it was a worthless point to brood over, he moved on. 'What happened to the steps which were being excavated on the eastern side of the temple perimeter wall?'

'The excavation has been stopped temporarily. The site has been handed over to the state archaeology department. They have sought the state government's approval for carrying out excavation on site. They'll resume work once the approval comes.'

'Assuming that it leads down into the temple . . . what lies on that side of the temple?' Khan asked. 'It is the vaults, right?'

'Yes.'

'It's really impressive how the entire city was planned so well in those days. Quite at variance with the way town planning happens nowadays.'

'I couldn't agree with you more.' Krishnan nodded. 'In the olden days every city was planned. Down to escape routes for the royal family. And at times even for the population at large.'

'We have seen evidence of this across the country, sir. In Mumbai too, such secret underground routes have been discovered. Recently a passage was discovered which extended from the GPO—where the Bombay Fort once stood before it was demolished—to Apollo Bunder. Apparently the British built this passage in the eighteenth century, fearing an attack from Napoleon.'

'We have them here as well. They were used for the royal family and their entourage to escape or hide in, in case of an attack. A lot of them were integrated with the drainage system, and ran parallel to the drainage pipes. Large drainage pipes facilitated the movement of people and goods from the palace to a safe haven close to the port. This discovery next to the temple seems to be one of those, hitherto unknown.'

'Some day, I tell you, your Dharmaraja Varma will take his family and all the riches and scoot. You will be left with the temple and empty vaults and your lord's blessings. Mark my words.'

'You say this outside the four walls of this room, Mr Khan, and you will be lynched.'

'I'm not stupid,' Kabir replied with a smile. And then suddenly the smile disappeared from his face. 'What if that is actually what is happening here? What if the king is actually using these passages to systematically loot the temple wealth?

Who would know if such a passage exists, from the king's palace? Would you?'

'No, but the state archaeological department should know.'

'Can we meet them? Just to make sure that we have that end covered? As it is I'm sure Varma is smuggling temple artefacts through sand-laden trucks. How's he doing that? Obviously the trucks are not coming into the temple. So someone is stealing the artefacts from the vaults or elsewhere in the temple and taking them to Varma's mansion, or to some other secret spot from where they are loaded on to sand trucks and dispatched to various ports, to be sold in the international markets.'

'We have a team which deals with the archaeological department. Mr U.R. Murthy is the ACP in charge of all such issues.' Krishnan reached out for his landline to call in Murthy.

A short stout man with an impressive handlebar moustache arrived shortly after. Krishnan began to make the introductions, at which point Murthy admitted to knowing Kabir. He was a much-spoken-about man in Kerala Police circles. His aggressive stance towards Dharmaraja Varma was quite the talk of the town, albeit in hushed voices.

When Krishnan asked him for information on the secret passages, Murthy said, 'I have a fair idea of where the secret passages are, but give me half an hour and I will check and get back to you.'

Half an hour later, Murthy returned to Krishnan's chamber. 'Okay, so here we are,' he said, pointing to a map of the city. 'There is an underground passage, well, it is not a passage so much as an escape route integrated with the city drainage, from the king's palace to just below the Swati Thirunal Palace which is a stone's throw from the Padmanabha Swamy Temple. It is a large drain; people can easily step in and wade through in a crouched position. There is no documented evidence of it having been used, ever. It was intended to evacuate the Padmanabha Dasa from the temple in case of an attack on the temple and its vaults.'

'This Swati Thirunal Palace . . . it's the museum, right?'

'Yes, the same one. It is called a palace because at one point in time it was the official residence of the king. Now it is a museum. Long ago it was a part of the temple precinct. The doors connecting the complexes still exist, though these days they have been locked for safety. And though it is speculated that one exists from the temple vaults to the Swati Thirunal Palace, no underground passages have been discovered till date.'

'Oh, okay!' Kabir Khan said. 'So the best Dharmaraja Varma can do at present is escape to the Swati Thirunal Palace, in case there is an attack.' He smiled. 'He can't escape to the port or away from the city.'

'Oh, but he can,' Murthy said, dashing Kabir's optimism. 'There is an escape route.' He indicated the map in front of them. 'It goes from the Swati Thirunal Palace to the Kowdiar Palace, the official residence of the king. From the palace there is another route which leads to the sea. No one has explored this path. It was sealed years ago to prevent unwanted access to the palace.' He marked the coordinates on the map in front. 'From the Swati Thirunal Palace to the Kowdiar Palace and from there to the sea.'

The path Murthy had marked ended at a point close to the sea. As Kabir took a closer look at the map, a nameless fear took hold of him. He lunged for his phone and dialled a number. As he waited for the call to connect, he looked at the map again and then at Krishnan. The DGP too had realized what Kabir had seen.

The point where Murthy had drawn a large X to indicate the exit point of the escape route was labelled on the map as Kuzhivilakom Temple. The temple which Madhavan had gone to inspect. The temple in whose vicinity both Subhash and Kannan were seen before they were murdered. Was there a connection?

'The phone is switched off,' he said grimly.

87

Krishnan immediately sent a message to the car that had taken Madhavan to the temple. Within five minutes Madhavan called back on Kabir's number. He was on the road outside Taj Kovalam.

'Wait for us. We'll be there in twenty minutes.'

'You want me to wait on the road?'

'Wait in the coffee shop.' Kabir hung up and turned to Krishnan. 'Let's go, quickly. We don't know what is in there.'

'Reinforcements?'

'I don't think so. I just don't want Madhavan to go in there alone. He is a Tamil Nadu Police officer. If something untoward were to happen to him you'll have lots to answer for. That's why I asked him to wait. We don't even know if we are overreacting.'

Just as they were leaving Krishnan's office the head of the mobile intercept and telecom surveillance team came in. 'I have Mr Parikh's phone records. I can bring them in whenever you are free.'

'This evening. We are just heading out. I'll call you the moment I am back,' Krishnan said, rushing out of his office.

In twenty-five minutes they were outside Taj Kovalam. Just as he was driving in, Krishnan spotted Madhavan and slowed down. The latter was standing at a cigarette kiosk outside the hotel and smoking. There were a few people around him, mostly locals. Madhavan was in plain clothes. Nobody seemed to have figured out that he was a policeman. As Krishnan brought the car to a halt, Madhavan subtly gestured, asking them to move on.

They parked the car in the visitors' parking and headed for the coffee shop. They had barely settled down in their chairs when—

'Hello! How are you doing, Mr Khan? Wonderful to see you again.'

'Same here!' Kabir smiled delightedly at Pallavi.

'Was the video of any use?' she asked.

Kabir looked at her sheepishly, for he had forgotten to thank her. 'Oh yes.' He grinned. 'Very.' As if it was an afterthought, he added, 'Thank you.'

'Finally!' Pallavi smiled. She turned to Krishnan then and introduced herself. 'Welcome to the Taj, sir. I'm Pallavi, the general manager.'

Krishnan didn't bother to introduce himself. He just shook her hand and sat back in his seat.

'So are congratulations in order?' Kabir asked Pallavi. He had noticed the change in her job title when she introduced herself to Krishnan.

She beamed in response. 'What can I get for you today?' she asked.

Kabir asked for filter coffee and Krishnan asked for green tea.

Madhavan and the beverages arrived at the same time.

'What the hell happened?' Madhavan asked the moment he reached their table.

Unlike him, Kabir waited for the waiter to leave and then filled him in on what they had learnt from Murthy.

'All the more reason to go there right away!' Madhavan stood up again, raring to go.

'Don't be crazy, Madhavan!' Krishnan chided. 'Let's not hurry this and mess it up.' He pointed to the chair, imploring Madhavan to resume his seat. 'Doing anything silly will tip off people. The royal family has unimaginable clout. One wrong step and we will be doomed.'

'But didn't *you* know about the royal family's connection to this temple, sir?' Madhavan asked Krishnan, surprised.

'Don't be an ass, Madhavan!' Kabir looked at him angrily. 'We left some important follow-up work and came to fetch you. Trust us when we say now is not the time to go poking about here.'

'Well, then you should have stayed and done your follow-up work. Why come all the way?'

Kabir didn't bother to explain to him the rationale that he had discussed earlier with Krishnan. Hurriedly he changed the topic. 'What were you discussing with the men at the stall outside?'

'I was just beginning a discussion on the temples in the vicinity. I pretended to be a trader in antiques and asked them if they knew someone who had something I could buy. In Chennai the paan shops outside five-star hotels are a hotbed of such activities. The foreigners staying in those hotels are perfect clients for smuggled goods.'

'What did they have to say?' Krishnan was curious.

'They don't have anything now. But they keep getting stuff every now and then.'

'From where?'

'That he doesn't know. They get a few pieces a month and he helps sell them off to foreigners staying at the hotel.'

'How does he get his client?'

'I asked him. He relies on the hotel staff to net him a client.'

'You mean to say that all these guys are involved?' Kabir was sceptical.

'If the fellow is to be believed, everyone is.'

'Unlikely,' said Kabir. 'He was probably boasting, trying to snare a new buyer.'

'I don't know about that.' Madhavan rolled his eyes.

Krishnan paid the bill and the three of them left. As they exited the gate and turned left Kabir looked out of the car window. The CCTV camera caught his attention. He turned to see what the camera was pointed towards. It was the cigarette kiosk. Tucked away in a corner of the road, the kiosk was placed in the most unobtrusive manner—people could buy cigarettes, stand there and smoke, without causing any trouble.

'Stop the car!' he said urgently.

Krishnan applied the brakes with a screech and stopped the car. Kabir got out and darted back into the hotel, leaving Krishnan and Madhavan wondering what happened.

88

Back in Krishnan's office, the mood was one of excitement. They had stumbled upon something wholly unexpected.

When Krishnan's assistant knocked on the door, a sense of calm descended on the three men. 'The head of mobile intercept and telecom surveillance is here to see you.'

'Send him in,' Krishnan instructed as he was the one who had sent word for him to come in.

'What do you have, Kutty?' Kabir asked the tall, gangly man who walked in. They had met before.

'We have analysed the data from Mr Parikh's phone,' Kutty began speaking. 'There are seventeen such numbers to which he made a call in the last two weeks, but the call wasn't answered. Of these, he spoke to six of them at various other points in time. That means that those six numbers are not his second number.'

'Obviously!'

'That leaves us with eleven numbers. Of these, three were in the vicinity of his own number whenever he called. Within thirty metres. One of them was Ranjit Dubey's. Understandable because he was in the room next to Subhash's. The second was Nirav Choksi's. He was in the room diagonally opposite.'

'And the third?'

'Kannan Ramalingam's.'

'Kannan?' All three of them exclaimed simultaneously.

'Yes, sir,' Kutty answered, somewhat taken aback by their chorus. 'The number was issued about two and a half weeks ago.'

'This isn't the regular number that Kannan used?' Krishnan verified.

'No, sir. This number is different.'

All three men wore similar expressions of shock on their faces. Kabir looked at Krishnan. 'Why would Subhash be calling Kannan? Unless . . . '

Kutty said, 'By mapping the geo location of Subhash Parikh's actual number and overlaying it with the locations of the new number we can safely say that this was Subhash's second number. The locations match most of the time except for when Subhash was in the temple. Then, the phone was switched off.'

'Makes sense,' Kabir said. 'When Subhash was in the temple he would not be carrying the second phone.'

'What about calls made from the phone?'

'Only one number,' Kutty responded.

'Whose?'

'Padmanabha Dasa.'

'Whaaat!!!' A shocked Kabir looked at Krishnan, who had bent down in frustration and his head was almost between his knees.

'I am beginning to believe in your hypothesis' was all he could say.

89

Dharmaraja Varma was resting in his bedroom when Krishnan and Kabir came calling again. They had earlier interrogated the owner of the shop that sold the SIM card to Kannan, but the shopkeeper had no recollection of who had picked it up. There were no CCTV cameras to go back to either.

The king didn't like to be disturbed while he was resting, so Krishnan and Khan had to wait. Krishnan was still reeling from Kutty's revelation that Subhash had called Thirumanassu. He was beginning to think he had no choice but to believe Kabir's hypothesis.

Almost an hour passed before the king arrived, completely unapologetic about the delay.

'Under normal circumstances I wouldn't have encouraged such an unannounced visit. However, I understand that these are trying times,' he said, a note of condescension in his voice.

'Thank you for being so considerate.' Kabir Khan's sarcasm was not lost on Varma, but he merely glared at him.

'You said you didn't know Subhash Parikh.'

'Is this an interrogation? Again?' Dharmaraja Varma was visibly annoyed.

'Well, not exactly, but not a casual conversation either,' Kabir said. He wanted to take the lead in the conversation.

Varma turned towards Kabir, a menacing look on his face. 'I might be old, but my memory hasn't failed yet. I had said that I had known him only for a week, maybe two.'

'Had you ever spoken to him over the phone?'

'Is there any restriction on that?'

'No.'

'Then?'

'Our records show that he spoke to you at least seventeen times in the two weeks leading up to his death.'

Dharmaraja Varma looked at him blankly and didn't offer any comment initially. But finding Kabir staring at him expectantly, he casually asked, 'Did he?' There was a grin on his face.

'That's what his telephone records say.'

'His?'

Kabir nodded.

'Well, so many people call me. Every day. How do you expect me to remember everything?'

'Didn't you just say you have a great memory?'

'Perhaps it has begun to fail me.' He guffawed.

'Did you ever meet him outside the temple?'

Dharmaraja Varma stood up suddenly. 'It is time for my evening walk, gentlemen. Next time, if you give me adequate notice, I will make sure my lawyers are present when we talk.' He extended his right hand towards the two of them. 'Just to make sure that nothing I say is misrepresented. I'm sure you understand.' He started walking back to his chambers. A maid walked in with glasses filed with cold drinks.

'It is okay,' he said, sending her away. 'Our friends were just leaving.'

Just before he exited the room, he looked at the DGP and said, 'Don't you think it is a bit foolish to expect me to stay disconnected with what is going on in my Padmanabha Swamy Temple. The entire wealth of generations is stored there, and you expect me not to make efforts to get to know what is going on inside.' He chuckled derisively. 'As if the CBI was not enough, you too have joined them in their stupid endeavours, Krishnan.' And he disappeared behind the door which shut by itself.

90

The drive back to the police headquarters was a traumatic one for Krishnan and Kabir.

'So Subhash was his mole?' Kabir was incredulous.

The fact that the discussion with the king had not gone too well was worrying Krishnan. He knew that Dharmaraja Varma was not the forgiving kind. He would pull strings to make sure Krishnan's indiscretion didn't go unpunished. 'But you know what,' he added after a prolonged period of silence, 'I still think he is not guilty.'

'For the sake of humanity, for the sake of Kerala and for the sake of those who believe in him, I hope and pray that you are right.' They were both quiet for a while, till Khan spoke again. 'If Subhash was his mole . . . if he was feeding Varma all the information about what was going on inside the temple vaults, then what was Kannan's connection? Why was the phone in Kannan's name? Was he also a part of the clique?'

They did not have any answers.

'I hope Madhavan has something good for us,' Krishnan prayed as he floored the accelerator. Madhavan had stayed back to interrogate the cigarette vendor, whom they had picked up outside the Taj.

A detailed analysis of Subhash's two mobile phones was waiting on Krishnan's table when they returned to his cabin. One look at it and Kabir figured out what the issue was.

'Between 9.30 and 10 p.m. on the night Kannan died, Subhash's phone shows an increased use of data. Which probably means he was not calling through his carrier; he was calling over the Internet. WhatsApp possibly,' he declared, showing the analysis to Krishnan. 'See,' he said. 'The time that he was on the call, the data usage has gone up. Clearly he was smarter than we think. Mobile calls can be monitored. WhatsApp calls can't.'

'But we still don't know whom he called.'

91

Pallavi had sent across the CCTV feed from outside the gates for the entire week. Kabir wanted to check the activities at the cigarette shop, particularly of the kind that Madhavan had spoken about.

He spent the whole night watching the tapes, analysing every individual who came to the cigarette shop, the money that changed hands. Occasionally, at night, he noticed a few foreign tourists spend a little extra time with the shopkeeper and eventually leave with a small packet. Every now and then, it was an Indian. It didn't take Kabir long to figure out that the shopkeeper was trading in meth. Narcotics trade was banned, but this was not Kabir's immediate concern. He was fighting a different battle. After making up his mind to forward the relevant clipping to Krishnan, he watched the entire week's video footage on fast-forward. When he didn't find anything, he started playing it all over again.

At 6 a.m. Madhavan walked in with two cups of coffee. 'Anything?'

Kabir yawned, raised his hands above his head and stretched. Accepting a cup, he said, 'Waste of time. What does our man have to say?' he asked, referring to the cigarette vendor.

'Not much. He claims to be an intermediary who just prospects. In case someone is interested, he refers them to a supplier who then calls the customer.'

'Interesting!' said Kabir. He yawned again.

'Have you been at it all night?' Madhavan asked, pointing at the screen. Kabir nodded wearily. 'Well, watching it again isn't going to get you anywhere. Take a break!' Madhavan nudged him off the chair and started randomly watching the footage on the laptop.

Kabir gratefully stumbled off to the bathroom to freshen up.

A few minutes later, Kutty arrived, carrying two folders. 'Krishnan sir is on his way. He'll be here in fifteen minutes. These came last night,' he said, setting the folders on the table. Then he left declaring that he was going to get himself some coffee.

Kabir emerged from the bathroom and walked up to the table. He casually glanced through the file that Kutty had left on the table. It was the analysis of the call records of Lakshmi Narain Sharma and Dallu Driver, whose real name was Dilip Patankar. Kabir had asked for them just before he left Mumbai. There was nothing in the report which stood out. No correlations, no common numbers, no patterns. Sharma's electronic trail was cold. Either he had covered up his tracks brilliantly or he had no role to play, and was just an innocent bystander. It was more likely he was the latter. Experience had taught Kabir that amateur criminals found it difficult to cover their tracks successfully in the modern age.

The analysis of Patankar's records was far more interesting. The most common numbers he had called were of five other cab drivers in Mumbai. All of them Ola drivers.

'Did you find anything?' Krishnan walked in, followed by Kutty.

Kabir nodded absently and continued to read the report. Halfway through, he looked up and asked, 'If someone calls you for a carpentry job, and you have a number of carpenters working for you, would you give the job to one of them or to a third party.'

'Obviously my own carpenter. Why will I pass an opportunity to make money?' Madhavan said.

'Unless, of course, your carpenters are not free or not skilled enough to carry out the job,' Kutty commented.

'Hmm.' Kabir kept reading. 'Why would Dallu give the job of picking up Subhash Parikh to Lakshmi Narain Sharma and not to one of the five Ola cabs that he runs?'

'What?' Madhavan paused the video and looked at him.

'According to this'—he held up the file—'Patankar is a one-time cab driver himself. His fortunes changed for the better when he bought five cabs and enrolled them with Ola. His lifestyle improved tremendously, and now he is the proprietor of a small cab company. Still he gave the task of picking up Subhash Parikh to Lakshmi. Isn't that strange?'

'There's something fishy here,' agreed Madhavan.

'It might be worth finding out when he went from being a driver himself to an aggregator for Ola. Were his cabs already booked the day Lakshmi was at the airport? Sending another driver is understandable if all five cabs were plying elsewhere at that time, otherwise it is a bit strange.' He looked at Madhavan and said, 'Can I have my laptop? I need to mail Mumbai Police. I'll call them in a couple of hours.'

Madhavan turned to the laptop. He was about to exit the video app when he noticed something on the screen. 'Did you see this?'

As they gathered around the screen and peered at it, Kabir took out his phone and called Pallavi. 'I need to know the identity of someone. Can you help me?'

92

Rajan was at the police headquarters that day to meet Kabir Khan and DGP Krishnan.

As soon as he entered Krishnan's office, Kabir pointed to the lounge chair in one corner of the room and said, 'Please make yourself comfortable, Mr Rajan.'

Rajan did as he was told.

Kabir strolled up to him with a few papers and said, 'HSBC Geneva?'

'What about it Mr Khan? We have spoken about it. Haven't we?'

'Oh yes, we have.'

'I remember mentioning to you that there must have been a mistake. There is no way Kannan could have a Swiss account—'

'Yes, there has been a mistake,' Kabir interrupted. 'The account should have been in your name, right?'

'What nonsense?' Rajan burst out indignantly. 'How dare you accuse me of swindling money and holding it in a Swiss account! How can this be mine?'

'Well, the only person close to Kannan was you. And Kannan didn't know how to read and write.'

'So? How does that make me the offender? What evidence do you have?'

'By association. This is pure conjecture. But given that he is your father's son . . .' He paused. 'Who else could it be?'

'The gold you found on him was not mine. If he could get half a gold bar from someone, he could get someone else's black money too!' Rajan countered.

'But who could that someone else be?'

'How should I know?'

'Dharmaraja Varma?' Kabir said, his eyes never leaving Rajan's face. He wanted to see the change in his expressions. This was just a test to see how much he was willing to share on his own.

Rajan merely shrugged. 'Maybe.'

'But it was not Dharmaraja Varma who met with Andrew Mormon, the HSBC relationship manager, at the Taj the night Kannan was killed, was it? It was *you*.' Kabir spoke in measured tones that belied the rising anger within.

'Meeting wh . . . who?' Rajan asked. For the first time that night, he stammered. 'I have no idea what you are talking about.'

'Andrew Mormon, right?' Kabir looked at Madhavan, who was standing in the corner, as if for confirmation. The latter nodded, his eyes gleaming. 'That's what the booking register at the Taj says.'

'You went there with Kannan that night—' Krishnan stepped into the conversation—'and met with the private banker. Why would you do that, unless the account that was in Kannan's name actually contains your money?'

'I did not meet Andrew Mormon,' Rajan insisted.

'Fuck you, moron!' Kabir Khan shouted, his impatience getting the better of him. 'We have CCTV footage of the Taj coffee shop where the two of you met! Want me to show it to you?' He reached for the pen drive that Pallavi had sent earlier in the day.

Rajan was defiant. 'Now you will say that I was the one who killed Kannan!'

Kabir nodded. 'Well, we would have. You were our number one suspect, after all.' Kabir was enjoying the conversation in between bouts of irritation. 'But the same meeting with Andrew

Mormon, which gave you away, saved you. At the time Kannan was killed, you were with Mormon in the coffee shop. Your meeting ended at two that night. The hotel's phone records show that you called Kannan's mobile afterwards, but the call didn't go through. You then returned home by a hotel cab.'

Rajan sighed. 'You have all the details, but you are mistaken. I met Andrew Mormon because I wanted to get to the bottom of Kannan's account. I had known Kannan his whole life. Money did not interest him. He was never one to chase riches. Honesty and integrity meant everything to him. If I had to pick one guy to fight for my life, I would've picked him. You operate on evidence. That's why you are chasing the bar of gold found on him. I go by belief. That's why I know that the account could not have been Kannan's. I knew that my chances of establishing this were slim. After all, there is a reason people keep their money in Swiss accounts. But for Kannan's sake, I wanted to give it a try.'

'And were you able to figure anything out?'

Rajan shook his head. 'No. Nothing came out of it, but at least I know that I tried.'

93

Kabir Khan checked his mail the moment Rajan left. He had done so several times already that day. Twelve mails beeped their way into his inbox. Facebook, Twitter, credit card companies, banks, companies selling libido-enhancing drugs, insurance, furniture . . . and nearly lost in the midst of all this a mail from ACP Patil. Hurriedly, he clicked on it.

Khan,

Checked out Patankar. He was a taxi driver with Travel House for six years. A month and a half ago, he was sacked for running an Ola cab service while being on the rolls of Travel House. He enrolled with Ola in June and his cabs started plying in July. By the end of July he had five cabs operational. Attached are the forms he submitted to Ola for enrolment.

    Do let me know in case you need any further information.

Patil

Khan clicked on the documents attached and perused them quickly.

    'Well? What is it?' Krishnan asked.

    'This guy, Patankar—'

'The one who gave instructions to Lakshmi Narain to pick up Subhash from the airport? What about him?'

'He bought five cabs and enrolled them with Ola in July. Because of which he was fired from Travel House.'

'How did a driver get money to buy *five* cars at once?'

Khan looked at the forms submitted to Ola Cabs and said, 'The cars are all hypothecated to Axis Bank. Looks like a loan from them.'

'Even then!' Madhavan argued. 'A loan of twenty lakh for a taxi driver. Is it so easy to get a loan these days?'

'Fair question,' Krishnan said.

Kabir thought for a minute and then turned on his phone. The screen sprang to life. He brought up the Google app on the screen and typed: June, July, 2016, mumbai. Over two lakh search results appeared. He quickly scrolled through the page.

'This should have been pretty obvious,' he sighed. 'This story is taking a different trajectory.'

He picked up his mobile phone and dialled a number. 'Patil,' he said when the call connected. 'Thanks for what you sent . . . but that's not enough.'

94

Kabir was about to tell Krishnan and Madhavan his theory when there was a knock at the door.

Krishnan looked up, annoyed. 'Yes, Kutty, what is it?'

'Sorry, sir, I just wanted to tell you that there was a small mistake in what I told you earlier.'

'What do you mean!' Krishnan roared, rising out of his chair.

'Okay, okay!' Kabir stepped in between them. He turned to Kutty and snapped, 'Out with it! Fast!' He knew that what they had been told earlier was not relevant any more. He just wanted Kutty to say his piece quickly and leave.

Kutty seemed visibly shaken by Krishnan's reaction. He cleared his throat nervously and said, 'The second escape route from the palace that I had mentioned is not from the palace to the Kuzhivilakom temple.'

'Excuse me!' Madhavan rounded on him.

'Let me explain, please! Centuries ago, when the palace was built and the temple was in existence, the second underground passage emerged inside the Kuzhivilakom temple complex. The complex covers an area of over two acres around the sanctum sanctorum. The underground passage extended from the king's palace to the southeastern corner of the temple complex. When the Privy Purse was abolished in 1971, the control of the temple land passed to the government . . . Well, for all temples except the Anantha Padmanabha Swamy Temple, which stayed with a private trust. At the time a significant portion of the temple land was used for public utilities like roads and other services.'

Kutty pulled out a map from his bag and spread it out on the table. 'This is where the underground safety route emerged. And this'—he pulled out a more recent map and laid it over the historical one—'is what this area looks now. This is where it is.'

A surprised Kabir Khan picked up the map and studied it carefully, an intense look on his face. 'So you are saying that of the two acres that belonged to the Kuzhivilakom temple, only half an acre remains with the temple? The rest has been taken over by the government?'

Kutty nodded. 'Yes. And the passage from the palace to the temple which emerged inside the complex, is now under the road that abuts the temple wall. The road that leads from the temple to the Taj Hotel.'

'Aah. That is very interesting. I think I know where this is. Come on, let's go. Let's get this one niggling option out of our consideration subset.'

95

The four of them were standing outside the Kuzhivilakom temple twenty-five minutes later. This time they had come prepared. Krishnan had initially objected to them going on this mission, but he fell in line soon enough.

Khan, as usual, stayed outside the temple while the other three went in. The idol of Ganesha looked very similar to the one found in the Wafi Mall heist, but was not the same. One look at it and Madhavan could see that this was a different idol.

Kutty laid out the map and pointed to the southeastern corner of the temple. 'The passage from the king's palace used to emerge somewhere there.' Madhavan and Krishnan looked in that direction. There was a boundary wall, and beyond it was the road that connected Taj Kovalam to the temple complex.

They came out of the temple and joined Kabir. 'The passage is right under the road where you are standing,' Kutty said. In one hand he had the historical map that he had obtained from the land records division, and with the other hand he was pointing to the road ahead.

'So to get to the passage, we will have to excavate. Like the steps that were found on the eastern side of the Anantha Padmanabha Swamy Temple,' Khan said. 'This also means that there is no way to escape from the palace to the coast, or, for that matter, smuggle goods from the palace to the coast through the elaborate drainage system.'

'Well, that's what it looks like. If I juxtapose the old maps with the city master plan, then the place where the drainage chute from the palace ends should be right under the road. So yes, there is no escape.'

'Then there is no point lingering here. Let's head back,' Krishnan said.

A dejected Kabir followed the others to the jeep. He had hoped that the exit point of the escape route would give him some insight. But if the drainage line was under the road, there was no point in pursuing his hypothesis. Another theory down the drain, literally. He looked around him—at the Kuzhivilakom temple to his left, the construction site to his right and to the road in between. The road that covered a thousand secrets.

Krishnan waited until Kabir climbed into the jeep, then stared driving towards the Taj. A little before the hotel, they got stuck in a traffic jam. The cigarette shop was closed; the shopkeeper was in custody. A car was trying to park and had held up the traffic in the process.

'Why do they have such narrow roads? A tourist destination needs proper infrastructure,' Madhavan lamented.

'But it's the same story throughout Kerala,' Kutty replied. 'Narrow roads.'

Kabir added. 'Pallavi, at the Taj, was also cursing the government when I last saw her. The road was not supposed to be so narrow. It was supposed to be a sixty-foot-wide road. But apparently everyone along the road has usurped the land. So now the road is only half its intended width.'

'One day we will take over and demolish all unauthorized construction on this road,' Krishnan declared. 'India needs a benign dictatorship to rid itself of everything illegal.'

'Benign dictatorship—isn't that an oxymoron?'

'Shut up, Kabir!' Krishnan said. 'We are talking about the road and traffic.'

Kabir looked up as if he had been struck by lightning. 'Hold it! Stop! Stopstopstop!' he cried.

'We are not moving, my friend! Can't you see the traffic?' Krishnan agonized.

Kabir turned and looked at Kutty. 'Kutty, the map that you are referring to, that's the master plan, right?'

Kutty nodded warily.

'Come with me!' Kabir leapt out of the jeep and ran back. Kutty followed, leaving Krishnan and Madhavan in the car. They had no choice but to wait until the traffic jam cleared and then take the first available U-turn.

Khan was standing with his back to the Kuzhivilakom temple gate when a huffing and panting Kutty joined him. 'What happened?'

'Kutty, your master plan had provision for a sixty-foot road, but the ground reality is a thirty-foot road. Thirty feet of what should ideally have been road has been taken over by the construction site.' Kabir pointed to the construction site opposite the temple. He had seen it a few times in the past but had never imagined it could be so significant. 'Is it possible that the escape route from the palace is not under the road, but inside that construction site?'

By that time, Krishnan and Madhavan had also reached. They were standing in the middle of the road, looking at each other.

'The passage has to be inside that construction site,' Kabir reiterated.

'We can check that out, Kabir,' Krishnan offered. He called his deputy and asked him to send backup to the Kuzhivilakom temple immediately. 'We'll need backup if we want to go inside.' He looked at Kutty and added, 'Kutty, you are from intelligence, you can choose to go back.'

Meanwhile, Kabir was scanning the barricades outside the site. They looked old and worn down, yet they hid everything behind them from public view. There were no hoardings, no notices proclaiming the site to be an apartment complex under construction, no signage. No effort seemed to have been made to draw the public's attention to the upcoming apartment complex. They waited on the corner for about ten minutes. The reinforcements were taking time. Khan was getting restless. Every now and then he would urge Krishnan to let them go inside. Krishnan resisted the first few times, but then he relented. They were about to go in when Krishnan's phone rang.

'Damn!' he muttered and took the call. 'Yes, sir.' A few seconds of muted conversation later, he hung up and looked at his team. 'That was the chief minister.'

'What?' Kabir was anxious. 'Why?'

'He doesn't want us to go in.'

96

They were huddled around Krishnan's table. The look on Kabir's face was one of elation. 'I was right!' He thumped the table with his right hand. 'See! I was right,' he repeated, waving the piece of paper that had just come in, in Krishnan's face.

'Calm down. Calm down.' Krishnan tried his best to settle the rush of adrenalin that had made Khan go pink in the face.

'I need to meet him. Now!' Kabir said, grabbing the sheet of paper and walking out of the cabin.

'Wait,' called out Krishnan, 'I'll come with you,' and rushed after him.

Within minutes, they were standing outside a door. Krishnan swiped his card and walked in.

'So!' said Kabir.

Radhakrishnan Nair wore a blank look on his face.

'What is this?' Kabir held out the piece of paper and waved it in front of him.

Radhakrishnan Nair took the paper and read it. He chuckled. Kabir gritted his teeth in response. 'I didn't know owning property is a crime in this country.'

'Why this particular property?' Kabir asked testily.

'My father bought this property years ago. Only he can answer this question.'

The sarcasm was not lost. Both Khan and Krishnan knew that Nair's father was not alive.

'Who sold it to him?' Kabir looked at Nair, anger in his eyes.

'Well, if you have got this far, then I'm sure you know the answer to that question. Why are you even asking me?'

Nair was not wrong. The entire document transferring the title of the property, the construction site outside the Kuzhivilakom temple, to Nair's father was in the investigators' possession. Days before the entire temple property was taken over by the government, the temple trust had sold it to the Nair family.

'Where did you get the money to buy such a large property? It's half an acre, isn't it?' Krishnan asked him in a steely tone.

'Like I said, I didn't buy it. I inherited it.'

The discussion was going nowhere.

'I think I will go and ask Dharmaraja Varma instead,' Kabir said and turned to leave.

'You definitely stand a better chance there, Mr Khan,' Nair remarked casually. 'But let me tell you one thing, he is not a bad man. Definitely not as bad as you make him out to be.'

'For you, "bad" is relative, Mr Nair, it has degrees.' Kabir had a wry smile on his face. 'For us, it is absolute. Black or white; no grey.'

As he walked out of the room, his phone rang. 'Yes, Patil?' he said, as he marched back to the DGP's room. 'Yeah, Patankar's cabs . . . Okay, so they *were* funded by Axis Bank? . . . Any chance of getting the forms? . . . I just want to see on what basis the bank approved loans for five cabs to one person . . . Really? You mean to say they approved it because these were meant to run as Ola cabs?' The expression on Kabir Khan's face was one of curiosity mixed with surprise. 'Ah! Now I get it. They assumed the five cabs, when plied as Ola cabs, would generate enough revenue to pay back the loans.'

Walking beside Kabir, Krishnan could overhear only his side of the conversation. Although he could fathom a fair amount of what they were talking about, he couldn't help but wonder what new information ACP Patil had got.

'But what?' Kabir asked, and then fell silent as he listened. 'One hundred per cent!' he blurted suddenly. 'The bank funded the full value of the car, when their norm is eighty-five to ninety per cent! Is that normal? . . . Hmmm, I didn't think so. Then what made them do it in this case? All right, can you find out for me? . . . Okay. Let me see what can be done. Thanks a lot, Patil . . . Hey, hang on! . . . Yes, yes, I am a pain! I know! But I need some more help, Patil, and only you can help me,' he said and went on to explain what he wanted done. 'You got that? Thanks, man! . . . Yeah, bye!'

Kabir disconnected the call, and immediately dialled another number. He didn't like pulling strings normally, but in this case, he had to.

'This is Additional Director Kabir Khan, CBI. Can you connect me to Mrs Sharma's office?' He kept the phone on the table and put it on speaker so that Krishnan could also hear the conversation.

A brief bank jingle played while he was transferred, and then: 'Mr Khan! What a pleasant surprise!'

'How are you, Mrs Sharma? I always only seem to remember you when all my other options have failed and I am desperate.'

'Not at all, Mr Khan! Tell me what you need. I don't require a preamble. Least of all from you.'

'Patankar, loan number LA468923401. Bought five cabs and put them for use with Ola Cabs in June or July this year. Axis Bank funded him. You guys gave him full funding for the on-road value of the car.'

'Did we? That's surprising.'

'I'm sure you had good reasons for it. I want to know what they were.'

'Let me check.'

'Do you want me to send you the forms?'

'Come on, Mr Khan!' Mrs Sharma laughed. 'You got the forms from us, and you are asking if you need to send them to me?'

'Thank you, Mrs Sharma!' Khan smiled and disconnected the call. Mrs Sharma and he went back a long way—she had been his relationship manager at one point in time. And he had helped her out in a case of domestic violence.

Mrs Sharma called back within half an hour. 'I think I know why we did that.'

For the next five minutes, Khan didn't utter a word. He quietly heard what Mrs Sharma had to say. With every passing moment he could feel his heart beat faster.

'Are you there, Mr Khan?'

A shocked Khan could only whisper into his phone, 'I think you have just managed to complicate the entire scenario for me. Thank you for everything.'

He hung up.

'What do we do?' he asked Krishnan after explaining everything that Mrs Sharma had told him.

'Vikram Rai and his team have gone back for the long weekend. Let them come back. We will do what we have to on Monday morning.'

97

The next morning, a Friday, Kabir Khan travelled to Mumbai for a day. He had some unfinished business with ACP Patil.

'Did you file the charge sheet?' Khan asked him the moment he saw him. 'I need to take a look at it.'

'What is the matter, Khan? What's playing on your mind?' Patil asked, gesturing to his team to bring the three-thousand-page charge sheet in the Mumbai blasts case.

'Nothing,' Kabir replied distractedly. 'Let me see it. Maybe I will be able to tell you what I think.'

Four cartons full of the paperwork that had gone into the charge sheet were brought in. Khan went through them in a very cursory manner. It didn't take him longer than forty-five minutes.

'Can we meet Lakshmi Narain Sharma? The old guy?'

'Sure. When? Now?' Patil asked Khan.

'If you're free, we can go now. Else we can leave in fifteen minutes.' Khan smiled.

'You are impossible.' Patil grinned. He picked up his cap and his service revolver from the table and walked out to his jeep.

'Do we know where Patankar is hiding?' Khan asked Patil. He knew that Patankar was an important cog in the wheel.

'Dallu Driver?'

'Yeah.'

'Not yet, but soon,' Patil replied. 'It is just a matter of time.'

Khan nodded.

At the jail, Khan talked to Lakshmi for about half an hour. Afterwards, Khan made one more request, one that Patil was not prepared for.

'I want to meet the families of everyone who died in the Mumbai blasts. Seven people died right? I want to meet all their families, if possible.'

'What?' Patil was shocked. 'Khan, everything we have done thus far is on the basis of my personal equity. If we go out and meet the public at large, someone might call the press. We will be in a soup for having spoken to them without mandate.'

'Leave that to me. You line up the meetings. I'll meet all of them between today and tomorrow. I have a late night flight to Thiruvananthapuram.'

'Okay, let me try,' Patil said.

Khan was back in Thiruvananthapuram by Saturday evening. When he landed, he saw a WhatsApp message from ACP Patil. 'Patankar in custody.' While the message brought a smile to Khan's face, he rued the fact that he was not in Mumbai to interrogate him. 'Possible to bring him here for a few days?' he typed.

Within seconds, his mobile beeped. 'I know you will not take NO for an answer,' Patil had replied.

98

THIRUVANANTHAPURAM

On Sunday morning, much to Khan's and Krishnan's dismay, the home secretary of the Government of Kerala arrived at the police headquarters to secure the release of Nair. No one had a choice. Instructions to release Nair had been issued straight from the state home ministry.

'Damn, this only proves that there is something fishy going on with Nair,' Khan complained the moment the home secretary left. 'There is only one way to take him out of the equation. For our satisfaction.'

'And that is?' Krishnan asked.

'We have to raid his construction site. I know the chief minister ordered us to leave that day, but that was then. Is there an option now?'

'You need to relax, Khan. Let's not rush this.' Krishnan was worried because he had received specific instructions directly from the chief minister. Despite wanting to get to the bottom of this, his hands were tied.

'I'm not rushing anything. But I need to put this issue to rest before we head down any other path. I need to know. The fact that the home secretary himself came to have Radhakrishnan Nair released shows that he is an important cog. They couldn't have let him stay here. They had to pull him out before he told us something.'

'And we need to know what that something is.' Madhavan understood what Khan was saying.

'Ideally, before they smarten up and succeed in hiding whatever it is they are up to,' Khan said. He was pleading now. 'We need to raid the site. And we need to do so before activity resumes at the temple tomorrow.'

'Kerala Police won't be able to support you in this without adequate permission. We'll be getting into a direct conflict with the administration if we were to do it.' Krishnan sounded adamant.

'So you are saying there is no way we can do that.'

'If information is all you need, then you don't need Kerala Police. Do you?' Krishnan winked at Khan. 'Besides, who can prevent a stranger from Tamil Nadu Police innocently loitering on to the site. People do get confused and lose their way, right.'

'But where is the iss—' Khan started to protest and then abruptly stopped. He looked at Krishnan who was innocently poring over the papers on his table, a small smile on his face. 'Seriously!' he exclaimed and looked at Madhavan who was looking confused. Khan took him aside and explained what was expected of him.

Later that evening, shortly before sunset, Madhavan, dressed as a local, pushed the barricades aside and walked on to the construction site opposite the Kuzhivilakom temple. A few hand-picked officers, dressed in regular clothes, who were loyal to Krishnan, kept watch from a distance to make sure there was no trouble.

The only risk Madhavan was running was finding Nair there, for he was the only one who could have recognized him. To make sure that Nair did not show up at the site, Krishnan was sitting in Nair's office in Attingal, trying to sweet talk him into believing that the police didn't mean him any harm when they had dumped him in the lockup.

99

On Monday morning, when Nirav and Vikram walked down to the hotel lobby to board their transport from the hotel to the temple, there was a Kerala Police team waiting for them. From the hotel, they were led straight to the Thiruvananthapuram police headquarters, where Kabir Khan and DGP Krishnan were expecting them.

'Mr Rai, how are we today?' Krishnan asked when they walked in.

'Good . . . very good,' said Vikram. There was a touch of irritation in his voice. 'What is the meaning of bringing us here in this manner?'

'My apologies, Mr Rai.' The DGP brought his right palm to rest on his chest and inclined his head to the right, as an apology. 'But I couldn't have done it in any other manner.'

'So Mr Choksi,' Kabir began the interrogation. 'Do you normally advise banks to provide loans to certain underprivileged people or was there a specific reason you did so a few months ago?'

'I don't know what you are talking about.'

'Have you ever recommended to your bankers that they sanction loans to certain individuals in the past?'

'I don't remember any specific instance where I might have done that.'

Kabir Khan threw down a loan application on the table in front of him. It was an Axis Bank loan application, and along with it was an internal credit memo signed by the person approving the loan. An email from a relationship manager was attached with the credit memo. Nirav read through the entire document. Slowly and carefully. And when he looked up, his eyes were red. Whether from anger or embarrassment, Khan couldn't tell. 'What does this have to do with you, Mr Choksi?' he said. 'Why did you recommend to your relationship manager that the bank approve a loan for five Maruti Dzire cars, to be run as Ola cabs, for one Mr Patankar?'

Nirav Choksi didn't respond. The paper dropped out of his hand and fell to the ground. Krishnan bent and picked it up.

'Tell us, Mr Choksi, what did Patankar do for you to earn such a recommendation?'

'What does this Patankar have to do with anything?' Nirav asked finally. Almost in a whisper. He turned and looked at Vikram, who appeared to be equally clueless.

'Well, Mr Choksi?' Khan asked him again.

Just then there was a knock on the door.

'ACP Patil from Mumbai Police is here,' Krishnan's PA informed them.

'Why don't you take this time to think about what you are going to tell us?' Kabir suggested. 'We'll be back.'

Nirav's cell phone was confiscated and Vikram Rai was allowed to leave. However, he decided to stay till the discussion with Nirav ended. He knew how these conversations could get messy.

As Khan left the interrogation room, his phone rang. 'Kabir Khan,' he said, taking the call.

'Officer, what kind of joke is this?' It was a woman's voice.

The abruptness of the tirade took him by surprise. 'Sorry, who is this?'

'Divya Choksi. Nirav Choksi's daughter. Mr Rai just informed me that you have detained my father. May I know under whose authority you've detained him?'

'Well, Ms Choksi, we have been having some discussions with him, that's all. Don't worry. He'll be home this evening.'

Kabir knew this was a flimsy answer, but he didn't have a choice. He didn't want to let Nirav Choksi go till he had answers to his questions.

'I am coming there with our legal counsel, Officer. My father is an influential man. He knows everyone around. If anything inappropriate has been done to him, I will haul you over the coals.'

'I look forward to meeting you, young lady,' he said and hung up.

Kabir pushed open the door to Krishnan's cabin and walked in. ACP Patil was waiting for him. In the corner of the room were two men. Khan had met one of them on his trip to Mumbai and had seen pictures of the other.

100

'So, Patankar,' Khan said to the person who had come with ACP Patil. The man didn't respond. His face was swollen, and his knees were buckling. He struggled to stand straight. It looked as if he had spent the night in prison, being thrashed. 'Patankar, right?' he asked.

The person nodded.

'So, who asked you to get Subhash Parikh picked up from the airport?' Khan came straight to the point.

He looked at Khan with eyes open half their normal size. He folded his hands and brought them up to his forehead. 'I just got a call, sir. I am an ordinary taxi driver. I got a call and I organized a pickup.'

Kabir looked at him, his eyes shooting fire. 'Ordinary taxi driver, my foot!'

Whack!

Kabir's hand rose above his head and came down swiftly, connecting with Patankar's cheek. Patankar landed on the floor and rolled to his right. 'I want the truth, Patankar! Tell me, why did you send this guy to pick up Subhash Parikh. Who asked you to arrange for a taxi to pick up Parikh? As per the information we have, Subhash Parikh had spoken to Travel House for a cab. How did you come into the picture?'

Patankar kept silent. Blood oozed from his split lower lip and his body was wracked by pain. Still he didn't speak. This was the first time he was being brought face-to-face with Lakshmi Narain Sharma.

'You called your contacts at Travel House, found out who the driver was and got him drunk the night before. You sent Travel House an SMS from the driver's phone saying that he couldn't go, and that Lakshmi Narain would go in his place. Isn't that the story?' Kabir demanded. 'That explains why Travel House sent a message to Subhash giving him Lakshmi Narain's details.'

Patankar had a horrified look on his face. He didn't know what hit him.

'Actually, we don't need you to confirm that this is what happened. The Travel House driver has already given a statement. He is filing a case against you for spiking his drink,' Patil said. He had done the homework that Khan had requested him to do.

Sharma looked at Patankar, scared. He then turned to Kabir and said, 'This is the second time this has happened to me.'

'What?' Krishnan said.

'Yes, that's exactly what happened before the Mumbai blasts. He'—Sharma pointed at Patankar—'called and asked me to come to Thani's Bar in Dharavi. There he showed me a drunk man lying on the floor and told me that fellow was supposed to drop someone at the airport and asked if I would go instead. I thought it was an opportunity to make money and went. We were near the airport when there was a blast in the car. I thought it was a terrorist attack. The passenger died. I nearly died.' His hand came up to cover his mouth. He looked genuinely taken aback.

Kabir looked at both of them and then focused on Patankar. He was the key. He knew a lot more than he was letting on. The story was now becoming clear.

'So who were you working for?' Kabir asked. Patankar shrank into a corner. He was down on all fours. Beaten and scared, he began to fear for his life. 'Who called you?'

'Look, Patankar,' Patil said. 'You were a pawn; you were used. All of us know that. The more you shield the people behind this, the more you will suffer. I have all the time in the world. So has the DGP. We can sit with you till you die of the pain. Do you want us to do that?'

The look of fear in Patankar's eyes intensified. Kabir's mentor had once told him, 'Almost all the criminals in this world are foolish. Driven by greed, they commit a crime. They assume that the crime is a harmless one, for invariably they don't know the full story.' Kabir realized that Patankar wouldn't know the entire story, but the fact that he was a crucial cog in the wheel made him an important riddle to solve.

'If you tell us the entire story, we will request the courts to be lenient with you.' He walked up to Patankar and placed his hand on his shivering shoulder. 'And,' he said, increasing the pressure of his grip on the shoulder, 'if you don't, then you will be arrested and held responsible for the murder of seven people in the Mumbai blasts. Being called the mastermind is not as sexy as it sounds, is it?'

Patankar panicked. Mastermind of the blasts was too serious a crime. He started sobbing. 'I didn't do anything. I just followed instructions.'

'Whose instructions?'

'I don't know his name. We just called him Saheb.'

'Have you met him?'

'Many times.'

'He's the one who helped you get the loans for the cabs that you run.'

Patankar nodded.

Kabir crossed to his table and rummaged through a few papers kept on it. He grabbed a photograph and shoved it under Patankar's nose and asked, 'Is this that person?'

Patankar squinted at the photograph for several moments, and shook his head. 'No, this is not him.'

'What?' A surprised Kabir looked around the room. Visibly embarrassed. 'Look carefully,' he insisted, waving the photograph in front of Patankar.

'No, sir. This is not the person. I have met him many times.'

Kabir turned and looked at Krishnan. The latter came up to him, took the photograph from his hands and looked at it.

'If the person is not Nirav Choksi, then who is it?' he muttered as he dumped Choksi's picture back on his table.

From the corner of the room a scared Patankar said, 'Give me my phone; I will give you his number.'

101

ACP Patil fished out Patankar's mobile phone from his bag. He had confiscated it from Patankar when he had arrested him.

Patankar hurriedly took it from him and keyed in his password. He opened the contacts and began tapping on the screen.

Madhavan walked in at that moment. 'Did these bastards speak?' he asked. 'Our friend in the other room is really worried. He seems to be sweating a lot,' he said, referring to Nirav Choksi.

Kabir Khan smiled. 'I hope all of them sweat for the rest of their lives. We are about to get the phone number of the person who is the mastermind behind Subhash Parikh's death and the Mumbai blasts, considering he used the same MO in both cases. It is big—' He turned towards Patankar. 'Hey!' he shouted and lunged at him. The latter quickly turned and hid his phone behind himself, refusing to hand it over to Kabir. 'Hey, give me the phone,' Kabir thundered, mentally berating himself for not following up on his instinct sooner. He had sensed something was amiss when he noticed Patankar fiddling with the screen in the manner that didn't seem like he was searching for a contact.

Patankar was stronger than Khan had anticipated. By the time he was overpowered and the phone taken away from him, it had been reset. All the data had been wiped. Khan was furious. His lapse of concentration, albeit for a moment, had cost him a very significant clue. He grabbed a length of rope lying in the corner and started whipping Patankar. The latter squealed in agony. Krishnan ran up to Kabir and tried to restrain him. Madhavan too joined him. But Kabir was like a man possessed. It took them a while to bring him back to his senses.

Krishnan called in the forensics team. Fortunately, after thoroughly examining the phone, they said that the data could be restored. But they would need twenty-four hours to do it.

A constable opened the door and walked in. 'Sir, Mr Choksi wants to talk to you,' he said looking at Kabir Khan.

'I'll be there in five minutes.'

102

'I had never imagined that my last case would be so emotionally draining,' Krishnan confessed as they waited for the lift.

Kabir laughed in response.

'Given what Madhavan found, do you think we should stop treating the king like a suspect?'

'DGP!' Kabir said in mock outrage. 'Who do you work for? The king or the state?'

Krishnan grinned at Kabir's theatrics and the latter merely rolled his eyes as they got into the lift.

'I need to speak to my relationship manager,' Nirav Choksi demanded the moment the two of them walked in.

'What for?' Kabir Khan calmly asked him.

'I remember the case where I had recommended a loan for the Ola cabs. However, I don't have any evidence to support my case.'

'How will the relationship manager help?'

'Well,' Nirav explained, 'I always speak to my bankers on their recorded line for investment-related instructions. I want to see if in this case too I spoke to them on a recorded line. If indeed I did, you will have evidence of what I said.'

'Please do, provided we listen in on that call,' Kabir said, not taking any chances this time.

Nirav readily agreed. A phone was brought in and Nirav called his Axis Bank relationship manager.

'Yes, sir. I remember those loans. In fact I remember because we normally do not fund Ola cabs. However, in this case, we made an exception for you. After all, if we don't do it for you, whom will we do it for.'

Kabir snorted at the relationship manager's obsequiousness.

'Thank you! Thank you, it's very kind of you to say so.' Nirav smiled as he spoke, secretly hoping his stature with the bank would lead Khan and Krishnan to take a softer stance on him. 'I was wondering if we had spoken on a recorded line, or was it a mobile phone conversation.'

'Let me check,' the relationship manager said. 'May I put you on hold?'

'Of course!'

The relationship manager returned to the call a couple of minutes later. 'I checked, sir. You had called on our landline. All calls to the wealth management unit of the bank are recorded. As I mentioned earlier, we normally don't do such loans, however, this one was done specifically based on your recommendation, as you are a VIP customer.'

'Could you give me a copy of the conversation?'

The friendly relationship manager suddenly became a bit cagey. 'If you don't mind my asking, why do you need the recording, sir?'

'Just so that I too have a record of the discussion.'

'I will have to check bank policy, sir.'

'Yes, of course, I understand. If at any point you think this is becoming an issue, let me know. I'll speak to your CEO.'

'That won't be necessary, sir!'

'Can you please send the clip to my email ID and to another email ID that I will give you?' Nirav glanced at Kabir, and at his nod gave his email address, and disconnected the call.

It took the relationship manager half an hour to obtain the recording and send it. Dropping the CEO's name during the conversation had done the trick.

Back in the DGP's cabin, Krishnan, Kabir and Madhavan crowded around Krishnan's laptop to listen to the conversation between Nirav and the relationship manager.

It was a five-minute-long conversation about some investments that Nirav was authorizing the bank to make. The Ola cabs featured in the last few minutes of the conversation.

'You guys don't fund Ola cabs?' Nirav was heard asking the relationship manager.

'I'm not sure, sir, but I can check it out for you.'

'Someone I know wants a loan for five cabs at once. It won't amount to a lot, roughly twenty-five lakh.'

'Can you give me some details about this person, sir?'

'His name is . . .' There was a few moments' silence. Then Nirav's voice was heard again, softer this time, asking, 'What's his name? Your taxi fellow.' From the question and his manner of speaking, it was clear that Nirav was speaking to a third person.

That's when a third voice spoke: 'Patankar. Dilip Patankar. Stays in Dahisar.'

Nirav repeated the information to the relationship manager. 'Can I give him your number? I'll be obliged if you could help him out. I'll even make sure the repayments come in on time.'

'Sure, sir. Give him my number. Or else if you give me his number, I will make sure someone contacts him.'

'Great! That won't be necessary. He will get in touch. Thank you,' he said to the relationship manager before hanging up.

The moment the call ended, Khan turned to Nirav. 'Who was that?' he asked.

Nirav Choksi looked at him, lines of worry creasing his forehead. 'Aditya,' Nirav said. 'The other person on the line was Aditya.'

103

'If there is one man in this world who has not committed a crime, let him stand up,' a frustrated Kabir said.

A knock on the door distracted them momentarily.

'Yes!' he barked.

It was Kutty. 'There was a call from the chief minister's office,' he said.

'Hmm.' Krishnan nodded, raising his hand and asking him to wait. He looked at Khan. 'If we are done with Choksi, let's send him back. We can always call him again if we need anything.' Khan concurred. Krishnan gave instructions for Nirav to be taken back to his hotel and then turned to Kutty.

'Now tell me,' he said.

'They have decided to allow the excavation on the eastern side of the temple,' Kutty announced. Suddenly realizing that he had not given Krishnan the complete picture, he added, 'The site where they discovered two steps near the eastern wall of the temple. The chief minister is now keen to give the go-ahead to excavate further. He is afraid that in light of the multiple issues cropping up at the temple, if he doesn't give approval it will devolve on him.'

'So what do they want from us?'

'Any excavation needs to be signed off by the police chief from a law and order perspective.'

'Is that normal protocol?'

'Not normal, sir. However, since the area falls within the zone that has been cordoned in accordance with the Supreme Court order, they require your sign off.'

This was a distraction Krishnan didn't like. He wanted to get away from the extraneous temple drama and focus on the actual murders. Monitoring an excavation was the least of his problems.

'Tell them to go ahead. They can send me the paperwork later.'

'Okay, sir. Thanks.' Kutty walked towards the door.

'And listen,' Krishnan called out; he had just remembered something. 'These are the steps close to the vault, right? Make sure we are adequately covered from a surveillance perspective. Cameras covering all angles. Security personnel 24x7. Personally brief the ACP.'

'That will not be an issue, sir,' Kutty replied. 'We already have them.'

'What?' Khan asked.

'As a matter of precaution, the ASI had installed CCTV cameras on site when the digging of the road began. Standard protocol, sir. They have rules for all sorts of digging around monuments like the Padmanabha Swamy Temple. Accordingly, work cannot commence unless CCTV cameras are installed.'

'Okay, thanks,' Krishnan said, dismissing Kutty.

'Aren't the eastern wall and the excavation site close to the place where Kannan was murdered?' Kabir wondered out loud.

'Yes, they are.' Madhavan stepped in.

'How on earth did we miss the excavation site? And the cameras there!' Khan remarked.

Krishnan walked up to the table and rummaged through a few sheets of paper. He pulled out the list of CCTV installations in and around the temple. There was no mention of the ones at the excavation site.

'I think I know why it is not there,' Khan volunteered. He had been thinking hard. 'The ASI comes under the Ministry of

Culture, Government of India. They installed separate CCTV cameras on the site, apart from what the temple had. Given that there is hardly any collaboration between the state and the government at the Centre, there is a massive communication gap. Our list didn't show the installations by the central teams.'

'We need to get them ASAP. The CCTV cameras there are closest to the murder site.'

Kutty and Madhavan were promptly dispatched to get the feed from the Archaeological Survey of India.

The footage from the cameras around the ASI excavation site was easy to obtain. Madhavan had contacts in the relevant offices which enabled him to get the feed without having to make too many explanations.

Although Krishnan and Kabir were hoping for fresh leads from the footage, they were not prepared for what they saw—at 2.58 a.m. on the night of Kannan's murder.

Khan reached out and paused the video. He had a shocked look on his face.

'Can we zoom in?' he asked Krishnan bleakly.

The DGP just shook his head, too shocked to speak. Madhavan pressed play.

On the screen a scuffle was taking place between two people. One of them was Kannan but it was the other who raised eyebrows. Kabir and the others watched in horror as the murderer searched in the autorickshaw for something. Moments later, he emerged with a small tube and inserted one end of it in the vehicle's exhaust pipe and the other end into an unconscious Kannan's nostril. He waited for some time, nervously looking around to see if anyone was coming that way. Then he pulled out a small bottle from his bag, and poured its contents into Kannan's mouth. Although Kabir, Krishnan and Madhavan knew what would happen next, watching the killer part lift, part drag Kannan's lifeless body and push it over the tank wall was not easy. Clearly the killer did not share their sentiments, for he stood there and observed the body roll down, till it hit the water. And then Subhash Parikh turned and calmly walked back, as if nothing had happened.

Madhavan and Krishnan stepped away from the screen, wearing matching expressions of disbelief on their faces. Kabir, however, was still staring at the screen. At a point on the bottom left.

Someone was hiding and watching everything.

'Who—?

'What is he doing there . . .? How can he just stand there and not help poor Kannan?' Krishnan was aghast.

Kabir looked at the video intently. He paused the video and moved closer to it. 'He is not watching,' he said, a note of revulsion in his voice. 'He is recording. He is clandestinely recording the murder.'

104

The mood in the police headquarters was sombre.

'This case is getting weirder by the day!' Kabir remarked. 'Everyone seems to have a secret. Damn it! What is this? A murder fest?!'

Krishnan was pacing up and down when Sundari called. He answered the call with a curt 'What is it?' He didn't appreciate his thought process being disturbed. However, he realized his mistake almost immediately; Sundari was not in the best of health. He had to be sensitive towards her. He walked to the other end of the room, and spoke in soft tones.

'But then everything is unprecedented till it happens the first time,' Khan said, looking at Madhavan. When the other man gave him a blank look, he realized that he was responding to his own thoughts and not to a question Madhavan had asked.

'So Subhash Parikh,' Madhavan began, ignoring Kabir's flight of fancy. 'Now that we have clinching evidence that he killed Kannan, can we at least claim that we have solved one murder?'

'Technically, yes,' Khan said impassively. 'But we still do not know the motive. And catching the murderer without a clue about the motive is pointless. Particularly in this case, given that the murderer himself is dead.'

'And we don't know who killed him.'

'Or why.'

Kabir rose from his chair and paced around the room, distractedly running a hand through his hair. 'Subhash was killed a couple of nights after he murdered Kannan. The only person who knew that Subhash Parikh killed Kannan didn't utter a word about it. Why? We have no clue. Obviously Parikh was killed because he knew something which the killer didn't want the world to know. What *did* Subhash know that got him killed?'

'Let's go over what we know about that night.' Krishnan had finished his call with Sundari.

'Nothing,' Khan retorted. Their complete lack of information about the night Subhash was murdered was frustrating. 'The only thing we know is that he was awake at 12.30 a.m. when he called Lakshmi Narain Sharma by mistake.'

'The driver.'

'Yes,' said Khan. 'Sharma heard multiple people speak, and the only thing he could make out in the conversation was something about land in Surat. But what does Subhash Parikh have to do with Surat?'

'He was a known trader in bullion and jewellery. He had an antique showroom on Fifth Avenue in Manhattan. Not much is known about his clientele except that they were mostly foreigners and included the high and mighty of the world. He imported stuff from all over the place. He was raided a few times by the FBI, but they never found anything amiss.'

'All this information is available on the Internet.' Krishnan was dismissive.

'True,' Madhavan agreed.

'Who can help us make sense of the Surat link? Who would know?' Khan wondered out aloud.

'Let's talk to Nirav Choksi. Wasn't he Parikh's oldest friend? I think we should call him here,' Madhavan said.

Khan picked up the phone and dialled Nirav Choksi's number. It was switched off. 'Let's go to the hotel. We will meet him in his room.' And he walked out of the room with Krishnan. Madhavan stayed back.

Twenty minutes later, they entered Hotel Lotus Pond. Khan tried Nirav's mobile again, but it was switched off. On their way to the hotel, Krishnan had checked with the reception and had been told that Nirav was on the premises. Kabir checked the hotel manifest and called Nirav from one of the house phones. There was no answer. He tried leaving voicemail, but the message box was full. Annoyed, Kabir went back to the reception and told them that he was trying to reach Nirav Choksi. He mentioned that he was with the DGP, investigating the recent death of one of the hotel guests. The receptionist was spurred into action. She asked a colleague to man the desk and escorted them to the floor where the audit team was staying.

She knocked softly on the door to room 545.

'Coming!' Nirav answered from within the room.

Kabir looked at the manifest in his hand. The room number listed for Nirav Choksi was 543. He looked at the receptionist questioningly and passed the manifest to her.

'We changed his room, sir. The AC in his earlier room, 543, was giving trouble. So we shifted him here. Temporarily.'

'Have you got it repaired?'

'Not yet, sir. No unauthorized personnel are allowed on this floor. That's why we cannot get that done till the team leaves. In any case, we are not allocating rooms on this floor to anyone else.'

The door opened just then. Nirav stood in front of them in a towel and a T-shirt. 'DGP. Mr Khan. What a surprise! What brings you here at this hour?'

'We have a few questions,' Khan supplied shortly.

'Of course! Come on in,' he said, holding the door open for them.

Once they were all inside, he added, 'Though I can't help but wonder what it is that you could not have asked me when I was at the police station for the most part of the day.' He smiled.

'We tried calling. Your phone was switched off,' Khan responded, rather curtly.

'Well, I always switch off my phone at night. Old habit.'

Khan ignored that and came directly to the point. 'Mr Choksi, this is about Subhash Parikh.'

'What else could it be about?'

'Did Subhash Parikh have any connection with Surat that you are aware of? Any family ties? Any enemies? Business interests?'

'I don't know much, except for the fact that he had recently bought some land in Surat. A few acres.'

'How do you know that? Did he normally tell you whenever he made these investments?'

'No, he didn't. He had offered to help Aditya, told him that in case he wanted to start anything in Surat, he would happily give him a part of the office that he intends to build there. Apart from that, I have no idea about his connection with Surat.'

'Interesting. Did Parikh offer him a job?'

'He just offered him the space and infrastructure in case he wanted to seriously pursue jewellery designing and diamond trading.'

'If he had intended to build an office complex, it must be a large parcel of land?'

'Twenty-five acres, I think he said. Though I must confess, he tended to exaggerate quite a bit.'

They spoke for a few more minutes and then left.

As soon as they were out of the lift and in the lobby of the hotel, Kabir took out his phone and made a call. It was over in ninety seconds. By then the driver had brought the police jeep around and they climbed into it.

'Home secretary of Gujarat,' Khan explained when Krishnan gave him a pointed look. 'I have requested him for some help with recent large property transactions in Gujarat and asked him to check out the property that Parikh bought. Let's see if that gives us something to work on.'

105

It was midnight when they reached the police headquarters. Madhavan was awake and going through the Mumbai blasts charge sheet. Patil had brought photocopies of all three thousand pages of the document upon Khan's insistence.

'You're back! Good!' Madhavan said as Kabir and Krishnan walked in. 'I have been through these documents and don't have any intention of continuing with it.' He pushed the boxes to the side and asked, 'Anything interesting?'

'The only thing we've got is that Subhash Parikh owned a large parcel of land in Surat, something he bought a few months back.'

'How does that help?'

'Did I say it helps?' Kabir snapped.

'Chill! Chill!' Madhavan responded. 'You need a cup of coffee.' He had become good at this—diffusing tension.

Kabir realized his folly and patted Madhavan's back. 'Sorry,' he said. 'I—' His phone rang. 'Who is calling me at this hour?' he wondered, pulling it out to see who it was. Surprised, he looked at Krishnan and whispered, 'Home secretary. That was fast.'

He quickly walked to the other side of the room to get some privacy while he spoke to his old friend. 'Jadeja!'

Within a couple of minutes he was back with the team. 'Strange,' he said. 'They have checked all property transactions over the last two years for land parcels larger than one acre.'

'And?'

'Subhash Parikh's name does not figure in the list,' Kabir announced grimly.

'What!' Krishnan was stumped.

'Hmm. That's what it shows apparently. No property over an acre has been bought in the name of Subhash Parikh in the last two years in Surat.'

'Are they sure?' Krishnan sounded doubtful. 'That was real quick. I hope they haven't made a mistake.'

'Unlikely. There is an audit going on at their main data centre. So their key staff was on standby. Jadeja asked one of them to spool a report for us. Apparently there were only one hundred and twenty transactions in the last two years. He is sending the entire list across. It's possible that Parikh bought it in the name of a company. He felt that it might help if we went through it.'

'Wonderful,' Madhavan remarked dryly.

Two minutes later Kabir's phone beeped—a new mail had arrived. He quickly accessed his inbox: it was from Jadeja. He opened it and read what the home secretary had to say. Kabir was extremely impressed by the way relationships worked in this country. If you knew someone it was so easy to get things done. He downloaded the attachment on his phone and started going through the list.

Meanwhile, Krishnan briefed Madhavan on their visit to the hotel and the conversation with Nirav. His tale was interrupted by a loud expletive from Kabir.

'This is not possible!' he exclaimed from where he stood, phone in hand. Madhavan and Krishnan turned towards him in anticipation. He did not disappoint. 'Neither Subhash Parikh nor any company he was directly involved in bought any large parcel of land in Surat. But guess what!' he asked with barely suppressed excitement.

'Shreyasi Sinha!' he blurted before either man could hazard a guess. 'She recently bought a twenty-acre plot in Surat.'

Krishnan grabbed the phone from Kabir and looked at the document himself. There it was: Shreyasi Sinha, 20.3 Acres. Bought from the Gujarat government. It was land designated for use as a diamond or jewellery bourse.

'Why would she buy land which has been allotted for use as a diamond bourse?' Kabir asked, looking around for Madhavan who had gone back to the sofa and was reading something.

'Let's ask for a copy of the property papers,' Krishnan recommended. 'They should shed some light on the transaction.'

Kabir nodded, constantly glancing over his shoulder to see what Madhavan was up to. 'I presume what you're doing is of more interest to you than what we are discussing,' he sniped angrily.

Madhavan didn't respond. In the next few minutes, Kabir went through the entire property transaction list two more times, just to make sure that he was not missing something. He kept sneaking peeks at Madhavan. The latter's lack of interest was irritating him as well as distracting him.

'Is it possible,' Madhavan finally looked up and said, 'that Subhash Parikh's murder has nothing to do with what is going on in the temple or in Thiruvananthapuram?'

Kabir set down his phone and turned towards him. 'What makes you say that?' He was slightly irritated that Madhavan was going on a tangent.

'There's something about the connection between Lakshmi Narain Sharma, Patankar and Aditya that's bothering me. Aditya's recommending the loan for Patankar through Nirav Choksi, Patankar's changing drivers during the Mumbai blasts and for Subhash Parikh's recent visit to Mumbai—it all points to a larger plan. Clearly Aditya is involved. We need to arrest and interrogate him.'

Krishnan nodded his head. 'Our security personnel at the hotel have been asked to keep a watch and arrest Aditya if he leaves the hotel. In any case we will bring him in once we are done with what we are doing.'

'Okay.' Madhavan continued, 'Look at the guys killed in the Mumbai blasts. Gokul Shah, the head of the BKC Diamond Bourse. Akhil Shah, leader of the Zaveri Bazaar traders movement against the BKC bourse. According to the charge sheet, even Nirav Choksi was nearly killed in the blast. And now Subhash Parikh, who was floating a Surat diamond bourse. Ever wondered why people connected to the diamond trade are the ones dying?'

Kabir had a shocked look on his face. He had never even considered that angle. 'Why didn't I think of it earlier?' he muttered.

'Tamilians!' Madhavan said and tapped the side of his forehead with his index finger. Then, seeing the lost look on Kabir's face, he added, 'We're naturally smarter. No offence!' he said. Krishnan smiled.

'What rubbish!' Kabir retorted. Moving on, reasonably quickly, he asked, 'How do we figure out what's the connection?'

Krishnan's phone rang at that moment. Seeing who it was, he hurriedly answered. 'Thirumanassu?' He walked over to the other side of the room. Meanwhile, Madhavan continued his conversation with Khan.

'The cab drivers are just pawns in the entire game. Too small to be of significance. Aditya is an involved person. So it's unlikely he will say anything. The only one who remains is Nirav Choksi. He can possibly tell us. But he didn't say anything when we met him.'

'But wasn't he the one who told you about Subhash Parikh having bought some land in Surat?' asked Madhavan. 'So, chances are that he won't hide anything from you, if you ask him the right questions.'

'Boys, Dharmaraja Varma is on his way,' Krishnan announced, interrupting their conversation.

Kabir swore angrily. 'I have no interest in meeting him. I will wait in the canteen. Call me after he has left.'

'You don't have to. I am going down to the portico to receive him,' Krishnan said, leaving the two of them in his office.

Khan turned and looked at Madhavan. 'Getting back to our earlier conversation, let's bring him in. We'll send someone tomorrow morning and get him here. Otherwise we'll meet him at breakfast tomorrow.' It was almost 2 a.m. 'He is in room 545,' Kabir reminded Madhavan. 'Coordinate with Krishnan and the team. I am going to visit Kannan's widow tomorrow.'

'Room 545, eh?' Madhavan asked him. 'Is this the old room number or the new one?'

Khan was surprised. 'New one. How do you know they changed his room?'

'The DGP told me about this when you were perusing the list your friend Jadeja sent.' He pressed the button to call the lift; it arrived within a few seconds. There was no one else in the lift, yet it stopped on every floor before it reached the lobby. All through the ride, Madhavan kept eerily silent. Very unlike him.

'What happened? What's on your mind?' Kabir asked him as they stepped out into the lobby. He noticed a few of the king's entourage standing there. Dharmaraja Varma and Krishnan had probably gone up in the other lift. 'Well?' He nudged him.

'Just wondering,' said Madhavan and momentarily looked towards the ceiling. 'Why was his mailbox full when you called room 543? Anyone who is used to staying in a hotel invariably checks the mailbox otherwise the flickering light on the phone next to their bed will constantly irritate them all night.'

'Hmm . . .' Kabir waited for Madhavan to continue.

'Or . . . it could be that he didn't even know about the messages because they were left for him *after* he changed rooms.'

'But if someone had called him from outside, the hotel operator would have put them through to the correct room.'

'Unless someone called from *inside* the hotel, in which case they needn't have gone through the operator at all.'

'No point speculating,' Kabir said as he pulled out his phone and dialled a number.

'Who are you calling?' Madhavan asked, only to be ignored for his trouble.

Kabir stayed on the call, waiting for someone to answer the phone. Not many people were expected to be awake at that time of the night. Finally when it was answered, a pleasant, yet groggy voice came on the line.

'Well. The CBI doesn't normally call good people. And I know I am not bad. And if you are calling in your individual capacity, you need to remember that no one calls a good single girl at this hour.'

'For someone who just woke up, you sound remarkably sorted.' Khan smiled.

Madhavan raised his eyebrows.

'I am.'

Kabir Khan realized that this was not the time for flirting. 'I called because I need some help.'

'Don't you always? Tell me.'

Kabir ignored her jibe and asked, 'The telephone instrument in hotel rooms, how does the messaging system work?'

'As in?'

Kabir Khan hurriedly explained the context of the question to her. Pallavi was smart. She understood quickly.

'Well, the Lotus Pond has just upgraded their entire technology platform. Their servers, software solutions, key card mechanism, everything has changed. Believe me, it was long overdue. I specifically remember because we had a problem with our systems around the same time. We use the same vendor. Because he was busy with their upgradation, he messed up our schedule.'

'Okay,' Kabir said firmly which Pallavi was smart enough to understand meant 'Move on!'

'Whenever someone checks in, he gets allocated a message box centrally, which resides on the central server. The messages are saved there. Whenever anyone calls a room telephone and leaves a voice message, a light flashes on the instrument. If the room guest retrieves the message and listens to it, he or she is given an option to delete it. In case the guest does not check it, the voice message stays there till he checks out. The check-out process clears the mailbox automatically and moves the messages to a temporary folder on the server. After thirty days the temporary folder is overwritten and the voicemails purged. This is the default configuration of the system that they have installed. It is the same with us as well.'

'So the message stays there till it is deleted by the guest or after thirty days, whichever is earlier.'

'More or less,' she said. 'Each chain has its own benchmark, but it is all clustered around the thirty-day mark.'

He asked a few more basic questions. Satisfied with the information for the moment, he thanked her for her help and apologized for having woken her up.

'It is always a pleasure talking to you,' Pallavi said.

Kabir wondered if she really meant it. He was still wondering when he turned and looked at Madhavan who gave him a naughty grin. 'Oh stuff it! Let's go,' he said.

'Where to?' Madhavan asked.

'To our hotel,' said Khan. 'I need to check on something.'

'The king is here. Krishnan might need you,' Madhavan argued.

'That's his problem, not mine.' He grabbed Madhavan by the hand and dragged him away. In no time they were driving through the empty streets of Thiruvananthapuram, on their way to Hotel Lotus Pond.

106

At the hotel, after checking with Nirav, the receptionist sent someone to escort them to his room. Nirav was standing at the door. 'Back so soon, Officer? I thought we were done for the day.' He smirked.

'We need to go to your previous room.'

'It is no longer my room.'

'I know that, but we thought you could take us if you have the keys,' Madhavan said, suddenly feeling very stupid. They could have asked the reception for the keys to 543. Kabir would tell him later that he didn't ask for 543 at the reception because they would not have been granted access without proper paperwork. Now it would seem like Nirav had asked for the room key card as it was his room previously.

Nirav looked at the steward who had accompanied Kabir and Madhavan to the floor and asked him to bring the master key. The steward, who was probably from the housekeeping department, pulled out his own master key and opened 543 for them.

Kabir dismissed him with a quick 'Thank you'; he didn't want him hanging around. He followed Nirav and Madhavan into the room and shut the door.

'Do you access the messages that people leave for you in your room?'

'I do. But these days who leaves messages on your room phone? Especially when you have mobiles.'

'I wonder who left you these messages then?' Kabir said, walking to the phone on the bedside table.

Nirav turned towards the phone. The red light was blinking. Kabir activated the speakerphone. After a glance at Madhavan he took out his phone, tapped on the screen a few times and placed it next to the landline. He then reached out and pressed the message button on the hotel phone.

A voice crackled over the speaker: 'You have ten new messages.'

107

For the second time that night, Madhavan and Kabir sped through the deserted streets of Thiruvananthapuram. A tense Kabir was at the wheel, and in no time, they had reached the police headquarters. He got out of the car and rushed inside. Thankfully the lift was on the ground floor, else he would have run up the five floors to the DGP's office.

As soon as he entered the room, he stopped. Dharmaraja Varma was sitting on the sofa with Krishnan, Radhakrishnan Nair from the transport company standing beside him.

'I'm sorry,' Kabir apologized and turned to go.

'Stay!' Dharmaraja Varma called out. 'I am leaving. I came because I wanted to speak with Krishnan.' He stood up. Krishnan wanted to accompany him down the lift, but Varma stopped him.

'What did he want?' Kabir asked the moment the lift door closed, and the king was out of sight.

'He was angry.'

'Looked it,' Khan said. 'But why?'

'He was furious that someone went to check out the construction site next to the Kuzhivilakom temple, even though we'd been told not to.'

'Be careful.'

'I know. The king can be vengeful. His ego is hurt. And he will hit back.' He exhaled loudly and settled into his chair. 'Where did you guys disappear to?'

Kabir Khan pulled out his phone, placed it on the table and played the messages he had recorded in room 543.

By the time the last message finished, beads of sweat had broken out on Krishnan's forehead. The messages revealed a saga that, though not entirely unexpected, shook them out of their skin.

'What do you think we should do?' he asked Kabir.

'Confront him,' Kabir said without a moment's hesitation. 'We need to bring him in. We have enough evidence against him.'

Krishnan looked at Kabir and Madhavan grimly. 'Pick him up.'

A team of six police officers descended on Hotel Lotus Pond and arrested Aditya Kumar that night. He was quickly hustled out through a side entrance. The few journalists who had waited all night outside the hotel had no clue about what was going on.

108

Aditya was pacing in his cell nervously. His entire world had come to a grinding halt. He had been unceremoniously woken from his sleep and carted away by a group of six policemen, led by the ACP, Thiruvananthapuram Range, and brought to the police headquarters. No one had told him why he was being arrested.

'Why am I here? What have I done?' he demanded the moment Krishnan and Khan walked in.

'You don't know?'

Aditya didn't reply.

'I am so sorry! They should have told you. My sincere apologies,' Krishnan mocked. 'Let me dispense with the suspense then.' He glanced at Kabir before turning the full force of his glare on Aditya. 'Tell us now!' he barked. 'What is your connection with Dilip Patankar?'

'Patankar?' Aditya thought for a second and replied, 'I know him as a regular driver.'

'How did Lakshmi Narain Sharma end up going to the airport to pick up Subhash Parikh the day he was supposed to travel to Mumbai?'

'Huh? How the hell do I know? I didn't fix it up.' Aditya was adamant.

Krishnan could not counter that; Patankar had still not admitted anything. And the forensics team hadn't recovered the data that he had erased from his mobile phone.

'Then tell us why you killed Subhash Parikh.' Kabir took over.

'WHAT!' Aditya looked shocked. 'Are you crazy? I did not kill him!' There was no sign of remorse on his face.

'Don't lie!' Kabir oozed fury, in his expression and his voice. 'We know you wanted him dead. Tell us why.'

Aditya coolly rose and walked up to Kabir. 'Being asked the same question multiple times, in different tones, by different people will not change my answer,' he said, staring at him. He ambled back to his seat. 'I have said this before: I did not kill him.'

'Oh really?' It was Krishnan this time. 'Maybe you'll change your stance after this.'

'Nothing will make me change my stance. Because. I. Did. Not. Kill. Him.' He spoke slowly, enunciating each word carefully.

Kabir took out his phone and played the messages that he'd recorded.

'Trying to reach you. Call me back. It is urgent!'

'Where are you? Have been calling you on your mobile. It's switched off. Call me!'

'Nirav, I need to speak with you. It is urgent.'

'Nirav, I am worried. I am scared. Call me back. It is urgent.'

A few more similar sounding messages played out, and finally,

'Nirav, we need to talk. Aditya wants me to convince you to get out of the Zaveri Bazaar Union and get the other merchants to move to the BKC bourse. In return, he will give me the chairmanship of the bourse and a three per cent stake in the company. But the Surat bourse has been my dream. I can't give it up. He has a video of me which he is using to blackmail me. He is not to be trusted. If you don't agree, he wants me to hurt you. He . . . I don't know how to handle this. Please call me. I fear he will carry out his threat of killing me. Keep Divya away from him. He is extremely dangerous for all of you.'

At a nod from Krishnan, Kabir stopped the audio.

'So,' the DGP said. 'What's the story here?'

'I have no clue what he is talking about.'

'Are you sure?' asked Khan.

'Yes.'

'What video is he referring to?'

'I have absolutely no idea, Mr Khan.' Not a single line of worry creased Aditya's forehead as he faced Kabir and Krishnan.

'What were you doing at Padma Teertha Kulam on the night Kannan Ramalingam was killed?'

'Me?' asked Aditya, apparently stupefied. 'Why would I be there?'

'Look, Aditya,' Krishnan said very softly. 'We know that recording a murder is not on everybody's agenda. People normally step in and save the victim. You didn't. The least you can do now is tell us why you were clandestinely recording Subhash Parikh killing Kannan. We have you on camera.'

Aditya abruptly stood up and began pacing up and down the cell, nervously rubbing his hands over his face. He seemed worried, frightened even, like an animal that's been cornered.

Krishnan started to say something, but Kabir held up his hand and asked him to keep quiet. Sometimes, when left to themselves and forced to introspect, even hardened criminals softened up. Aditya was quiet. Very quiet. When he finally turned to face them Kabir Khan could see that his eyes were red. Blood red.

'I wanted to kill that bastard! I was scared that he would expose me to Nirav Uncle and Divya. I love Divya! I felt the only way to get out of this mess was to get rid of him. But I didn't kill him. Believe me!' he insisted. 'I didn't kill him.'

'Expose you? Expose what?' Khan demanded. Aditya didn't respond.

Krishnan picked up the conversation. He wanted the flow of information to continue. 'Well, if you threaten to kill someone, and the person ends up dead next morning, you better have a damn good alibi.'

'I—' Aditya paused. He was measuring his words and speaking very carefully. 'I did want to kill him. I even went to his room that night.'

Kabir and Krishnan exchanged tiny smiles. They were almost there.

'But . . .' Aditya trailed off.

'But what?' Kabir prompted.

'When I went to his room, I couldn't.'

'What do you mean you couldn't kill him? How did Parikh die then?' Krishnan asked, a touch of impatience creeping into his voice.

'Because he was already dead when I got there.'

109

Aditya's interrogation left everyone confused. He firmly denied threatening Subhash and wanting him to harm Nirav Choksi and put it down to the hallucinations of an old man.

'He is lying!' Madhavan declared the moment they were out of the interrogation room. 'There is no way that he did not kill Subhash Parikh! Absolutely no way.' He shook his head. 'It has to be him.' Madhavan was excited. 'Did you see how he evaded the question about how he got the key to Subhash's room? He is hiding a lot of things.'

'Well,' Khan said calmly. 'That apart, most of what he said ties in with what we already know. Let's take it with a little bit of caution. I have asked Mumbai Police to conduct a thorough search of his residence and scan the area for clues. We should be hearing from them any time now. Even the Kerala Police team that has gone to search his room at the Lotus Pond should be returning soon.'

'Warrant?'

'We will deal with it, Madhavan.' Kabir dismissed Madhavan's objection.

Krishnan joined the conversation. 'If for a minute we assume that Aditya is telling the truth, then who could have killed Subhash?'

'There aren't too many people who could have killed Subhash. It has to be an insider. Someone who chose the most opportune moment to commit the murder and palm it off on the wrath of the lord,' Khan said with a grimace.

'You are right,' Krishnan agreed. 'Murderers are almost always someone on the inside. Someone who knows the lay of the land and also has access to the potential victim. In this case, three people together met Subhash the night he died. A fact corroborated by Lakshmi Narain. If it is true, and if Aditya is not the killer, then it has to be one of the other two.'

'Our nth hypothesis,' Madhavan lamented.

'We can't ignore it even if it is the nth.' Khan went up to the window and opened it. He wanted some fresh air. They had been awake all night. It was morning now. The newspapers had come in.

Krishnan rang the bell to summon a constable and asked him to get them some coffee. He stretched and yawned. 'Let me call Sundari and tell her that I'll be late. I have an early morning meeting with the home minister.'

110

By noon, a Mumbai Police representative flew into Thiruvananthapuram carrying videos, photographs, documents and other items which had been seized in the raid on Aditya's apartment. Thanks to Kabir's relationship with ACP Patil and DGP Krishnan's conversation with the Mumbai Police chief, things had moved quickly.

Kabir was perusing all of those. There was an image of a trophy, an award that Aditya had won at Amsterdam, a few certificates, some credit cards, a few random hotel key cards, an envelope from Dior which contained an appointment letter—he had not lied to Divya about it—and a few photos of his worldly possessions, of which he had quite a few.

After some time, he casually picked up his phone and dialled a number again.

'Are you free now? Can you come? I need your help. I'll send the car.'

'I don't need the car. I'll be there. Just text me where you want me to come,' Pallavi said and hung up.

Krishnan returned from the state home minister's office in a very irritable mood. The sight of Kabir Khan sitting with Pallavi in his office irked him even more. He was about to give them a piece of his mind, when better sense prevailed. 'I need you for a minute Khan' was all he said.

'Sure,' Pallavi rose and walked out of the room.

'What happened?' Khan asked. 'You don't sound too good.'

'They are transferring me.'

'What?' Khan was shocked. 'You have a month left until you retire.'

'Yes. I am being transferred to the traffic department,' Krishnan said with loathing.

'Why on earth?'

'Inept handling of the Padmanabha Swamy Temple murders.'

'You are kidding me!'

'Does it look like I am?'

'But we are almost there!' Kabir was visibly distraught. 'We are closer to the culprit than we have ever been.'

'I think Dharmaraja Varma lobbied for it and he's pretty powerful. Clearly our going after Radhakrishnan Nair and Madhavan's visit to the construction site riled him. Our taking him on had to have some collateral damage. They can't touch you, so they are coming after me.'

'Damn! When is it effective from?'

'A couple of days, I guess. They are waiting for the chief minister to return from Delhi. Only he can sign the orders.'

'So we don't have much time to crack this.'

They were interrupted by a knock on the door. Krishnan scowled when he saw it was Pallavi. She ignored him completely and addressed Kabir. 'Tanveer, my technology head, just called. I may have something for you.'

111

'How is that possible?' Kabir was flummoxed. 'Could there be an error?'

'Unlikely.'

'Damn!' Khan was both excited and worried at the same time. He had to wrap up the investigation before Krishnan was transferred. Otherwise he would not get any support from Kerala Police. And without their support he wouldn't be half as effective. More so, he didn't want Krishnan to fade away like this. Officers of his calibre deserved to be celebrated.

'Is there a way to validate this?' he asked Pallavi.

'The only way is to call.'

'Call them?'

'Yes. Call as a tourist, saying that you forgot something there. It was not too long ago, right?' Pallavi asked.

Kabir gave her a wide smile. 'When you quit the hotel industry, come and join me.' He adored her.

'Do I have to quit the hotel industry for that?' she asked coyly. It took Kabir a few minutes to understand what she meant. And then his smile became even wider.

Khan looked at the key card in front of him. It had the hotel name and contact details. He looked at his watch. It was almost noon. Amsterdam was three and a half hours behind. It would be morning there. For a minute he contemplated waiting until it was night there. The late night shift in hotels was normally staffed with inexperienced and new staff, many of them trainees. It would be easier to talk his way through their ignorance of procedure. But he decided not to wait. They were running against time.

'Okay,' he said. 'Let's call now.'

Pallavi picked up his phone and keyed in the telephone number on the card. There was silence for a moment and then the line connected.

'Hotel Okura, goedemorgen!' came the operator's voice.

'Good morning,' Pallavi said. 'I'm calling from India. I need some help.'

Realizing that she was talking to someone who would not understand Dutch, the telephone operator switched to English. 'How may I help you, madam?'

'I was there in March this year, 16 March. Room 2160. I may have forgotten a photo album in the room. It is filled with my memories of Amsterdam. I was looking for it today, but I can't find it at home. In fact I haven't seen it since I came back. Could you please check if I left it behind?'

'You said room 2160?'

'Yes. Shreyasi Sinha. Room 2160. Although, could you double check the room number before you speak to Lost and Found? Just in case I've got the room number wrong.'

The receptionist could be heard tapping a few keys on her system. 'Yes, madam, it is room 2160.'

Pallavi looked at Kabir and smiled. She gave him a thumbs-up.

'Just one more thing, miss. My friend was staying at the hotel around the same time. If you can't find the album under my name in your Lost and Found, can you check if it was left behind in his room? His name is Aditya Kumar.'

Again the receptionist tapped a few keys. 'Can you spell out the name for me, please?'

Pallavi spelt out the name and the receptionist went back to work.

A few moments later she asked, 'Are you sure he was staying here? In this hotel? I can't find anyone by that name in our guest list.'

'That's all right. Don't bother. Now that I think about it, I don't think I took it out of my room; I must've left it there.'

'Sure, madam. Let me check. If you could give us some time?'

'Thank you, miss. I will call back in an hour.'

The moment she hung up, Kabir asked her, 'Is it what we think it is?'

'Worse. She certainly stayed at this hotel. But our friend didn't. Given that he won the award in Amsterdam, it is safe to assume that Aditya was in Amsterdam on those dates. However, he must have stayed at a different hotel. But then how did Shreyasi Sinha's key card end up with him?'

'Unless they stayed together and he unintentionally carried the key card back.' Kabir looked at it. 'It looks quite neat. Maybe he brought it back as a souvenir.' He walked to the window and went through the sequence of events in his mind. One of the items Mumbai Police had confiscated from Aditya's home in Mumbai was a pack of key cards. One of them was the key card of a hotel in Amsterdam. When Tanveer ran them through a card reader that hotels have, he discovered that all the key cards had been issued to Aditya Kumar—all except one. The hotel key card of the hotel in Amsterdam was issued in the name of Shreyasi Sinha. And the dates of their stay in Amsterdam also coincided. How had Shreyasi Sinha's hotel room key card landed up in Aditya's room? How did Aditya know Shreyasi? Was there an angle there which they couldn't see? If Aditya indeed was the one who killed Subhash, was Shreyasi an accomplice? His head started spinning at the number of possibilities this discovery of one key card had thrown up. The more he tried to unravel the different threads, the more entangled he got.

'Shreyasi Sinha!' he exclaimed. 'Where are you? You are the domino I am looking for. The first domino. All I need is to topple the first domino. Where the hell are you?'

112

When Kabir narrated what he had found out to Krishnan, the latter did not believe him at first. 'Strange. Very strange,' he said. 'One thing is certain. Aditya is definitely involved. He knows a lot more than he is telling us.'

'Well, if you look at it, the post-mortem puts the time of death between 2.30 and 3.30 a.m. Aditya claims to have gone to his room to kill him at around 4.30 a.m. Why? We don't know. We have someone who heard Subhash alive around midnight. The last of the messages that Subhash left for Nirav was at 1.30 a.m.,' Kabir reasoned. 'But how do all these timelines tie in?'

'So what are you hinting at?'

'I am saying that Alprax, which is the poison suspected in the post-mortem report, takes three to four hours to act. The victim does not realize that he is dying. He just falls into a deep slumber. Considering the time of death is between 2.30 and 3.30 a.m., and he was sending Nirav a message at 1.30 a.m., it's unlikely that the Alprax was the cause of death. It has to be something else.'

'What about the three empty strips of Alprax that were recovered from his room?'

'Well, they could have been placed there by the killer in order to mislead the investigation. Moreover, to kill someone Subhash's size, the killer would need over two hundred Alprax tablets.'

'You sound like a killer yourself. Do you realize that?' Krishnan chuckled.

'Well, I was in Delhi during the Sunanda Pushkar case. I followed that investigation very closely; some of the investigators were my friends. It was a similar story—murder in a five-star hotel. They suspected it was Alprax, but as the investigation progressed, they figured out that it could have been something else as well.'

As they stood there, looking out of the window pensively, Kabir said, 'It was an insider who killed Subhash.'

'And he is still in the hotel. But none of these people are hardened criminals. They are not people who kill for a living,' Krishnan said. Though it did cross his mind that if Subhash could kill Kannan so mercilessly, there was no reason to believe that the others were not hardened criminals. 'They haven't left a single decent clue. I'm afraid this might just be a perfect murder,' he lamented mournfully.

'There's no such thing,' Kabir said firmly. 'They must have left a clue. It's just that we haven't found it yet. When we get to the bottom of this, you will see that just like a perfect diamond has a flaw, even your so-called "perfect murderer" leaves a clue.'

'I wonder how they can commit a murder so easily. Even if I wanted to kill someone, I wouldn't know where to begin,' Pallavi said.

Krishnan turned and looked at her. 'Exactly what I was thinking.'

'But,' Kabir asked, 'if you were desperate to get rid of someone, what would you do?'

'Figure out what would work?' Pallavi responded.

'How?'

'Google?'

'Exactly!' Krishnan thumped his hand on the table. 'Khan, if any of these guys committed the murder, I bet they did some research online.'

Kabir's interest was piqued. His back divorced itself from the chair and his elbows came to rest on the table in front as he leaned forward to listen to what Krishnan was saying.

'The killers are not experts. At least that's what it is beginning to look like. They must have done some research on how to kill, or on the impact of their actions. None of them is a medical student or expert. So they must have accessed the Internet to get some information,' Krishnan said.

Kabir was thinking out loud. 'And the only way to access the Internet would be the hotel Wi-Fi or mobile data.' And after a moment's thought he added, 'They could also use a dongle. Or even a data card.'

'Correct.' Krishnan nodded. 'Kutty will be able to track all the mobile connections that exist in their names. The challenge will be getting the hotel to cooperate.'

'Let me check with Tanveer if he can help. His fiancée works there,' Pallavi offered.

Krishnan looked at her quizzically.

'Tanveer, my technology head who helped you decode the Amsterdam hotel key card. He used to work at the Lotus Pond. His fiancée still works there. We can ask her if she has access to the data on Internet usage and websites accessed.'

'Why will she do it for you?'

'Let me talk to him,' Pallavi coaxed. 'Why rule out the possibility of him helping. If he doesn't, you can go directly to the hotel to seek this information.'

'But that will take time. And that's a luxury we don't have,' Khan said, looking at Krishnan, the latter's transfer weighing on his mind.

Pallavi stepped out of the room and called Tanveer.

'We need to get this done, Tanveer,' she told him.

'I will ask her if she will help,' Tanveer responded. 'But I'm not sure she'll agree. She may get into trouble.'

'Tanveer, if she does, we will hire her. You can tell her that. If you want, I will have her appointment letter ready tomorrow morning itself. We'll be helping nab a murderer!'

'Okay, ma'am. I'll speak to her.'

'Thanks, Tanveer. We will need the Internet access details of all the members of the audit team, Divya Choksi and Aditya Kumar, plus their credit card details so that we can pull out the kind of transactions they have been doing, and their room bills. I'm sure the key cards will also tell a story. We need that information too.'

113

That evening, the first set of data came in. It pertained to the core audit team. One by one, they went through the list of website URLs accessed from the morning of the day Kannan was killed to the night that Subhash was killed. Tanveer's fiancée had asked for some more time to run the query and pull the data prior to Kannan's death.

'Nirav is gay, man!' Madhavan announced with a laugh. 'He was searching for gay porn. Did you see how he was ogling Kabir's butt? Now I know why!'

'Shut up!' Kabir yelled. 'Focus.'

Vikram Rai had been visiting antique sites across the globe, investment sites, Netflix and some random sites.

Subhash had been busy googling his own name and accessing his Manhattan store website. Narcissism at its peak. He had also googled the steps that had been excavated next to the temple walls and the underground drainage network of Thiruvananthapuram several times, apart from accessing a few mail sites.

Kabir and the others went name by name. Every single person was covered. But they didn't come across anything that could have been termed suspicious. They were about to give up when Tanveer called Pallavi. Possibly because of her closeness to Khan, she had become an integral part of his team.

After speaking to Tanveer, Pallavi looked up. 'He is sending some more data. A few other rooms as well.'

Kabir looked up from the bills that he was perusing. Bills from Aditya's room. Subhash's bills hadn't come in by then.

The second set of data that Tanveer sent, rather his fiancée sent, was explosive. After combing through it, Kabir showed it to Krishnan. It didn't take Krishnan long to figure out what the data suggested.

He called the ACP. 'Let's get a team together. We need to go on a mission.'

'It can't be far from the hotel perimeter,' he said looking at Kabir. 'Let's check every possible option within seven hundred metres.'

It was 7.30 p.m. Everything would shut by 9 p.m. They had to move fast. In no time a team of eighteen officers led by an ACP assembled in the porch of the police headquarters, awaiting instructions. Khan and Krishnan arrived a few minutes later.

It was the beginning of the end.

Part 3

114

Aditya's thoughts were interrupted by the sound of the key being inserted in the lock. He turned and looked at the door of his cell. A constable stood there, gesturing him to follow. Aditya stepped out of the lockup and walked with the constable to the main hall of the police station, housed in the headquarters.

As he entered the hall, he saw Divya seated there. Her eyes were swollen as if she had been crying. He turned away. He didn't have the heart to say anything.

'Why?' asked Divya when she saw him. 'Why did you have to do this?' She started sobbing again. 'You wanted to kill Dad! He loved you. He loves me so much that he agreed to let me be with you. What did he ever do to you?' She hid her face in her hands and cried, her shoulders shaking.

Kabir was leaning against the table beside Divya. Legs crossed at the ankles, he was observing the scene very keenly. He was the one who had wanted Divya to confront Aditya. The latter had been quiet so far. They had tried questioning him a few times the previous day, but it hadn't worked. They had desisted from using torture as a weapon given the profile of the people being investigated. He had to be coaxed into talking, and being confronted by Divya could just do the trick.

Aditya still didn't say anything. He even refused to look at Divya. She stood up and walked towards him. The moment their eyes met, overwhelmed with guilt, he lowered his gaze. He had failed her. She stopped right in front him, raised her right hand and slapped him.

'Hold it!' Krishnan yelled from his chair. 'This is a police station, young woman. Leave the violence to us.'

Divya glared at him and then turned back. Aditya hadn't shown any signs of breaking down. Overcome, she slumped down in a chair. Just then, Nirav walked into the police station. He was accompanied by Vikram. As soon as she saw him, she rushed into his arms.

'What are you doing here, Divya? You should leave all this to me.' Nirav had said the same thing when Divya had called him that morning to inform him that she was going to the police station.

'I am sorry, Dad,' Divya said and hugged him. Her sobbing continued. Her faith had been shattered. Her love life was in a shambles.

Kabir allowed the tender scene between father and daughter to continue for a bit. After which he led all of them to a separate room within the police station. He didn't want people to interrupt their conversation. Nirav had not filed a police complaint against Aditya for conspiring to kill him. However, the police had taken suo moto notice of Subhash's messages and filed an FIR.

'So Aditya,' he began the moment they had settled down. 'Why did you want to kill Nirav Choksi?'

'One day you say I killed Subhash Parikh. One day it is Nirav Choksi. Why don't you make up your mind?'

'Answer the question, Aditya.'

'You are going by the words of a senile old man and accusing me of doing something I did not do.'

'Do you mean to say the messages Subhash left on Nirav Choksi's phone were nothing but the hallucinations of a senile mind?'

'Exactly.'

'Bullshit!' Divya spoke up. 'He is lying.' She looked really upset. And angry.

'And what makes you say he is lying, young lady?' Krishnan asked, a gleeful look on his face. Strangely he was enjoying the conversation.

'I know Aditya. If he weren't lying, he would not hesitate to lock eyes with me. The very fact that he is unable to do so, means that he is not speaking the truth.'

'That's hardly an explanation,' Kabir scoffed.

'Have you ever loved anyone, Officer?' Divya asked him abruptly.

Kabir's face became red.

Krishnan cleared his throat loudly and said, 'Let's not get melodramatic, Ms Choksi.'

'Well, if he has, he would realize that people become very perceptive when they're in love. When you know someone loves you, you are blind to everything. But when you suspect the person you love to be cheating on you, the same issues which you would have ignored earlier now begin to tell a story.' Tears streamed down her cheeks as she said this.

Kabir was beginning to enjoy this impromptu lesson in love. 'What made you believe he was not in love with you?'

Divya hesitated. 'It is a long story, Officer.'

'Take all the time you need.'

'I would rather not talk about the past, Officer. Suffice to say that I know he cheated on me.'

'Aaah!' Kabir exclaimed. 'And when one cheats, it is fair to assume that he doesn't love you any more. Fair assumption.'

'I am still hoping that he is in love with me, though.'

'If he comes back to you, will you take him back?'

Divya looked at Kabir, anger rapidly replacing the tears welling up in her eyes. 'He tried to kill my father! And you want me to take him back?'

'Well, sure he tried to commit a murder. But . . .'

'But what, Officer?'

'But you actually beat him to it.'

115

'What!' Aditya exclaimed. 'What was that?' There was a shocked look on his face. For a moment he thought he hadn't heard Kabir correctly.

Divya looked up. Kabir was looming over her, his face expressionless.

'Are you freaking crazy?' she shouted.

Krishnan discreetly rang the bell and a uniformed lady officer stepped in.

'How could you even insinuate that, Officer?' Nirav stepped up in between his daughter and Kabir.

'What's the hurry? We will get there . . .' Kabir smiled broadly. He pushed Nirav to the side, and asked Divya, 'So tell me, Ms Choksi, when did you learn about Shreyasi Sinha?'

'Who?' Divya asked feigning ignorance.

'Would you like some help remembering, young lady?' Krishnan took out a photograph from a folder and handed it over to her. He pointed to a woman in the picture and said, 'This is Shreyasi Sinha.'

'I have no clue what you are talking about. Who is she?'

'Look carefully. Does she look familiar?'

'No.' Divya glanced at the picture and looked away, shaking her head. Krishnan looked at Aditya. 'Sir,' he said sarcastically. 'Do you know her?'

Aditya didn't even try to take the picture from Kabir's hands. 'Yes,' he said. 'I know her.'

'That's all?!' Khan ridiculed. '*I know her.* That's all you have to say?'

'She was a judge at the International Jewellery Design Competition which I won.'

'Was there a link between the two?' Krishnan asked. 'I mean between you winning and her being there?'

Divya looked at Aditya. He was standing there silently. 'She had no role to play in my win.'

'Aah! Then it was after the competition, is it?'

Aditya remained quiet. His silence spoke volumes.

Kabir looked at Divya; she had started to sweat by now. 'Are you certain you don't know this lady?'

Divya looked away, refusing to acknowledge the question.

'If you don't know who she is, what were you doing outside her room a few days before Subhash Parikh got killed?'

'All of you have seriously lost it,' she responded. 'If I am saying that I don't know her, why would I be outside her room?'

'Leave her alone! If she says she doesn't know her, she doesn't,' Nirav defended her vociferously.

'Let's see, shall we?' Kabir said, ignoring Nirav's outburst. He crossed the room and plugged in a pen drive into the computer and clicked on one of the files that showed up on the screen.

It was CCTV camera footage that Kabir had obtained from the hotel. After Tanveer's fiancée's data came through, they had explored the feed across the entire hotel. From the supers on the screen one could make out that this was from the twelfth floor at Hotel Lotus Pond, outside room 1203, right next to the service lift.

'Have you seen this room before?' Kabir asked Divya. He dragged the cursor and fast-forwarded the video. The time stamp on the screen said 01:43.

Divya recognized the date: it was Nirav's birthday.

The lift on the floor opened and Divya stepped out. She tiptoed to room 1203 and stood outside the door. It seemed like she was trying to eavesdrop on the conversation in the room. Slowly she took out her phone and dialled a number. She inched closer to the door and pressed her ear to it. Something distressed her, for she covered her mouth and turned away. The slight shaking of her shoulders suggested that she was crying. She stood there for a few moments before making her way back to the lift.

'Okay, let's fast-forward this now,' Kabir said, dragging the video to 03:21. The door to room 1203 opened and Aditya emerged from within.

'Do you want me to show you more?' Kabir asked. 'If you are wondering, the person in the room is Shreyasi Sinha.' He looked around the room. There was a stunned silence. 'Similar CCTV recordings of the day Shreyasi Sinha arrived from Singapore show that she checked into this hotel.'

Aditya was shocked. Till this moment he had not imagined that Divya or, for that matter, anybody knew about his transgressions.

116

'What I am wondering is how you figured out the room number,' Kabir said to Divya. 'It was a different floor, completely exclusive, three suites. How did you know the correct room?'

Divya realized that there was no point denying anything. 'By chance,' she said. 'I've had my doubts for a long time. That day, on Dad's birthday, when I returned to my room, I called Aditya. When he didn't answer, I went to his room. I have one of the key cards. He was not there. On instinct I pressed the redial on the hotel phone in his room. Normally people use hotel phones for room service, laundry, housekeeping, etc. This time the phone connected to another room. I knew something was wrong. After that it was just a matter of time. Most men get away with their affairs, for the women in their lives are tolerant. But if the woman is hell bent on finding out, a man can't hide an affair, no matter how hard he tries.'

Kabir didn't volunteer any information on how they had learnt about the relationship. The Amsterdam hotel key card that was found in Aditya's house was for a room which had been booked in the name of Shreyasi Sinha. That coupled with the fact that Aditya hadn't stayed in the same hotel in Amsterdam had raised questions. It didn't mean much, but it did suggest that theirs might have been more than a professional relationship. It was only when they started tracking Divya and her movements through the hotel on the CCTV camera footage that they discovered that Shreyasi was in the same hotel. And what a prize catch it was. Tanveer's fiancée's data had worked.

'Even the best of men make mistakes,' Kabir said.

'Yes,' Divya said, nodding nervously. 'They do.'

'It never occurred to you that you could also make mistakes?' Krishnan asked.

'What? What mistakes are you talking about?'

'If you want to kill someone, googling how to from your phone is the last thing you should ever do.'

Divya was stunned.

'Succinylcholine,' Kabir said. 'Heard of it? It is also called Sux.' Seeing the blank look on everyone's faces, he added. 'Last year, Dr Santosh Pol was arrested in Maharashtra for killing six women using Sux. It was in the papers.' He turned towards Divya. 'Any particular reason you googled him?'

'What? Why would I? I've never even heard of him. I don't remember everything I google. Do you?'

Kabir walked to the table and pulled out the papers that Tanveer's fiancée had sent. It was the document detailing the websites visited by everyone in the audit team as well as Divya and Aditya.

'On your father's birthday, you googled Santosh Pol and then accessed the article in the *Times of India* which outlined how he killed his hapless victims.'

'It is a regular news article.'

'Oh that it is.' Khan agreed, nodding. 'Here it is,' he said, as he pulled out the article and placed it on the table.'

'Sux' hard to detect in system
Umesh.Isalkar@timesgroup.com
Pune: Succinylcholine or Sux is a neuro-muscular paralytic drug used by Santosh Pol who allegedly kidnapped and then killed an Anganwadi worker and five others by administering it.

The drug causes muscular paralysis, but has no sedative effects; the victims could have been wide awake when Pol injected them, experts said. Senior critical care expert Shirish Prayag said the drug is used to relax muscles along with anaesthetic drugs when a patient needs to be intubated. 'It acts so quickly that we have to immediately put the patient on a ventilator to support respiration or he or she may die. The drug paralyses all the muscles in the body including those used for breathing. The drug is less commonly used now because better substitutes are available,' he added. Forensic science expert Harish Tatiya of state-run B.J. Medical College said, 'The drug cannot be detected easily as it metabolizes quickly into the natural components present in the human body. This makes its detection tougher.'

The methodology to detect the drug is not commonly available in India because Sux is not used for poisoning or killing someone, Tatiya added, cautioning that since it is injectable, it cannot be used to kill someone by a common person.

Succinylcholine is not an over-the-counter drug. It is a scheduled drug under schedule H of the Drugs and Cosmetics Act 1940, accessed against a prescription from a registered medical practitioner, a senior official from the state's Food and Drug Administration said.

'When you google the article immediately after discovering that your boyfriend is cheating on you, it doesn't mean much. When, after reading this article, you continue to research what Succinylcholine does, it is still not very significant. Even when you google "painless means of killing + sux", it can be ignored. However . . .' Kabir looked at the people in the room. 'However, if on the day you guys return from Kanyakumari, you step out at night and buy the injectable drug along with four strips of

Alprax, that raises not some, but many questions. Do you deny that you went out and bought these drugs the day you came back from Kanyakumari?'

'Are you guys so desperate to close this case that you decided to pin it on a kid? You call yourself cops. You should be ashamed of yourselves.' Nirav sprang to his daughter's defence.

'We'll see about that,' Khan said and ignoring Nirav he asked Divya again, 'Do you deny that you went out and bought those drugs?'

'I don't know what you're talking about!' She was embarrassed and it showed. Nirav had a surprised look on his face. Vikram Rai, who had been a silent spectator, was busy on his phone texting. Asking one of his contacts for help, presumably.

Divya bowed her head; she didn't want to say anything. It was only when a worried-looking Nirav put his arms around her to reassure her that she tearfully looked at him and shook her head. 'You know this is not true, Dad,' she pleaded. 'I did not kill Subhash Uncle.'

'A few hours before Subhash Parikh was murdered and a little before the CCTV cameras in the hotel went blank, the camera in the hotel lobby captures you rushing out. About fifteen minutes later, you surface at Menon Medical Stores, about half a kilometre from the hotel, and ask for Succinylcholine. The chemist refused to give you the medicine at first, but you bribed him and got what you wanted. Everything is recorded on the store camera. Your mobile triangulation also puts you in that area at that time. Do you still deny it?'

Not to be left behind, Krishnan added, 'There are very few stores in Thiruvananthapuram which stock Succinylcholine. It is not a commonly available drug. So it was easy to find out which store you bought it from.' He pulled out a copy of the bill and flung it on the table. 'There you go!'

Attached to the Menon Medical Stores bill was a screen grab of Divya buying the drug from the store. Though the bill was for some other drug, the photograph showed her reading the text on the injection.

'Not only did you buy Sux from there, you also bought four strips of Alprax,' Khan added. 'The proprietor of Menon Medical Stores has been detained for selling prescription drugs without a proper prescription. He identified you!' Kabir said with a flourish.

Divya was quiet.

Irritated by her silence, Khan said, 'I have asked the coroner to re-examine Subhash's body and have asked him to specifically check for Sux. The post-mortem is most likely to be positive. Everything points to you. Time to confess!'

Divya began to shiver. Nirav was sitting right next to her. He looked confused. A bit dull too. Probably falling blood sugar levels were beginning to affect him.

Krishnan turned to look at Aditya. 'While she's confessing, maybe you'd like to shed some light on why you wanted to pack off Subhash Parikh *and* Nirav Choksi, both?' And he raised his right hand and pointed it towards Aditya. 'You got lucky. Plain lucky! She killed him before you did.'

Kabir looked at Divya and then at Aditya. Neither of them spoke. 'So you don't want to speak?' Kabir asked them. Divya looked at Aditya, a look of disgust on her face.

'In that case, I guess it's time for a tête-è-tête.' Khan led Aditya and Divya out of the room, marching them briskly to another room at the far end of the corridor.

He opened the door and ushered them inside. The moment they stepped in, they came to an abrupt halt.

Sitting in the room, dressed in an orange sari, graceful as ever, was Shreyasi Sinha.

'Game's up!' Kabir sounded triumphant.

117

A few hours earlier

Shreyasi Sinha was in room 1203 of Hotel Lotus Pond when Kabir Khan, accompanied by a team of Kerala Police, knocked at the door. She had been in that room ever since she arrived from Singapore. By severely restricting her movements—going out rarely, keeping away from the crowd, staying away from the cameras—she had hidden fairly successfully. She had cut her hair short and streaked it grey to avoid easy detection. Even the hotel staff hadn't seen much of her, which explained why they were unable to confirm if she was a guest when the police were hunting for her.

The Interpol notice against her came in handy. It was easy to take her into custody.

She just requested the police to wait, changed into a sari, and walked out of the room, a picture of grace and composure. Kabir could see why, despite the age gap, Aditya had fallen for her.

In the interrogation centre at the police headquarters, Shreyasi denied any wrongdoing in the case of the Dancing Nataraja statue that she had supplied to the National Museum of Australia. The transaction was done through the Singapore Freeport, and the statue was shipped directly from the Freeport to the museum. While the transaction itself was not illegal, the fact that the statue was shipped into Singapore, held at the Freeport and shipped out directly from there, thus evading sales tax and luxury tax in Singapore, made it a federal crime. 'Every art dealer in Singapore does it,' she claimed. Kabir had no knowledge of the laws in Singapore. However, when she laid out the contours of the transaction, it made sense.

'Whom did you buy it from?' Kabir asked.

'HK Global Artisans Development Company,' she replied. 'Subhash Parikh's company.'

Kabir was both surprised and relieved. Shreyasi's confession clearly established a serious business relation between her and Subhash Parikh. It also pointed towards Subhash Parikh's involvement in the temple scam in Tamil Nadu. Whether he masterminded the entire operation or merely bought the artefacts cheaply from the perpetrators was still uncertain. When he asked Shreyasi this, she feigned ignorance.

'Subhash Parikh's store on Fifth Avenue was a front for all his activities. It lent credibility to his nefarious activities. How he carried them out, I have no clue,' she explained.

'Why would he agree to risk everything and hide you in the hotel? Records show that he was the one who booked the room for you. True, he booked it through MakeMyTrip, but the credit card he used for the transaction was his,' Khan said, mentally thanking Pallavi for figuring this out. When Tanveer's fiancée was looking through the rooms for which she had to pull out the Internet usage data, she discovered that there were two rooms for which the same credit card number had been provided as a surety. Both rooms were in Subhash Parikh's name, albeit one of them was in the name of Subhash *Chandra* Parikh.

'Because we were to get married,' she said calmly.

'Married?' Khan was stunned. Then what was Aditya doing in her room, in Amsterdam and here!

'Yes. But somewhere down the line, I felt that he was using me as a conduit for his illegal antique trade and that didn't go down well. We had an argument.'

'Why didn't you go to the police?'

'No one would have believed me. He was rich. He had the money, the contacts.'

'What is your relationship with Aditya?' he asked point-blank when he couldn't think of a more sophisticated way of asking her.

'He is a . . . friend.' There was a faint pause before 'friend'. 'I first met him at the jewellery design competition, in Amsterdam. We got close.'

'How did he end up in your room?'

'Is it a crime, Officer?' Shreyasi asked with a smirk.

'No,' Kabir hastily responded. 'But it seems unlikely that he came to your room merely to pocket your key and walk off. And here? Is he spending nights in your room because he is just a *friend*?'

'You are getting too personal, Mr Khan,' she remarked icily.

'Well, Ms Sinha, a man has been murdered. And more often than not it is the personal stuff that leads to murders. So it might be *too personal* for you, but for me it is bloody work! So shed this damn arrogance and answer my questions!' Khan barked. The sophisticated ways of the art world were beginning to irritate him. 'Let me ask again: What was your relationship with Aditya?'

'Just a friend.'

'I see!' he snapped. 'The 2 a.m. friend takes on an entirely new meaning here, doesn't it?'

Shreyasi chose to remain silent, though anger was building up inside her.

Finally Khan came to the question he had wanted to ask her all this while.

'Gujarat?'

'What about it?'

'Ever been to Gujarat?'

'Yes, quite a few times. Why?'

'In the last two years?'

'Not in the last two years.'

'Business interests in Gujarat?'

Shreyasi seemed flustered. Beads of sweat dotted her forehead and neck. 'No,' she said, but there was no conviction in her voice.

'Maybe then you can explain the twenty acres of land you bought in Surat last year.'

'Just an investment. Had some free cash, so I bought it.'

'Who had some free cash?'

She didn't respond.

'Who had some free cash, Ms Sinha?' Khan repeated forcefully.

'If memory serves me right, this land was bought in return for some artefacts and antiques that we had supplied to some diamond jewellers in Surat.'

'Any reason why Mr Parikh had your power of attorney and executed the transaction on your behalf?' He sprang the surprise question. The property papers that he had asked for clearly showed that Subhash Parikh had bought the property using the general power of attorney given by Shreyasi Sinha.

'As I told you, we were going to get married. He used to take care of these deals for me in India. It was difficult for me to travel every few days to collect payments from customers.'

'Strange! Given that he himself was a New York-based art dealer.'

Shreyasi fell silent. The problem with lying was that while the first few lies were thought through, the subsequent ones tended to fall apart. That's why no liar ever emerged unscathed from a sustained interrogation. Their ability to connect all the lies in a cohesive story diminished with every subsequent lie. Shreyasi was fast reaching that point.

'Did you have any plans for the property or was it just an investment?'

'Subhash wanted to do something with it. I'm not sure what,' she replied, regaining some of her nonchalance. 'But now with him dead, I guess I will just sell it and move on.'

'Are you sure?' Kabir asked her, raising an eyebrow.

'Of course! *I* have no interest in Surat.'

'Have there been any more transactions like this? Transactions where he used your power of attorney to buy property?'

Shreyasi thought for a while, and then shook her head. A feeble 'No' escaped her lips.

Kabir asked her a few more questions and left. He wanted to put Aditya, Divya and Shreyasi in the same room and question them together and see where it all led to.

As he sorted through the ideas crowding his mind, one thought stood out: Did Shreyasi too have an interest in seeing Subhash dead?

118

Present

Aditya acknowledged Shreyasi with a subtle nod. Divya completely ignored her and walked to the far end of the table and sat down.

'So,' Kabir began. He had been through such situations many times in the past. 'Ms Sinha says that her relationship with Aditya was a *friendly* relationship.' He intentionally started off with a statement which was sure to rile up Divya.

There was a moment's silence and then—

'*Really?*' Divya drawled. She had taken the bait.

Kabir nodded. 'In which case, there was no need for you to have clandestinely eavesdropped outside her room.'

Shreyasi looked at Divya in horror. This was the first time she had heard that someone was eavesdropping on her.

'I have said before, I trust my instinct more than what anyone may have to say. What I heard in the room is enough for me to know that what was going on in that room was not between *just friends*,' Divya responded, dripping venom with every word.

'What's with her? She is talking crap, Officer.' Shreyasi was taken aback by Divya's tirade.

'Coochie-cooing with someone in your room while his girlfriend is asleep is not my definition of a friendly relationship,' she spat. 'Scheming, plotting, strategizing! Friends my foot!'

'Scheming?' Krishnan caught on to the word. 'Scheming about what?'

'The Surat diamond bourse!' she declared.

'Aah!' Kabir Khan exclaimed. His lips stretched into a wide smile. This is what he had wanted to hear. It was what he had imagined all along. The snatches of conversation that Lakshmi Narain Sharma had heard over the phone at midnight, a few hours before Subhash Parikh died, had given him the idea. There was no reason for Surat to be mentioned in a hostile conversation unless there was something big at play. Kabir liked the way this was playing out.

'So it was more than a romantic liaison?' He egged Divya on.

'They wanted to usurp Subhash Uncle's land.'

'Subhash Parikh?'

'Yes! Yes! Subhash Parikh,' Divya replied testily.

'Go on!'

'Apparently Subhash Uncle had a large parcel of land in Surat which was bought in her name.' She pointed towards Shreyasi. 'When they were in a serious relationship. Now both of them wanted to bump off Subhash Uncle to take control of that land.'

'That's not true.' Shreyasi reacted. 'I bought it. It was mine. It is in my name. I don't have to bump off anyone to take back what is mine.'

'Aditya has confessed to having schemed to pack off Mr Parikh, Ms Sinha. So there's no point denying it. His confession is on tape and is admissible as evidence in court.'

'What does that have to do with me?' Shreyasi asked. 'If he says he had planned it, then ask him. Why are you asking me?'

Aditya looked stunned.

Khan turned towards Shreyasi. 'So you're saying that you were not a part of his plan to kill Subhash.'

'Not at all. I have no clue what is being spoken of here.'

The door opened and Madhavan walked in. He crossed over to Khan and whispered something. The two of them left together.

Khan returned some moments later carrying a document. There was an uneasy silence in the room.

'How about you tell us what happened in room 1203'—he pointed towards Shreyasi Sinha—'the night Subhash Parikh was killed.'

No one responded.

Aditya looked down at his shoes. Shreyasi looked at Aditya. And Divya looked at both of them.

'Perhaps Ms Choksi could tell us . . .' Kabir suggested. 'Seeing as these two don't want to.'

'There was a huge argument going on in the room when I reached there.'

'What argument? Between who all?'

'Them and Subhash Uncle.'

'How do you know?'

'I recognized their voices.'

'And what was the argument about?'

'Like me, Subhash Uncle had also discovered their relationship a few days ago. There was a fair bit of unpleasantness. While I was happy that Subhash Uncle had found out about them, what got me worked up was that they wanted him to kill Dad.'

Khan looked at Krishnan, who had been silent all along. They were getting somewhere.

'Why would they want your father dead?'

'Apparently Subhash Uncle wanted to set up a diamond bourse on the land he had bought in Surat.'

'He? You mean he had bought the land in Surat?'

'Yes. That's what they were saying.'

A cynical smile creased Shreyasi's face when she heard Divya say this.

Oblivious to Shreyasi, Divya continued. 'There was a huge argument about that. Subhash Uncle felt that setting up a bourse in Surat would do wonders for the diamond trade. Compared to Mumbai, Surat would be a lot cheaper and more effective for a diamond bourse. Labour and realty are cheaper. The travel time is less. The space is larger. There are many of benefits. But the only hitch was that it would kill the already tottering BKC bourse. The diamond trade in Mumbai would be split between Mumbai and Surat. Most likely in favour of the latter. And that would sound the death knell for the Mumbai trade. This woman here, she didn't want any of that. She wanted to sell the land and keep the money. Aditya was more dispassionate. He offered Subhash an alternative. Kill Dad, sell the Surat property, split the money and become the chairman of the BKC Diamond Bourse.'

'How would killing your father help?'

'Dad is very influential in the diamond trade in Zaveri Bazaar.'

'Yes, so we've heard.'

'Today, only twenty per cent of the BKC Diamond Bourse is occupied. Dad calls it a bhoot bangla. Low occupancy has rendered it commercially ineffective. The bourse is losing crores every month. But no one is moving there, because the entire diamond and jewellery trade ecosystem is around Zaveri Bazaar. BKC has been plagued with issues—connectivity, traffic, apathy, high rental and capital values—which make recreating the Zaveri Bazaar model very difficult. Impossible, actually.'

'So why your father?'

'Dad has always been very vocal against the BKC bourse. And until he gives the go-ahead, the Zaveri Bazaar jewellery union will not move. Dad knows that while moving there will be good for the big and rich traders, a large number of the lower-end traders will go out of business. He has been talking to them and convincing them not to fall prey to it. Even our neighbour, Akhil Uncle, wanted to sell his property and move, but Dad talked him out of it. Poor man was killed in the Mumbai blasts, last year. Dad could have been killed too, but luckily he survived.' A single tear escaped from her eye and rolled down her cheek. 'This is what he gets for being so nice to them. For taking up the cudgels on their behalf. For helping out people whose life depends on Zaveri Bazaar.' She was sobbing now. 'Subhash Uncle protested for some time. But then they showed him some video, and . . . and he fell in line. I am not sure what was on the video. But I guess the position of a chairman of the BKC bourse was too good to pass up on. He agreed to kill Dad that night.' A steady stream of tears flowed down her cheeks.

Kabir unceremoniously shoved a box of tissues in Divya's lap and turned to Shreyasi. 'So the battle that you had in your room was because he wanted to set up the Surat diamond bourse and you didn't?'

'As I said, Mr Khan, the land is in my name. 'It is mine. Subhash was only helping out. Why would I need anyone's permission to sell my own land? What kind of stupid logic is this?' With her right hand she tucked her short hair behind her ears and continued, 'This girl here is jealous because of her boyfriend and—' She didn't complete the thought. 'What she's saying is rubbish! And you are believing her.'

Kabir had seen far too many tears and too much bravado during interrogations to be taken in by these two women. He turned to Aditya.

'And you, what do you have to say about this?' He waved the document he had brought with him a little while ago.

'Power of attorney. The one that is in Subhash's name. Given by Ms Sinha,' announced Khan. 'The only thing of significance here is that the power of attorney expires six days from now.'

'So?'

'Subhash had struck a deal for selling the property. He was stopping in Mumbai on his way to Surat. To sell the property. Why not kill him before he transferred the property to someone else using this power of attorney and pocketed the money himself? How's that for motive?' Kabir looked at Krishnan. The latter nodded in agreement. 'And what better than to threaten him into killing the thorn in your flesh, before you eliminate him?'

'I could have just withdrawn the power of attorney,' Shreyasi said reasonably. 'Wouldn't that have been easier to do than killing him?'

'You would have to go to Surat for that. And given the current state you are in, stepping out of the hotel would be fraught with risk. You could have been seen and arrested. Interpol has issued a notice for your arrest.'

'Mr Khan, had you not been a CBI officer, I'm certain you would have found your calling as a writer of crime thrillers,' Shreyasi Sinha remarked casually. 'What you are saying is a figment of your exceptional imagination.' She glanced at Aditya. 'For a minute assume that we did want to kill Subhash Parikh for the land. Why would we have any interest in killing Nirav Choksi? It is preposterous of you to even suggest that.'

'Well, wasn't that the discussion in your room that night? From what I have heard so far it seems the well-being of the BKC bourse can only be ensured if Nirav Choksi is out of the picture. What's your interest in the bourse? I will figure it out. Sooner than later.'

Kabir walked out, followed by Krishnan. They decided to give the three of them some time with each other in the same room. Putting them together in the presence of non-intrusive police personnel might make them talk. In any case the room was wired and they could track everything going on inside.

119

After Kabir Khan and Krishnan left, a visibly shaken Nirav waited in the visitors' hall of the police station, hoping for a miracle. 'I had not bargained for this when I signed up with you,' he told Vikram Rai. 'My life is falling to pieces,' he lamented. With teary eyes, he buried his face in his palms.

Vikram Rai gently patted his back. The man needs help, he thought sympathetically. His friend is dead. His daughter is being held for the friend's murder. His future son-in-law is being held for planning to kill him. Everything around him is collapsing. Vikram continued rubbing Nirav's back as if to offer solace. 'It will all be all right,' he said.

At the other end of the complex, in the DGP's office, Krishnan flung his cap on the sofa as he walked into the room. It had been a tiring morning for them. Interrogations were never easy for the interrogators—the strain was as much mental as it was physical.

The phone started ringing the moment he sat down. Normally all calls were routed through his secretary, but since she was not there, all the calls were coming directly to him.

'I warned you! It is karma. It is the will of the lord.' Dharmaraja Varma sounded hysterical. 'Can't you see what is happening to a happy family? If this is not the will of the lord, what is it?'

'We are still investigating, Thirumanassu. Let's see how it shapes up.'

'Tell the court-nominated team that this is what is in store for them if they continue with their blasphemous work. The best thing they can do now is pack up and leave. The lord's wealth needs to be left to Him to manage. Humans have no jurisdiction over it.' And he hung up just as abruptly as he had begun.

Madhavan was in the room. He had not joined the interrogation. Kabir briefed him on the happenings in the past few hours. Madhavan too appeared confused. 'So it was Subhash who was the temple raider?'

'That's what Sinha claims.'

'Somehow the story does not sound believable. Why wouldn't Divya tell Nirav what had happened rather than take matters into her own hands? Why would Aditya change the entire cab arrangement for Subhash, if he was going to kill him anyway? If he knew that Subhash wasn't going to make it to Mumbai, then why leave a trail?'

Khan kicked off his shoes, sat down on the sofa and put his feet up on the table in front. His eyes closed involuntarily. He went over the facts of the case again; there had to be something that he was missing.

Aditya was in a relationship with Shreyasi Sinha. They had evidence to prove that: the Amsterdam hotel key card and CCTV camera footage that showed him entering her room at the Lotus Pond in the middle of the night. There was no denying that he was cheating on Divya—a fact that she had figured out. The argument that night between Aditya, Subhash and Shreyasi was also something which she had overheard. The CCTV camera images showed her standing outside the room and listening at the door. She had rushed out well past midnight to buy certain drugs, which were in all likelihood used to kill Subhash. Aditya had confessed to entering Subhash's room at 4.30 a.m. with the intent to kill him, only to find that he was already dead. Aditya's confession was not backed by evidence, but it tied in with what they knew about Subhash's death. He was playing it safe. At best, he could be held for trespassing, but not murder.

Was it so simple? Why did all of it have to happen in Thiruvananthapuram? Why to the team handling the temple audit? He was a bit confused.

A knock at the door interrupted his flow of thoughts. 'What?' he demanded crossly.

An ACP stuck his head inside the doorway and asked, 'Can we take them back to the lockup, sir?'

'Hmm.' Kabir nodded. 'The three whom we interrogated. Let the other two leave.'

The ACP nodded and left.

Khan took out his phone and replayed the voicemails Subhash had left for Nirav. Just what was he trying to tell Nirav. One by one he heard all the messages again. Nothing stood out. No hidden meaning. No hidden message. He was about to turn off the audio when he heard a noise. Very faint, almost inaudible. He suddenly perked up. Where had that come from? He had missed it all along.

He played the last message over and over. It was sent at 1.32 a.m. Hurriedly he sought out Krishnan, and together they headed to the forensics department. The message was played on audio amplification equipment, at a decibel level fifteen times the original. Pallavi too had come by then. Khan had asked her to stick around as much as she could—her hotel contacts were proving invaluable.

The message was played again. Just before the end, Kabir paused it, asked everyone to be silent and then resumed it. The feeble noise that he had heard at the end of the message was quite loud, yet Kabir couldn't figure out what it was.

'Doorbell,' said Pallavi. 'That's the doorbell. A soft, non-intrusive doorbell.'

120

'Madhavan!' he called out.

Madhavan was at the far end of the room sorting out the Mumbai blasts charge sheet papers. They had to be put back into the box and stored away safely. He was taking stock of the core charge sheet document and the exhibits. He didn't hear Kabir.

Just then, Krishnan's phone rang. 'Home minister's office,' he said as he walked away to a corner of his room to take the call, as he normally did. He returned in forty-five seconds. 'I've been summoned,' he said making sure that only Kabir could hear him. 'The chief minister's back today. They want to issue the orders today as soon as possible.'

'Damn! Assholes!' Khan said. 'When do you have to go?'

Krishnan looked at his watch and said, 'It's a fifteen-minute drive, so I'll leave in two hours.'

'That's more than enough time. We will nail this before that,' Kabir said determinedly. He turned towards Madhavan and yelled. 'MADHAVAN!'

This time Madhavan heard him, 'Yes?'

'Can you quickly get me the Menon Medical Stores video?'

Within five minutes Madhavan was back with a pen drive, which had the CCTV images from the medical store. He plugged it into his laptop and played the video on the screen.

The moment the video began, Kabir swore viciously. 'Damn! What the hell is going on?'

'Why? What happened?' Madhavan asked him.

'I can't believe we missed this!' he muttered angrily. 'We made a hypothesis and went all out to prove it, without realizing the hypothesis could be flawed. We were looking for reinforcers rather than real evidence.'

'Missed what?' Madhavan asked patiently.

'Pallavi!' Kabir yelled, ignoring Madhavan's query.

'Not so loud! I'm right here!' Pallavi admonished.

'Sorry! Sorry!' he said sheepishly. 'Where is the key card report? The details stored in the key cards of the rooms.'

'Tanveer's fiancée had said she would send it this morning. Let me check if it has come.' She turned on her laptop and checked her mail. 'It has come,' she said.

Kabir came closer and peered at the screen.

'The key card captures movement in and out of the room, and records the times when the door is opened or closed, either with or without the key card. This is a recent upgradation, so not many know about it,' Pallavi explained while Kabir tried to make sense of the report.

'According to this report, Subhash Parikh's door was opened five times that night. At 12.36 a.m.—I guess that's when he came back to his room after meeting Aditya and Shreyasi. Then at 1.32 a.m., 1.46 a.m., 4.33 a.m. and 4.37 a.m.'

'So?' Madhavan asked. He had not understood a word of what Kabir had said.

Kabir motored on. He was excited. 'Divya left the medical store at 12.38 a.m. The store is ten minutes from the hotel. Add five minutes for walking from the hotel entrance to Parikh's room. She would not have been outside his room before 12.50-12.55 a.m. But there is a catch here.' He pulled out the data that had come from the lift sensors. 'Because of the increased security the only way to get to Subhash's floor is using the lift, but not a single lift stopped there between 12.45 and 1.30. Which means that no one came to the floor around the time we assumed Divya came and killed him. The post-mortem report is very clear. It says that he died between 1.30 and 2.30 a.m. We missed this simple connec—'

'Hold on!' Pallavi interrupted. She pointed to the door-opening pattern of Divya's room. 'Her door was opened at 12.53 a.m. using her key card—this is probably when she returned from the medical store. Then at 1.12 after which it wasn't shut till 1.28. But who opened it and why did it remain open for *sixteen minutes* at an hour past midnight? There's something fishy here. Clearly she left the door open, went somewhere—probably to kill Subhash—came back, shut the door and went off to sleep. No?'

'Unlikely, because Subhash's door is opened only at 1.32. The last time Divya's door opened or shut that night is at 1.28 a.m. Which means she could not have rung the bell outside Subhash's room at 1.32 a.m. Had she done that, her room door would have opened at least once more after that, but it didn't; not until morning, and then too from the inside. Divya was in her room at night. She couldn't have killed Subhash. Remember, they all overslept the morning after they returned from Kanyakumari?' Kabir Khan argued. 'She couldn't have done it.'

From Aditya's key card data, it was evident that he was the one who had walked into Subhash's room at 4.33 a.m. So he was not lying. They examined the data from the key cards of the other people in the audit team. It was painstaking work, but at least they were heading in the right direction. Khan was worried about Krishnan's transfer. It was playing on his mind.

'Madhavan,' he called out abruptly. 'Can you get me the calls made between the rooms occupied by the extended temple team that night? Extended means everyone including Divya, Aditya and Shreyasi. Both hotel phones and mobile numbers.' He went up to him and spoke in an urgent voice. 'Bulldoze your way through, Madhavan. We are short on time. If we don't kill this issue right now, I will always hold myself responsible for screwing up the retirement of a decorated officer.' He gestured towards Krishnan who nodded. 'Go personally to Lotus Pond and get this done,' Krishnan added.

Madhavan dumped the charge sheet papers he was holding and stood up. 'These have to go today. I promised ACP Patil that they would be with him tomorrow.' In the normal course they would have asked someone from the team to do this, however, since Patil had shared the papers with them at a personal level, they didn't want to get anyone involved.

Kabir nodded absently. 'I'll put them in the box,' he said as he began packing the stuff Madhavan had left, into the box. A few annexures to the charge sheet, the three-thousand-pages-long main document, a few press clippings focusing on those killed and their families and the impact on ground. He had met all of them when he had gone to Mumbai, especially the survivors. He flipped through the newspaper cuttings distractedly—interviews with families of victims a few days after the blasts and pictures full of grief and tragedy.

Suddenly Kabir stopped. One particular picture had caught his attention. He pulled out his phone, opened the gallery and scrolled it until he found a picture that he had saved many weeks ago. His hunch was right.

He called a number.

'Hello. Who is this?'

'Hi. My name is Kabir Khan, from the CBI. We met a few days ago. I hope you remember?'

'Oh yes, Mr Khan. How are you?'

'Fine, thank you, ma'am. I know we spoke at length when we met, but I have a small query. I just happened to see a picture of you with some other people in the *Times of India*. It was carried immediately after the blasts. Could you tell me who those people are? Do you recall the picture I'm talking about?' he asked, and after a pause added, 'I can WhatsApp it to you in case—'

'No, that won't be necessary,' she said softly. 'I remember the picture. A lot of newspapers carried just my photograph but only one newspaper which carried the family picture . . .' She fell silent.

'Ma'am?' Kabir prompted. 'Who are the other people in your picture that *TOI* carried?'

'My husband and my son.'

'He's a fine young man, I must say. Where is he these days?' Silence.

'Ma'am?'

He heard a slow sob. He held on. 'I am sorry, I didn't mean to upset you.'

'It's all right, Mr Khan,' she said stifling her sobs.

They spoke for a few minutes more after which Kabir disconnected the call and yelled out for the ACP.

'Are all of them still in the room, or have you taken them back to the lockup?'

'Still there, sir. I was on my tea break. I haven't been to the interrogation room. Should I—'

'That's okay, don't bother. I'll go down myself,' Khan said, looking at Krishnan who was replying to a few government diktats on his mail. The last few that he would respond to before being transferred to the traffic department.

'I think I know who killed Subhash Parikh,' he said nonchalantly. The confidence, which had sagged a bit, was back. As was his swagger.

'I am going to the interrogation room,' he said. 'Coming?'

'Don't you want to wait till Madhavan comes back?' Krishnan asked him

'We don't have time now. I only want to know if any calls were made from one specific room that night. If there were, I am on track. And don't worry. We will not go forward with the wrong hypothesis this time around. Come, let's go,' he said and walked towards Krishnan. When he was next to him, he slapped him on the back. 'This one is for you, DGP Krishnan. One of the finest human beings I have met.'

121

Kabir Khan breezed in into the interrogation room, with Krishnan close behind. On the way they had asked Nirav and Vikram to join them.

'So!' he said the moment the door shut behind him. 'If we are all done with our stories, let's focus on the truth now. What is the reality here? I need to know.'

Aditya was struggling to understand what had just happened. They had spent two hours, maybe more, going over it and now they were back to square one. Shreyasi frowned.

'So what did you do after you came back from Menon Medical Stores?' Kabir asked Divya. The interrogation had begun. Again.

'I went up to my room.'

'And. When did you go to Subhash's room?'

'I have told you! I DID NOT KILL SUBHASH UNCLE.'

'Well, you bought Sux from the store. You bought Alprax from the store. Alprax strips were found in Subhash's room and my hunch and circumstances both point to the fact that Sux killed him. Who else could it have been?'

'Am I the only one who bought the two medicines that you named?'

'Well, that day, from a chemist near the hotel, it was only you.'

'But I didn't kill—'

'Then why did you buy the drugs?' Kabir banged on the table in front of him and yelled. Divya got frightened. She started sobbing uncontrollably. Nirav rose from his chair and rushed to her side. 'Enough, Officer!' he said. 'You are harassing her.' Hugging her protectively, he shouted, 'She doesn't deserve this!'

'We'll know soon enough,' Kabir said as he continued with his queries. 'Why did you buy Sux from the medical store if the intent was not to kill Subhash Parikh?'

'I wanted to kill! I wanted to kill!' Divya cried hysterically. 'But not Subhash Uncle. I wanted to kill *Aditya*!' Everyone in the room was stunned. 'I wanted to kill him for cheating on me. And for plotting to kill my dad.' She sobbed. 'I can tolerate anything but not someone going after my dad. I told Aditya, I will choose my dad over everyone else in my life, every time! He has done so much for me. I love him.'

'We all love our fathers, don't we?' Kabir remarked. 'So drop the histrionics and tell us what happened next.' He had no time for family soaps.

'I bought Sux to kill Aditya. I thought it would be easy. But killing someone needs guts. I'm not glorifying murder, but I couldn't bring myself to kill him. I chose the next best option. Kill myself. My boyfriend cheated on me. My boyfriend wanted to kill my father. It couldn't get any worse than that. So I took fifteen tablets of Alprax. I told myself that I would inject myself with Sux just as I started falling asleep. But I got scared. And called Dad.'

'Ah,' Kabir said. 'And daddy came to help the little baby out?' This meant that the call he wanted Madhavan to confirm had happened. Now he didn't need the data that Pallavi's contact was running for them. 'So, Mr Choksi'—he turned to Nirav— 'you went to help her out?'

'Yes, I did.' Nirav was irritated. 'What else could a father do?'

'Why haven't you mentioned this to us before? We have had multiple conversations on the murders,' Kabir asked both Nirav and Divya.

'Probably because it was not relevant to the case,' Nirav snapped. 'And what did you expect me to come and tell you? That my daughter was trying to commit suicide?'

'We will discuss that later. Tell me, what did you do after that?'

'I went to her room. Scared that she would get locked in, she had left the door open. She had passed out by the time I reached. Fifteen Alprax tablets are not life-threatening. At best they put you to sleep for a long time.'

Kabir made a mental note. This probably explained why her door was open from 1.12 to 1.28 a.m.

'How did you get to her room?' Kabir asked him.

'The fire exit is right across my room. I ran up two floors.'

That was why there was no data suggesting that the lift had stopped on that floor during that time, Kabir thought to himself. He also figured that if Nirav could have run up the stairs to Divya's room, someone else could have used them to come to their floor too. He looked at Divya. 'Where is the Sux injection now?' he asked. 'After all, you didn't use it.'

'Must be in my bag,' Divya responded.

'Let's find out,' Kabir said, dialling a number on his phone. 'An ACP from DGP Krishnan's team is in your room right now.'

'Any luck?' he asked when his call was answered.

Within a minute he disconnected the phone and looked up. 'There is no trace of the injection in your room.'

'What?' Divya was shocked.

Kabir nodded, a dire expression on his face. 'Tell us, Ms Choksi, when did you inform your father about the fact that Aditya and Shreyasi were using Subhash to kill him?'

'As long as Aditya was cheating on me, I kept it to myself. I was too ashamed to tell anyone. But the day I heard them discussing a plan to kill Dad, I couldn't stay quiet any more. I had to tell him. I went straight to his room from the twelfth floor. I was furious. I told him everything, apologized for having fallen in love with Aditya and promised to break it off.'

'If that is true, then why did you look surprised when you heard the messages left by Subhash on your hotel phone the other day, Mr Choksi?'

'I . . . I was surprised that Subhash tried to come up to me and tell me about it himself.'

'That didn't seem to be the case, Mr Choksi,' Kabir retorted. 'You appeared, at least to us, completely ignorant of the fact that Subhash was asked to kill you.'

Instead of responding to Kabir's question, Nirav turned his attention to Divya and hugged her. She was devastated.

'Mr Choksi,' Kabir said. 'Your daughter almost committed suicide. Your prospective son-in-law schemed and wanted you dead. Your friend was tasked with murdering you, and yet the only thing you were bothered about was how to get even with everyone around.'

Nirav's grip on Divya slackened. 'What?' he asked, surprised. 'What do you mean, Mr Khan?'

'Mr Choksi, do you know someone called Ankit?' Kabir asked. He had an intense look in his eyes—one that scared the people in the room.

Nirav Choksi looked around the room, and then raised his eyes to look at the ceiling. He was thinking. Trying to put a face to the name.

'Ankit Shah?' he asked.

'Yes.' Khan nodded. The look on his face didn't change.

'Yes. I know him. Akhil Bhai's son. He went overseas for some work. Didn't want to be in the jewellery trade.'

'Is that so?'

'Or is it that *you* wanted him out of the country? Because you wanted Akhil Bhai under your control? Isn't it true that Ankit was pushing his father to move out of Zaveri Bazaar? And that's why you sent him overseas, so he would be out of the way?'

'That's not true! We were neighbours in the Bazaar. But Akhil Bhai came to me one day and wanted me to help him get some work overseas. I put him in touch with some of my clients in Dubai. One of them—I don't even remember who—offered him a job and he moved.'

'That's lovely. Who doesn't want to help one's neighbour!'

Nirav was quiet.

'Do you know where he is now?'

'No. He switched jobs once he went there.'

'Are you sure you don't know where he is?'

'Absolutely. But what does that have to do with anything?'

'Just curious,' Kabir said. 'I was speaking to his mother today. She said Ankit is overseas and that she still gets a monthly remittance from him, which now comes to you since his father is dead, and you pass it on to her. When I asked her about his whereabouts, she started crying. She doesn't know where he is.'

'Neither do I. I give her the money every month. Last two months in fact. Yes. But that's not something which he sends. I do it on my own. Just to keep her going. I just tell her that it is from her son.'

'Why?' Kabir asked him. He looked around the room and then at Nirav. 'Is he dead, by any chance?'

Kabir was not looking for an answer, he was looking for a *reaction*. A reaction is far more meaningful and visceral than a mere answer; a reaction is not as easily manipulated as an answer.

Nirav had a shocked look on his face. 'I have no clue.'

Kabir pulled out two pictures from his folder. And handed them to Nirav.

'The first one is a *Times of India* newspaper cutting with a picture of Ankit Shah and his family. Published in the papers after Akhil Bhai was killed in the blasts. The second is the reconstructed photo of a man who was killed in the Wafi Mall heist in Dubai. Both are the same person. Isn't it, Mr Shah?'

Nirav looked at both the pictures and slowly raised his eyes to meet Kabir's piercing gaze.

'You know, don't you?' Kabir asked. 'You are the one who sent him to the Alsafa gang that deals in jewellery and antiques. He was your eyes and ears in the Middle East. You ran your trade through him.'

'What rubbish is this?' Nirav started yelling. 'How dare you imply that I run a smuggling racket!'

'Because you do!' Khan said. 'Till weeks before the Wafi Mall heist, you were in touch with Ankit in Dubai. The day he was shot at and killed, your calls stopped. Why would you not tell a mother that her only son had died? Why would you deprive her of the right to grieve? And most importantly why would you hide it? Ajmal Jewellers was a large client of yours. We had your accounts checked for remittances. Ajmal Jewellers accounts for over forty per cent of your foreign inward remittances.' Khan had checked the bank statements as a routine part of the investigation. When he was investigating Dilip Patankar's purchase of five cabs, he had asked for Nirav's bank statements for the last one year. And when he specifically looked at it for evidence, it all came together.

'Ajmal Jewellers is an old client of mine.'

'That may be true, but that does not explain you not sharing the news of Ankit's death with either Akhil Bhai or his wife! Unbelievable!' Kabir was furious now. 'You promised to buy the property off Mrs Shah because you didn't want her to create a scene and expose you. She still thinks you are a good Samaritan.'

'I didn't know that Ankit died in the heist. Besides, you can't hold me guilty just because my acquaintances are guilty of misconduct. If Ankit does something wrong, I can't be the one held responsible.'

'Of course not!' Kabir nodded. 'I just wanted to set the context. Before I come to the issue right here in Thiruvananthapuram. Aditya clandestinely recorded Subhash killing Kannan. It turns out Kannan had seen Subhash strike deals with the cigarette vendor outside the Taj Hotel for stolen antiques. CCTV recordings from outside the hotel show Subhash frequenting the shop. They also show Kannan confronting Subhash the day he was killed. It is possible that he threatened to inform the king who is the ultimate moral authority in these parts. Subhash chased him and killed him.' He took a deep breath. 'Aditya recorded Subhash killing Kannan and used the video to blackmail him into agreeing to murder you. For he had a vested interest in the BKC bourse and wanted to avoid potential conflict with the Surat diamond bourse. The losses there are in tens of crores a day, and the only person standing in their way was you.

'And when Subhash walked out of the room, Aditya and Shreyasi made plans to eliminate Subhash after he had accomplished what he had agreed to do. Divya overheard that when she was outside their room. She came and told you about their plans. You were worried. When Divya called you after she took the Alprax, you went to her room. When you saw her sleeping, you decided to use the situation to your advantage. You saw the Sux and figured that this was a brilliant way of eliminating the competition—to put an end to the threatening Surat diamond bourse that Subhash wanted to set up. After all, the Surat diamond bourse would have been a very attractive proposition for many of the traders and merchants in Zaveri Bazaar. Despite your control on your people, they would have ditched you and gravitated towards the Surat bourse, thus severely undermining your control over the trade. These people hadn't moved to the Mumbai bourse because of a lot of factors that were genuinely not trader friendly—capital value, rents, space, distance, cost of operation. It would have pushed the cost of doing business up and made the trade less profitable. It was easy for you to convince people to not go. But the same would not have been true for Surat. He was making inroads into your antique trade. And now he was out with a mandate to kill you. Obviously, you had no idea that he was trying to warn you about

Aditya's intent. All his messages were going to the other room. So before he could kill you, you killed him, probably hoping that the blame for the entire episode would fall on Aditya since he planned on killing Subhash anyway. You would also have got your revenge on the guy who cheated your daughter and rocked your lives.'

'Nothing you are saying is making sense.'

'You left Divya's room and came down to your floor by the lift. You rang the doorbell in Subhash's room just as he was leaving a voice message for you in room 543. Subhash opened the door. He assumed you had heard his messages and come. You killed him. You injected an unsuspecting Subhash with the Sux. You watched him die and then went back to your own room. The only thing which remains unanswered for me is how and when you made him ingest the Alprax. That aspect is not critical in light of the rest, however, I would put my money on the fact that after you injected the Sux, a desperate and breathless Subhash asked for water, and you gave him water laced with Alprax . . . Am I right, Mr Choksi?'

He waited for Nirav Choksi to say something, but nothing happened.

'What you didn't bargain for was the fact that the hotel had upgraded its key lock mechanism only recently and hence did not rely on just the CCTV cameras to track movements. We don't know whether you bought off the CCTV vendors or Aditya did or if it was a sheer coincidence. It doesn't matter given the evidence we have now. You didn't bargain for Subhash being used as a weapon to kill you to take you out of the equation in the conflict of the bourses and Zaveri Bazaar. You didn't reckon on Subhash valuing your relationship of over forty years, and paying you back for the favour your dad did in keeping him out of the juvenile remand home, you didn't—'

'It was not me,' Nirav burst out. 'You are mistaken!' And then realizing it was futile, he added. 'I need to make a call.'

Kabir walked up to him, made a fist and punched Nirav in the face. Nirav tumbled to the floor. Divya started shrieking as blood spurted from his nostrils.

'Suits you, you bastard,' yelled Kabir as Nirav fainted and fell on the ground.

'Let's go,' he said to DGP Krishnan. 'Let's be ahead of schedule for the meeting with the home minister.'

As he walked out, he looked back. Madhavan, who had returned from Lotus Pond, was still in the room. He smiled, raised his fist, made a thumbs-up sign, then he stepped out, followed by the DGP.

'The home minister is in for a surprise,' he said as he affectionately put his arm around DGP Krishnan and hugged him.

Epilogue

The Wafi Mall heist was never solved. It is one black mark on the impeccable track record of Dubai Police. The authorities could never zero in on the temple from where the Ganesha figurine was stolen. But as in life, where one incident has an unexpected effect on another unrelated one, the Wafi Mall robbery and Kabir Khan's investigation into the stolen artefacts had the unforeseen outcome of bringing the key players together in Thiruvananthapuram and thereby the temple murder case to a closure.

Nirav Choksi was taken into custody for the murder of Subhash Parikh. The second post-mortem conducted on Parikh's body confirmed death due to injection of Sux. Since Succinylcholine is absorbed and broken down by the enzymes in the human body, there is very little Sux left in the body for the post-mortem to detect. However, when they tested for the breakdown products, called metabolites, the coroners had some success. They detected high quantities of succinic acid, a metabolite formed by the disintegration of Sux, which clearly pointed to its use in the murder of Subhash Parikh. Two important pieces of evidence nailed Nirav in the coming weeks. Key was the discovery of a syringe in the vault at the Anantha Padmanabha Swamy Temple. It had Nirav's fingerprints on it and a forensic analysis revealed that it had been used to administer the Sux. Unable to decide how to dispose of the syringe after using it to kill Subhash, Nirav had hidden it safely, deep inside the vault, hoping no one would find it. However, he had not accounted for DGP Krishnan's intuition—a closed-door search conducted in Vikram's presence led to the discovery of the murder weapon. Further investigations revealed that Nirav had been in touch with Ankit Shah in Dubai till the morning of the day Ankit was killed at Ajmal Jewellers. Old CCTV camera footage at the Wafi Mall confirmed that Ankit was a frequent visitor to Ajmal Jewellers. Nirav's phone and bank records showed that Ankit's visits corresponded with calls to Nirav and, later, an inward remittance from Ajmal Jewellers to Nirav Choksi. While that was not clinching evidence in itself, it was reason enough to begin another investigation into Nirav's involvement in the widespread thefts of artefacts from temples in Tamil Nadu. Madhavan suspects that Subhash's emergence as a dominant player in the business of smuggling antiques could have compromised Nirav's stature, giving him reason to be on the lookout for an opportunity to get rid of Subhash. Madhavan has begun an independent investigation into this hypothesis. Nirav Choksi is currently in Thiruvananthapuram Jail, waiting for the law to take its course.

Aditya was taken into custody for orchestrating the Mumbai blasts. It did not take the police long to figure out that his claim of being brought up by a single mother, was nothing but a smokescreen. He was the son of Jinesh Shah—brother of Gopal Shah, promoter and chairman of the BKC Diamond Bourse—and his estranged wife. Shah's wife had taken her son and left India after an acrimonious battle years ago, but father and son had always been in touch. Gopal Shah didn't have a family. Knowing that after Gopal Shah's death, everything would come to him, and that the BKC Diamond Bourse would be a white elephant unless the merchants from Zaveri Bazaar moved in, Jinesh Shah and Aditya planned the blasts, intending to kill both Gopal Shah and Nirav Choksi. The perpetrators almost got away with it till Kabir Khan interrogated the two taxi drivers. And once the police figured out that it was not a terrorist attack, it didn't take them much time to unravel the remaining story.

Aditya wanted to eliminate Subhash Parikh for he was a threat, regardless of whether or not he killed Nirav. Aditya's dalliance with Shreyasi had left him exposed. He was not aware that Divya knew about the two of them. Shreyasi was worried that Subhash Parikh would use the power of attorney to transfer the property to someone else, and carry forward his dream of a Surat diamond bourse, even more so after he learnt about Aditya and Shreyasi. Subhash was sure to take steps to not only protect his own interest, but usurp hers too. She chose the safe way out and, with Aditya's help, found a buyer. In fact, it was she who had lovingly accosted Aditya outside Divya's house when Aditya dropped Divya home after the dinner at St Regis, and sought his assistance.

Shreyasi and Subhash were to meet that buyer at the Taj in Kovalam to take the discussion forward. Aditya hung around at Shreyasi's insistence. While Subhash was waiting for Shreyasi to come, he had observed a few transactions taking place at the kiosk and figured out that it was a front for nefarious dealings in antiques and drugs. On the way out of the hotel, a slightly drunk Subhash got into a discussion with the cigarette vendor. Unknown to him, Kannan was there too. He had driven Rajan there for his meeting with Andrew Mormon, the HSBC relationship manager from Zurich. When he heard Subhash discuss antiques and temple jewellery with the cigarette vendor for a price, Kannan confronted Subhash and threatened to tell the king. However, he was not allowed to meet Dharmaraja Varma, who was fast asleep. A shocked Subhash had chased Kannan through the streets of Thiruvananthapuram, finally catching up with him at the Padma Teertha Kulam, late at night where he killed Kannan mercilessly. Subhash even planted the gold brick in a bag in Kannan's auto rickshaw, to deflect the investigation—a small price to pay, to keep his real identity under wraps. Aditya, who had been following Subhash on Shreyasi's bidding, clandestinely filmed him killing Kannan.

Shreyasi Sinha was also arrested in the conspiracy to kill Nirav Choksi. Most of the evidence against her is weak even though Kabir Khan is confident that Aditya's confession along with Divya's testimony will be enough to send her to jail for a reasonable time.

Divya, who had contemplated suicide when she realized Aditya was cheating on her, was shattered when she realized that her father was a power hungry, blood sucking, manipulative demon. She has now severed all ties with the people who made her life a living hell and moved to the US where she is pursuing a career in academics.

DGP Krishnan was offered an extension for a year—a result of solving what came to be known as the 'Padmanabha Swamy Temple murders'. However, he declined the extension, choosing instead to spend time with his wife and lavish on her all the love and attention that he had not been able to during his life as a public servant.

Kabir Khan went back to Delhi to take up his new assignment as additional director, technology, CBI. Pallavi joined him three months later. She was transferred to the Taj Mahal Hotel in Delhi. Khan had to pull some strings to orchestrate the move. The two of them meet each other daily, and are now considering marriage.

Dharmaraja Varma continues to be as powerful as he was earlier. His power and influence can be gauged by the fact that not only did he manage to infiltrate the audit team and plant a mole in Subhash, he also was able to send a team of loyal police officers to Kannan's house to question his wife, without Krishnan's knowledge. Incidentally Kannan's wife later confirmed that her husband had arranged for the alternate phone for Subhash after being requested to do so by Subhash during his visits to the temple to deliver lunch to Rajan. Though no doubts remain that it was done at the insistence of Dharmaraja Varma.

Krishnan and Khan still differ on the king and his conduct. Krishnan's opinion was driven by the fact that the construction site next to the Kuzhivilakom temple, where the underground escape route from the palace emerged, was suitably barricaded and sealed to prevent unwanted elements from accessing it. He felt that if the king had done that and handed over the land to Radhakrishnan Nair, it was an indication of his honest intentions. Khan felt that the fact that the king was not letting go of the power and riches that rightfully belonged to the people only went to show that he had an ulterior motive. Moreover the presence of the gold-plating machine in the temple and the recovery of temple riches from the sand truck in Madurai pointed to the king's involvement in something less than honest. The jury is still out on this one.

The amicus curiae submitted his report to the Supreme Court two months later. The final report omitted a lot of irregularities that the team had identified. Vikram Rai came under a lot of fire and was even accused of selling out to the king. The fact is that he was frustrated and had reached a mental state wherein he just wanted to complete the task handed out to him and exit. Somewhere deep inside he had also come to believe that it was god's will that had caused the deaths of Kannan and Subhash.

The state has made no efforts to take over the temple. Dharmaraja Varma, despite being kept out of the temple's affairs, still runs it by proxy, as all the other members of the Supreme Court-nominated team were bureaucrats from the local community. The security at the temple is now foolproof. CCTV cameras cover every corner. Blast-proof bolsters have been installed at every entrance. The fear of an attack from external forces has been addressed. However, what goes on inside the temple no one knows. Vault B has still not been opened. Everyone is waiting for someone to order the opening of the vaults again. The case is sub judice in the Supreme Court. However, it seems even the Supreme Court is now scared to take a decision, that too, *in the name of God.*